R. I

The Weather Book

A Manual of practical meteorology

SALZWASSER
VERLAG

R. Fitz Roy

The Weather Book

A Manual of practical meteorology

Reprint of the original, first published in 1863.

1st Edition 2022 | ISBN: 978-3-37500-442-2

Verlag (Publisher): Salzwasser Verlag GmbH, Zeilweg 44, 60439 Frankfurt, Deutschland
Vertretungsberechtigt (Authorized to represent): E. Roepke, Zeilweg 44, 60439 Frankfurt, Deutschland
Druck (Print): Books on Demand GmbH, In de Tarpen 42, 22848 Norderstedt, Deutschland

A MANUAL

OF

PRACTICAL METEOROLOGY.

THE WEATHER BOOK:

A MANUAL OF PRACTICAL METEOROLOGY

BY

REAR ADMIRAL FITZ ROY.

LONDON

1863.

CONTENTS

CHAPTER I

CHAPTER II

CHAPTER III

CHAPTER IV

CHAPTER V

CHAPTER VI

CHAPTER VII

CHAPTER VIII

CHAPTER IX

CHAPTER X

CHAPTER XI

CHAPTER XII

CHAPTER XIII

CHAPTER XIV

CHAPTER XV

CHAPTER XVI

CHAPTER XVII

CHAPTER XVIII

CHAPTER XIX

CHAPTER XX

CHAPTER XXI

APPENDIX

LIST OF ILLUSTRATIONS

AT END OF VOLUME

WEATHER BOOK

CHAPTER I

Introductory Remarks—General Notices—Special Considerations—View of World, represented by a Globe—Atmospheric Conditions—Meteorologic Instruments as Weather-Glasses; and Methods of Use practically.

UNDER so plain a title neither abstruse problems nor intricate difficulties should be found. This small work is intended for many, rather than for few, with an earnest hope of its utility in daily life. The means actually requisite to enable any person of fair abilities and average education to become practically 'weather-wise' are much more readily attainable than has been often supposed. With a barometer, two or three thermometers, some instructions, and an attentive observation, not of instruments only, but the sky and atmosphere, Meteorology may be utilised. The word we have just used may be unavoidable occasionally, however inconvenient in itself and in expression. The term applicable to that sublime science, which once included even astronomy, is now much too comprehensive for its modern application in general; although, indeed, an Arago, a Herschel, a Kaemtz, or a Dové, might justly claim for it, even now, as extensive a range as that comprehended by Aristotle.

From the philosophers' point of view — analysis of highest order, pure mathematics, scientific chemistry, electricity and magnetism, geology and natural history, are requisite, as their elaborate treatises show, and with those invaluable works scientific readers usually are conversant. This book is intended to be popular — not necessarily superficial — but suited to the unpractised and to the young, rather than to the experienced and skilful, who do not need such information.

To facilitate such objects, it seems advisable to consider meteorologic conditions of our world as if we looked down on it from without. When a terrestrial globe is before the eye, relative sizes, spaces, distances, extensions in area, and depths, are less inaccurately viewed. Islands, even our own, are no longer seen as it were in *perspective* only, continents have their due share, in the mind's eye, and oceans have their extensive magnitude displayed. It was calculated by one of the most eminent physicists of our age, that the *average* depth of great oceans may be about five miles ; that the height of Indian or Asiatic and American ranges of mountains reaches as far above the sea level, and that, on a sixteen-inch globe, a coat of *ordinary varnish* would represent a depth equal to *their height.**

For reasons explained in a following chapter, it does not appear probable that the air of our atmosphere, which we can live in, extends so many miles upward as in general may have been supposed. From ten to twenty seems a probable total of depth, and not too small for its extent, as air; while about seven miles seems to be the

* Sir John Herschel's 'Natural Philosophy.'

limit in which man can exist. It should be considered that no one has ascended in a balloon much above the highest mountain's summit level, that all aëronauts and mountaineers are familiar with *successive* horizontal currents of air, alike neither in temperature nor dryness —in electricity, or other qualities (excepting chemically as air), that clouds are passed through, and left below, while only on *rare* occasions have any, and those *very* high ones, been distinguished actually above the highest mountain summits. And when these facts are well weighed, we cannot demur to reason about horizontal motions of air, as those of a fluid, gravitating and therefore seeking equilibrium all around the globe we inhabit.

To some persons, it has been found that this idea of air having a level, horizontally, like water, and invariably tending to equilibrium, as an aërial ocean, is somewhat difficult at first — as is the reconcilement of ocean's *spherical* surface, with that which we are accustomed to call *level*, to beginners in mensuration. Not only has air every elastic and mobile quality indefinitely, while it is fluid tending to equilibration, but, unlike *water*, or most liquids, it *is* compressible to the greatest degree, and in proportion extremely *expansible* — facts to be kept constantly in mind, as they will enter into the explanations of many atmospheric conditions specified in following chapters.

Having our world thus in view, as it were, with an aërial ocean around it, in depth not exceeding a few miles, we are prepared to consider the consequences of heat, *solar* heat acting diurnally on the atmosphere as our globe rotates. To this great and constant agency, combined with its absence, or *cold*, and with unfailing gravitation, it is sufficient to ascribe all our atmospheric conditions and changes, without *at present* drawing in any powerful *lunar* influence, or other planetary relations.

It is remarkable that 'Astro-meteorologists' and 'Lunarists' have not observed that their supposed causes of weather must, if existent, affect entire zones of our atmosphere, in diurnal rotation, instead of one locality *alone*; and that such results are not proved by the facts observed.

That the moon, as well as, and probably much more than, the sun, causes a tidal effect in air, due to gravitation, cannot be doubted; but as the *solar* heating and electrical causes are very much greater, and act powerfully on elastic, expansible, and mobile air, all the effects caused by gravitation towards sun or moon have been found, by repeated observation, to be so greatly overborne or masked by recurring daily causes, immediately referable to solar heating, or electrical action, as to be almost undistinguishable even at places supposed to be most eligible for observation.

When persons who attribute changes of weather to the moon are asked, 'What periods of a lunation of four weeks are critical?' the reply is usually, 'the quarters—new and full moon especially—within two or three days of either.' But any day in a lunation *must* be within 'two or three' days of a quarter, one way or the other; therefore no satisfactory information can thus be gained, and we remain baffled.

Coincidences are much noticed, generally speaking; and but few persons treat them as merely casual.

Having premised these general considerations, it appears suitable to take a view of observed facts in connection with the use of meteorologic instruments, or 'weather-glasses;' and respecting indications of atmospheric change, previous to continuing the subject of horizontal movements or currents of air, with their results; and discussing methods, at present in application, for utilising acquisitions derived from multitudinous and very prolonged observations of authorities, acknowledged in practice, as well as in science.

Separated from the body of this work, in an Appendix, are various special papers in some detail; a few small tables, of frequent use in practical meteorology;* and some illustrative diagrams.

* Wherever the word 'meteorological' *would* be accepted, by most persons, the present writer asks leave to *shorten* it, by two letters; as the possible, but slight, incorrectness of doing so, in a few instances, seems trifling in comparison with the frequent convenience of abbreviation.

CHAPTER II

Meteorologic Instruments — Authorities available for Reference, and for fully detailed Information — Barometers, Thermometers, and Hygrometers, as Weather-Glasses — Rain-Gages — Wind-Vanes — Summary — Rules — Action and Range — Scales — Indications — The Chief Features—Instrumental Affections—Clouds — Animals— Signs — True Bearings — Levels — Kew — Average Temperatures.

In addition to a careful and judicious observation of any natural indications easily available — especially those of the atmosphere, as seen and felt, unassisted by man's inventions — but few, simple, and inexpensive instruments are required for ordinary purposes — such as occur to, and therefore concern, everybody. For higher objects, investigations of a purely scientific character, and the general duties of a regular observatory, extremely delicate, elaborate, correct, and consequently expensive, mechanical aids are indispensable.

Such beautiful instruments as these are familiar to the meteorologist, but are not requisite for general use; therefore we will here only advert to the specially descriptive and useful catalogues, and other lists, now readily available (in answer to letters and postage stamps), which contain not only correct drawings of every such instrument, with thoroughly reliable descriptions and directions, but their prices. In authentic treatises also, even of high class, such as 'Meteorology,' by Sir John Herschel; the 'Admiralty Manual,' edited and partly written by him; Sir Henry James's 'Instructions;' Drew's 'Practical' book; Glaisher's, Walker's, Daniell's, and Howard's works: there are such ample and *proved* stores of information respecting the best instruments, that one need only remind the reader of them, and pass on to the very few and cheap indispensable aids in the study of weather.

Perhaps a laudable anxiety to be correct and systematic in making and recording meteorologic observations has induced the prevailing idea that *extreme precision* is all-important, and that observations should be very numerous. In observatories, unquestionably, such should be the rule; but to treat all localities, all observers, all circumstances of time, climate, and opportunity, alike, and to require a similar registration from each, would indeed be Procrustean, while their application of very refined instruments might be like cutting wood with razors. Any kind of mercurial barometer, if fairly made, well divided to hundredths of an inch (or to millimetres), with enough vacant space in its cistern to allow the mercury to fall sufficiently, and without air above the column, may be used as a weather-glass, showing pressure (or tension) of air around. Such an instrument may cost from two to four pounds. Cheaper ones are sold, even at ten shillings each; but they are unreliable. Aneroids (if occasionally compared) are excellent as barometers for weather indications.

Good thermometers, on porcelain scales that will last, with *legibility*, may now be obtained from the best makers for a few shillings each. Cheap ones, a shilling or two in price, are not trustworthy.

Two thermometers are requisite, — one to be fitted with a water cup, and a piece of cotton or linen, to show evaporation (as will be further noticed).

A rain-gage may be had for one or two pounds, in zinc or copper. It is an interesting and useful, but not a necessary adjunct everywhere.

Wind-vanes, or weathercocks, should not be *trusted*; as they are seldom placed well or correctly. Sometimes their letters are set according to true north (by pole star); sometimes by a magnetic compass, having perhaps one, two, or three points of variation; sometimes by guess, according to neither,—occasionally with variation allowed for the wrong way, and therefore error doubled.

The sun's shadow at noon, a line toward him at rising or setting, about the equinoxes, or a line toward the pole star, will give *true* direction for a local *bearing* circle, easy of construction on grass, or a wall, or even a window-sill.

Directions of wind ought to be ascertained by observing the set, run, or horizontal movements of the lower clouds, when possible. Next to them is smoke, as a guide; but this *may* deceive, from local eddies of wind, as much as an ill-placed wind-vane or a rusty weathercock.

Movements of *upper* clouds should always be noticed likewise; and when different from those of the lower, as is often the case, notes should be made (as the wind will shift toward their direction); but the *registered wind* should be the lower or *surface current.*

A barometer, for a weather-glass, should be placed where it may be seen at any time, in a good light, at the eye level: and it should be set regularly, at least twice a day.

An explanatory card and a Manual should be accessible near the barometer, and should be carefully *studied* by the inexperienced.

In an aneroid, a metallic, or a wheel barometer, the motion of the hand corresponds to that of mercury in an independent instrument; but such *substitutes* should be occasionally verified by comparison.

The *average* height of the barometer, in England, at the *sea level*, is about 29·95 inches; and the average temperature of air in low situations, exposed, but shaded, is nearly 50 degrees. (In the parallel of London.)

In order to compare a barometer with others, at different places, each should be reduced, by allowances proportioned to elevation above the sea, and for respective temperatures.

For each hundred feet the barometer is above the mean sea level, add one tenth * of an inch to the observed height; and, for close comparison, when desired, *subtract* three hundredths of an inch for each *ten* degrees which the attached thermometer shows above 32°; or add proportionally *below* the freezing point. (Round numbers are used here.)

The thermometer is *usually* about one degree lower for each three hundred feet of its elevation *above* about fifty feet from the ground: but this varies locally.†

In general, wind appears to affect barometers more than rain; and temperature is influenced by the *direction* of wind, prevailing or coming, more than by time of day or night; or even by state of sky (while unexposed to *radiation*).

* +0·109 to +0·101 of an inch.

† Depending on currents of air, or wind, dryness or moisture, and radiation. It is very uncertain and variable.

THE BAROMETER RISES
for northerly wind

(including from north-west, by the *north*, to the eastward),

for dry, or less wet weather, for less wind, or for more than one of these changes: —

Except on a few occasions when rain (or snow) comes from the northward with *strong* wind.

For change of wind towards *any* of the above directions: —

A THERMOMETER FALLS.

THE BAROMETER FALLS
for southerly wind

(including from south-east, by the *south*, to the westward),

for wet weather, for stronger wind, or for more than one of these changes: —

Except on a few occasions when *moderate* wind with rain (or snow) comes from the northward.

For change of wind towards the *upper* of the above directions: —

A THERMOMETER RISES.

Moisture, or dampness, in the air (shown by a hygrometer) increases BEFORE or with rain, fog, or dew.

On barometer scales the following contractions may be useful in *north* latitude: —

RISE	FALL
FOR	FOR
N.ELY	S.WLY
NW.—N.—E	SE.—S.—W
DRY	WET
OR	OR
LESS	MORE
WIND.	WIND.
EXCEPT	EXCEPT
WET FROM	WET FROM
N.ED.	N.ED.

And the following summary may be useful *generally* in *any* latitude: —

RISE	FALL
FOR	FOR
COLD	WARM
DRY	WET
OR	OR
LESS	MORE
WIND.	WIND.
EXCEPT	EXCEPT
WET FROM	WET FROM
COOLER SIDE.	COOLER SIDE.

In other latitudes substitute the word South, or Southerly, or Southward, for North, &c.

Familiar as the practical use of weather-glasses is, at sea as well as on land, only those who have long watched their indications, and compared them carefully, are really able to conclude more than that the rising glass * *usually* foretells less wind or rain, a falling barometer more rain or wind, or both; a high one fine weather, and a low the contrary. But useful as these general conclusions are *in most cases*, they are *sometimes* erroneous, and then remarks may be rather hastily made tending to discourage the inexperienced.

By attention to the following observations (the results of many years' practice and many persons' experience) any one not accustomed to use a barometer may do so without much difficulty.

A barometer shows whether the air is getting lighter or heavier, or is remaining in the same state. The quicksilver falls as air becomes lighter, rises as it becomes heavier, and remains at rest in the glass tube while the air is unchanged in weight (tension, or pressure every way). Air presses on everything within about ten miles of the world's surface, like a *much* lighter ocean, at the bottom of which we live — not feeling its weight, because our bodies are full of air,† but feeling its currents, the winds. Towards any place from which the air has been drawn by suction,‡ air presses with a force or weight of nearly fifteen pounds on a square inch of surface. Such a pressure holds a limpet to the rock, when, by contracting itself, the fish has made a place without air § under its shell. Another familiar instance is that of a fly which walks on the ceiling with feet that suck and stick.

* Glass, barometer, column, mercury, quicksilver, or hand.

† Or atmosphere, the atmospheric fluid which we breathe.

‡ Or exhaustion. § A vacuum.

The barometer tube, emptied of air, and filled with pure mercury, is turned down into a cup or cistern containing the same fluid, which, feeling the weight of air, is so pressed by it as to balance a column of about thirty inches (more or less) in the tube, where no air presses on the top of the column.

If a long pipe, closed at one end only, were emptied of air, filled with water, the open end kept in water, and the pipe held upright, the water would rise in it nearly twenty-eight feet.* In this way water barometers have been made. A proof of this effect is shown by any well with a sucking pump, up which, as is commonly known, the water will rise about twenty-seven feet, by what is called suction, which is, in fact, the pressure of air toward an empty space.

The *words* on formerly devised scales of barometers should not be so much regarded for weather indications as the height and rising or falling of the mercury; for, if it stand at *changeable* (29·50), and then *rise* towards *fair* (30·00), it presages a *change* of wind or weather, though not so great as if the mercury had risen higher; and, on the contrary, if the mercury stand above *fair*, and then fall, it presages a *change*, though not to so great a degree as if it had stood lower: besides which, neither the direction, nor force of wind, nor elevation above the sea level, are in any way noticed on such scales: which seem to have been calculated for an *average* elevation of about 400 feet above the sea, to suit inland localities.

It is not from the point at which the mercury may stand that we are alone to form a judgement of the state of the weather, but also from its *rising* or *falling*, and

* *Practically*, owing to air, and mechanical difficulties, which prevent a rise to near *thirty* feet (as often assumed).

from the movements of immediately preceding days as well as hours, keeping in mind effects of change of *direction*, and dryness or moisture, as well as alteration of force (or strength) of wind.

The barometer is said to be *falling* when the mercury in the tube is sinking, at which time its upper surface (if large and not well *boiled*) is *sometimes* concave or hollow; or when the hand (see page 9) moves to the left. The barometer is *rising* when the mercurial column is lengthening, its upper surface being convex or rounded; or when the hand moves to the right.

In temperate climates, toward the higher latitudes, the quicksilver ranges, or rises and falls, nearly three inches — namely, between about thirty inches and nine-tenths (30·9), and less than twenty-eight inches (28·0) on *extraordinary* occasions: but the *usual* range is from about thirty inches and a half (30·5) to about twenty-nine inches. Near the Line, or in equatorial places, the range is but a few tenths, except in storms, when it *sometimes* falls even to twenty-seven inches.

The sliding-scale (vernier) divides tenths into ten parts each, or hundredths of an inch. The number of divisions on a vernier exceeds, *or* is less than that in an equal space of the fixed scale, by one.

By a thermometer the *weight* of air is *not* shown. No air is within it. But the bulb is full of mercury, which contracts by cold or expands with heat — according to which effects the thread of metal in the small tube is drawn down or pushed up so many degrees, and thus shows temperature.*

When a thermometer has a piece of linen or muslin

* Thirty-two degrees is the point at which fresh water begins to freeze, or ice to thaw. Salt water freezes at twenty-eight degrees, if quite still, and accessible to air.

tied loosely round the bulb, wetted enough, by a strip or thread dipping into a cup of water, to keep it *damp*, it will show less heat than a dry one, in proportion to moisture in the air and quickness of drying.* In very damp weather, with or *before* rain, fog, or dew, two such thermometers will be nearly alike.†

For ascertaining the dryness or moisture of air, the readiest and surest method is the comparison of two verified thermometers—one dry, the other *just* moistened, and *kept so.* Cooled by evaporation as much as the state of the air admits, the moist (or wet) bulb thermometer shows a temperature nearly equal to that of the other one, when the atmosphere is extremely damp or moist; but lower at other times — in proportion to the dryness of air, and consequent evaporation — as far as twelve or fifteen degrees in this climate; twenty or even more elsewhere. From three to eight degrees of difference is usual in England, and about seven is considered healthy for inhabited rooms. These thermometers should be near each other, but not *within* three inches.‡

The thermometer fixed or attached to a barometer (intended to be used only as a weather-glass) shows the temperature of air about it *nearly*, but does not show the temperature of mercury *within* exactly. It does so, however, near enough for ordinary practical purposes —provided that neither sun, nor fire, nor lamp heat is allowed to act on the instrument *partially.*

Mercury in the cistern and tube being affected by cold or heat, makes it advisable to consider this when

* Evaporation.

† Their difference, subtracted from the lower, or moistened one, gives the DEW POINT (nearly)—when between about 70° and 40°.

‡ See notes on Meteorologic Telegraphy, in Appendix, on this subject.

endeavouring to foretell coming weather by variation of the column, and indispensable when making comparisons with other instruments, or for science.

Briefly, the barometer shows weight, tension, or pressure of air; the thermometer, heat and cold, or temperature; and the wetted thermometer, compared with a dry one, the degree of moisture or dampness.*

It should always be remembered that the state of the air *foretells coming* weather, rather than indicates weather that is *present* (an invaluable fact too often overlooked)—that the longer the time between the signs and the change foretold by them, the longer such altered weather will last; and, on the contrary, the less the time between a warning and a change, the shorter will be the continuance of such predicted weather.

To know the state of the atmosphere, not only barometer and thermometers should be watched, but *appearances* of the sky should be vigilantly noticed, invariably.

If a barometer has been about its ordinary height (say *near* thirty inches at the *sea level*),† and is *steady*, or rising — while the thermometer falls, and dampness becomes less — north-westerly, northerly, or north-easterly wind, or less wind, less rain or snow, may be expected.

On the contrary, if a fall takes place, with a rising thermometer and increased dampness, wind and rain

* The two thus combined, making a (Mason) hygrometer; for which, however, some kinds of hair, grass, or seaweed may be a substitute, though very inferior.

† It differs, or stands lower, about the tenth of an inch for each hundred feet of height directly upwards, or vertically, above the sea; its *average* height being 29·95 inches at the mean sea level in England on the London parallel of latitude; which height may be called 'par' for that level. Allowances should therefore be made for barometers on high land or in buildings; each different elevation having its own (normal) line of pressure, or *par height*.

may be expected from the south-eastward, southward, or south-westward.

In winter, a considerable fall, with rather low thermometer (from 30° to 40°) foretells snow.

Exceptions to these rules occur when northerly winds with wet (rain, hail, or snow) are impending, before which a barometer often *rises* (on account of the *direction* of the coming wind alone), and deceives persons who, from that sign only (the rising), expect fair weather *immediately*.

When the barometer is rather below its ordinary height (say down to near twenty-nine inches and a half *at the sea level*), a rise may foretell less wind, or a change in its direction, toward the northward, or less wet; but when it has been very low, say about twenty-nine inches, the first *rising* usually precedes or indicates *strong* wind, at times heavy squalls, from the north-westward, northward, or north-eastward, *after* which violence a gradually rising glass foretells improving weather, if the thermometer falls. But if warmth continue, probably the wind will back (shift against the sun), and *more* southerly or south-westerly wind will follow; especially if the barometer rise has been sudden, and considerable, or if it is unsteady.

The most dangerous shifts of wind, or the *heaviest* northerly gales, happen *soon* after the barometer *first* rises from a very low point; or, if the wind veers *gradually*, at some short time afterwards, although with a *rising* glass.

Indications of approaching change of weather, and the direction and force of winds, are shown much less by the height of the barometer than by its falling or rising —yet a height of more than thirty (30·0) inches (at the level of the sea) is indicative of fine weather and *moderate* winds ; *except* from east to north, *occasionally*, whence it *may* blow strongly, even with a *high* glass, for a time.

A rapid rise of the barometer indicates unsettled weather; a slow movement of some duration, the *contrary*; as does likewise a *steady* barometer; which, when continued, and with dryness, foretells very fine weather, lasting for some time.

A rapid and considerable fall is a sign of stormy weather and rain (or snow). Alternate rising and sinking, or oscillation, always indicates unsettled and disagreeable weather.

The greatest depressions of the barometer are with gales from SE., S., or SW. ; the greatest elevations with wind from NW., N., or NE., or with calm.

Though the barometer *generally* falls for a southerly, and rises for a northerly wind, the contrary *sometimes* occurs ; in which cases, the southerly wind is usually dry with fine weather, or the northerly wind is violent and accompanied by rain, snow, or hail ; sometimes with lightning.

When the barometer sinks considerably, much wind, rain (perhaps with hail), or snow, will follow, with or without lightning. The wind will be from the northward if the thermometer is low (for the season), from the southward if the thermometer is high. Occasionally a low glass is followed or attended by lightning *only* ; while a storm is beyond the horizon.

A sudden fall of the barometer, with a westerly wind, is occasionally followed by a violent storm from NW. or N. to NE.

If a gale sets in from the eastward, and the wind veers by the S., the barometer will continue falling until a marked change is near, when a lull *may* occur;

after which the gale will soon be renewed, perhaps suddenly and violently, and the veering of the wind towards the NW., N., or NE., will be indicated by a rising of the barometer with a fall of the thermometer.

Three causes (at least) appear specially to affect a barometer:*—

First. The direction of the wind—the NE. wind tending to raise it most, the SW. to lower it the most and wind from points of the compass between them, proportionally as they are nearer one or the other extreme point.

NE. and SW. may therefore be called the wind's *poles* (as Dové suggested).

The range, or difference of height shown, due to change of *direction only*, from one of these bearings to the other (supposing strength or force, and moisture, to remain the same), amounts in these latitudes to about *half an inch* (as read off).†

Second. The amount—taken by itself—of vapour, moisture, wet, rain, or snow, in the wind, or current of air (direction and strength remaining the same), seems to cause a change amounting, in an extreme case, to about half an inch.

Third. The strength or force alone of wind, from any quarter (moisture and direction being unchanged), is preceded, or foretold, by a fall or rise, according as the strength will be greater or less, ranging, in an extreme case, to more than two inches.

Hence, supposing the three causes to act together, in extreme cases, the height would vary from near thirty-one inches (30·90) to about twenty-seven inches (27·00),

* Electrical effects are yet too little determined, however evident.

† Very important, but too seldom considered.

which has happened, though rarely (and even in *tropical* latitudes).

In general, the three causes act much less strongly, and are less in accord; so that ordinary varieties of weather occur much more frequently than extreme changes.

Another remarkable peculiarity is—that the wind usually *appears* to veer, shift, or go round *with the sun* (right-handed, or from left to right),* and that when it does not do so, or backs, *more* wind or bad weather may be expected, instead of improvement, after a short interval.

A barometer begins to rise considerably before the conclusion of a gale, sometimes even at its commencement. Although it falls lowest before high winds, it frequently sinks very much before heavy rain. The barometer falls, but *not always*, on the approach of thunder and lightning.† Before and during the *earlier* part of settled weather it usually stands high, and is stationary, the air being dry.

Instances of fine weather with a low glass occur, however rarely, but they are always preludes to a *duration* of wind or rain, *if not both*.

After very warm and calm weather, a squall, or storm with rain, may follow; likewise at any time when the atmosphere is *heated* much above the *usual* temperature of the season; and when there is, or

* *With* watch-hands in the northern hemisphere, but the *contrary in S. latitude*. This, however, is only *apparent*; the wind is actually circulating in the *contrary* direction: as a circle, or circular figure, turned horizontally, while moved across a map or chart, will explain better than words.

† Thunder clouds rising from *north-eastward*, against the tropical wind, do not usually cause a fall of the barometer, because they are in an advancing polar current.

recently has been, much electric (or magnetic) disturbance in the atmosphere.

Allowance should *invariably* be made for the previous state of the glasses during *some days*, *as well as some hours*, because their indications *may* be affected by distant causes, or by changes close at hand. Some of those changes may occur at a greater or less distance, influencing neighbouring regions, but not visible to each observer whose barometer feels their effect.

There may be heavy rains or violent winds beyond the horizon and the view of an observer, by which his instruments may be affected considerably, though no particular change of weather occurs in his immediate locality.

It may be repeated that, the longer a change of wind or weather is foretold before it takes place, the longer the presaged weather will last ; and, conversely, the shorter the warning, the less time whatever causes the warning, whether wind or a fall of rain or snow, will continue.

Sometimes severe weather from the southward, *not lasting long*, may cause no great fall, because followed by a *duration* of wind from the northward ; and at times the barometer may fall with northerly winds and fine weather, apparently against these rules, because a *continuance* of southerly wind is about to follow. By such changes as these one may be misled, and calamity may be the consequence, if not duly forewarned.

It is not by any means intended to discourage attention to what is usually called 'weather wisdom.' On the contrary, every prudent person will combine observation of the elements with such indications as he may obtain from instruments; and will find that the more accurately the two sources of foreknowledge are compared and combined, the more satisfactory their results will prove.

A few of the more marked signs of weather, useful alike to seaman, farmer, and gardener, are the following: —

Whether clear or cloudy, a rosy sky at sunset presages fine weather; a sickly-looking, *greenish* hue, wind and rain; a dark (or *Indian*) red, rain; a red sky in the morning, bad weather or much wind (perhaps rain); a grey sky in the morning, fine weather; a high dawn, wind; a low dawn, fair weather.*

Soft-looking or delicate clouds foretell fine weather, with moderate or light breezes; hard-edged oily-looking clouds, wind. A dark, gloomy blue sky is windy, but a light, bright blue sky indicates fine weather. Generally, the *softer* clouds look the less wind (but perhaps more rain) may be expected, and the harder, more 'greasy,' rolled, tufted, or ragged, the stronger the coming wind will prove. Also — a bright yellow sky at sunset presages wind, a pale yellow wet: therefore by the prevalence and kind of red, yellow, or other tints, the coming weather may be foretold very nearly; indeed, if aided by instruments, almost exactly.

Small inky-looking clouds foretell rain; light scud clouds driving across heavy masses show wind and rain; but if alone may indicate wind only.

High upper clouds crossing the sun, moon, or stars, in a direction different from that of the lower clouds, or the wind then felt below, foretell a change of wind *toward their direction*.†

* A 'high dawn' is when the first indications of daylight are seen above a bank of clouds. A 'low dawn' is when the day breaks on or near the horizon, the first streaks of light being very low down.

† In the tropics, or regions of trade winds, there is generally an upper

After fine clear weather, the first signs in the sky, of a coming change, are usually light streaks, curls, wisps, or mottled patches of white distant clouds, which increase, and are followed by an overcasting of murky vapour that grows into cloudiness. This appearance, more or less oily or watery, as wind or rain will prevail, is an infallible sign.

Usually, the higher and more distant such clouds seem to be, the more gradual, but general, the coming change of weather will prove.

Light, delicate, quiet tints or colours, with soft undefined forms of clouds, indicate and accompany fine weather; but unusual or gaudy hues, with hard, definitely outlined clouds, foretell rain, and probably strong wind.*

Misty clouds forming, or hanging on heights, show wind and rain coming, if they remain, increase, or descend. If they rise, or disperse, the weather will improve or become fine.

When sea-birds fly out early, and far to seaward, moderate wind and fair weather may be expected. When they hang about the land, or over it, sometimes flying inland, expect a strong wind with stormy weather. As many creatures besides birds are affected by the approach of rain or wind, such indications should not be slighted by an observer who wishes to foresee weather, or compare its variations.

There are other signs of a coming change in the weather known less generally than may be desirable, and

and counter current of air, with very light clouds, which is not an indication of any approaching change. In middle latitudes upper currents are not often evident, except before a change of weather, being generally more or less polar, and therefore dry, because their vapour, *uncondensed, is invisible.*

* See Clouds — in Appendix.

therefore worth notice; such as, when birds of long flight—rooks, swallows, or others—hang about home, and fly up and down, or low, rain or wind may be expected. Also when animals seek sheltered places, instead of spreading over their usual range—when pigs carry straw to their sties—when smoke from chimneys does not ascend readily (or straight upwards during calm)—an unfavourable change is probable.

Dew is an indication of fine weather, so is fog. Neither of these two formations occur under an overcast sky, or when there is much wind. One sees fog occasionally rolled away, as it were, by wind, but seldom or never *formed* while it is blowing.

Remarkable clearness of atmosphere near the horizon —distant objects, such as hills, unusually visible, or raised (by refraction)* —and what is called 'a good *hearing* day'—may be mentioned among signs of wet, if not wind, to be expected.

More than usual twinkling of the stars, indistinctness or apparent multiplication of the moon's horns, haloes, 'wind-dogs,' † and the rainbow, are more or less significant of increasing wind, if not approaching rain, with or without wind.‡

Near land, in sheltered harbours, in valleys, or over low ground, there is usually a marked diminution of wind, during part of the night, and a dispersion of clouds. At such times an eye on an overlooking height may see an extended body of vapour below (rendered

* Much refraction is a sign of easterly wind, veering southward.

† Fragments or pieces (as it were) of rainbows (sometimes called 'wind-galls') seen on detached clouds.

‡ *Remarkable* clearness is a bad sign. The 'young moon with the old moon in her arms' (Burns, Herschel, and others) is a sign of bad weather in the temperate zones or middle latitudes (probably, because the air is then exceedingly transparent).

visible by the cooling of night) which *seems* to check the wind.

The dryness or dampness of the air, and its temperature (for the season), should *always* be considered, *with other* indications of change, or continuance, of wind and weather.

On land, generally, there is more difficulty in ascertaining the real direction of the wind, in practice, than there is at sea, where sails, or a vane and a compass are always at hand, uninfluenced by heights or eddy winds.

Some persons notice smoke, others clouds (seldom going with the *local* wind, *below*, though generally correct as respects the *prevailing* wind), some mark the vane or weathercock, while only a few of the very numerous general observers know how their points of reference bear by the world (or map) or even by a magnetic needle, of which the *variation* is still less often known within a point of the compass (if indeed *understood*).

Observers should be advised to *mark* a true E. and W. line, *about the time of the equinox*, by the sun at rising or setting, and by it give their bearings or directions of wind. And they should take its direction from that of the *lower* clouds (when they are not very distant), compared with that of vanes and smoke, in preference to any other indication.

Much more care is required in noticing the veering, backing, shift, turn, or gyration of the wind, than has usually been thought necessary. Very rarely has the way the wind *went round* been noticed in ordinary registers, though of material consequence.

These shiftings or veerings of wind—being caused, generally, by the progression of circuits or cyclonic movements of the atmosphere, which succeed or *coun-*

teract each other, variously impinging against air at rest, or moving differently — require much attention, especially in *forecasts* of weather.

With respect to the 'normal' levels, or lines, or barometric heights (namely, the *means* — above and below which instruments range, at places of *various* elevations), often, indeed generally, used on the continent of Europe — it may be repeated that our word 'par' may be a synonym for use: thus (say) twenty-four hundredths (or whatever it may be) above or below par.

Wherever practicable, the vertical difference between any such level, and that of the ocean, should be ascertained, as each ten feet of rise lowers the barometer about eleven thousandths of an inch.* This sea level should be that of the ocean itself, at half tide — a *mean* level which should be the universal standard of reference throughout the globe; varying less than any other.

'Weather-glasses' were used even before the eighteenth century.† Among others, De Foe watched and registered them in 1703 (see his account of 'The Great Storm'); but it is an instance of the necessity for *repeating* information, that, generally speaking, even *now* so little complete use is made of these instruments, however inexpensive, familiar, and common they have become.

As all these barometric instruments often, if not usually, show what may be expected a day or even days in advance, rather than the weather of the present or next few hours, and as wind, or its *direction*, affects them much more than rain or snow, due allowance should always be made for days as well as for hours to come.‡

* Through a few hundred feet vertically, at about 50° average temperature.

† Torricelli invented the barometer in 1643.

‡ See 'Wind-Currents' subsequently.

Marked distinction is advisable between such instruments, observations, and instructions as are intended only for indicating changes of weather or its duration, and those of a superior kind required for comparisons and elaborate deductions for scientific purposes.

To know whether a tube with mercury has been well boiled (as it is called) by holding and turning it over a charcoal fire, it is unnecessary to *watch* the tedious process. Subsequent examination of the metal in the glass tube, with a lens, and its 'click' at the *top* of the tube, give unfailing evidences of the presence or absence of air (whether *boiled* or otherwise prepared).

To verify the graduation thoroughly, not a few casual heights *only* (by comparison with another barometer), artificial pressure or exhaustion must be obtained, by placing the instrument under the receiver of an air-pump.

This is done at Kew Meteorologic Observatory very completely; and it is *necessary* for accurate scientific barometers, though not for mere weather-glasses.

While saying so much of the mercurial barometer, it would be an injustice to the Aneroid not to mention that fourteen years' experience of this small and *very* portable barometer — at sea, on land, and travelling — has induced its *high* recommendation (when *set properly*) as an excellent weather-glass for small vessels or boats.

Annexed is a table of average temperatures between 8 and 9 o'clock A.M., near London, which may be used (with allowance for *ordinary differences* between Greenwich temperatures and others) to assist in foretelling the direction and nature of coming wind and weather.

The thermometer (shaded and in open air) when much

higher, between 8 and 9 A.M., than the *average*, indicates southerly or westerly wind (tropical); but when considerably lower, the reverse or northerly (polar) currents of air.

These indications are not yet so generally familiar as they ought to become, being easily marked, and very useful, practically.

The average temperatures at Greenwich, in the shade and open air, between 8 and 9 A.M., are nearly the *mean temperature of each twenty-four hours*, taking the year through, around London; and, with allowance for the *differences* between the *means* of Greenwich temperatures and those of other places, they may be taken for the British Islands, generally, as follows, for about the middle of

January	37°	July	62°
February	39°	August	61°
March	41°	September	57°
April	46°	October	50°
May	53°	November	43°
June	59°	December	39°

and proportionally between each such middle period.*

* This brief abstract is taken from Mr. Glaisher's elaborate and extensive tables of temperature, which were prepared from records of more than half a century of Greenwich observations.

CHAPTER III

Meteorologic Instruments — Observations — Registry — Forms — Scales — Objects of most Importance — Limits of Utility in practice — Wind-Charts — Simultaneous Observations — Synoptic Charts — Beaufort Notation — Practice at Observatories — Liverpool and Greenwich — Gyration of Wind — Definite Subjects.

Besides the meteorologic instruments we have specified as indispensable, some of a better kind, and many for different objects, are used at Observatories, or by amateurs who can afford time and expense.

Barometers of various kinds, standard, self-registering, and mountain; various kinds of thermometers, some most delicate, some for extreme heat, others for the greatest degrees of cold (many being self-registering); actinometers for measuring the sun's heat, and ozonometers — are employed: hydrometers are used at sea, and hygrometers everywhere. Of these, on Regnault's, Daniell's, or Mason's plan of construction, the most satisfactory, for ordinary purposes, is that of Mason, being simple, easily made, used, and recorded, while quite accurate if carefully employed.*

Hydrometers have been in extensive use during the last few years in all oceans, with the resulting conclusion, that sea water is of very nearly the same density, and equal in saltness, throughout the general expanse of each ocean and the larger seas, only differing by a few parts (say ten to twenty) in one thousand and thirty, near the

* See Memorandum in Meteorologic Telegraphy — Appendix.

mouths of large rivers, or in those rainy regions where at times the whole surface of the sea is freshened by recent heavy rains. Distilled water being taken as the unit, or as 1000 grains, the heaviest sea water yet tried has been 1·040, or 1040 (equal parts) in the Red Sea and Indian Archipelago, the average 1·027, and the lightest, at sea, 1·012, or 1012 grains.

Ozonometers have been variously constructed and tried, but no clear and consistent results have yet been obtained by *ordinary* observers, so much individual tact is essential to dealing satisfactorily with the test papers and their alterations. Variations of light, draught, time, and paper, may cause changes attributed only to ozone, and there are no reliable means of checking them.

Hitherto the general conclusion appears to be that ozone prevails at sea, and that when much noticed over land it is during sea-winds, and at places most swept by them, as high ground near an ocean.

It is coincident with healthy winds—and is supposed to be a modification or combination of oxygen with gases exhaled from the sea, especially chlorine acid gas. It has a tanning quality, and a slightly sulphurous smell.

Rain-gages,* or pluviameters, have been tried of many sizes and at various elevations. A preference is now given to those of rather small size, either on the ground, or but a few feet above its surface. Some are fitted with graduated glasses, others have dipping tubes, graduated artificially; which are very convenient, though not quite so reliable, under all the possible conditions, as those which have independent measuring glasses.

Wind-gages have been tried;—that by Lind—also a

* Some write 'guage,' others 'gauge;' Brande prefers 'gage.'—See his 'Chemical Dictionary.'

modification of it by Sir W. Snow Harris — and the well-known pressure-plate; but these seem to yield only partial, if not equivocal, results. The beautiful cup and dial anemometer (due to Robinson chiefly, if in some degree suggested by Beaufort or Edgeworth) is more approved, after having been tried experimentally through several years of exposure.

The principle of the cups employed with Osler's self-registering machinery, improved and simplified at Kew,* is one of those facts of nature that are such prizes when discovered.

Dr. Robinson showed (in the 'Transactions of the Irish Academy') that a current of air is opposed by a concave hemisphere, one-fourth more than by a convex one of the same size. Thence experimental trials and mathematical reasoning induced him to adopt the arrangement now general ; namely, four hemispherical cups, on horizontal arms, revolving on a friction rollered axis, at a known proportional rate one-third slower than the passage of air or wind current. Hence velocity, and, from it, pressure, are readily calculated.†

The compact self-registering apparatus now well arranged, and proved by trials of some years at distant stations (Halifax and Bermuda as well as in England), indicates direction as well as velocity of wind, and requires attention only once a day. But it is expensive, from 50*l.* to 70*l.* being the cost.

The small cup and dial anemometer, as made by Mr. Adie, may be obtained for about 3*l.*

Yet, excellent as these well-devised instruments are, the practical, and now common, mode of estimating force of wind by arbitrary scale, ranging from 0=a calm, to 12=a hurricane, is found generally sufficient for

* By Mr. Beckley.

† Directions and Tables in Appendix.

descriptive purposes; and it is surprising how closely practised observers agree in such estimations. All honour to Beaufort, who used and introduced this succinct method of approximate estimation by scale, expressed in numbers instead of vague words, about the beginning of this century. By the kindness of his family, we have them now before us, in the log of H.M.S. 'Woolwich' in his own handwriting, dated 1805.

Being provided with the most requisite instruments, and having a sufficient acquaintance with their practical use, our attention is necessarily drawn to a consideration of the best system of making and registering observations, however few or many.

Everyone who has interested himself in meteorology is aware of the difficulty, delay, and annoyance caused by variety of scales used, by want of accordance in times of observation, by difference of language, and by the expense, as well as trouble, if not labour, of extensive intercommunication.

It seems hopeless to expect *unanimity* where habits and climates are so various. To break through accustomed ways and adopt others is always more or less irksome, if not inconvenient; and perhaps such sacrifice will be less necessary if certain general principles can find favour by their own merit, and may be more commonly established.

First. As to the variety of scales.

Excellent as the centesimal division is theoretically, and deservedly cherished on the continent of Europe, the *fact* is that America, India, and Australia do not use it on their instruments (excepting those of a very few scientific men, widely separated).

Fahrenheit's scale is so popular that neither Reaumur's,

nor even the centigrade, can easily displace it in general estimation; but tables for their conversion are very common: and this first cause of discordance, namely, variety of scales (including all those used for barometers), may be now almost irremediable.

Double scales on one instrument add to expense, and are liable to cause occasional errors in reading off; but if an international scale should ever be deemed advisable, such a graduation might be added to all instruments, in *addition* to each respective national scale.

Secondly. The want of accordance in *times* of observation has been much felt, but might be considerably remedied in future arrangements.

There are certain special hours, agreed on by all who are considered authorities in meteorology, and some of these might be preferred as most eligible.

It seems to be a mistake to seek for more than a limited degree of observation for general purposes of extensive cooperation. Loading the mind, as well as shelves, with overwhelming accumulations of facts, only causes distaste, if not oppression, even among the most zealous; and then the progress of science suffers among its misdirected, though earnest, votaries.

Broad distinction might be made between such minute and frequently repeated observations as are required for special or local objects, and those which are wanted for elucidating the greater outlines of nature's laws, or for knowledge of weather. Time may be wasted, great trouble and pains misapplied, by unavailing repetitions, or unnecessarily minute niceties in reading off, recording, and reducing general observations. In consequence of the unwearied investigations of able men, especially at regular observatories, it is now known that there are certain hours in every place at which the temperature is nearly an average, or mean, a maximum or a minimum, day by day; and these hours might be chosen for observations of a general or extensive character, in co-operation with others elsewhere.

In tropical latitudes, the barometric maxima are about 9 o'clock, and the minima between 3 and 4. But in middle latitudes, or near the poles, no such regularity occurs (except *very rarely* during the finest and most settled weather); therefore precise time for reading off a barometer is of far less consequence than frequency of observation; because, to compare with others, difference of time (or longitude) must be allowed for *simultaneous observations*, and the successive readings should be duly reduced by interpolation. Mean results, however valuable for certain special objects, are nearly useless in the comparison of simultaneous observations. For this purpose single observations, at known times, unadulterated by averages or means, are alone desirable.

Here the question may be asked—'What results should be periodically published?' Some persons who take the trouble to keep meteorologic registers say, 'Publish them in full.' But this would be as impracticable in general as unavailing. The *combined data* from many sources are wanted by the majority of those who are interested in such matters, not isolated diaries or extracts, except in special cases. But what extent or kind of combination is advisable? Some scientific men require original observations, singly or in numbers, still preserving their individuality. Others prefer means or averages for certain periods, say 'five-day,' monthly, or yearly; and as each has special objects in view, perhaps of equal importance, it appears to be advisable to tabulate all data in such a manner as to be available for the advocates of either method, and on no account to diminish the value of any original observation by recording it (duly corrected or reduced) otherwise than individually, whether subsequently published or not.

As one illustration of what may be speedily effected by combination, a plan was submitted in 1857, which has been executed, and has thrown a light on the atmospheric changes over the British Islands and their vicinity, which had been unattainable previously. We refer to ascertaining the simultaneous states of the atmosphere at certain times remarkable for their extreme and sudden changes, at very numerous stations on land as well as at sea, within an area comprised between the parallels of 40 and 70 degrees N., and the meridians of 10 degrees E. and 30 W. longitude.*

For each selected time (referred to *one* meridian) a chart has been compiled of the atmospheric conditions within these limits, and from such charts a great amount of information, practically as well as scientifically useful, has been derived. Their inter-comparisons already tend to show the course, progress, and nature of those changes which had seemed so uncertain, and had caused so much anxiety to farmers and travellers, as well as to those concerned in navigation or fishery. Scientific men have obtained facts immediately applicable to theories of wind and weather, and to a more distinct elucidation of the nature and progress of *supposed* atmospheric waves; or of varying pressures or tensions of atmosphere, whether extending in lines or areas, and to what extent. The meteorologic history of selected periods by such a combination is one object now steadily followed.

* Besides more than a hundred places of regular observation within the British Islands, registers are kept at the lighthouses, now very numerous; and generally there are ships passing across the above-mentioned area, which keep official Logs!

When Sir John Herschel proposed 'term days' for general use in the combination of magnetic and meteorologic observers, which was instituted in 1838, that great philosopher recommended united efforts to be made at *definite limited times*. The principle of observing at certain *terms* rather than constantly, if adopted generally — besides being otherwise advantageous — might induce many persons to cooperate who now cannot undertake to observe continuously.

In accordance with this principle, the series of charts adverted to was intended to exhibit simultaneous states of atmosphere over the British Islands and adjacent seas — especially the direction of wind current, and its strength at certain times (8 to 9 A.M. and 2 to 3 P.M.); rain also, and fog, besides other features.

The investigation of changes, and order of variation, in currents of the atmosphere, being one particular object — in these synoptically dynamic wind-charts, the direction of the wind is shown by a line drawn (to leeward) from the place of observation, in length proportional to its strength or force; and the unit of scale is one division of longitude.

Directions of wind are laid down by the true meridian, two points of westerly variation being allowed as a general average. The pressure or tension, and temperature, are shown, duly corrected and reduced.

Among the results already obtained from these synoptic charts (many hundred in number) is the *apparent* N. and S., or meridional direction of atmospheric wave-lines (*so-called* — those of the *troughs* as well as those of the *crests**), but *real* proof of *areas* of depression — of the diminution of the wind's strength,

* Compare with Espy's Fourth Report.

or force, over land *—and evidence of a continuous alternation with opposition of the great, and more or less *parallel*, † polar and equatorial, or tropical, currents of the atmosphere.

In the progress of these charts, observations published in France, Holland, and Germany have been used, where available; but delay and doubt have sometimes been caused by the continental practice of using normal lines, or levels, of pressure, without specifying the *heights of places above the sea level.* This practice, accurate in theory, when the normal line is *sufficiently* ascertained from a series of observations, is inconvenient, practically, when endeavouring to combine abnormal quantities (as given in tables) with the actual barometric readings observed at lighthouses, on board ships, or at fixed stations on land, where the height above the sea is known, but the normal line of pressure has not been obtained. And a minor cause of temporary perplexity has been, the variety of ways in which directions of wind have been recorded, without stating (if known) which meridian was referred to, whether magnetic or true—the variation of the compass sometimes exceeding two points.

But a more serious source of doubt, and one which requires deliberate consideration with reference to anemometric observations, is the varying manner of estimating or measuring and recording the force, strength, or pressure of the wind, and its revolutions or gyrations. Some general understanding with respect to measurements of wind is urgently required.‡

At present the gyrations of wind are called direct or retrograde, and are registered and combined accordingly; but the results are unsatisfactory, because whether

* Shown remarkably at Wrottesley Hall in Staffordshire.

† Dové in *Law of Storms.*

‡ See Lloyd and Robinson in *Transactions of Irish Academy.*

the wind veers directly, or retrogrades (*backs*), is consequent on the central part of a circulating portion of atmosphere passing on one side or the other of an observer: or results from the varying and alternating impulses, or motions, of the main currents.*

The following method (Beaufort Notation) is now generally used to indicate the state of weather and force of wind at sea, and gradually has been adopted on land at many places:—

b Blue sky.
c Clouds (detached).
d Drizzling rain.
f Foggy.
g Gloomy.
h Hail.
l Lightning.
m Misty (hazy).
o Overcast.
p Passing showers.
q Squally.
r Rain.
s Snow.
t Thunder.
u Ugly (threatening) appearance of weather.
v Visibility. Objects at a distance unusually visible.
w Wet (dew).

Note.—A bar (—) or dot (.) under any letter augments its signification; thus $\underline{f}$ very foggy, $\underline{r}$ heavy rain, $\underset{\cdot}{\underline{r}}$ heavy and continuing rain, &c.

0 Calm.
1 Steerage way.
2 Clean-full from 1 to 2 knots.
3 " " 3 4
4 " " 5 6
5 With royals.
6 Top-gallant sails over single reefs.
7 Two reefs in topsails.
8 Three reefs in topsails.
9 Close-reefed topsails and courses.
10 Close-reefed main-topsail and reefed foresail.
11 Storm staysails.
12 Hurricane.

From 2 to 10 being supposed 'close-hauled.'

On land a gradually increasing estimate between 1 and 12 may be used as an approximation.

The above method is now become common, and that, in practice, it answers well, at all events for seamen, is shown by its having grown into general use during half a century of very critical trial.

* See diagram—Veering Winds.

Another method of indication is the following:—

Scale of wind:						
Beaufort . . =1 to 12	1 to	3	Light .	. 0 to	1
corresponding to land=0 6	3	5	Moderate	. 1	2
	5	7	Fresh .	. 2	3
	7	8	Strong .	. 3	4
	8	10	Heavy .	. 4	5
	10	12	Violent .	. 5	6

WIND

PRESSURE — VELOCITY

Lbs. (avoirdupois)	No. (Land Scale)	Miles (hourly)
1	1	10
4	2	25
9	3	40
16	4	55
25	5	70
36	6	85

Some time after this summary was first used, many registers of wind were received from careful observers on land, who, it was then noticed, used the scale 0 to 6, not only in a manner differing from the above, but variously.

Out of forty observers, twenty used decimal fractions below unity, to represent the weaker winds, yet not in exact accordance with the scale authorised by Mr. Glaisher, and employed by many well-known observers, besides Mr. Hartnup, of Liverpool.

At Greenwich, Wrottesley, Kew, Cambridge, and other places, the force of wind is given in pounds (avoirdupois) on a pressure plate, the assumed ultimate standard.

0 representing a calm, and decimal fractions being used with or without integers corresponding to the actual increase of pressure ascertained, as far as the number 6;

a moderately fresh breeze will be represented by unity or 1, which is inconvenient, to a certain extent, as sailors are accustomed to take unity for representing the lightest air, 6 a rather strong wind (which *they* call a fresh breeze), and 12 a hurricane. Moreover, seamen are reluctant to use *fractions* for expressing what any two people may differ in *estimating*, even at the same whole number.

The correspondence between the land scale given above (0 to 6) and that devised by the late Sir Francis Beaufort, now used over all the oceans, is not agreeable to the usage of land observers *generally*. These two scales increase arithmetically, and without fractions; while that used by some few good authorities on land, in accordance with the geometrical progression of forces on a pressure plate, subdivides the integers decimally, beginning at one-tenth, and progressing as far as the integer 6. In practice, probably, the scale to which an observer is accustomed is the best for him to use (and it is *his* convenience that ought to be first considered), supposing its principle correct. But it is absolutely necessary that all records, to be *used by others*, should contain exact accounts of such particulars, as indeed of all those that are required by cooperators in meteorology respecting times, scales, and instruments.

In reply to enquiries on this subject, Mr. Hartnup wrote:—

Observatory, Liverpool: July 14, 1858.

When this observatory was first established, I adopted the scale for wind (0 to 6) in consequence of it being in use at observatories generally in this country. The advantage of the numbers is, that when *squared* they represent the pressure in pounds on the square foot; so that the force, estimated in this way, may be compared with an instrument like Osler's anemometer, which registers the pressure in pounds on the square foot.

When we compare the forces from estimation with those shown by the instrument, we find them agree very well for all the light winds; but when the pressure gets up to 8 or 10 pounds on the square foot, the estimation appears to be very uncertain, and individuals differ much in their opinions.

As our anemometer gives us a continuous record of the pressure, and also horizontal motion of the air, we take only a single observation daily from *estimation* (0 to 6) merely for comparison with the recorded pressure.

Mr. Glaisher wrote as follows:—

Greenwich: July 23, 1858.

Beaufort's notation, 1 to 12, will do for sea use, because it is accompanied with definite reference to the power of the sails, &c.; but the notation I consider best for observatories is that of 0 to 6.

This notation was carefully compared with simultaneous records, by means of Osler's anemometer, for several years, and the results were discussed and published in the Greenwich volumes for the years 1841 (p. 55), 1842 (p. 88), and 1843 (p. 115), of the 'Abstracts.' Enclosed is the general result of these comparisons.

From the Greenwich Magnetic and Meteorologic Volume for 1843.

Estimated force	Observations	Lbs. pressure	Mean pressure in lbs.
½	1,010	227½	0·2
1	1,326	1,396	1·1
1½	370	1,055¼	2·9
2	215	860⅓	4·0
2½	85	526½	6·2
3	41	325	7·9
3½	6	65	10·8
4	11	113	10·3
4½	2	25	12·5
5	4	74	18·5

And the error that arises from assuming that the square of the estimated force corresponds with the pressure in pounds on the square foot is as follows:—

The force by estimation			the error is		
The force by estimation	$0\frac{1}{2}$,	the error is	0·05	lb. in	defect.
"	1	"	0·1	"	excess.
"	$1\frac{1}{2}$	"	0·6	"	"
"	2	"	0·0	"	"
"	$2\frac{1}{2}$	"	0·0	"	"
"	3	"	1·1	"	defect.
"	$3\frac{1}{2}$	"	1·4	"	"
"	4	"	5·7	"	"
"	$4\frac{1}{2}$	"	7·7	"	"
"	5	"	6·5	"	"

With respect to the forces 4 and 5, the estimations are of gusts in gales, and they are so few in amount as to be of little value, and cannot be considered as of much weight.

Considering the strength of the wind by estimation to be reduced to pressures on the square foot, by the above rule—

$0\frac{1}{4}$	or	0·25	by estimation is	1 oz.	pressure on the square foot.
$0\frac{1}{2}$	"	0·5	"	4 "	"
$0\frac{3}{4}$	"	0·75	"	9 "	"
1	"	1·0	"	1 lb.	"
$1\frac{1}{2}$	"	1·5	"	$2\frac{1}{4}$ "	"
2	"	2·0	"	4 "	"
$2\frac{1}{2}$	"	2·5	"	$6\frac{1}{4}$ "	"
3	"	3·0	"	9 "	"
$3\frac{1}{2}$	"	3·5	"	$12\frac{1}{4}$ "	"
4	"	4·0	"	16 "	"
$4\frac{1}{2}$	"	4·5	"	$20\frac{1}{4}$ "	"
5	"	5·0	"	25 "	"
6	"	6·0	"	36 "	"

and this rule has been found to hold, where understood.

During this investigation it was found that there were 1,598 cases of estimated force of $\frac{1}{4}$, and that in 1,513 of these cases there were no pressures shown at the anemometer, while the sum of the pressures in the other 85 cases amounted to 31 lbs.; and there were 376 cases of estimated force of $\frac{1}{2}$, 65 cases of $\frac{3}{4}$, 26 cases of 1, and one case of $1\frac{1}{2}$, in which no pressures were shown at the anemometer.

From these results, which agree closely in their several

characters with those of 1842, it appears that the wind may frequently blow with a pressure of ½ lb. on the square foot, and occasionally with a pressure of 1 lb. on the square foot, and yet no pressure may be shown by the instrument.

The subsequent comparisons, even up to the present time, more closely agreed with the formula:—

(Estimated force)^2=pressure in lbs. on the square foot.

Estimated force	0·0	calm.	Estimated force	0·9	fresh breeze.
" "	0·1	very light airs.	" "	1·0	
" "	0·2		" "	1·1	
" "	0·3	light breeze.	" "	1·5	very fresh wind.
" "	0·4		" "	2·0	
" "	0·5		" "	2·5	
" "	0·6	moderate breeze.	" "	3·0	strong wind, gale.
" "	0·7		" "	3·5	
" "	0·8		" "	4·0	strong gale.
			" "	5·0	heavy gale.
			" "	6·0	hurricane.

Those observers who have used the pressure represented above have worked uniformly; but for the most part we cannot compare the forces estimated by one observer with those of another, but rather should compare results by the same observers together; and in many cases we are reduced to the necessity of saying, merely, that in those instances where the numbers are *greater* the wind has been stronger than when it has been *less*. There is great necessity for a cheap and effective instrument for the register either of velocity or of force, so as to be entirely independent of estimations.*

By the frequent use of such a wind-gage as this, a close approximation to the force, or pressure, and the velocity of the wind, may be attained;† but at present estimations at sea are often inaccurate; and even some of those made on land are liable to mislead, when used for general purposes, on account of the following reasons:—

Observatories are variously situated as to height,

* The small cup and dial anemometer is such an instrument. See its description in Appendix.

† As by Sir Fred. Wm. Grey, in 1860, on board H.M.S. Boscawen, his flag-ship.

exposure, distance from the sea, and influence of neighbouring heights, or even buildings, which more or less interrupt or alter the wind that passes close to the observer.

There is evidence in Mr. Hartnup's published and very valuable anemometrical results * which seems to prove that to his observatory, in a valley, with buildings and hills to the north-eastward, the real polar current does not blow from NE., but from nearer SE. By his reliable digest of winds experienced there, it appears that those most prevalent were from WNW. and SSE. But in England, generally, the prevailing winds are proved to be westerly, inclining to south-westerly and north-easterly, while of all winds the south-easterly is about the rarest. This being so, it would seem that observations in the valley of the Mersey cannot be quoted as showing the wind generally prevalent even in that part of England; and similar effects may occur elsewhere.

At Lord Wrottesley's observatory, in Staffordshire, about 530 feet above the sea, there appears to be considerably less strength of wind at any given time, when a gale is blowing *generally*, than occurs simultaneously at places along the sea-coast: whence the inference is, that undulations of the land's surface, and hills, diminish strength of wind materially by frictional resistance.

While there were very heavy gales on the coast, Lord Wrottesley's anemometer registered no greater force, at any time, than fourteen pounds on the square foot; though at Liverpool, and at Greenwich, as much as twenty-eight pounds' pressure had occurred, if not *more.*

All the synoptic charts hitherto advanced at the Board of Trade exhibit a marked diminution of force *inland*, compared with that on the sea coast. Indeed, the

* 1852–1857.

coast itself offers similar evidence, in its stunted sloping trees, and comparative barrenness.

Should not such facts as these induce *much* care in selecting *positions for anemometers*? and, when considered in connection with local peculiarities of many places, their mountains, or other peculiar character, their land and sea breezes, the diminution of wind at night, and uncertain care,—may not they lead one to doubt whether reliable information respecting the general winds of ocean, on the largest scale, such as is now required by meteorologists, might not be obtained from ships at sea even more accurately than from anemometers set up on islands in the ocean (unless, indeed, very carefully located, and unusually well attended)?

It has already been said that on land *generally*, there is more difficulty in ascertaining the real direction of the wind, in practice, than there is at sea—where sails, or a vane and a compass, are always at hand, uninfluenced by heights, or eddy winds, or local attraction.

It may also be repeated that some observers notice smoke, others clouds (seldom going with the local wind, below, though generally correct as respects the wind prevailing above, *and soon to be felt below*, along the surface)—while only a few persons know how their points of reference bear, accurately.

Various forms or schedules for registration are in use. Generally speaking, the less complicated, and the larger in scale, are the more productive, because more encouraging and actually useful to the observer.

What *appears* best in them, as most comprehensive and accurately devised, may be found, perhaps, too exigent in cold, wet, darkness, or night; too troublesome, in fact, for a labour of love — even of science.

Objects of known importance should take precedence of any speculative or merely curious observations. However true may be the principle of accumulating facts in order to deduce laws, a reasonable line of action, a sufficiently *apparent* cause for accumulation, is surely necessary, lest heaps of chaff, or piles of unprofitable figures should overwhelm the grain-seeker, or bewilder any one in his search after undiscovered laws.

Definite objects, a distinct course, should be kept in mind, lest we should take infinite pains in daily registration of facts scarcely less insignificant for future purposes than our nightly dreams.*

Familiar atmospheric conditions and changes affect all, are intelligible to all, and can be defied or despised by none. Wind and weather, temperature, and dryness or moisture, have first claims to the consideration of all; however common or popular, rather than scientific, they may be deemed.

For arrangements suited to one of the least onerous, although immediately practical methods of observation and record, at present in use, reference may be made to the Appendix, in which the Board of Trade experimental system is described.

Of course independent observers will adopt such lines of proceeding as may best suit their own objects, and the promotion of useful knowledge: bearing in mind that collections of facts, siftings, reductions, or *means* of observations, however valuable or numerous, are not, as such, necessarily *results*.

They are *prepared materials*, ready for use, inductively, or otherwise, from which such conclusions can be derived as may indeed be correctly termed results.

* Herschel's saying.

CHAPTER IV

Historic Sketch — Works and Authorities anterior to this Century — Between 1800 and 1850 — Since 1850 — Department of Government for some Meteorologic purposes established in 1855 — Essays since made towards Application of Meteorology more practically — Coast or Fishery Barometers — Examples followed — Also on Continental Shores — Evidently beneficial Consequences.

HERE it may be advisable to interpose a brief historic sketch of what had been effected in meteorology before the middle of this century.

Unquestionably, from the oldest antiquity, this 'sublime science' * was studied by all men of observant and reflective dispositions; including, as it did at those far remote times which preceded the day of the Stagyrite philosopher, all astronomic, electric, chemical, and atmospheric phenomena. It was then observed with awe and wonder, realised in modern times only among the most illiterate, or indeed the savage of our race. Combined with the earliest mythology, and always allied to astrology — the study of all that was seen above the earth, in an inanimate condition, or felt by atmospheric influence on the senses, must invariably have engrossed a large share of intellectual attention.

In the oldest and most authentic records, so frequent are the references to wind, weather, rain, thunder, lightning, hail, or the heavenly bodies — besides those supreme luminaries the sun and moon — that the deep interest then taken in such subjects is evidenced distinctly.

* Aristotle.

Very interesting and most instructive it is to mark the expressiveness, the beauty, and, above all, the absolute accuracy of all those numerous sentences, of a meteorologic character, interspersed among the writings so wonderfully and truthfully handed down through more than 4,000 years.*

That the mythologic accounts of stealing fire from heaven referred to a Franklinian essay by Prometheus, and that Pythagoras actually used lightning rods (or conductors), probably few classical authorities who have compared the accounts entertain a doubt.

It is strange, however, that in no country does the Greek sage's skill appear to have been followed by any results of a practical kind; while in the far East, from Ceylon to Japan, instead of attempting to collect or carry off electricity, the practice from time immemorial has been an endeavour to avert the stroke of lightning by a lump of glass, or a ball of silk at the highest point of each important building.†

In the middle ages and since, astronomy took ground above and apart from other sciences; chemistry was studied exclusively; and meteorologic investigations alone almost ceased, till Hadley, Halley, and Dampier roused a spirit of enquiry into atmospheric conditions and laws. Dampier's admirable (but *now* too little appreciated) descriptions and intelligent explanations were text-books among the navigators of that and the following century (as Cook, La Pérouse and Flinders showed in their works), being then the only systematic and reliable general account of winds, weather, and climate around the world.

Early in the eighteenth century Franklin turned his

* See passages in Appendix.

† Extracts in Appendix respecting Japan, China, and Ceylon.

sagacious intellectual ability towards atmospheric phenomena, especially those more immediately electric. In his various letters and works between 1740 and 1770, scarcely any of the more important questions arising out of enquiries into air, water, and electricity, seem to have been unnoticed by him; although the science of that day did not admit of explanatory solutions since become familiar.

Toward the end of last century, and during a few years of the nineteenth, much meteorologic information was acquired by Spanish marine surveyors, out of whose books many a valuable leaf has been taken by English, French, and other navigators employed in scientific missions. Then, in the earlier years of the present century, the great Humboldt threw his intellectual light on the physical characteristics of our atmosphere, which has been augmented by bright original rays from Arago, Herschel and Dové. Besides these philosophers, a galaxy of distinguished names occurs to mind as having largely contributed to the meteorologic knowledge now generally available.*

In 1853 the celebrated Maury visited England with a view of endeavouring to rouse public attention to the desirability of undertaking, as an extensive international enterprise, a systematic collection of observations over all the habitable world, commencing with meteorologic observations at sea. Some years previously that active-minded, able, and industrious officer of the United States navy, had taken pains to inform

* Airy, Bache, Beccaria, Biot, Blodget, Buist, Capper, Crosse, Dalton, Daniell, De la Rive, Delmann, Drew, Espy, Faraday, Ferrell, Forbes, Glaisher, Harris, Haughton, Henry, Higgins, Home, Howard, James, Jenyns, Johnson, Kaëmtz, Kreil, Kupffer, Lamont, Lartigue, Le Verrier, Lloyd, Loomis, Maury, Meldrum, Miller, Piddington, Pöey, Prestet, Quêtelet, Redfield, Regnault, Reid, Robinson, Ronalds, Russell, Sabine, Secchi, Smyth, Strüve, Thom, Thomson, Tyndall, Walker, Webster, Welsh.

himself of all that had been done at the hydrographic offices of France, Spain, Russia, and England; had collected all the voyages and travels of recent date, and, generally, had accumulated all the printed information, at that time available, which could be of use for his grand project. Having induced the then powerful Government of the United States to provide ample funds, and a staff (varying from ten to twenty persons) of efficient assistants,* their sagacious instructor accumulated all the journals, diaries, ships' log books, and every such sea record that he could obtain, and commenced that useful system of deducing general or average conclusions, from multiplied observations, which has been productive of such unquestionably beneficial results to seamen, to their employers, to commercial intercourse. and to the world. The writer of these words is aware, from personal knowledge, how coldly Maury's views and applications were received in this country prior to 1853, when they first found earnest and adequate supporters in Admiral Smyth † and Lord Wrottesley.‡

In the early part of this century, while Mr. Marsden was Secretary of the Admiralty, the want of collected and combined information respecting the ocean was so often felt by that able public servant, that he suggested a plan for arranging, or grouping, all that could be obtained, in certain convenient divisions of the seas. He then proposed the method of squares, so suitable and convenient in practice, as subdivisions.§

In 1831 a systematic commencement of a collection

* See lists in Maury's 'Sailing Directions,' 4to, first to eighth edition.

† The eminent Astronomer, Antiquarian, Navigator, and Marine Surveyor, then Foreign Secretary of the Royal Society.

‡ Lord Wrottesley's exertions, in the House of Lords and elsewhere, induced Government to take active measures.

§ General Sabine has the documents.

and discussion of meteorologic observations, made at sea, was undertaken at the Hydrographic Office of the Admiralty, upon a similar principle, by Captain Becher; but pressure of other duties, and the limited extent of means then applicable, impeded the collection, which was scarcely more than commenced.

This very useful arrangement, a division of the ocean into squares, which affords the means of grouping and averaging observations, as well as identifying spaces of sea like provinces of land, was thus originated at the Admiralty.

In the year 1838 a system of meteorologic observations on an extensive scale was strenuously advocated by the author of the *first* 'Law of Storms' (Sir William Reid); and, chiefly in consequence of *his* exertions, officers of the Royal Engineers at detached stations, and Consuls in foreign ports, were requested to collect and transmit such observations to this country.*

But probably the more immediate object in view at that time was the investigation of storms affecting the safety of ships rather than the duration of their passages; and it was not till Maury, of the United States, fully appreciating what had been previously done in the wide field of research which he was then contemplating, commenced those extensive undertakings, already so useful, which have earned deserved praise for their accumulation of facts, for their useful advice, and valuable results.

* As it has been said that 'we want observations in unknown, unfrequented places, rather than in the beaten tracks,' it may here be remarked that we require to know all particulars about the most frequented localities, as a *first necessity*, besides what can be collected about other places *generally*. Mercantile navigation cannot be too much facilitated by information of the most complete description. The wants of inexperienced persons should be kept in view, not the (fleeting) acquirements of those who have passed their ordeal, and have acquired adequate information by long years of practical learning.

The maritime commerce of nations having been extended over the world to an unprecedented degree, and competition having reached such a point that the value of cargoes and the profits of enterprise depended more than ever on the duration and nature of voyages, it was obviously a question of the greatest importance to determine the very best tracks for ships to follow in order to make the quickest as well as the safest passages. The employment of steamers in such numbers, the prevalent endeavour to keep as near the *direct* line between two places (the arc of a great circle) as intervening obstacles, currents, and winds would allow, and the general improvement in navigation, caused a demand for more precise and readily available information respecting all frequented parts of the oceans.

Not only greater accuracy of detail, but more concentration and arrangement of the existing though scattered information (so difficult to obtain speedily), were required. Besides which, instrumental errors vitiated many results, and prevented a considerable portion of the meteorologic observations made at sea from being better than rough approximations.

'It is one of the chief points of a seaman's duty to know where to find a fair wind, and where to fall in with a favourable current;'* but with means hitherto accessible, the knowledge of such matters has only been acquired by individuals after years of trial and actual experience at sea, of which the results have not been conveyed adequately to their successors.

By the Wind and Current Charts published of late years, chiefly based at first on the great work of the United States Government, superintended by Maury, and by studying his Sailing Directions, navigators have

* Said the able and much-lamented Basil Hall.

been enabled to shorten their passages materially—in many cases as much as one-fourth, in some one-third—of the distance or time previously employed.

Although much had been collected and written about winds and currents by well-known Authorities, attention had not been sufficiently devoted to the subject, however important to maritime countries, and especially to Great Britain.

In 1853, the principal maritime Powers authorised a Conference to be held at Brussels, on the subject of meteorology at sea. The Report of that Conference was laid before the British Parliament, and the result was a vote of money for the purchase of instruments and the discussion of observations, under the superintendence of the Board of Trade.

Parliament having voted the necessary expenditure, arrangements were made, in accordance with the views of the Royal Society and the British Association for the Advancement of Science, for a supply of instruments so constructed and tested as to be strictly reliable and inter-comparable. A communication was made by Government, in consequence of which the Royal Society obtained the opinions and suggestions of many eminent meteorologists in Europe and America, and then addressed an elaborate letter to the Board of Trade,* expressing their views of the principal objects sought for and more especially desirable, in the investigations of meteorologic science, with the hope of ascertaining important laws.

A naval officer was appointed to execute the duties of this new department (assisted by other persons), and at the beginning of 1855 an office was established at the Board of Trade.

* In Appendix.

Agents were appointed at principal ports, through whom instruments, charts, and books might be furnished to a limited number of very carefully selected ships; and the supply commenced. Since that time about a thousand merchant ships and numerous men-of-war, in which officers have undertaken to make record, and transmit observations, have been so supplied.

Many more ships might have been similarly provided with instruments, had the willingness of their captains alone affected the supply; but as only a certain number of good instruments could be purchased by Government annually, with due regard to the Parliamentary vote of money, and as the agents require instruments, to be kept for the purpose of comparison with those sent or returned, besides those wanted for occasional supply at numerous stations, the number was necessarily limited.

Wind-charts were prepared for the four calendar quarters, rather than for the four commonly received seasons of the year, because, in fact, the extreme variations of the atmosphere and of the ocean occur some time after the equinoxes and solstices; so that February, May, August, and November approximate to the actual extremes nearer than those months which respectively precede them, and are *usually* considered the middle of each season.

This arrangement was adopted for another reason also, which is, that all parts of the world, all varieties of climate and season, should be considered, besides those most familiar to Europeans.

It is obvious that by making a passage in less time there is not only a saving of expense to the merchant, the shipowner, and the insurer, but a great diminution of the risk from fatal maladies; as, instead of losing time, if not lives, in unhealthy localities, heavy rains, or calms with oppressive heat, a ship properly navigated may be speeding on her way under favourable circumstances.

Such information, duly classified and rendered easy of access, is invaluable. At present it exists to a much greater extent than is usually supposed; but is too diffused among a variety of books and documents to be popularly available.

Changes in the atmosphere over the ocean, as well as on the land, being intimately connected with electric or magnetic action, besides wind and weather, all seamen are interested by such matters, while the facts which they register become valuable to philosophers.

Meteorologic information collected at the Board of Trade is therefore discussed with the twofold object in view — of aiding navigators, or making navigation easier as well as more certain, and amassing a collection of accurate and digested observations for the consideration of men of science.

There is no insuperable reason why every visited part of the sea should not be known as well as the land; if not, indeed, generally speaking, better, because more accessible and less varied in character. And it is expected that in process of years every frequented square of ocean will have been investigated sufficiently to enable digests to be given, which will afford such guides to the inexperienced as much time and practice only could give them otherwise.

As it is desirable that observations of the wind and barometer should be made and recorded more frequently than those of other kinds, and as every vigilant commander requires them to be made regularly for his information, at least once in each watch, there can be no great additional trouble caused by the Meteorologic Register, or Weather Book (or 'Abstract Log,' of the American States Navy).

Regular attention to the barometer tends directly to the safety of the ship, as well as the comfort of all on board, and the economy of material; but to make such an inspection of full value, the reading should be *recorded*, in order that the movements of the mercurial column may be known during previous days as well as hours. These prolonged comparisons, and judicioùs inferences drawn from them, afford the means of foretelling wind and weather during the next following period of more or less time, and therefore have an immediately important, as well as a future value.

Their records, subsequently compared with many other accounts, assist the meteorologist in tracing and investigating atmospheric changes, circulating winds or cyclones, storms as well as ordinary gales — subjects in which every seafaring man is vitally interested.

Great improvement has taken place of late years, in passages across the ocean, no doubt partly due to the improved construction of ships and eager competition of their owners and captains; but a large share of it may be attributed to publications by which the experience and acquirements of a few persons have been rendered available to many. By collecting and digesting observations already made, but not yet turned to account, and by means of more correct and extensive investigations in future, the 'highway of nations' may yearly become more safe, and the intercourse between distant parts of the world remarkably facilitated.

To the well-informed and experienced Seaman there may be comparatively little to offer; but property and life, to a great extent, must at times be entrusted to inexperienced men. Every commander of a ship must have a beginning.

During late years the great increase (by the wider diffusion) of nautical knowledge has not only much shortened sea passages, but has rendered them more secure and less liable to mistakes, as well as to such uncertain delays as occurred so often formerly.

The great advantages of making a quick passage are admitted, in a general way, no doubt; but we do not always realise to ourselves the shipowner's, merchant's, or even the public interest in the question. If a frigate, with important despatches, is some days later in arriving at her destination than might be the case, the possible consequences may be disastrous; but the *expense* is not thought of, because it does not affect individuals, and because the ship is maintained in continuous service for a considerable period, probably some years; but for *every day* that a merchant ship is delayed beyond the expected or an average time of passage, not only do passengers suffer more or less inconvenience, affecting health, it may be, if not life itself, but the merchant loses, and the shipowner loses. The expense of pay, provisions, and wear and tear of a large ship, full of cargo and passengers, is from 50*l.* to 200*l.* daily; besides which direct expense, there is the diminution of that ship's annual earnings, by the delay unnecessarily caused before she can commence another voyage. Thus the injurious effects of a long passage are compound, and, though well known to the owners of clipper ships, are not so clearly recognised by the public at large.

The importance of accumulating and discussing observations of wind, weather, climate, currents, temperature, and nature of sea water, with other matters usually included under the term Meteorology, having been fully recognised by Government in the department established in 1855 for the collection and discussion of meteorologic observations, made principally at sea; and in order to secure methodical reduction and tabulation of such observations, so arranged that the philosopher may use them with confidence and facility, and that the navigator may acquire from them practical information without avoidable delay, —much consideration was given to the system of record to be adopted, which is now (briefly) the following: —

The surface of the globe being supposed to be divided into squares, which are numbered and lettered on maps for reference—numbers showing the principal squares, and letters their subdivisions — these separate spaces serve for grouping observations, and their respective centres are as points of particular reference for averages, or mean results, like observatories.

Large books, agreeing in tabular arrangement, are numbered to correspond with the squares, and are so methodised that every individual entry made from any register or log of uncorrected observations, after being duly reduced, can be recorded in its appropriate table, in such a way that it may be used singly or otherwise, and identified or traced at any future time.

When averages are required, of course these data are equally available; but the general principles of operation are to allow no details to be lost or confused, and to leave no doubt as to the authority for any fact recorded.

There are in use many collecting books of forms, called data-books, appropriated to the following principal subjects: — barometer, thermometer, hydrometer, winds, weather, currents, variation, soundings, crossings, passages, storms, ice, shooting stars, and meteors, aurora, electricity, and miscellaneous occurrences.

Entries are made in these tabular forms, as the logs, or meteorologic registers, are successively examined, the various data being extracted, reduced, and recorded by different persons, and remarkable passages of immediate interest being noted for publication.

Perhaps here reference may be made to a result already obtained from the comparisons *at sea* within the tropics, of a great many reliable Kew model barometers.

Within certain limits of latitude, near the equator, the barometer varies so little from a normal height now ascertained, that (allowing for its tidal change) any ship *between those parallels* may ascertain the error of her barometer, aneroid, or sympiesometer, to nearly two hundredths of an inch, and this without incurring risk by moving the instrument, and without any trouble, beyond making the usual observations.

By this fact, which could only have been proved by employing such instruments as those recommended by the Kew Committee, a value is given to all barometric observations made by ships crossing the equator, equivalent to that derivable from comparisons with a standard instrument; and as this applies *to past* as well as to *future* observations, it may be the more appreciated.

Having shown what has been effected to the present time, and having given an outline of *some* future proceedings contemplated,—a reference to the Royal Society's letter in the Appendix may be requested as an exposition of the views of that learned and scientific body (in 1854) with respect to these subjects.*

* The Parliamentary Papers connected with Meteorologic Observations at Sea were presented in February 1853 (No. 115), and in February 1854 (No. 4), the latter containing a Report of the Brussels Conference.

In 1857, the Board of Trade commenced that practical measure which has been followed by such extensive and beneficial consequences—namely, lending barometers to the most exposed and least affluent fishing villages on the coasts of Great Britain and Ireland, and distributing (*gratis*) instructions for their use. About sixty good instruments have been so *lent* (by special arrangements in each case) to responsible parties, who have charge of those well-appreciated monitors. They are located, from the Shetlands to the Channel Islands, on the eastern and on the western shores.

Since their establishment, some generous benefactors, headed by the Duke of Northumberland, have fixed barometers at many other places, for *public* use. His Grace alone most kindly contributed more than half the expenses, and all local facilities for permanently fixing about fourteen barometers along the coast of Northumberland. The British Meteorologic Society, with their valued Secretary, Mr. Glaisher, did the rest.

Then the Lifeboat Institution took up the cause of our seafaring coasters, and a considerable number of similar barometers, with instructions, have already been placed at many of their stations.

The French Government has also cooperated, having translated and distributed the 'Barometer Manual,' while instruments, specially made in Paris, have been conveyed to their coasts, for fishermen.

At a few places public barometers had been fixed, so as to be available by the community, several years before the Board of Trade moved in the matter; but no popular instructions or directions for their use had been available, except at one place—Eyemouth near Berwick—where Mr. D. Milne Home had not only set up a barometer, but had distributed printed directions for its beneficial use.

At Aberdeen, Peterhead,* and other places in Scotland, there were such instruments some years prior to 1850. In 1842, much discussion about barometers, and their value, took place at a Committee of the House of Commons, on Shipwrecks.

Valuable as a barometer is if understood and duly watched, its indications often mislead those who are uninformed; therefore *wherever* it is offered, as a weather-glass, a brief abstract of instructions should be attached —*invariably*.

It is not easy to ascertain what total of effects in saving life and property such extension of these accumulating measures may have caused already—under Providence; but there is no doubt the casualties on our coasts, as well as at sea near them, have diminished very much during *the last few years* (excepting by collisions), considering the *great* increase of vessels employed—and it is certain that seamen as well as fishermen *now* much value the barometer.

* Placed there for the Earl of Aberdeen, by Admiral W. A. Baillie Hamilton, and elsewhere by other persons, anxious to save *lives* which no *Insurance Office* can protect.

CHAPTER V

Brief general Glance at Climates around the World—Atmospheric Conditions and Movements—Great Circulation of the Atmosphere incessantly caused by Heat—Consequent on Action of the Sun—Motions of Air around and about our World—Normal Winds—Prevalent Winds also, and their Effects on Climates.

Before endeavouring to trace and explain the characteristics and general movements of our atmosphere, a considerable knowledge of which is essential in judging of weather, however little studied hitherto, scientifically, it may be useful to place a terrestrial globe before the eye, and not only compare the *small* British Islands with other portions of the world—with continents and oceans—but to think of the marked differences of climate and atmospheric conditions appertaining to those well-known divisions or zones, the tropical, the temperate, and the polar. Clear ideas of these general features, and of relative areas or magnitudes on the world's surface, are indispensable preliminaries.

Now, let us consider the world as it really exists—in *rotation*—the directions of atmospheric currents being more or less diagonal, across instead of along meridians—owing to solar influence acting all around, consecutively, and *continually*; therefore occasioning atmospheric circuits or circulation, and causing a grand general exchange of air over all our globe.

These currents of air near the equator are neither eastward *exactly with* the earth's rotation—in speed—nor *much* in a contrary direction. Affected by the *sub-solar tendency* at the same time, although in varying degrees, the *sensible* movement is intermediate between the extremes of diurnal solar *drag* and equatorial rotatory motion to the eastward (antagonistic impulses), the results being equatorial motion of air *very* much less in speed westwardly than the sun's daily course (or that of the sub-solar *position*), *rather less eastwardly* than the earth's surface, and therefore *really slow* along it towards the *west*, in the equatorial zones.

Thence, raised by heat, expanded, having *nearly* the centrifugal or rotatory *eastward* motion of the equator —held down, however, always by gravitation—towards the poles the upper currents flow, with (for a time) their equatorial impetus carrying them more and more across the converging meridians until it is lost, gradually, near the poles; whence, again drawn, they move, not only towards the equator, but—more and more diagonally as they meet the augmenting velocity of rotation, and cross the expanding meridians, their direction becoming more and more easterly, or from the eastward, until so much checked and influenced by the earth's rotation *towards* the east, that they become gradually intermediate in movement between the antagonistic motions, as above described.

Another view of this subject has also been expressed by the writer, but as it harmonises in its results, and is almost distinction without difference, he will only advert to it by saying that a globe uniformly covered with fluid, water, air, or gas, must hold any such fluid in a level or horizontal equilibrium by force of gravity, and that no *local* disturbance, such as that of sub-solar heat, can affect the mass dynamically, without occasioning counter-currents proportional to constant forces, and areas of surface passed over, horizontally.

According to this view, the inter-tropical perennial (or trade) winds from the eastward should be counterpoised by the (prevalent) *anti-trades* or westerly winds, of both hemispheres; — and a continual alternation or conflict between the currents going *poleward*, and toward the east, with those advancing from colder to warmer regions, and *westward withal*, would be the consequence, as under the previous expositions.

This great general circulation, affecting all the atmosphere round the whole world (and therefore always to be considered in connection with any limited or special meteorologic case), is, however, affected, and exceedingly modified, locally, by continents, oceans, mountainous ranges, and deserts; which much augment conflicts of air currents, and occasion the varieties of winds, storms, and climates experienced in each hemisphere; all alike in origin, all in accordance as to general principles, and all now explicable by the same natural laws.

Wherever currents of wind, either the main currents, tropical and polar (of which all others are more or less compounded), or any other streams of air, meet or mutually oppose, their tendency is to cause a calm, or a gyration; and if the latter, always in one direction, *against* watch hands in the northern hemisphere, but *with* them in south latitude.

Currents *from* a pole move towards the equator and towards the west also, it has been shown; and those from the equator move towards the east while going towards a pole. Their mutual approach occasions a movement of the intermediate air, rotatory, in one direction only; a consequence of antagonistic air currents, as well as of *convergence of meridians and differing latitudes.**

In the southern hemisphere a contrary effect, or *with* the watch, is obviously certain, on similar principles; and it is very important that these gyrations should be clearly understood and relied on by seamen, so many mistakes having been made by confusing the cases of cyclone centres passing *between* the pole and observer, or the *contrary*; but of this in other places.

Successive, or rather *consecutive*, gyrations, circuits, or cyclones, often affect one another, acting as temporary mutual checks, until a combination and joint action occurs; their union causing greater effects: as may be seen even in water, as well as in winds.†

Between the tropics and the polar regions, or in temperate zones, the main currents are incessantly active, and more or less antagonistic, from the causes above mentioned; the *return* current, or westerly (*from* the westward), being *prevalent* in the temperate zones.

Wherever considerable changes of temperature, development of electricity, heavy rain, or these in combination, cause temporary disturbance of atmospheric equilibrium (or a much altered *tension* of air), these grand agents of nature, the two great currents, speedily move by the *least resisting lines*, to restore equilibrium, or fill the comparative void. One current arrives, probably, or acts *sooner* than the other ; but invariably collision occurs, of some kind or degree, usually occasioning a circuitous sweep, a cyclonic (or *ellipsonic*) gyration, little *noticed* when gentle or moderate in force, but nevertheless occurring.

* Herschel, Dové, Ferrell, and other authorities.

† See Diagram — Interfering Cyclones.

As there must be resistance to moving air (or a conflict of currents) to cause gyration, and as there are no such causes on a large scale near the equator, there are no storms in very low latitudes (except local squalls). It is at some distance (ten to twenty degrees) from the equator that hurricanes are occasionally felt.

They originate in or near those hot and densely-clouded spaces, sometimes spoken of as the *cloud-ring*,* where aggregated aqueous vapour is at times condensed into heavy rain (partly with vivid electrical action), and a comparative vacuum is suddenly caused, towards which air rushes from all sides. That which arrives from a higher latitude has a westwardly, that from a lower an eastwardly, tendency, due to the earth's rotation, and to the change of latitude: whence a chief cause of the cyclone's invariable rotation in one direction, as above explained.

The hurricane or cyclone is impelled to the W., in *low* latitudes, because the tendency of *both* currents there is to the westward, along the surface; although one—the tropical—is *much less so*, and becomes actually easterly near the tropic, after which its *equatorial* centrifugal force is more and more evident, while the *westwardly* tendency of the polar current diminishes; and therefore, at that latitude, hurricane cyclones cease to move westward (re-curve), then go towards the pole, and, subsequently, almost eastwardly (in some cases), though commonly towards the north-eastward, till they expand, disperse, or ascend. It is a mistake to suppose they travel very far, or last many days—however, details on this subject may be deferred to future pages, in which they will be more apposite.

* Maury's Physical Geography of the Sea.

The laws are sure and uniform to which all atmospheric conditions and changes are accordant, and only require to be familiarly known to be appreciated and to become practically useful.

In order to assist in explaining those laws, and to aid in attaining a distinct view of their operation, the following brief considerations are submitted to the reader:—

Looking at a globe, as an eye in space beyond our atmosphere would see the earth — marking its relative features, polar regions, equatorial and intermediate zones, its diameter (8,000 miles), its swift rotation at the equator but slow motion near its poles, the convergence of meridians, and the small depth of *sensible* atmosphere, (about ten to fifteen miles, above which may be some miles of *very light* gas) — bearing in mind the nature and extension of numerous ranges of mountains, some being four or five miles high; the relative proportions of sea and land in each hemisphere; the constant cold of polar regions, and the constant heat of inter-tropical zones — *all around the world* (not in one place, under the sun, or *sub-solar*, for a short time only) —and then (for simplification) *imagining* the earth to be still (not *rotating*), *other* conditions of atmosphere, heat and cold being the same (*without* the sun), what would the movements then be? They would be *convective*, like the convection of water heated at one place — the action of water in a kettle on the fire.

From equatorial to polar regions there would be an action, like that of fluid heated unequally, in direct lines (or meridians) from equator to pole, and back to the equator. Expanding in the inter-tropical zone — *all around* — checked by gravitation from rising above a certain height, and overflowing towards the poles —

thence cooled, the air would again move, chiefly along earth's surface, toward the equator.

But the equatorially heated spaces, or masses of air, require more extent of area, even irrespective of expansion, than there is in the polar regions toward which they tend; therefore compression — a contest with air moving below in a contrary direction — and a considerable union with it, even *before* reaching middle latitudes, must occur. Thence much would return toward the equator, the *remainder* only continuing toward a pole, and descending (gravitating) to earth's surface whenever the flow from the pole became diminished, or even temporarily interrupted. These contrary currents (here *supposed* in meridian lines) would occasion comparative stagnation, with tension or pressure, on the *equatorial* side of '*middle*' latitudes (variables, or 'horse latitudes'), and commotions (if not storms) in or beyond the *middle* and even higher latitudes, quite into the polar regions. (Still *supposing* the earth not rotating.) The *ab-polar* current *may* expand as it goes toward the equator, having increasing space, though it is checked considerably by the return current, just mentioned, that descends near the tropics. Hence comparative freedom from storms, and usual tranquillity of inter-tropical latitudes might be expected near the equator. Hence also one might look for greater prevalence of storms in the winter half of a year in temperate or high latitudes, and for their comparative infrequency during the summer half; because each would approximate at those seasons more toward the characteristics of polar and equatorial regions. Thus far (*permissively*?) with an *imaginary* case.

Now, *returning* to a consideration of the world in its *actual* state, always rotating, and to the circumstances shown in the first four pages of this chapter — it may be stated that comparisons of accumulated facts have induced the conclusion that winds move in parallel currents, or circulate around *centrical* areas; and that whether the extension of such movement or circulation be immense, as between the tropics and the polar regions, or whether it be small even as the dust-whirl, the *laws* of circulation, or gyration,* are *uniform*, except in such very rare and *limited* cases as to be unimportant.

When movements of the atmosphere, such as those of the perennial trade-winds, or those very prevalent westerly winds, the 'anti-trades,'† are on the largest scale, the wind appears, at any one place, to move in straight lines, owing to the really circular arc having so little curvature; but when circulation is comparatively limited, as in a cyclone, rapid changes in the wind's direction are obvious to every observer.

When such movements are not horizontal, but inclined to the surface, more or less, perhaps nearly vertical, or partaking of various directions, they are exceedingly difficult to trace, except by upper clouds seen crossing heavenly bodies, or by visits to high mountains, or by balloons, or by 'dust'‡ (so called), carried from far distant places through the higher regions of our atmosphere.

Nevertheless, it appears from the facts ascertained, that the current, from polar regions, tends *upward* when *arrived between* the tropics, and then as a tropical current *above*, to the eastward, while the lower *ab-polar* movement is southward and apparently westward. *Apparently*, because it is caused by the earth turning towards the E.; not by its own inclination or impulse, which is

* Dové. † Herschel. ‡ Ashes, or Infusoria.

almost southerly. Near the equator it has indeed acquired the equatorial (rather than centrifugal) impetus, which, as it rises into an upper region, causes it to move *eastward* while returning towards either pole, but losing this impulse gradually, by gravitation, and by friction along the surfaces, as it approaches that centre.

This circulation, therefore, closely followed out, is similar to that of all the smaller cyclonic motions (*ellipsonic*?) *against* watch hands in N. latitude, *with* the hands of a watch in the southern hemisphere.

A practical, important, and too little noticed consequence of these facts is, that lines drawn on a map, at right angles to the *right* of the wind's direction *toward* any one *facing* it (*left* in S. latitude), all tend more or less toward the *centrical* area (whether oval, elliptic, or circular), around which there is then a movement of circulation, more or less varying; and, therefore, that a fair average of such lines of direction (as radii), drawn from various stations, will show (where they intersect each other *most nearly*) the approximate centre of general circulation, which, even thus roughly ascertained, may enable any person, acquainted with the subject, to complete the circles on paper, show how the wind is then blowing, with its probable relative strength at any parts around, and over what countries or coasts the central part of such circulation will probably pass.

Having this knowledge, it obviously follows that telegraphic warning may be sent in any direction reached by the wires, and that occasionally, on the occurrence of very ominous signs, barometric and other, including always those of the heavens, such cautions may be given before storms as will tend to diminish the risks, and loss of life, so frequent on our exposed and tempestuous shores.

It has been proved that storms, indeed all greater circulations of atmosphere, between the tropics and polar regions, have eastward motion, bodily, while sweeping around a centrical area. Within the tropics they move otherwise, or westward, till they recurve.

This universal motion (however irregular or modified in some *few* localities, by exceptional and minor causes) is *additional* to the regular and grand circulation above mentioned, which, *constrained* by the earth's surface, or otherwise, by gravitation, &c., occasions movements like 'parallel currents' (first spoken of by Dové). These circulations of the polar and tropical currents, with their attendant peculiarities of dry, cold, and heavy air, or moist, warm, and light air, raising or lowering the barometer, as they pass over any country, have caused the *appearances*, often noticed, of 'atmospheric waves,' corresponding to barometrical oscillations; as well as to the 'gyrations' of wind, so well elucidated by that eminent meteorologist.

Such currents, excessively broad and prolonged, are always flowing, in nearly *opposite* directions: if near the earth's surface, side by side, or parallel; but if overlapping, or entirely superposed, *crossing* in various directions, and more or less impinging on or *intermingling* with each other. These greater currents, incessantly in motion, occasion with their eddies the minor movements of cyclones, successive, and perhaps *numerous* —one cyclone following, impinging on, and more or less *counteracting* another, thus causing those complicated changes of wind, sudden shifts and *apparent* contradictions of general laws, which have so baffled some investigators, and have caused temporary doubts of the reliability and the universality of laws of storms.*

* See Diagram of Interfering Cyclones.

While these normal (*ab-polar*, and tropical) currents are respectively moving, toward the wide inter-tropical regions, and toward those very *limited* spaces around the poles of our world, they have also, as has been mentioned, but may be repeated, a general movement, in mass, *laterally* towards the east.

The body of air raised (rarefied by warmth, loaded with vapour, and expanded) around the whole globe, about its equatorial bulk, is vastly greater than the aggregate of cold, dry, condensed, and heavy air in the polar regions. This inter-tropical mass of air, surrounding the world, has a temporary impulse *eastward* with *nearly* the rotating velocity of that zone. Prevented by gravitation from rising *above* a certain distance, pressed on continuously by air in motion below (or behind), toward either pole it must go, to seek its level and equilibrate the atmosphere.

While moving toward either pole — retaining for a time, though gradually losing, its acquired *eastward* motion, which is continued only till the momentum of its weight and velocity fails in effect towards polar circles — there must be a continual impact, a constant impulsion from the westward laterally against the *polar* current, as it is drawn *toward* and *after* the rising *sub-solar* or inter-tropical part of the atmosphere.

The polar current has no *lateral* impulse of *its own*;* it is *drawn* towards the W., *in appearance only*, because the earth's surface has a greater rotatory velocity eastward than the polar current, proportionally to its nearer approach to the equator: though, on the other hand, that current is gradually acquiring equatorial motion, the greatest *westward* effects being near the tropics (where the trades *are* generally found strongest).

* The inter-tropical zone is heated permanently, and nearly alike, on an average, all round the world.

Therefore the sensible result on the *whole system* of circulation in temperate zones must be continual *easterly* progression, a *general* motion of the atmosphere toward the East, except in the lower latitudes and (perennial) trade winds, where its motion is different from that in higher latitudes, being to the West.

This continuous impulse of the upper tropical current *eastward*, while that of the polar stream is nearly southward, *in itself*, seems to be one cause of that universal law of gyration — *against* watch hands in N. latitude, *with* them in the southern hemisphere — which is now generally recognised, though not explained nor accounted for *originally* previous to Dové's publications.

Thus, however frequently altered or masked, the normal state of our atmosphere appears to be a regular alternation or circulation of currents between polar and tropical regions — the polar *usually* advancing along the earth's surface, the counter current *generally* above, at higher elevations.*

Sometimes, even for weeks together, a polar current prevails — excessively broad — many thousand miles in width, and in latitude reaching from icy regions through the perennial trade-winds, quite to the sub-solar zone. The more marked characteristics of this current, where it does not blow over an expanse of comparatively warm ocean, are (relative) cold, dryness, and heaviness or tension, with positive, or an excess of electricity.

During such a steady condition of atmosphere a return, or tropical, current, passing above, is often made evident by light upper clouds seen crossing heavenly bodies, and by the sensations of feeling (or temperature), at high elevations, on mountains, or in balloons.

At other times, and by far the more prevalent, there is a more or less conflicting alternation, along the earth's

* In the temperate zones *either* current may be superposed.

surface, or in the upper air, of these great principal currents, in such a variety of proportion and combination, that observers, however careful and discriminating, cannot be otherwise than perplexed until more is ascertained, not only of the mechanical, but the chemical and electrical, laws of the atmosphere. With the tropical current there is little, if any, plus or positive electricity manifested in the air; but sometimes, particularly with moist deposit, including hail, there is minus or negative electricity in a greater or less degree.

Part of the tropical current certainly *descends*, between the latitudes of 20 and 40°, turns there toward the equator, and combines with the perennial winds or the periodical monsoons. The rest flows on toward the polar region, invariably coming down, or descending, toward the earth's surface, wherever the *ab-polar current fails*; and then having obtained access, like an elastic wedge, it increases in breadth and strength till a revival of the *polar* current's energy enables that wind to turn, overcome, and eventually displace its usurping antagonist.

As the *ab-polar* current diminishes or fails, *gradually*, and irregularly (in outline or shape like tongues of flickering flame), while moving *southward*, and as the first descent of the upper tropical stream is more or less *from* the westward, the feeble extremities of the polar current are turned *to* the eastward, and, as they become combined with the advancing tropical stream, turn actually northward till *lost*—thus causing a rotatory movement, *against* watch hands—a movement as constant in the northern hemisphere as its analogous motion, in the contrary direction, is general in southern latitudes.

When the polar current recovers strength, being recruited from far remote sources, it usually presses suddenly if not violently against the *polar* side of the current which is flowing *from* the tropics, and from the *westward*, making it diverge in direction by curving away from the place of most pressure, and thus increasing the *tendency* to circulate, as above mentioned, in one direction rather than another. These currents combine, or mix, variously, in their nature as well as in direction. There is also an electrical action, not yet traced distinctly, though frequently indicated, and fully ascertained by instrumental means.

Although these appear to be *general outlines* in accordance with observed facts, it ought to be borne in mind that, while similar features or peculiarities occur on even a *small* scale in some localities, there are apparent exceptions or contradictions in others (such as *temporary* land or sea breezes, occasional gyration of a *local* whirlwind or waterspout, *contrary* to usual law); so exceptional, however, that they may truly be said to prove the *generality* of those great laws so necessary to be carefully studied and sufficiently mastered,—particularly by seamen.

The more marked characteristics of the polar current, where it does not blow over an expanse of comparatively warm ocean, are (relative) cold, dryness and heaviness, or *tension* with positive electricity. By relative heaviness is meant specific gravity, the weight of a given bulk (say a cubic foot) of polar air compared with an equal bulk (by dimension) of air in a tropical current; and, by tension, we mean its confined, or resisted elasticity.

When such a body of atmosphere as a wide tropical current flows against high land, it is speedily deprived of much aqueous vapour (condensed into rain or snow), and if it afterwards crosses a considerable tract of country it is *dry*, though still *specifically* light; with inferior tension, until *mixed*, by degrees, with polar air.

Masses of land, with arid deserts or large forests — high, perhaps snow-covered ranges of mountains, extensive valleys, or rivers on a great scale, influence atmospheric currents, as they cross, in almost every conceivable way; and it is exceedingly difficult in some localities to eliminate effects of a special or peculiar kind, from the great general, or normal conditions of the world's atmosphere, which should always be kept in view.

That there are *waves* of air, atmospheric undulations, or *pulsations*, we have authorities for accepting; but that they are not such as have been sometimes supposed, while looking at barometric curves of oscillation, seems clear. Vibratory undulations may exist on a greater or less scale in all elastic fluids that are not at rest; but the direct consequence of such motions, in the atmosphere, on those of the mercurial column, appears inconsistent with the facts that, sometimes while either polar or tropical current lasts *several weeks*, with settled weather (the former much more frequently), there is little or no sensible change in the column of mercury, while the wind remains steadily in one quarter; yet with, or shortly before, a change of wind's *direction only*, the mercury falls or rises; and this, while there are notable abnormal motions in *other* regions of atmosphere, amply sufficient to cause the transmission of undulatory vibrations, or atmospheric waves.

What has been termed the 'trough' of the wave, being the lightest air, ought to mount *highest, as it does between the tropics*; while the (so called) 'crest,' being in the middle of heavy dry air (which we find to be the case with polar current, *invariably*), should have a lower position.

The effects of icebergs on our climate have been much

questioned, especially with reference to recent seasons. It would seem that when they are numerous, or large, and are under currents of wind that blow to our shores, a chilling influence may be felt, and aqueous vapour may be borne from their vicinity to be condensed in rain on our western high lands. The heat absorbed in thawing ice or snow, and converting its water into invisible vapour or gas, is well known to be very considerable in quantity.

But similar effects occur annually — not, indeed, from icebergs only, but on an infinitely grander scale—around the arctic and antarctic circles, affecting all the adjacent temperate zones. As either pole is turned more toward the sun, after the vernal equinox, heat increases in the direction of that pole until a thawing effect is produced on the exterior ice, when an interval of comparatively cold weather occurs, caused by absorption of heat near those circles, affecting more or less the contiguous regions; and thus, perhaps, the frequent cold of April or May in this country (and other parts of our hemisphere also), especially after a warmer *early* spring than usual, may be accounted for *generally*.

The converse of these conditions ought to occur (if the facts be as above supposed) — namely, a short second summer, or rather an interval of comparatively fine warm weather soon after the autumnal equinox, caused by liberation of latent heat (during condensation of vapour, and formation of ice) and precipitated moisture. Is not this the case all over the world, in temperate zones? The expressions 'St. Martin's,' 'St. John's,' and the 'Indian' summer, advert to this period, which is recognised in each hemisphere everywhere.

CHAPTER VI

Lower, Upper, and Intermediate Currents of Air — Consequent Varieties and Variations of Climate — Barometric Curves — Wave Theory — Winds affecting Climates — Influenced by Oceans — Sea Temperatures — Specific Gravity — Ozone.

We have been considering the grander and more general atmospheric circulation, irrespective of minor motions; but as these greater and normal movements occasion a variety of inferior off-sets, intermediate currents, and eddying circuits, it is indispensable to take due notice also of them.

Any person who has watched clouds crossing heavenly bodies in unsettled weather, may have observed them moving in perhaps more than two directions. Aeronauts have found as many as four simultaneous currents, successively superposed, and differing in character as well as direction.

Mr. Glaisher's recent ascents have corroborated the results of Gay Lussac, Rush, Welsh, and Green, besides other less generally known air-voyagers. These minor or intermediate currents have not qualities depending on elevation *solely*. Far from it, temperature, tension, and moisture vary quite differently from the formerly supposed regular progression upwards. For example, Mr. Glaisher found temperatures increasing with height after much diminution; then again falling, and with varieties of moisture. These and other similarly irregular variations proved intermediate currents, irregular in character, though corroborating *normal* decrease of temperature as well as pressure. As this subject will be further and fully discussed, it may suffice now to remark only — that these superposed, and varying currents of air, either colder or warmer, drier or more moist, than those adjacent (above or below, or both), must affect the climate and vegetation of high lands, against which they impinge; and modify greatly the effects of any lower or surface stream of air; whether limited narrowly, or extending over hundreds, even thousands, of miles.

Hence it is that in Switzerland, Scotland, and other mountainous countries, the temperature is sometimes warmer at a considerable elevation than it is on lower grounds; and that *descending* gusts of wind are sometimes very much warmer than the air then generally moving along earth's (or ocean's) surface.

So much has been said during the last few years about 'atmospheric waves,' that we may again refer to them here, and in rather more detail.

If wind veer round the compass in the course of two or three days (more or less), or is many days in making a circuit, — invariably, as it goes round, the barometer rises or falls according to the direction or strength of the wind. Supposing a diagram to represent 36 hours, and to be divided into spaces of three hours each along the upper horizontal line, while below, points of the compass are shown (from N. around by E. to N. again, — continued to S.); and at the side a scale of inches and decimals, from 28 to 31. Next, let us suppose that the wind has gone round the compass once, or say once and a half, as happens occasionally, and that it has been an extreme case of depression, as in a storm.

Then, if from (say) 30·3, with the wind at N., a veering occurs, first towards the NE. and then onward in the same direction around the compass—as the wind so shifts to the NE., and is about to shift towards the E. and S., the barometer foretells it or falls beforehand. When the wind is NE. the mercury is lower, probably, than when it was at N. As it gets to the E. the mercury falls:—it gets lower still at SE., and falls still more to S. and SW., where it is probably the lowest, because it feels the effects of the south-westerly or tropical current most then, and may be down, let us suppose, to 28·2 inches. As the wind shifts round to SW., W., NW., the column in the tube rises, till, perhaps, the wind is N., or even NE., when it may be as high as 30·8. It has been known in this country as high as 30·9. As the wind goes round again to the E. and SE. and S., the barometer falls as before, and a line or curve traced upon paper, representing these falls and rises, or oscillations of the barometer, during a certain time (*say* some 36 hours), has an appearance like the outline of a wave of water; but as these apparent waves, or undulations, take place *exactly* as the wind shifts, and proportionally to its strength, and as, if the wind remains in one quarter for some days, or say two or three weeks together, the curve approaches to a straight line, remaining at about the same elevation, it seems that there is an intimate and immediate connection between such a curve, or wave-line, and the oscillation of the *mercury*, though not necessarily between the curve and any undulatory movement of the atmosphere above our heads.

If a body of the atmosphere above us swelled upwards, like a wave, and fell again, as has been supposed (as it were in 'crests' and 'troughs'), how should we reconcile it with the fact of there being various currents passing over each other in different directions through the atmosphere? Aeronauts who have been up in balloons say that from one stratum of air they passed into another, and another, and at times even a fourth also, moving variously. There cannot be *vacancies* between the undulations of various strata of air. Those different bodies of atmosphere could not be undulating like waves, while having spaces between them, and interferences of cross movements. Waves of ocean have only elastic air above them, which does not impede their rise and fall materially; and they are only superficial, not reaching far down.*

With any actual raising of particles, or masses of air, the lighter or tropical portions of winds should rise the highest, and would expand; but, according to the 'Wave theory' (here controverted), the reverse is asserted; the lowest part of the *apparent* trough of the wave occurs, with the lowest barometer, that is, with the air, which is the *lightest* and most *expanded*, and ought (therefore) to rise up the *highest*; and, coincident with the heavy dry air, the highest part, or what is called the 'crest' of the wave, is observed. Considering then these facts, and the exact correspondence of the movements of the mercury with the wind's direction, besides the extreme variability traceable in *such* an atmospheric wave — which can hardly be conceived motionless for *weeks* (as in the case of a *steady northeasterly* wind), and then going into extraordinary irregularity during *a day or two* — we are led to the belief that what are *commonly* called 'atmospheric waves' are delusive; and that, although there are waves in any line

* Deep sea soundings and explorations — Pearl and Sponge divers — besides very deep work in diving bells (as at Cape Frio, for the Thetis's freight) — have proved this to be general.

indicating oscillations of the barometer, there are not such movements in the atmosphere itself as are usually adverted to by the expressions 'trough' and 'crest.'

Pulsations, or variations in *tension*, occur continuously, and have not yet been explained satisfactorily,—but are they, strictly speaking, *waves*?

Before referring even briefly to the effect of winds upon climates generally, I would allude to a few considerations connected with oceanic conditions. It may not be generally known that over ocean in most parts of the world, the average temperature of superficial water is nearly that of air near the surface. In the tropics sea-water temperature ranges from 70° to 80° or more, and the air is much the same. In some equatorial parts of the world the surface water is as warm as 86°, for instance, near the Galapagos Islands; and in some confined localities it is even *more than* 90°, as, for example, in parts of the Red Sea and Indian Archipelago. But although so warm on the surface, it is very much colder at a few hundred fathoms below, where the cold increases to 35°, or perhaps less. It was long considered that 39° must be the greatest cold that could be found in the lower ocean (being nearly that in which water was said to be most condensed), but reliable observations during the last few years have shown temperatures considerably lower than 35°.* We do not yet know exactly what effects are caused by *great* pressure, or other deep sea agencies *besides* want of *air*. The effect of great variation of temperature, and, therefore, quality of water, or the varying state of the water itself, — the action of winds upon the surface, also of evaporation, of rain, and lunar influence — combine

* See Maury's Physical Geography of the Sea; or his Sailing Directions.

to cause constant movement analogous to a *circulation* of the ocean (like that of the atmosphere), though on a much more limited scale, and, perhaps, not sensibly so much affecting very great depths. There is, for instance, the well-known current called the Gulf Stream, which runs from the Floridas across the Atlantic towards Europe, with a temperature ranging from 80° to 60°, underneath which is a current which several observers have found to be as low in temperature as 36°, or less. So closely do totally different waters sometimes approach there, and pass without mixing, that Admiral Sir Alex. Milne once found H.M.S. Nile's bow in water of 46° temperature while the stern was in the Gulf Stream at 70°. General Sabine (now President of the Royal Society) has given remarkable cases of *persistence* in sea currents.* Off the Cape of Good Hope also is a similar remarkable mixture of extremes of temperature within a very short distance of each other. The Lagulhas stream running from near Madagascar, by the coast of Africa and that Cape, has a temperature of 70°, but near the Cape, meets with cold water, from the Antarctic regions, at a temperature ranging from 40° to 50°; and these currents occasionally intermingle, sometimes near the surface, sometimes below it, so that one may dip a thermometer in the water at one hour, and find 45° or 46°, and an hour or two afterwards find from 65° to 70°. Similar places occur in the Pacific Ocean, and there is one very marked near the Galapagos Islands, on the N.W. and S.E. sides of that group.

The obvious effects of such warmth of sea water, particularly that of the Gulf Stream, upon our own climate, and the waters that are near the shores of other countries

* Sabine's Pendulum Experiments.

upon land adjacent to them, need hardly be much dwelt on in passing, except to remark that *wind* blowing over a body of warm sea water is warmed and otherwise affected (perhaps chemically).* Those countries which are exposed to the sea winds (of the lower and middle latitudes all round the world, in the northern as well as in the southern hemisphere), bringing moisture and warmth with them, are milder in climate, and more favourable to vegetation, than those countries which are exposed to dry land winds, whether hot or cold. Tropical, or other east winds, from over an expanse of ocean, carry vapours and rain. But they differ in some respects from the westerly. Polar currents in general carry but little moisture excepting where, immediately before reaching the land, they have passed over a considerable expanse of ocean, whence they have taken up evaporated moisture, and, therefore, have acquired a character more like that of ordinary sea winds, though not so moist and beneficial. Where ice or snow is melting on a great scale, air carries off vapour even from a *usually* dry quarter. Generally speaking sea winds are more or less charged with vapour, but land winds are usually dry, very different and various in their qualities, according to the country traversed.

It has been much discussed, especially in Scotland, whether the Gulf Stream has really so much effect upon our climate as has been usually thought. It has been chiefly questioned because experiments have been made with thermometers close in shore, within twenty or thirty fathoms, where the water has been affected more or less by rivers or the land near it, and has not been found nearly so warm as the winds or water of the Atlantic—but this seems to be rather a fallacious

* Ozone indicates some such peculiar effect.

ground of argument. There is no doubt that along the coast of Norway, as well as the coasts of Scotland and the Hebrides, the warming effect is such that all ice is kept out of the harbours there. The climate is mild all the year round, even at the North Cape; while on the western or the opposite side of the Atlantic, ice comes down in-shore to a very much lower latitude, even below Newfoundland.

The Consul General for Norway (J. R. Crowe, Esq.) says, that within the last few hundred years ice has increased along the east coast of Greenland very much, according to authentic records which he has consulted. We know that there were colonies, many centuries ago, on the shores of Greenland, then an open coast, which were destroyed by being blocked up by ice, and have never been heard of since: but the precise site of those settlements has been doubted. Late authorities state that they must have been on the west side of Greenland.

The space between north-west Iceland and Greenland is now blocked up usually, although some centuries ago it was quite open; while between Spitzbergen and Nova Zembla there is a very large space of open water, and for 200 miles round the North Cape of Norway, *no ice is ever seen.* The Gulf Stream is found to communicate its effects across the Atlantic by more or less narrow streams of warmer water, even to the eastward of the North Cape, where none of the harbours are frozen up at any time of the year, and where fishermen work in lighter clothes than they use further to the southward and eastward.

In some countries, where the wind blows almost constantly in one direction, vegetation is abundant on the side against which the wind blows from the ocean (an inexhaustible source of moisture), while on the other side there is scarcely any vegetation at all; as in Peru, Patagonia, parts of Arabia and Africa, various islands, parts of Asia, and of Australia, where all the moisture from the sea winds has been previously condensed or abstracted: and in passing across extensive land, the other sea side, as in Peru, receives only dried air from the land, and the country is more or less barren. So in many other places, wind carrying moisture affects one side of a hill or mountain and does not affect the other equally. Our own climate being exposed to westerly and southerly winds for about three fourths of the year, is remarkably favoured in this respect, as these winds are not only moist, but warm, and pass over warm waters of the ocean, if not the tropical, at least those of the more expanded part of the Gulf Stream.

There may be cause to suspect a gradual change in our average climate under such peculiar circumstances, and it may be very questionable how far the northern regions,—those in the latitude of Iceland and from Newfoundland across to Norway,—how far those countries may be directly though slowly affected by increase or diminution of ice in the Arctic regions; and this is a subject which should also have its weight with reference not only to considerations of our own seasons, but to temperate climates adjacent to polar regions around each hemisphere.

The temperatures of the surfaces of almost all seas and oceans has been generally ascertained, and those of their depths here and there. Thermometers peculiarly constructed, self-registering, and showing maximum as well as *minimum* temperatures, or minimum only (which is sometimes sufficient, and admits of the instrument being *narrower*, a considerable advantage in *sounding*), strong enough to resist the pressure of the ocean at three or four miles depth, where there may be a force exerted to compress them, exceeding three or four hundred atmospheres (of 15 lbs. to the square inch), have been employed.

The specific gravity of the ocean has been tried lately in nearly all parts of the world, by small glass hydrometers; and the general result is that the specific gravity of the salt water is very much the same in all places, except where affected by recent heavy rains, or by water from the mouths of large rivers; the differences in the specific gravity being found to be less, usually, than errors of observation, such as may occur if the hydrometer is put into water without being carefully wiped. From mere carelessness in not thus cleaning it a difference of two or three divisions of the scale may be caused. The instrument is, however, *very accurate if correctly used*, and by its means a general result seems to be established — that the surface of the ocean is almost everywhere within one or two divisions of 1,027 (taking distilled water at 1,000 grains), sea-water thus *averaging* 1,027 grains in weight. The difference between various parts of the ocean, taking the whole world, being not more than 2 or 3 of these divisions, or from 26, in short, to about 28, rather less than the difference between using the instrument carelessly and accurately. In the Red Sea a specific gravity considerably higher than 1,028 seems to have been found; and some of the eastern seas show similar *exceptional* instances (*said* to extend to 1,080 in the Red Sea).

Interest has been caused by ozone, which has been thought to affect health considerably. Whatever may be the real chemical or philosophical explanation, the known facts at present appear to be that ozone is chiefly found on or near the sea, and that winds which blow towards the land from the nearest sea bring the most ozone. Lieutenant Chimmo lately observed that in the Hebrides, and on the north-west coast of Scotland, there is more ozone than he had found in other places, including the great ocean; and, on comparing notes from different parts of our own coasts, it is remarkable that the winds which accompany the greatest indications of ozone are those which blow from the nearest and largest sea. When Captain Jansen, of Holland, and Dr. Mitchell of Edinburgh, made observations in India, in the Atlantic and in Algeria—Jansen's being between Batavia and England — they found by independent methods that over the sea, clear of the land, there was most ozone, and that over land or hills near the sea—hills against which the sea-winds blew—there was more than in the valleys or in other places which were separated from the sea; and that inland, about towns, and in inland places generally, there was exceedingly little. These observers employed the methods advised by Dr. Moffatt and by Professor Schönbein.

This may seem to point to a connection between ozone and chlorine gas, which is in and over sea-water, and which *must* be brought by any wind that blows from the sea. We will not here make any further reference to its peculiarities, except one—its possible affection of the gastric juice—as it is a question rather too purely chemical. Certainly at present the results of various different observations of ozone show— that the greater prevalence of it is with wind that blows from the nearest sea; — that it prevails more over the ocean and near it than over land, especially land remote from the sea:—that it improves digestion, and has a tanning effect.

CHAPTER VII

Recapitulation and further Explanations — Qualities of Air — Vapour — Convective Action — Alternations — Tropical or Juxta-Tropical Zones — Action of Currents — Results of Experience — Barometric Curves—Atmospheric Waves—Currents specified by Dové as 'parallel,' by others as 'successive' — Law of Gyration —Electricity —Polarisation of Air — Mechanical Views of Redfield, Reid, and Barlow.

With the hope of being clearly understood, although risking a repetition of ideas, if not expressions, some degree of recapitulation will be offered in this chapter before an advance is ventured into an explanation of the reasons for predicting, or, rather, *forecasting* weather, as a practical application of meteorologic science tending to its utilisation in daily life.

Pray imagine or place a globe before you, and look at it from east or west, at right angles to the polar axis. Consider the globe as rotating: your eye being in space a long way outside of the earth's or globe's atmosphere, which may be supposed to extend eight or ten miles from the surface, *nearly* as we feel it — and farther in a much lighter condition, perhaps even less ponderable than that of hydrogen gas, the lightest of our elements, which, *light as it is, still gravitates.*

Bear in mind the difference between actual and relative gravitation, or *weight.* Lead, feathers, gas, even the lightest of all, gravitate toward the centre of mass — one more forcibly or heavily than another, which is, therefore, *forced* to rise, or sink *less*, against *its own tendency*. Air is an *elastic, a highly elastic fluid*, having not only the equilibrating properties of water, *but a resilience, or tendency to expand at even the least diminution of pressure.* Its (atomic) particles being more nearly *mechanically* than chemically combined (in the proportion of one part of oxygen to four parts of hydrogen), they are always liable to chemical change, caused by more or less heat (caloric), electrical action, or mere gravitation. In gravitation is included *cohesion*, the cohesion of particles being only a lesser effect of the general law of attraction or gravitation, whether as Newton viewed it, or a *magnetic* action, as has been suggested by high authority.

Air under diminished pressure expands on all sides, becomes *lighter*, bulk for bulk, like the air on a high mountain, which presses so lightly on mercury, compared with that near the sea.

Air *also* expands from increase of *heat*, that subtle and mysterious agent which acts mechanically, *and* in an unexplained manner: but a manner which is *felt* through the very densest as well as the lightest matter, yet no more explicable, to the *general* senses, than sight, or the electric touch, or the moral emotion in one human being caused by a look or a word from another.

Again, air expands from an increase of vapour, aqueous or watery vapour, in an invisible state. This gas, *lighter than air* (like expanded but not condensed *steam*), mixed among the particles of air, renders any given bulk, say a cubic foot, lighter than a cubic foot of *drier* air; while, from its elasticity, resilience, and fluidity, it fills equal space: partly as a bale of cotton occupies a larger space, *naturally* (though not larger if *artificially* compressed), than a mass of earth equal in weight: and partly as *warm* water occupies *proportionate* space among bodies of cold fluid, such as the Gulf Stream at 80° meeting currents at 40°.

Vapour rising, which is water in a gaseous state, (water being one part oxygen, and two parts hydrogen by *bulk*), may undergo more or less chemical change as it rises through air, thus adding to or taking from the weight of that air. Such changes are accompanied probably by electrical action, more or less sudden, or visible ; or felt only in its effects.

An electrician at a table can cause a little breeze of wind that moves toy boats in a trough, and can make rain, in drops, by an electric current through the air we are breathing—a miniature analogy to operations of Nature.

Having thus shown the more special properties of air— Suppose the torrid zone of our earth (or the globe imagined before us) to be considerably heated, while the polar regions are cool, an action like that in water set on the fire to boil takes place in the atmosphere. The warmed parts rise; their places are filled by the cold; in turn, the now *chilled* parts (which were warmed) descend, where they can, and a circular rather than a vertical alternation is 'set up.' This is almost the process of convection, which generally proceeds in fluids, by a circulation *nearly* vertical.

Now, bear in mind that the warmed *mass* of torrid-zone air is vastly greater, even without any expansion, than the polar cool bodies : and that, once in motion, the greater mass *must* go somewhere (owing to its momentum, and to condensation and increase of weight, in the upper and colder regions of our atmosphere); and it will not appear improbable that a very considerable portion of the air raised near the equator *descends* just beyond the tropics, and there makes its way, *between* opposing polar currents, or *under* or *over* them, towards the north and east; while another, perhaps the greater part, turns *southward* in the calm variable latitudes, and helps to supply the perennial trade winds, which *cannot* be sufficiently maintained from the comparatively small polar regions (where the meridians all converge so rapidly).

But the *varying* states of equatorial and polar regions, consequent on the earth's rotation, on immense precipitation of vapour (rains)—on daily, as differing from nightly, action of the sun—on great electrical changes and chemical action, and other perplexing causes: these varying states must be accompanied or followed by alternations, or, as it were, *pulsations* of the atmospheric greater currents—those towards and from the equator or poles. Such *pulsations*, so to speak, must be accompanied by more or less onward movement of air along the earth's surface, by absolute calm, or by a *tendency* towards a vacuum. Mind, only a tendency, because no sooner does either current, polar or tropical, yield or fail, than immediately the *resilient* properties of the other are actively developed to equilibrate the mass. Thus, directly a polar current (our north-east wind) becomes less decided, and draws towards east, the barometer by falling, and the thermometer by rising, indicate a lessened tension, a raised temperature, and a coming tropical current. The change may follow by south-east and south to south-west, or it may be masked by other influences, and back round, by the north, or shift across at once.

After an interval the polar current, having, as it were, acquired strength, approaches, either suddenly with a great conflict, perhaps storm, lightning, and hail, or *gradually*, causing only a change from S.W. through

W. to N.W., and afterwards again by N. to N.E. These are the *usual* effects, but anomalies occur often, from counter-eddies in the atmosphere, more or less *resilient*, which, however, are all explicable in connection with these few general principles and the rotation of the earth, for which reference should again be made to the globe.

As the earth (or globe) turns on its axis from W. to E., particles or bodies of air drawn towards the equator from either pole, are more and more left behind, as it were, on the surface, which is turning continually to the E. more and more rapidly as nearer the equator, where the rotary movement is greatest. Hence air, starting from either pole, and always moving directly towards the equatorial regions, is felt on the earth's surface as a current between N. and E. (a diagonal line being traced across the globe), and thus a wind felt as N.E. was, perhaps, really a north wind; and a north wind, as felt, may have been almost a north-westerly current.

The opposite case differs considerably. A particle or a mass of air raised at the equator and impelled towards either pole, has the *momentum* of that part of the globe where it *ascends*, and as it goes polarwise it passes over portions of the surface moving slower and slower compared with equatorial rotation. Such an equatorial mass (or particle) goes eastward *faster* than the surface, and causes westerly wind. Hence the *prevalent* west winds of middle latitudes, which are, however, frequently in contest with, or considerably affected by, polar currents — the two *combining* — from the westward causing all varieties of warm or cold, wet or dry, wind from *that* side (south to north by the *west*), while their mutual action from the opposite side (north to south by *east*) causing the fluctuations and variations observed with winds from that half of the compass.

The basis of this theory is Dové's 'Law of Gyration,' supported by Sir John Herschel; but its illustration in some measure, and this application of it to the peculiarities of the calm variable, or *horse* latitudes, were the present writer's, originally.*

Some of those 'peculiarities' are — remarkable stagnation or quiet of the atmosphere near the earth (while high light clouds, rapidly crossing heavenly bodies, show upper currents *toward* polar regions)— frequent, but temporary rains—squalls, often *descending*, and (generally, all the year round) a remarkably high barometer, or much atmospheric tension.

Exceptions to this general condition, between 25° and 35° of latitude, are those occasional but comparatively rare hurricanes, or storms, which, like all great temporary winds, are more or less cyclonic or circuitous.

The high barometer and general tranquillity of those juxta-tropical zones of all the world (where not much affected by continental masses of land, having heated plains or snow-covered mountains) are caused by the opposition of descending equatorial air cooled (to a certain degree) by the higher regions, and the horizontally moving polar currents drawn usually towards the equator. The combination of these two causes pressure and raises the barometer.

When, in middle, or other latitudes, pressure or tension is relaxed — from *comparative* failure of polar supplies — *immediately* the air becomes lighter the barometer falls, and the prevailing opponent, equatorial or tropical current, begins to be sensible — its approach being generally gradual, preceded by warmth, and by an overclouding of the sky — altogether different

* They were first expressed in the third number of Meteorologic Papers, published by the Board of Trade in 1857.

from the accompaniments of a sudden or rapid, cold, and, perhaps at first, stormy polar wind.

The more salient features have alone been here sketched; as to include more details at present might only confuse. The general circulation and alternation of atmospherical currents being understood, it is easy to see how a circular or cyclonic character must obtain with all storms, which are the vortices, or eddies on a large scale, at the edges of great moving *breadth* or masses of the atmosphere.

The currents of a large river illustrate these motions, in a certain sense, but the fluid *water* has neither *resilience*, nor much *electrical* agency operating in it — nor *chemical* changes — nor mechanical alteration from absorption or precipitation of *vapour*, like the *fluid*, and elastically, as well as otherwise, most *changeable air*. Circuitous sweeps or cyclonic eddies are horizontal, or vertical, or inclined at a certain angle to the horizontal plane. One part of the meteoric curl may touch, sweep, or press along the surface of the globe — while another side of the cyclone may be in an upper region, and unfelt, though often traceable, through its upper current, carrying clouds across the heavenly bodies in various directions — successively — differing from those of the surface wind felt by the observer.

Land and sea breezes — of fine weather, and tropical climates — are local, and small circulations, vertically, on principles exactly similar to those already mentioned. They are cases of 'convection' — the cool sea air moving to the heated land, by day — rising, becoming cooled, and returning seaward to the *then warmer* ocean at night, or towards morning. The sea varies so very little in its normal temperature, in respective latitudes and localities, that it is everywhere a great modifier, or moderator of climate; besides being perhaps the source of that interesting peculiarity, ozone — so beneficial to health — which is found to *prevail* over sea or with winds from the sea (and, as we have said, *seems* to be oxydised chlorine gas).

A few more words, by way of recapitulation, may be here added respecting 'atmospheric waves' (so-called).

Particular attention was drawn to these *supposed* undulations of atmosphere, by papers read at meetings of the British Association, and by an article in the Admiralty Manual of Science. Great authorities then countenanced the theory, and apparently sanctioned such opinions. Yet there is so much argument against those views, that even the highest names may scarcely warrant their implicit adoption. That there must be undulations or pulsations in the atmosphere — constituted as it is — cannot be doubted, but that the curve traced on paper representing the oscillations of a barometer, as the wind veers round the compass, corresponds to a mechanical, watery, wavelike, undulation of the body of atmosphere — is not sufficiently proved.

Summarily, one may demur to it on these grounds. First, the curve so traced on paper, varies not only with the barometer, but with the *direction* of the wind, which is invariably accompanied by change of pressure or tension, consequent on the greater or less action of polar current.

Secondly, while the wind *remains* in one quarter, the curve or line, taken as that of the superficial outline of a wave section, *remains* almost unvaried, except in consequence of altered *strength* of wind or *much rain*, which have each a *comparatively* small effect.

Thirdly, the lowest part of the curve (*called* the

trough of the wave) always corresponds to the lowest barometer, or *lightest air*; whereas it is the lightest air that rises highest, as instanced at the equator; and therefore the crest of an atmospheric *wave* (so to speak) ought to be over the place of lowest barometer.

Fourthly, aeronauts always find, and the upper clouds often show, currents *above* very different from those below. These superposed and successive strata, in rapid cross motion, must tend to check if not to destroy undulation. To what has been stated on this subject (atmospheric waves) in the invaluable Essay on Meteorology in the last edition of the Encyclopædia Britannica, the utmost deference is due; but the experiment there described, of the undulations transmitted through successive *passive* strata of fluids (coloured) *in a vessel*—did not meet the case of fluid strata of *air moving* horizontally, in *various* directions, across each other.

That there are *tidal* waves in the atmosphere, caused by the sun and moon, experiment has proved; but that they are so *very* small as to be, practically, almost insensible, seems also to have been demonstrated. This subject, however, has still to be much investigated. Such waves as these follow their causes, in periodic times, *not* diurnally *alone*, as influenced by sun and moon, but in *semi-lunar* intervals affecting both *direction* and *force* of wind.

Among constant agencies are the formation, growth, or decay of ice in polar regions, and its effects. The comparative qualities of *polar* winds (north or south)—their electrical and other peculiarities, and the *relative depths* of the atmosphere at the poles and equator—are very curious and little known subjects in meteorology.

As it has been *ascertained* that the sun's rays *are* more powerful in high latitudes than they are in tropical regions, perhaps the *depth* of atmosphere is diminished near the poles, owing to less centrifugal force; while it is not so much charged with aqueous vapour: and thus there may be at least these two reasons for increased penetration by the sun's rays.

Electricity has been referred to, and often will be again, in these pages—ubiquitous agent as it assuredly is. With polar winds or air currents, its influence varies towards a maximum, and is *plus*, positive, or vitreous. With the opposite (tropical, moist, and southerly or south-westerly) winds, electrical indications are almost insensible, minus, or negative. With rain or snow there is usually less, (minus, or negative) electricity in the atmosphere—if *any* can be distinguished at all (without experiments of a peculiar and special nature). This all-pervading agency, latent and tranquil if equilibrated, equally diffused or specifically apportioned — excited, or made evident to our faculties by action, change of temperature, friction, collision or pressure —is so intimately engaged in every atmospheric change, opposition, movement, or combination, that it should never be left out of mind. Imponderable, intangible, ubiquitous — nay, *materially*, almost omnipotent, this most marvellous of all the elements of our wonderful world, is under control, subordinate to man, and yet as unknown and even as mysterious as 'his glassy essence.'

The circulations of *magnetic* currents are so similar to atmospheric circulations in their remarkable outlines, and the *electrical* state of each main current of air, tropical or polar, is so regularly minus or plus according to the north-eastward or south-westward direction — these currents having also, invariably, *tensions* of more or less mechanical *pressure*, shown by the barometer, averaging from a quarter to half an inch everywhere—that one may ask whether polar cold and tropical heat may not affect the condition and relative *position* of the atoms, particles, or molecules of air, so that those from polar regions are polarised in position, *inter se*, deprived of much heat, or electric fluid, and therefore also of aqueous vapour, closed together, and made denser, drier, and heavier, bulk for bulk. Supposing this to be the case, and that the particles of an *ab-polar* current are ranged (say) north and south (whatever their actual ultimate form may be), while those of a tropically-affected body of air are not only separated farther apart by heat and vapour, but ranged in a different direction (suppose), east and west—their form may be such as to *prevent*, under *those* circumstances, so close an adhesion or packing together.

The particles would be more separated, more mobile, even more fluid; and, as vapour is lighter than air, each cubic quantity would be lighter and moister than equal cubes of ab-polar or north-easterly atmosphere. Such considerations as these might go toward explanation of the barometric oscillations—as varying currents extend or move along earth's surface.

But there is another cause of barometric oscillation besides actual lateral and vertical pressure or tension; (themselves effects of depth and lateral elasticity of atmosphere, acting more in a calm than at other times, especially when currents or winds are mutually tending from opposite directions towards the place of observation). This cause is the diminution of air tension or pressure caused by its *expansion*, in consequence of freedom to move horizontally, or otherwise (like water let out of a reservoir, were water *also* elastic as well as fluid). Sir William Reid's explanation, after Redfield's, adopted and therefore supported by his very high authority, is that the pressure of the atmosphere is diminished by *motion* in some places; increased, by the same cause, in others, according as the depth varies vertically. But they applied this view specially to rotatory storms, and did not include the general question.

And there may be a further consideration:

Experiments made by Mr. Barlow in 1849, instituted to discover how far vertical pressure is diminished by horizontal speed, *seemed to show* that a velocity of fifty miles an hour caused about one seventh less vertical pressure than when the movable body was stationary. Now, in the familiar instance of *skating*—ice will bear a man in rapid motion which would break if he stood still. If air, in swift motion, have its vertical weight, and therefore total tension, diminished, the Torricellian column must show it. If moving with horizontal velocity of thirty miles an hour (about one-third of its swiftness in a storm), and the tension diminished only one-thirtieth instead of one-seventh, the column might fall about one inch from this cause only;—but, probably, it would fall much more—on the assumption of this view of diminished pressure being tenable,—which, however, *high authorities deny.*

In treating of remarkable and happily but infrequent occurrences, such as great storms, a tendency has prevailed to permit attention to be so much engrossed by those *exceptions* to the general course of nature, that ordinary weather, prevalent winds, and, as one may say, the meteorology of everyday life—has been neglected.

An endeavour to lessen the vacancy, in this respect, left by those admirable teachers, Redfield, Reid, Piddington, and even by higher authorities, namely, those true philosophers who have written on meteorology, is the present writer's aim. He has felt the want of aid in daily *weather-work* and knows how others often feel.

In 1839, the following passage was published in the Beagle's Voyage, with reference to Reid's Law of Storms, then first exciting general notice among sea officers. It was thought by the author of that voyage, then recently returned from seven years' exploring and surveying duties in many quarters of the world, including its circumnavigation, that too much stress was laid on the *exceptional* storm, and too little notice given, too few facts stated, respecting the normal or regular course of atmospheric conditions or changes, and ordinary movements of the air.

His words *then* were: 'are not storms *exceptional* to the general winds or atmospheric currents—not the CAUSES of them? Some persons may have laid too much stress upon such exceptions, and have rather overlooked the principal *general* features—those of the conditions which *prevail almost continuously*. Common winds occur throughout the year, except during short intervals; but hurricanes, or even ordinary storms, are comparatively rare. May not opposing or passing currents cause eddies or whirls on an immense scale in the air, not only horizontal, but inclined to the horizon, or vertical?'

'In laying a ship to during a storm, there are *other* points to be considered besides the veering of the wind, such as the direction of the sea, perhaps against a current. I never myself witnessed *one* storm that blew from more than sixteen points of the compass, either successively or by sudden changes. In most, if not all of the storms to which I can bear testimony, currents of air arriving from different directions appeared to succeed each other, or combine together. One usually brought the "dirt" (to use a sailor's term), and another cleared it away, driving much back again, often with redoubled fury. One of these currents was warm and moist, another cold and dry, comparatively speaking. While one lasted the barometer fell or was stationary; with the other it rose. At all places I have visited, or from which I have obtained notices on the subject, the barometer stands high with easterly, and comparatively low with westerly winds, on an average. Northerly winds in the northern hemisphere affect the barometer like southerly winds in the southern hemisphere.' *

A quarter of a century's attention to the subject *since*, has convinced the writer that consideration ought to be given *first* to the great general order of circulation, with alternating, and more or less 'parallel,' currents, and afterwards to *their* consequences, when disturbed — namely storms, and other occasional phenomena.

* Voyages of Adventure and Beagle.—Appendix, 1839.

CHAPTER VIII

Means employed to collect Information — Simultaneous or Synoptic Charts — Ready Co-operation — Inferences since proved true — Barometric Curves — Atmospheric Currents: their Translation Eastward — Commencements of Changes — Alteration and Deflection of Currents — Effects of Land — Cyclones: their Duration — Authorities — Capper — De Foe — Comparison of Storms.

SIMULTANEOUS observations of our own atmosphere had been recommended by some of the most eminent men, who had turned a part of their attention to meteorology, even before Dr. Lloyd undertook and executed his valuable series, extending through ten years, in Ireland. From these, from Mr. Stevenson's three years in Berwickshire, and from many fragmentary notices, some of very old date, some in the last two centuries, and others of our own time, it was obvious that, over and around the British Islands, storms had an eastward course, or, in other words, came from the west *generally*. Exceptions, however, *seemed* to occur with easterly winds (from the east), which were not then understood.

In 1857 the Board of Trade invited general co-operation around and upon the North Atlantic, between the tropic of Cancer and the arctic circle. United States, Norwegian, Danish, Dutch, German, French, Spanish, Portuguese, and Italian observations were collated with those of our own coasts, ships, and observatories. The lighthouses (admirable points for such enquiries) were in the front rank, by Trinity House direction. Ships traversed the sea, provided with the few instruments indispensable, while, for central operations, the principal observatories afforded an unquestionably sound basis.

A series of charts was then commenced by Mr. Babington, which, in three years, increased to many hundreds. These outline charts have *no mark* on them *unnecessary* for expressing atmospheric condition or time, or locality by latitude and longitude. An outline only of land, and as few names as possible, are shown. Being intended to express consecutive simultaneous states of atmosphere — as if an eye in space looked down on the *whole* North Atlantic *at one time* and afterwards took similar views (much more extensive than '*bird's eye*') at regular intervals of hours or days, so as to obtain sequences of synoptic conditions — we called them 'synoptic charts.' It was subsequently suggested that 'synchronous' would be a better term, and it was adopted. Now, however, it appears to the writer that *this* word is less appropriate. In General Sabine's recent lecture at Cambridge, on Magnetism, the term synchronous is applied to observations made at the same local hour around the world: but these are not simultaneous. Truly indeed they are synchronous, but not in the sense that is required for occurrences happening simultaneously or synoptically, referred to time or view, at one place only, and one meridian. Therefore it is that we now abandon our erroneous appellation and revert to '*synoptic* charts.' Their principles of construction, and many other details respecting these very useful documents, are in the Appendix, and in accompanying diagrams.

Among the most instructive and permanently valuable, are those of the period which included two notable storms, that of October 25–26* and November 1, in 1859. This series was published as an atlas, with the Tenth number of the Board of Trade Meteorologic Papers.

First comparisons of such observations around our own coasts *seemed* decidedly to show consecutive '*waves*' of atmosphere, by the curves indicating *altitudes* of the *barometric* column.

Espy's great works, and his multitudinous curves closely covering many large sheets, *seemed to prove* the case indisputably.

Yet the present writer ventures to submit a very different view of the subject—one that, at all events, is in no degree contravened by any facts hitherto publicly recorded as having been anywhere reliably observed.

The two principal currents of air being different in their qualities, obviously cause states of pressure or tension, temperature, and other peculiarities, at any given place, corresponding to those of the air then present—a portion, however small, of a passing current. This current does not continue, in the temperate zones, for a long time; it may be a mere streamlet, as it were, of a few hours duration; it may continue during some days; it may persistently last through several weeks; but, while it is present, the statical conditions of air around an observer are of the same character, however different in quantity, or force—excepting when there is a *mixture* of air currents at the place of observation, in which very common, if not prevalent case, statical conditions vary with the relative proportions of elements intermingled.

(Such elements are now sufficiently known, and trace-

* Royal Charter.

able, to admit of their being stated in a mathematical manner, and managed algebraically.)

It has been proved that great atmospheric currents circulate, extend to various distances horizontally in length and breadth, or either only, are sometimes side by side but moving in opposite directions, sometimes superposed or overlying. And it has also been proved that the mercurial column has an average height, in presence of one current, differing considerably from that which is the normal, average, or mean elevation under opposite influence, that of the contrary main current.

What must be the results of observation at any one place? As one of the principal air currents, polar or tropical, approaches, its peculiarities are gradually felt, and barometers alter (other instruments also.) The alteration continues in one direction as the current passes, until its greatest influence is past, and a contrary change begins, which increases as the opposite current advances, or extends its effects. Thus the barometer rises and falls, or falls and rises, more or less regularly —as it is influenced by the passing currents of air; and as these movements are more or less directly with the surface *wind* which goes round the compass, 'gyrates,' or shifts with those currents (of which it is the effect and evidence), a line traced on paper, co-ordinating the barometric heights, will have a wave-like form, in which the crests will correspond to one current and the hollows (or troughs) to the opposite.

But this appearance *on paper* in no way demonstrates a real mechanical undulation of atmosphere, a body composed of many layers, or overlying strata, different in qualities, and moving in *various* directions simultaneously.

The Gulf Stream, with its dense, and heavy, though

warm water, exists side by side, in equilibrium, with the less saline, lighter, and cooler water of arctic regions.

Sabine describes currents of water running thousands of miles *parallel* to other currents setting in contrary directions, *without mixing*, one having qualities very different from those of the other. Every navigator of experience knows several cases of a similar kind. The Orinoco, the Amazon, the Plata, Niger, Congo, Ganges, Hoanho, the Japanese current (like our Gulf Stream), the Lagulhas current, and the Straits of Magellan, are familiar instances, immediately occurring to mind.

Generally speaking, the more rapid the motion of passing currents, either of water or air, the less they mingle; and, contrariwise, the more gentle, the quieter their appulse, the more readily, intimately and quickly their intermixture takes place. Thus the observed facts show that *gradual* alterations always accompany slow motions, and abrupt rapid changes are observed invariably with strong winds. Simultaneous observations show that the lines uniting places of equal pressure or tension (isobarometric) usually extend NW. and SE.* across the directions of those main atmospheric currents which agree so remarkably with the directions ascertained to be those of magnetic currents,† whether in earth or air.

This accords with the views expressed here of mutual action from opposite directions, either retreating, and so *diminishing* tension (*apparent* pressure), or advancing, condensing, and therefore augmenting it, not only horizontally, but by the intrusion or rush of either advancing current, as a wedge, above that next the

* In this hemisphere.

† Herschel, Kreil, Lamont, Lloyd, Loomis, Quételet, Sabine, and Walker.

surface (though *below* other air), *or along the bottom.* It is in these transitions that tempestuous weather occurs,—storms and all minor atmospheric commotions being occasioned chiefly by these opposing currents, causing eddying or cyclonic sweeps, sometimes continuing for several days in succession. These huge eddies in the atmosphere have been too often regarded as erratic meteors, starting from some place (not defined) and whirling round and round, like a wheel, while going across a whole ocean. For many reasons (some already stated in these pages, others to be yet adduced) this *cannot be.*

As the contesting currents move along earth's surface, they must carry such eddies, *which they cause,* with them, between their contiguous sides, just as eddies in water are carried along (translated) bodily, by a stream, while whirling round.

Soon after a few of the earlier synoptic charts were partly filled, it became apparent that while there are *various* currents, sweeps, or circuits, in any given area of our temperate zone, intermixed and incessantly moving—the whole body of them (as a connected group), the entire mass of the atmosphere in our latitude, has a constant, a perennial movement toward the east, *averaging* about five miles an hour.

This induction from facts observed at a great number of places having since been fully proved, and amply corroborated, has induced the Board of Trade to provide means for daily forecasts of weather, and occasional warnings of expected gales of wind, or storms.

It is certainly remarkable that, until lately, attention had been so much attracted to the *exceptional* occurrences of our climate—to storms, to extremes of temperature and extraordinary falls of rain, hail, or snow—

that the ordinary course of nature, the less disturbed and normal condition of atmosphere, though by far the more prevalent, had so slight a share of thought bestowed on it, so little consideration of a comprehensive kind given to its usual state, that there was no clue, *apparently*, to the common alternations or changes of wind and weather; and even the ablest philosophers almost derided the idea of foretelling them, except on occasions of great storms. Now that we have a key to the subject, some light may be thrown, and the difficulties of darkness partly dispersed. Some perplexing questions still are unanswerable, and obstacles occur often, no doubt, but they are of minor importance, in a practical point of view, and do not interfere materially with what has become a daily public duty — namely, giving general notice of *probable* winds and weather, for two days in advance, around the coasts of Great Britain and Ireland, with such occasional cautionary premonitions as may diminish loss of life and destruction of property.

When one contemplates the grander circulation of our atmosphere, effected by a continual progression towards the West, inter-tropically,* and Eastward in temperate zones — when these originating movements are viewed in connection with the permanent conditions of equatorial and polar regions, and with the meridional or cross currents occasioned by their respective heat and cold — admiration of the providential arrangement for incessant change of vital air may well be unlimited.

By these continuous changes a malarious or pestilential region is ventilated, and air raised or carried from it does not pass more than once over any other place before it is intermingled with the atmosphere, as land drainage is carried out to sea, by constant tidal currents.

* Not overlooking occasional, and but temporary interruptions, easily explicable; but marking, as it were, great *outlines*.

Among the most striking consequences of this normal tendency toward the east, in the temperate zones, is the apparent anomaly of east winds sometimes beginning in the west, and west winds occasionally to the eastward of any place — which may be thus explained.

A stream of polar wind traverses the North Atlantic near Ireland and Scotland. As it advances southward it also moves (or is carried with the whole atmosphere) eastward, so that its effect is felt first in Ireland and Scotland. Advancing southward still, before approaching Norway, it is impeded by Scotch highlands (4,000 feet) and then affected by Norwegian mountains (8,000 feet). The increasing current, of air (or *wind*) — advancing, widening, and augmenting in momentum, passes around Scotland, between it and Ireland, along the Scottish eastern shores, and, urged from behind, while in front checked, and *deflected* by Danish, Dutch and French shores, this *polar* wind becomes more or less *easterly* on our east coasts.

There is no *true* east wind in our zone, that has come from any *considerable distance due east*, moving toward the west. Polar winds deflected by local configuration, and the earth's rotation, become more or less easterly. When a tropical current is advancing, its extremes intermix with the yielding or diminishing opposite (the polar), deflect them, and (affected also by local configuration of land) become south-easterly before they turn to southerly and then to south-west.*

This is the usual order, but the force of each current varies, the *vis a tergo*, or, as it may be, the *indraught* of a change in *advance*, a diminished tension not at once altered by a current from elsewhere, causes successive actions, expansions, impulses, or pulsations, of an otherwise failing movement — occasioning *retrograde* motions,

* See Polar Current diagram.

sudden shifts, squalls, or even violent gales of *short* duration.

The mutual action of horizontal, or any currents of air, may be likened to the shooting out, or flickering, of long tongues of flame, *in their form*, though of course *totally* unlike in *degree*, or direction of motion, and otherwise. There can be no vacancy, nothing like a vacuum between opposing, or adjoining air currents, under *ordinary* circumstances, although there may be diminished or increased pressure, according as they tend towards and compress each other, or incline away from and so lessen mutual *tension*. When a tropical current is advancing from the S. and W. it approaches in an irregular manner by such (as it were) flickering sallies, either from *above* a diminishing polar stream, or horizontally along the surface of earth or ocean.

Touches of the coming wind are therefore felt, in various places, before its main stream has occupied the area. This applies equally to an advancing polar current, as the *new* occupant usually comes *above*, and displaces the exhausted one, by local and perhaps far-separated action, previous to general usurpation. Hence it happens at times that the tropical wind extends a stream across South England, to perhaps Heligoland, *before* it has touched Ireland; after which it may increase in its spread northwards to the west of Ireland, and so gradually include all the British Islands; or, it may not touch them *more*, but pass off eastward. These variations are dependent on the great causes of the conflicting currents — of which we know but little, as yet, that enables us to *calculate* their occurrence and duration.

Very great differences and deflections, or changes in direction, are caused in the lower air currents by *land*. One cannot more readily realise the view of this subject, that is found to be accordant with fact, than by looking at the action of flowing tide around rocks, or a river under a bridge.

Viewing our islands, or any lands, as impediments to the free horizontal motion of air currents, and recollecting that—however impeded, checked, or deflected (perhaps upward) air *may be* in places—the main body, the great, wide, and deep portion of atmosphere flows on resistlessly—local anomalies, squalls, eddies, or calms are more readily explicable. In general the tropical current is so unimpeded, comparatively, in the North Atlantic, that it advances much more *northward* there, than at the *same time* it reaches across Spain and Portugal; and the consequence is that the first appulse or influence of a south-wester is usually felt in Scotland and Ireland, and even occasionally Norway or Denmark, owing to such *preceding* local '*touches*' as have been just mentioned.

Conversely, the very first effects of a polar current advancing, are sometimes shown in Portugal—although *generally* on the west coast of Ireland, its north part, and in Scotland. Useful proofs of these effects are attainable, not only by comparisons of published weather reports, but by a curious and generally unnoticed means. The *Steamers* arriving at Queenstown, Londonderry, Liverpool, or Southampton, sometimes publish short notices of the wind and weather prevalent during two or three days before arrival,* and such kind of weather may not only be expected to follow in Ireland, but generally it will reach and cross England, though not always, as coasts are more or less barriers. Against the high hills of Ireland, the mountains of Wales, and

* These steamers have *crossed* the *places* or *lines* of wind and weather so described; the *lateral* progression of such currents not nearly equalling powerful steamers, advance *across* them.

the highlands of Scotland — against the heights of Cornwall, Devonshire, Westmoreland, and Cumberland, many a current of wind, heavily charged with vapour, is impelled (by its momentum from remotely acting force), but *there* has its moisture precipitated and its direction changed, either by the land or by *opposing* air-currents.

Storms occur in such localities which do not last long or travel far. They are violent and locally dangerous, but are not extensive and far reaching, like those cyclonic commotions which sometimes begin in the Atlantic, and pass over us, sometimes originate *hereabouts* and last a day, or, *rarely*, two to three days, as they move along eastward.

Whatever *may* have been the duration of any one cyclonic storm in the Atlantic, in the West Indies, or in the Indian Ocean, no instance has yet been obtained *here*, of a definite and reliable character, of a rotatory gale lasting or *travelling* beyond four days.

Redfield, Sir William Reid, Piddington, and their immediate followers, certainly refer to cyclones of *apparently* many more days in duration, but, after looking through their works, examining carefully their facts, and comparing them with other data, it is difficult to believe that occasionally *consecutive* cyclones have not been treated as continuous storms. In the works of those authors, so full of facts, and everywhere evidencing the integrity of mind dictating their expression, it is highly satisfactory to study; whether recently acquired light induce other conclusions from their researches, or, on the other hand, ratify them fully.

There have been authorities, however, whose works, though published, have not been known sufficiently, and the chief of them is Capper. Mentioned, and even quoted, indeed, he has been, but not sufficiently. For original and valuable ideas, Colonel Capper deserved more credit than he received in his day, or has yet been awarded.*

Nor should De Foe be remembered otherwise than with gratitude, for his interesting accounts of great storms.† De Foe's name, better known by 'Robinson Crusoe' than by 'The Storm,' may induce a remark that *his* statements *may* be more or less over-coloured, if not exaggerated, nevertheless they *will* bear criticism.

Those who have never witnessed the power of wind in a violent tempest, or concentrated whirlwind, are naturally reluctant to give full credit to 'traveller's tales:' but as it happens that the writer of these words has himself seen effects exceedingly marvellous, and has often found truth stranger than fiction, he will add a few extracts in the concluding chapter from various authorities, showing some consequences of storms which he believes to be correctly described and perfectly true.

And here may occur a question not easy to answer, respecting tempests of former days, and those occurring now, occasionally. Were there greater storms some hundred years ago? Was that of 1703 really much more remarkable than any other known, historically, or by tradition? Ought we to anticipate such extreme visitations again?

When analysed carefully, the facts of the greatest storms on record do not appear to exceed those occasionally witnessed now: but there are, in the present day, better buildings, better ships, and more precautions. Experience, education, instruments, and diffusion of knowledge, with the now understood laws of storms, have enabled us to withstand, although they have not disarmed the tempest.

* Capper on Winds, &c.

† The Storm, &c., published in 1704.

CHAPTER IX

Effects of the greater Currents of Air and their Offsets around the World — Glancing intertropically first — West Coast of Africa: Its Islands—Atlantic Trade Winds — Rains — Harmattan—Tornadoes — Brazil — West India Hurricanes — Gulf of Mexico — Northers — Rains — Isthmus — Mexico — Papagayos — Tapayaguas — Peru — Galapagos — Digression about Mountains — Pacific Ocean — Polynesia — Indian Archipelago — China Sea — Northern Australia — Indian Ocean—South-western Asiatic Coasts — Eastern Shores of Tropical Africa.

Having considered the facts of a great atmospheric circulation, and their apparent connection, it may be advisable to glance around the world at their salient effects. In meteorology, almost more than any other subject, it is requisite to comprehend a wide range of phenomena within one general view, rather than to limit the mind by few or minute details — the atmosphere itself, of which we treat, being only limited or restrained by gravitation, and by the world's superficies — between which concentric surfaces it is specially free to move in any way. *Extreme* mobility, elasticity, and permeability, are *marked* characteristics, in addition to properties of fluids in general.

Near the equator, in Africa, are heavy rains and great heat, much thunder and lightning, particularly twice in the year, soon after the sun has been vertical. When he is farthest north or south there is less rain, with a prevalent easterly wind (from the east); while *returning* southward, or about September, exceptional westerly winds occur, with excessive rains on the west coast. Inland, on high tracts, especially when far from the sea, less rain falls, excepting on the eastern side of high ranges of mountains, near the tropics. In North Africa especially, but likewise in a less degree in South Africa, rain is rare. The perennial winds, north-easterly and south-easterly, blow over so much heated and dry land in crossing Arabia and Asia, that no moisture reaches the deserts.

Southward of the equator, towards Capricorn, and in the interior, away from sea influence — thence also to about the parallel of thirty degrees, aridity prevails so much that the 'rain-maker' thrives by his impositions on the credulous savages.

Crossing towards the west, from Africa, it is well known that between about five and fifteen north latitude is a space of ocean, nearly triangular, the other limit being about twenty (long.) and ten (lat.), which used to be called by the earlier navigators the 'Rains,' on account of the calms and almost incessant rain always found there, in which unfortunate ships used sometimes to be detained for many weeks. They are caused by the meeting of the trade winds and the upper return currents. Sometimes between the 'trades' a westerly wind blows, even with the strength of a gale, in this space, and near the Cape Verde Isles, even to the African coast, to which it takes rain. Formerly this wind, which occurs about September, was called (when England traded for slaves) the Line westerly Monsoon.

At other times of year, a dry wind blows from Africa, near Cape Verde, carrying clouds of fine dust. It is the Harmattan. Another peculiarity of that coast is the tornado,* a brief local whirlwind, very violent

* Spanish and Portuguese for *twisted*.

but not extensive. The southerly trade wind, drawn in towards Africa by the expansion of heated air inland, imparts its sea moisture incessantly to the central western shores. There, under the Line, are forests scarcely tenanted, except by the gorilla, while on each side northwards and to the south, are mangrove swamps, low river banks, and the pestilential haunts of the genuine black, the ebony-coloured man of Congo.

The 'red fogs,' and the dust that falls on ship's sails and decks in sailing near Cape Verde Isles has been said by Ehrenberg to have been carried in upper (return) currents from Northern Brazil. It appears much more probable that the adjacent coast of Africa should have such animalcules as he examined microscopically, than that they should have been raised from Brazil and transpersed through upper air without falling anywhere except near the coast of Africa, where this red dust is *frequent.* Elsewhere, or near Brazil, it is not observed. *Tornadoes* and the Harmattan are frequent on the west coast of Africa, near Cape Verde. On the opposite boundary of the Atlantic, along Brazil, towards the West Indies, there is continual, almost perennial, easterly wind, moderate, but with much rain at times. The shores are thickly wooded, there are no arid deserts. Certainly such insects as Ehrenberg examined *may* be found in Brazil, but does it follow that they are not also in Africa under nearly the same parallels?

It is a question of some interest—not only because similar 'dust' (animalcules) had fallen in the Mediterranean and Italy, which also was supposed to have been wafted from Brazil (although Africa lies between them), but because a celebrated authority partly based on it his theory of the trade winds *crossing* near the equator and then becoming upper or counter currents.*

* Maury.

How two nearly equal and similar bodies of air always advancing from opposite directions, could pass through or *permeate* each other, each one maintaining momentum and bulk, *without change*, instead of intermingling and becoming mutually neutralised, does not, however, appear in evidence.

Physically such a permeation of aqueous air may be deemed impossible. Dalton, it is true, and other philosophers since, have showed the inter-permeability of certain *gases*, but even then, and under special conditions, very slowly and gradually.

On the west side of the Atlantic, between the tropics, steady easterly winds blow always, except in occasional calms of short duration, and in the hurricane season of the West Indies. The two trades meet in about thirty (W. long.) and cross the Mexican Gulf, with directions varying from local causes, between S.E. and N.E.

Great heats in the northern parts of Brazil, Guiana, Trinidad, Venezuela, and Columbia—likewise also those of Central America and Mexico, draw very strong gales, at times furious storms, from the cool north, from over North America: and besides these so-called 'Nortes' there are in the West India regions, especially their eastern part, those awful hurricanes of which every one has heard so much. They are cyclones of the most distinct and, so to speak, complete kind; and they have been traced through several days of apparently continued gyration. Respecting the power and nature of these storms, some notices will be found in a following chapter.

Redfield thought that he traced two or three notable hurricanes even from the coast of Africa to the West Indies, and then actually across the whole Atlantic to our European islands; but these hurricanes occurred at periods when the northern hemisphere was much disturbed, namely, the autumnal equinox, the time of 'Line westerly Monsoons,' and of gales in other parts of the Atlantic.

Judging from Redfield's evidence, published in charts and books, it appears to the present writer that one or two shifting gales in the 'Line westerly,'* two or three distinct cyclonic gales, each of brief duration, as usual in the Atlantic, and some West India hurricanes altogether unconnected with them, were linked together on paper because happening near the respective times, and near one another. How is it that no one such hurricane, or gale, has been met or crossed by the almost innumerable vessels that have passed along that frequented thoroughfare between 20° and 30° W., 10 N., and the equator? *Facts* are entirely against Redfield's theory in those cases.

It may be here observed, in passing, that no hurricanes occur on or within a few degrees of the equator, in any part of the world. The occasion of this special peculiarity will be subsequently explained.

Proceeding to Central America. It is found that the Cordillera, or range, of the Andes, interrupts persistency of wind, and causes great local variety. On the eastern sea-coasts, superabundance of rain is brought by the easterly perennial: along the eastern sides of the mountains, from North Mexico to Grenada, forests everywhere spread; and vegetation corresponds to the heat with an excessive quantity of rain.

Westward of the heights along the Pacific coasts, sterility is the prevalent feature; all moisture is depo-

* So called by Horsburgh &c.

sited by the easterly winds on the weather side, and along the leeward flanks of the ridges there is *comparatively* an arid tract of country.

There, however, as around *all the world*, *inter-tropically*, short intervals of *westerly* winds, a few weeks or a month or two in their duration, occur every year, at about the same time, near or soon after the September equinox. Sometimes strong, if not violent, northern winds, blow from Mexican heights across the sea-shores, within a few hundred miles south and west of those coasts.

They are coincident with, and correspond to the Nortes of the Gulf of Mexico. These winds sometimes reach the Galapagos Islands. Unless so disturbed by the 'Papagayos,' as these strong but clear winds are called, or by the *rare* westerly winds, all the western coasts of Central America are truly *pacific*. There is very little wind, and the sea is smooth. As you recede from land the perennial easterly winds again become regular, almost without an interval of calm.

We must not proceed farther without a notice of the tropical currents across those northern breadths of South America that are covered with the most abundant vegetation, and the most extensive forests, and are watered by the longest rivers, in the world. All the perennial wind there brings moisture from the Atlantic; which is stopped, precipitated, and, *from* the mountains, returned by the rivers. Across the Andes to Peru, not a shower reaches, and the country there is absolutely sterile: while in the vast territories, extending from those mountains to the estuaries of the Amazon and Orinoco, rain is abundant all the year, forests spread everywhere, and animal life abounds. In Peru the houses have no roofs to keep out *water*;—rain is a prodigy; and everywhere, unless artificially irrigated from a mountain torrent, the country is uniformly barren and brown; producing no vegetation (naturally), maintaining no conspicuous animal life except llamas (vicuñas or guanacoes), condors, and seals; though by artificial expedients and immense labour formerly, now a productive, rich, and in some places a populous region.

Similar harsh sterility extends both ways from central Peru — northward, as far as Payta, near the equator, and toward the south, along part of Chile.

On those shores in particular where, in former ages, such multitudes of sea-birds swarmed as in their seemingly interminable flights actually darkened the air, guano abounded; no rain washed away its accumulations, age after age; and not until the comparative civilisation of those countries, under Ynca rule, were those deep deposits at all disturbed by man.

In consequence of the Andes interrupting easterly winds between the equator and the tropic of Capricorn, the usual, if not perennial, atmospheric current is along the coast, rather toward the heated land by day; and from it, from the cooler heights to the then warmer sea, by night. But these alternations occur only near the coast. At sea, the trade-wind blows with more or less regularity, according to the offing.

It should be observed that the grand Cordillera rises, in Chile, if not in Peru, to about 23,000 feet above the sea level. One-third higher than the Swiss mountains or Teneriffe, higher considerably than Ararat or Demavend, it is only exceeded by the magnificent Himalayas (29,000 feet). Eastward of *these* Andes, so remarkable in geographic, geologic, and meteorologic points of view — politically also, and ethnographically important — in the regions extending from their slopes to the Atlantic, as far as the zone of calms and light variable winds usually extends, or to about 30° S., forests everywhere prevail.

Here it may be convenient to draw attention to a very remarkable geologic conformation, common to a great part of our world approachable by sea, though not so much to the far interior of extensive continents—namely, gradual slope up from east toward west, and comparatively precipitous steeps, from summits, westward. Norway, Europe generally, Africa, with its outlying islands, both Americas, the Galapagos, the (elevated) Polynesian islands, the ranges of Australia, China, and Asiatic sea-coasts generally—when viewed extensively in profile from south or north, have the wedge-like outline that is familiar to Englishmen in the Bill of Portland.

To the physical philosopher and the geologist we must turn for reasoning on this striking peculiarity—one that the writer has often noticed and considered with extreme interest. His attention was first drawn to it by seeing the Galapagos group, from a distance, appearing like *several* 'Bills of Portland,' all exactly similar in their profile outline when many miles distant. Since that time (1836) many opportunities have occurred for enquiries and careful comparisons, of which the result is a belief that, excepting those greater east and west ranges of mountains embodied within continents, or continental islands (such as Australia and Borneo), the general average direction of ranges or chains of mountains is nearly meridional, and their section approaches that of a wedge (pointing *eastward*).

This wedge-like shape is common to every little sand-ridge, every shifting shingle bank, formed along shore by wave or tidal action. It is also that of sand-ridges on a plain, drifted by wind alone, and it is the form of snow-drifts—the point of the wedge being towards the source of action. Whether water, or wind, or both, acting *continuously*, have been agents in these conformations: whether, in contracting or expanding, the earth's surface, or crust, has had a tendency to scale-like fracturing, must be left to the consideration of competent judges.

In meteorology the facts are immediately important, only as affecting wind and climates. One geologic consideration however may be offered here, namely, the *apparent* explosion of volcanic eruptions, in *general*, along the steeper ridges to the westward; the frequency of earthquakes among the broken and upheaved strata of the steeper, or more precipitous sides of mountainous ranges; and their rarity, comparatively, on the much more extensive sloping ascents, on their east side.

To this last a recent instance at Mendoza is one of the very rare exceptions. The inhabitants had supposed themselves as safe from earthquakes as if at Buenos Ayres. In one minute, however (in 1860), their large town was shaken to the ground—and part of it entombed. This may have been a vibratory shock from the Andes, rather than a volcanic action, under Mendoza, or in the plain country near.

Whether Sir Humphrey Davy's *earlier* view of volcanic causation abandoned by him, but *said* to have been again favourably considered in his later years, was well-founded, or otherwise—the facts are incontrovertible, that all the great volcanic craters, all the principal originating places of earthquakes, are near the sea or some great lake-supply of water. On noticing a newly placed volcano in central Asia, on the lamented Atkinson's map, he was questioned, and his reply was, that it is dormant now, but said by the natives to have been active *before* their time — and that near it there is a very *large lake.*

The few active volcanoes known in central Asia, on the great chains extending from Persia to China, are *probably* near lakes, or unfailing supplies of water from ice or snow melted, either by the sun, or by action of internal volcanic heat affecting the *surface* and its superposed glaciers.

Perhaps, in *glacial theories*, the effects of such heat, and that occasioned by immense *pressure* (even of *ice*?), in thawing or softening, and, as it were, lubricating the under sides of glaciers, has scarcely been estimated sufficiently.

This rather geologic digression may be pardoned, because some meteorologic effects are occasioned by volcanoes, and because the forms, as well as the natures of lands, have so much local influence on winds and weather.

Looking along earth's surface horizontally, and recollecting that elevations of land range from a few hundred feet up to about five miles vertically (Himalayas), that the *lower or surface* currents of air are sometimes less than a mile, seldom more than two or three miles in depth, and that other currents are variously superposed, the possible effects of such barriers as ranges of mountains, or even high hills, are obvious. Impelled against them by persistent cause behind, while overlaid above, increased tension (barometric pressure) is occasioned to windward, and to leeward an opposite result, where, under the lee (as it were), sensibly less pressure is found, experimentally, than on the weather side of such a barrier — at the same time.

Perhaps such effects are nowhere more remarkably

evident than in Patagonia, where westerly winds *prevail*. While the barometer is *high*, *comparatively*, yet with *warm* westerly winds, accompanied with much rain, blowing *strongly* on the western coasts, *towards the Andes*, there is, simultaneously, a comparatively low barometer, with *westerly* wind, still strong, but without rain, and very cold, in the almost deserts of eastern Patagonia. These anti-trades are forced against the meridional barrier, recoil, and then pass *over* it, having lost moisture and warmth. Everywhere similar effects occur under like conditions; and it may here suffice to allude, in passing, to our own high western and comparatively low eastern lands, also to India, to South Africa,* to the Rock of Gibraltar, and to the Straits of Magellan.†

Reference may be made here to Sir Henry James's experiments at Edinburgh, in 1852,‡ to windward and to leeward of (even) a house, with an aneroid barometer. If his scrupulously careful trials, with a delicate instrument, showed distinct differences of tension, in consequence of being to windward or to leeward, how much more sensible must be the effects of extensive winds against high ranges of land, *not temporary obstacles*.

In all cases of wind blowing against land, whether a continent or an island, the first and the chief effects are felt to windward, on the *exposed* shore. After impinging against such obstacles, and passing over more or less uneven or rugged land, the force of wind is much diminished, for a certain time or distance, although eddies, and at times *very violent squalls*, may be caused by the wind forcing its way over a barrier, while resisted by *upper currents* as well as by the barrier itself, and then

* Table Mountain, &c.

† Magalhanes, or Magalhaens.

‡ Transactions of the Royal Society of Edinburgh.

rushing suddenly into the space to leeward (where tension is much less) with elastic expansion like that of air from a gun.*

Proceeding now across that vast space of ocean, which no charts sufficiently realise to the mind (because numerous islands occupy such disproportionate space on paper), that extensive spherical area, of almost half the world's surface—the 'Great South Sea' of the early navigators—we find uniform trade winds on each side the equator, almost uniting near it; and without a space of continuous '*rains*:'—a limited interval only of *variables* and calms being found, during about ten months of the year. In the other two, westerly winds and rains *are* frequent (about October) near the equator, and among the Polynesian archipelagoes, but not even then near the 'heart' of either perennial wind.

A word about the Galapagos islets should be added here, before quitting the east side of the Pacific.

All volcanic craters, seemingly recent, scantily covered with vegetation and trees to windward, deserts on the lee side, the climate of those islands is healthy though hot. The sea on the north side is more than 80°, while that on the south is 60°, distinct currents of water meeting there from the hot Gulf of Panama and the cool coast of Chile. They join, and flow westward together, from four to two miles an hour. Doubtless it is their influence, and the continual easterly breezes, that make these islets very salubrious, although under the equator. When the distant 'Papagayos,' or 'Nortes' are blowing, a heavy swell rolls against the northern shores: and, on the south, the influence of far

* Thus are caused those whirlwind squalls, formerly called by the sealers in Tierra del Fuego, 'williwaws.' They may be termed truly *hurricane squalls* — like those at Gibraltar, in a violent *Levanter*.

away southerly gales, in the South Pacific, is similarly felt—occasionally.

Although intertropical parts of the Pacific have usually fine weather, with light or moderate easterly winds, inclining from north on one side, and from south on the other side of the Line; there are the occasional though rare interruptions of bad weather, and even storms, already mentioned. From the equator *northward* these occur about, or a month or two after, the autumnal equinox, but to the southward of the Line (at the Friendly and Society Islands for example) they occur after *their* corresponding season,—namely in May, or June. During such interruptions of the regular wind and weather of these seas and islands many a frail vessel, laden deeply (a double canoe), has been driven out of her *intended* course (as *shaped* by stars, and *usual* wind) from island to island, and *obliged* to run to leeward, to perish in the ocean—if no land could be found before their food and water failed. Several such instances are related by the earlier navigators; many are detailed in Burney's great work on the South Sea. The peopling of very remote isolated spots, such as Easter Island, (or such as the Andaman Islands, *passim* *), can be thus explained, but not those *alone*—(*à fortiori*) great continents, in *various* places, successively but irregularly.

On the west side of the Pacific there are more and longer interruptions to the otherwise prevalent easterly trade winds. In the Indian Archipelago, including the Arafura Sea, westerly winds are the monsoon that blows during October and three following months, at times stormily, and often with much rain.

Towards China, the effect of a continent much heated

* Lately much discussed.

in summer but very cold in winter is shown by monsoons south and north, and by hurricanes, or typhoons, about the periods of change, *especially* about October, *occasionally* in May, soon after the equinox.

Very healthy and delightful climate, owing to continuous easterly sea breezes, is a property of north-eastern Australia, but toward the west, along the north coasts of that continental island, heat and droughts are great. From the Indian Archipelago across to the east coast of Africa, there are very different winds and weather at opposite seasons of the year. When the sun is *south* of the Line, north-east and south-east trade winds blow, with settled weather—till hurricanes occur, in the *southern* autumn, near the Mauritius, and in the Southern Indian Ocean. When the sun has crossed the equator northward (in April) a change follows, and, instead of the north-east trade, a south-west monsoon is drawn into its place by the heated surfaces of eastern Asia—and then continues several months.

The atmospheric contests at changes of monsoons are always occasions of heavy rains and storms, with thunder and lightning. With the monsoon itself—from the south-west, the tropical region, and the sea—great quantities of moisture are carried—to be deposited on the Himalayas, and other high ranges of eastern Asia.*

It should be particularly noticed that these great air currents of the Indian and China seas are simultaneously *toward* the north-east, while Asia is heated by the sun: and that when that continent is comparatively cold, snow-covered mountains adding to its frigidity, the greater currents of air are *polar*, *from* the north-east,

* Five or six hundred inches of rainfall, at one place, have been *measured* in *half* a year only — by Colonel Sykes and other well-known observers.

towards the warmer seas, and *always* heated southern parts of Africa, India, Malacca, China, and Borneo.

South of the equator, eastern Africa and Madagascar have continuous easterly winds, a fine climate, and abundant rain.

At the Seychelle Islands, north of Madagascar, storms are unknown; so beautiful, healthy, and untroubled a sea climate is not to be exceeded, if equalled elsewhere.

The Mauritius is well known to be otherwise at *intervals*, but its notoriety for hurricanes has been exaggerated. True it is that once in a w years a *violent* storm occurs at Mauritius, but the hurricanes heard of so frequently range over that extent of ocean which lies from Madagascar to Australia, and many gales of wind in it, however far off, are called *Mauritius* hurricanes. Nevertheless, such cyclonic tempests occur, like gales of wind elsewhere, most frequently in (*their*) autumn, but occasionally at other times, with as much fury as West India hurricanes.

CHAPTER X

General View of Climates in Temperate Zones — Eastern Coasts of North Atlantic — Western — North America: Central Land, and Western Coasts — North Pacific — Islands — Japan — China — Tartary — Central (temperate) Asia — Western Regions — Sea of Azof — Caspian — Black Sea — Turkey — Greece — Italy — Mediterranean — Adriatic — Archipelago — Syria — Egypt — North Coast of Africa — Spain.

HAVING glanced around the inter-tropical regions, we may now go westward again in the northern temperate zone, between Cancer and the Arctic circle.

Commencing at the union of the Mediterranean and the Atlantic, a mixed but comparatively fine and temperate climate, hot only in summer, is characteristic of north-west Africa (along the *coast*), in Spain, and in Portugal. During, and after summer, the calm variables extend 10° to 20° further north (and the NE. trade wind also) than they do at the opposite season. The effect is that the parallels of forty and fifty N. in their summer, have weather resembling that of thirty and forty, when the sun is far south of the equator.

This shifting (or libration) of climate, *generally*, all round the globe, ought to be kept in mind, because its effects, however much modified by local causes, are of a universal nature. From Portugal to Ireland, to the Isles of Scotland, and to Norway, greater variations, stronger winds, and less settled weather prevail, as the latitude increases, even in summer.

The latitude in which the main currents are most in

opposition below, where there are consequently more squalls, gales, or storms, varies with the seasons, and with local circumstances. It is important to observe and compare these *nodal* lines — or averages drawn through the *nodes*, or central calm areas, around which the principal air currents seem to turn or circulate when in mutual antagonism.

At one season these points are considerably further north than at another,— in *extensive* winds, when only a very few such central spaces are observed to co-exist in some thousand miles of superficial area; but in light breezes they are as numerous as irregular.*

In the temperate zones there are, at times, intervals of the very worst as well as of the very finest weather in the world, though such *extremes* are rare.

Some local whirlwinds, or hurricane-squalls, are as furious as those of the tropics, but they are usually less extensive, and in general less violent.

Beautifully serene and delightful days occur, not to be excelled anywhere in the world, but they are few, comparatively, and far between.

Generally speaking, the later spring, the summer, and *early* autumn are less troubled by gales, have finer and more regular weather, and less rain, than other seasons of the year. There are frequent exceptions to this rule assuredly, but they are generally compensated in adjoining or immediately subsequent periods. Of course there are marked differences in climate, even in the same latitude, not only between sea and land, but in that of the land under different conditions.

Mountains, plains, open or sheltered localities affected by directions of winds (with *their* characteristics), are

* Reference may be made, with regard to this subject, to a paper in the Appendix, respecting some notices of wind gyrations at observatories.

cold or heated, arid or moist, in the *same zone*. As examples, compare the climates of Norway and Greenland, of Ireland and Labrador, of Portugal and Pennsylvania. Unquestionably much, indeed most of the characteristic qualities as to climate, of the climatology of any place, depends on latitude, and *elevation;* but next to these are prevalent air currents, or *winds*, even before local conformation, which always has so much influence.

It has been observed, and has been the subject of recent discussions, that temperature is sometimes higher at a considerable elevation than below. In Switzerland, in Scotland, and other places, besides in balloons, these apparent anomalies have been noticed—difficult to account for on the supposition that temperature diminishes uniformly and regularly with elevation, but obviously easy by allowing for upper currents, at various temperatures. That there are usually such alternating currents, and that they vary much in tension, temperature, moisture, and other qualities, has been proved by ascents of high mountains, and in balloons. Crossing clouds show them even to the casual observer below.

In changes of weather, accompanied by differences of temperature, how little, ordinarily, is attributed to the body of air enveloping a place—how much to the sun's action!

Sometimes it is remarked as *strange*, that during a cloudy, perhaps windy and rainy night, the temperature should be *many* degrees higher than during (perhaps the previous, or following) days of bright sunshine. The *directions* of air currents, whether southerly or northerly, not having been sufficiently, if at all considered.

Hence it is that so many *mistakes* are made about

clothing and fires; their consequences being colds, coughs, and too often fatal illness.

Looking now at the Atlantic, between Europe and North Africa, with North America in the temperate zone, and bearing in mind the peculiarities already noticed, one cannot but be struck by the great facilities its winds, and even the water currents, afford for communicating between the continents. Their greater circulations (as elsewhere in other oceans) expediting the voyager in one direction here, while aiding his return, by another route, there.

It is impossible to know these facts, and to contemplate the çondition of various nations in early ages, without a conviction that migrations in various directions *across the oceans*, occurred long before the era of Christianity.

We may recover, by the research of a Rawlinson, and by the will of an enlightened Ruler, undestroyed tablets showing how, where, and when, Etruscan, or Phœnician, or Pelasgic argonauts explored other lands than those of which we now have early histories. In the mounds of Assyria, in Mosul itself (that ancient site), from among the dust of Babylon and Nineveh*— greatest cities of antiquity—Indian and Mexican and Chinese history may yet be largely disentombed.

Prevailing easterly winds across the lower half of the North Atlantic impel surface water, incessantly, through intervals of the West India Islands, into the Gulf of Mexico. There they are *heaped* (as any one may

* When the writer first visited Tahiti (in 1835–6), a ceremony occurred among the heathen natives which Mr. Nott (then a missionary there) told him was an *annual* custom — a 'lamentation for Nineveh.' He knew no more.

observe that water is raised at the leeward end of a large lake, a canal, or an estuary, while strong winds are blowing along its length), and, as fluids, seek equilibrium by rushing through their easiest escape — the Gulf of Florida — into the North Atlantic. Their accumulated action amounts to that of a vast river of warmed water running along the coast of America, over or against opposing currents (still nearer the shores and then below) this Gulf Stream, so well known now, yet only brought into useful notoriety by Franklin, about a century ago. (1760-70.) It would be mere repetition to say much more here, about this influential oceanic current, than to recommend an examination of Keith Johnston's admirable illustrations of that, among *many* other physical peculiarities of our world's superficies; and to urge a student of such subjects to study the 'Physical Geography,' and the 'Meteorology' recently given to the world by Sir John Herschel.

In the illustrious Humboldt's works are such inexhaustible mines of knowledge, that extreme gratitude is due to those who have rendered them so pleasantly accessible by translations everywhere pronounced excellent. Arago's Meteorology, similarly available and acceptable, should be also remembered, by a student, among the first of numerous works on the atmosphere. One word more. Whatever effect the Gulf Stream may have *locally*, it is obvious, on comparing its extreme limits, source and direction, that the great bodies of tropical air which incessantly traverse *both* temperate zones, toward the poles and eastward, must have far more effect on climates than air from over any *comparatively* small tract of ocean.

Where winds from sea approach—still more when they blow *against* land, their characteristics are more or less altered; and these changes are more obvious at or near the boundaries. Currents of air accumulate, blow round or over, are stopped or deflected by land (as has been shown elsewhere) which, at the same time, absorbs much, if not all, of their moisture. Hence the windiness of headlands, projecting capes, or very salient promontories, and the comparative wetness of those shores or high lands against which the vaporous or moisture-bearing winds usually blow, such as Portugal, Western France, Ireland, Wales, Cumberland, Scotland and Norway.

Inland, such winds are more and more moderated and dried. Hence it results that within Portugal, and much in Spain, in France, on the east side of England and Scotland, as well as in Europe generally, there is less wet, and far less wind, on an average, than along the immediate seaboards of the Atlantic, exposed to every first onset of the anti-trades. Along the eastern coasts of Great Britain, and, partially, those of Ireland, the localities may be considered (by a seaman) as *under the lee* —less exposed, and drier during westerly winds. But when the polar current is in force from north-west to north-easterly, the coasts exposed to its onset feel most wind; though they have not necessarily the most rain or snow, as *their* fall depends on meetings of currents solely, when heights of land do *not* chill the *vapour-bearing* one (as is the case during a polar current along the surface), unless their summits reach upward, above the lower wind, into the vaporous tropical one.

It is a common remark among observers of weather in England, that *usually* it snows *only when* the thermometer ranges between 30° and 40°, or rather with the air temperature about 35°. This seems to be a consequence of influence on either current by the other, which tends to diminish an extreme of temperature, while causing deposition of vapour in snow or rain.

At the western islands of the Atlantic and Bermuda, especially the latter, storms are but too well known.* Sir William Reid's works† are as ample as truly reliable, respecting the facts of meteorology thereabouts, in the West Indies and in North America. But his views of one cyclone travelling far, instead of having successors,‡ his adoption, so far, of Redfield's expositions, and his slight attention to great permanent or constant movements of atmosphere, are not to be reconciled with now proved facts—*facts*, be it observed with thankfulness, accruing out of observations suggested and encouraged by himself. On the western side of the Atlantic, although often visited by storms, the coast is not by any means so tempestuous as its eastern opposite. Winds are more *offshore*, and are drier in general. Causes operate there on a grand scale, analogous to those above mentioned as occurring in western Europe. Neither there, nor elsewhere in the *temperate* zones, does the wind *prevail* from east (true). It may be north-easterly, or south-easterly, but from true east it does not blow except rarely, and only for a very short time as it veers or shifts into other quarters, south-east or north-easterly.

It was observed by Franklin§ that north-east winds began to leeward on that coast (which trends south-west and north-east) (true), and he accounted for it by supposing that the first movement of air began to leeward, like that of water in a canal drawn off from one end. But he did not then show where the water, so set in motion to leeward, went, or what originated the

* 'Still vexed Bermoothes.'

† Law of Storms, second edition.

‡ Stevenson of Dunse.

§ Letter, May 12, 1760.

movement. On the principles explained in these pages, a polar current ought to be felt at the westernmost place first, if not very far south of the eastern one. And (in *his* example) a reference to the globe will show that a polar wind (called NE. but truly NNE.), ought to reach Philadelphia before advancing *eastward* to Boston (400 miles ENE.), irrespective of mountainous ranges or other local features. References to cases of northerly winds first beginning in Ireland, and then felt *successively* to the *eastward*, shown by numerous simultaneous observations, and to the polar (north-easterly) winds crossed by fast steamers to the west of Ireland, which *afterwards* are found to traverse the British Islands and western Europe, may illustrate and tend to corroborate this view. Professor Henry* and the lamented Espy have lately published abundant evidence of a general motion from west towards east, over the Northern States, and the testimony of each experienced aeronaut is strongly confirmatory. This, as a 'great fact,' is insisted on here — at the risk of supererogation. As the prevalent winds in temperate North America are westerly — crossed at times by tropical or polar currents, and as they blow over vast extents of land, *cold* and dry in one season, hot if not moist in another, extremes of winter and summer temperature are felt, unmitigated by sea winds. Ranges of mountains, lying nearly in meridional directions, and of height to influence the lower air currents, induce a remarkable parallelism frequently, and a *narrowness* of stream, in proportion to its length, that has not been described in any other region of the world, but appears to be quite in accordance with such ideas and principles as have lately obtained currency. Professor Henry said, in a remarkable letter to General

* Of the Smithsonian Institution.

Sabine (dated July, 1861), 'We find that not only do the storms of wind and rain come to us (at Washington) from the west, and enter our territory from the north (near the Rocky Mountains in British possessions, about 110° west), but also the cold and warm periods. The early and late parts traverse the country in the form of a long wave extending from north to south, and moving *eastward*.'

'When this wave arrives at a given meridian during the night, a killing frost is experienced along a band of country extending north and south, it may be in some cases more than a thousand miles, while in an east and west direction it is not more than fifty or a hundred miles.'

'At first sight it may appear somewhat strange that our warm spells (periods) should begin at the NW. point of our map,' and then Mr. Henry offers an explanation which is not satisfactory to the writer of these words,—but he gives it verbatim, and will then venture to suggest another.

'The south wind (says the professor) is warm and light, and as probably, it is, in all cases, a wind of *aspiration*, the solution of the problem is not difficult.

'A rarefication probably takes place in the north, which draws into it the air next to it on the south, and this again gives motion to the portion of air still further south, and so on till the current reaches the Gulf of Mexico, while at the same time the same heated air from the south is wafted eastward by the prevailing westerly upper current of the temperate zone.'

This argument *supposes* a very improbable, but yet continually recurring *cause* of first motion in the NW. What is this cause? Why do not similar causes (if such exist) occur *elsewhere*, and occasion analogous effects?

Let us revert, rather, to first principles—to the action, the continuous action, of polar and tropical currents caused by tropical heat (solar) and polar cold — *veræ causæ*?

Looking at a globe — it is evident that an advance of either main current, from polar or from tropical regions, may reach a high latitude in any given meridian before it touches a lower one. But this will depend, not only on the *diagonal* line of advance more or less south-westward or north-eastward, but on the facilities or impediments either current encounters. Tropical currents, in force, arrive at the west of North America from the south, along and over the Rocky Mountains, whence they are deflected by the *increasing* anti-trade towards the east, and thus their first indications, their first appulses (which are *lateral*) at Washington, come from the NW. across the direction of their length.

The polar winds, air currents from NW. to NE. flow south-westward, and while so moving in that direction, have also a sidelong or lateral progression (as elsewhere described), slow but constant and general, toward the east.

Hence the first advent of polar winds to any of the very numerous meteorologic stations set up by the Smithsonian Institution is from the NW. quarter, although the wind itself is more northerly, even north-easterly, or almost easterly in direction.

Thus it occurs also in Ireland, Europe generally, and *around the world*, under similar conditions.

The laws of nature being uniform, must of course apply to all places similarly; and that those which we believe to be such laws are found generally applicable, *cæteris paribus*, is their crucial proof.

Before quitting America, it may be observed that, although very many hundred stations were provided with meteorologic instruments, and directed by the Smithsonian Institution, natural difficulties and sources of error unavoidably occurred among the incidents of new and extensive countries. Of but few places in the interior has the level, or elevation above that of the sea, been ascertained geometrically. Approximate heights, assumed from barometric readings themselves, of course afford no standard to which they can be referred, and, however useful normal levels (as adopted by Dové), may be for comparisons, they require years of continuous observation for their determination, and, after all, indicate no independent measure of elevation.

Temperature observations, within a continent, at *various* elevations, are likewise difficult of *inter-comparison*, besides being so liable to error.

With a general reference to the *latest* editions of works published by Espy, Blodget, Bache, Henry, Ferrel, Loomis, Redfield, Russell, Maury, and, above all, those of Franklin —

We may now proceed to the west side of America, and across the North Pacific.

Very similar is the climate, and nearly do the winds correspond to those of Spain, Portugal, Ireland, Norway, and, indeed, the west of Europe generally corresponding in latitude. And much the same may be said of the North Pacific compared with the North Atlantic, and of the coasts of Japan as well as China, considered in quality with eastern North America. Local *peculiarities*, special differences there are, in detail, but the broad general character is similar. Intermediate islands have no such cold, nor such heat, as the continents.

Along the northern coasts and islands, storms and bad weather are as frequent as on Irish, Scotch, and Norwegian shores. In the ocean itself, its central extent especially unimpeded by land, winds are less sudden and violent; and they veer or shift much less irregularly. But there are cyclonic gales, and at times severe tempests, as in the North Atlantic.

There is also a kind of gulf stream—the Japanese current which sets toward the NE., and a general circulation of that ocean in consequence, with a sort of *central eddy* also (*mare sargassum*) in which sea-weed, drift wood, birds, and fish, are abundant. Japan and its adjacent islands have much less extremes of temperature than China near them, but are very stormy in winter, very foggy, and subject to great earthquakes,* besides eruptions of volcanoes.

From E. to W. in Asia and Europe, between Chinese Tartary and the Mediterranean, the ordinary features of a temperate continental climate are much modified, in various regions of that vast continuous space, by elevated districts, steppes or table-lands, chains of mountains, or low plains.

Remote from ocean, no such supplies of moisture are received as those which fertilise sea-coasts and islands generally. But on the windward slopes of mountainous ranges, and hills of fertile soil, forests extend—the level or table-lands being usually without trees, often arid deserts, but occasionally rich prairies, abounding in pasturage. From the mountains and those tracts where rain or melted snow feed rivers and lakes, ample supplies of water combine with other natural advantages to render those regions among the finest on the globe for the developement and health of all animal creation.

The Black Sea, that of Azof, and the Caspian, may be regarded as large lakes influenced by their limited

* *Alarum*, described in Appendix.

local conditions. Sudden changes, squalls, storms of short duration, though very violent, are consequent on their expanse of water, immediately contiguous to land sometimes heated excessively, at others snow-covered and frozen. From the Black Sea, currents *always* set into the Mediterranean, being the drainage of those great steppes and mountain-ranges held by the Cossack and the Circassian, under Russian (nominal) dominion, though scarcely control.

To say much here of climates and seas, so well-known as those of Turkey, Italy, western Europe, the Adriatic and the Mediterranean, would be superfluous, were not this book intended for those who may not have been there, as well as for others.

Generally, one may describe the Mediterranean, the Archipelago, and the Adriatic, as fine-weather seas, in beautiful climates. But they have their storms, and heavy ones, at times; short, however, in duration; and all are in accordance with the laws obtaining elsewhere. That notorious storm of November, 1854, in the Black Sea, was demonstrated to be circuitous, or cyclonic,* and comparatively local.

Many tempests have been investigated in the Mediterranean, bearing testimony to the unity of character remarkable in meteorology when accurately viewed. Squalls, however, are of frequent occurrence, and their origin is of course local, however violent. Barometric indications are as useful there as in other regions, allowing for latitude range.

The Maestral, the Bora, Gregala, and Levante, are polar currents, with more or less easting. The Sirocco, Libeccio, and Ponente, are tropical. Their respective peculiarities are as well known to pilots, and are as

* Meteorologic Paper, Board of Trade, First Number, diagram.

constant, as the gyrations of wind over the British Islands.*

But the snow-covered Alps, Etna, and the Appenines, many Spanish high ranges of land, Greek mountains, Syrian and Arabian heights, and the hot deserts of Africa — each so near the great Mediterranean basin — must, at times, influence atmospheric currents suddenly and violently, though, if unsustained by remote and general causes (inter-tropical or polar), not lasting long, like gales over an extensive ocean.

Before advancing farther, it may be here mentioned that very interesting barometric results have been collated by Dové, from Russian and other reliable observations, chiefly directed by Kupffer. According to which, as now viewed, it would *seem* that the tension of air is so much less *ordinarily* in the northern parts of Russia, within the temperate zone (latitudes 40° to 50°) that the *normal* pressure is said to be only about *twenty-nine inches*, in the parallel of 45° N. lat.

However, — before relying on this result, and on others of a similarly-obtained kind, it would be satisfactory, and doubtless is indispensable, to know the levels or elevations of many stations — very difficult questions, when inland districts, unsurveyed *sectionally*, are their foundations.

* Smyth's 'Mediterranean.'

CHAPTER XI

Temperate Zone — South of Equator — African Coast — South Atlantic — South Pacific — South Indian Ocean — Africa — Cape — Southern Ocean generally — South America — East Coast — Interior — Andes — West Coast — Patagonia — East and West Tierra del Fuego — Falkland Islands.

South of the equator, in the *temperate* zone, Africa has a delightful, but rather dry climate. In the extra-tropical region of calm variables, aridity prevails; but to the southward, and as far as the Cape of Good Hope, sea-winds carry moisture, and this adequate irrigation maintains much fertility. Animal life is extraordinarily abundant, and artificial crops succeed well.

On the west coast, toward the Tropic of Capricorn, the southerly trade wind blows along shore, usually; and during the summer, or rather more than half the year, south-easterly winds prevail from about the latitude of the Cape of Good Hope, or a few degrees southward. They are alternate with the NW. anti-trades, which, in the winter of those regions, cross Africa some distance north of the Cape, and at times blow most tempestuously. The shifting of these stormy winds from a tropical to a polar current (*there* from north-west, to south-west and south-easterly), against watch hands, accords with the law of gyration.*

Several causes combine to make the Cape of Good Hope a stormy promontory. High, steep, and salient, every wind must be more or less affected by it, as a mechanical obstacle, and by the relative temperatures

* Dové, 1827—1862 (Scott's edition).

surrounding, as well as immediately above, its ranges of mountainous land. It is also frequently a central place, or nodal mass, *around* which opposing currents of wind *turn* more readily than when unobstructed.

Heated tracts of arid land, cool summits of mountain ranges, and an ocean, are there contiguous. In the north are African deserts — toward the south, Antarctic ice, beyond a wide range of open sea, in which strong currents, like the Gulf Stream, run from thirty to eighty miles a day or more (off Cape Lagulhas). And this in that zone where incessant alternation occurs between the two greater air-currents : all which causes contribute to make that famous promontory truly 'El Cabo Tormentoso' or the 'Cape of Storms,' as described by the early voyágers, and not in exaggerated terms.

Complaints of the barometric indications have often been made there (as in most of the stormier regions), but probably the faults were not *instrumental.* Persons who think the barometer intelligible without some intimate acquaintance, who draw hasty conclusions from insufficient observation, are unlikely to judge correctly in unsettled weather, and then they blame the barometer.

In that part of the year when the sun is south of the Line, — from September to March, or about a month or two after that period, the south-east trade is, bodily, several degrees southward of its medium range, and is strong, blowing rather toward Africa on the east side, and toward America, near Brazil; those regions being then most heated. At that time it encroaches on, or occupies part of, the temperate zone; and the *calm variables, usually* just extra-tropical, are then found between 30° and 40°. In *their* winter the contrary occurs, and those variables are found between fifteen and thirty degrees south.

South of those parallels, or reaching into them, heavy gales *may* occur at any season, but they are *prevalent* in winter; even more than prevails in the northern zone.

There are two distinct winds especially affecting those southern temperate regions, the *northerly* or tropical, and the southerly or polar.

On the Brazilian coast, about and to the south of the tropic, there is so much regularity in the alternation of winds, although but for a few points, that the two prevailing currents, from south-east to north-east, are often called monsoons. The latter prevails when the sun has been farthest, if not longest, south — and, therefore, has heated the interior country excessively.

Much rain — and electric action — thunder and lightning — accompany the stormy periods of those winds, especially the times of their shiftings, though the change of direction does not vary more than about a quadrant in general. In the vicinity of all these coasts an excess of lightning is remarkable.

As in the southern hemisphere there is *much* less land than in the northern — as the oceanic expanse is scarcely interrupted, except by the southern Andes, by the promontory of Africa, by Tasmania, and New Zealand — the courses, the breadths, and the successive combinations (after opposition) of the main currents of wind are far more regular, self-demonstrative, and easier to trace, than those occurring anywhere in the northern temperate zone; their gyration being frequent and *regular*.

A very marked consequence of this uniformity is the great similarity, and equability of climate, around the globe (in the south temperate zone) and its resulting perennial, or evergreen vegetation, almost unmixed (except far inland) by any deciduous trees.

The anti-trade prevails — those 'brave west winds' as

Maury calls them — and a remarkable fact corresponds (whether it be their cause or their effect), the barometer *averages* about an inch less than in equal northern latitudes: though it *does range* as high, or nearly so, when the (rare) south-easterly winds blow. Very interesting questions hang on this remarkable average depression of the barometer.

Theories have been hazarded as to pressure (or tension) at the poles, on account of proved diminution of pressure, from the calm variables of each juxta-tropical zone to the Antarctic and (in a less degree) the Arctic regions. Tropical currents (the anti-trades) are *prevalent* in temperate zones, and are stronger toward higher latitudes. With them the barometer averages a less height *everywhere* on the globe. The greater their strength, or force, the lower is the mercurial column (or its substitute).

But *these* currents cannot circulate *near the poles* as they do around them, thirty to sixty degrees distant.

What *proof* is there of *polar depression*?

Another consideration may be offered to the reader.

All explorations of *high* southern latitudes have been made in the summer or autumn of those regions, when *westerly* winds are prevalent. But it is in their winter and spring, when nights are long and the cold is greatest, that easterly — *south-easterly* — gales blow, with a *comparatively* high barometer *frequently*. At other seasons they are rare: and as the *greater* number of our observations have been obtained during summer and autumn, of course a comparatively low average has been deduced hitherto from the figures.

A *few* voyages, such as the Chanticleer's and Beagle's, in *winter*, show *high* barometers with *easterly* winds in 50° to 60° S. *repeatedly*.

Many, also, of the passages made by ships from

Australia round Cape Horn or — going towards our antipodean colonies through high latitudes, show high barometers, with winds from south-west to south-easterly (polar); but as those winds with easting are exceptional and as the westerly winds (mixed tropical and polar) are *generally* strong, the barometric averages are comparatively low.

Assuredly, however, it is as unphilosophical to infer, solely on account of a diminution of pressure from the calm variables towards polar regions, that proportionally lessened pressure exists towards a pole, as it would be to expect a pressure at the equator, similarly *greater* than that near the *tropics*.

Instead of proceeding across to the east coast of South America, it may be now more convenient to add a few remarks on the Great Southern Ocean.

Not only in the southern part of the Atlantic and the Indian Ocean, but throughout the circumferential expanse of sea between the circles of Capricorn and the Antarctic, generally similar winds, weather, and climate, may be truly said to prevail, varying only in (a few degrees of) temperature, with the latitude.

A voyager round the Cape of Good Hope, Tasmania, or Cape Horn, finds the turn of the winds, their character, and the climate, correspond throughout remarkably.

Indeed, in describing any one southern region much beyond the tropic, a whole zone is described, as far as the oceans and continental seaboards.

Inland, however, over African, Australian, or Patagonian deserts, in the vicinity of mountains, or near ice, extreme differences exist: — while elsewhere the causes already mentioned, and the moderating or equalising effect of such a predominating body of ocean, nearly alike in temperature, probably occasion the evergreen vegetation that is so remarkable.

It is there the mariner sees swelling waves on the grandest scale, a quarter of a mile apart, and rising sixty or seventy feet vertically. There, likewise, enormous icebergs are sometimes encountered, not only in high latitudes, but even occasionally near the parallel of forty degrees. By reliable angular measurements some have been found to be at least eight hundred feet high, and several miles in circumference.

In that ocean it is easy to make rapid passages eastward, before the prevailing wind and sea: but easterly gales *are sometimes* found, and, when heavy, they raise a great irregular sea, crossing the perennial swell from the westward.

As we have said, easterly winds may be rather expected in the winter of those latitudes, namely, June, July, and August, but occasionally, also, though rarely, at other times of the year.

Fogs are comparatively rare, except near land, or far south. Thunder and lightning are very infrequent, but indicative of bad weather.

For the use of a few seafaring readers, one may remark here that, in crossing the Pacific *toward the east*, in southern latitudes, a ship should not go beyond 50° S., till near Cape Horn, as there is usually much ice southward of that parallel, especially in the eastern part of the South Pacific; and occasionally it is met with some degrees farther north, in autumn (February, March, and April), after long continuance of westerly gales.

A few hundred miles *may* be saved in distance, out of about twelve thousand, by going into very high southern latitudes, but at the risk of encountering ice, and with the certainty of a very cold disagreeable climate. This applies equally to Australian passages by the Cape of Good Hope, where Great circle Sailing has been carried too far by many ships.

Immediately near Cape Horn, and the Falkland Islands, ice seldom remains, as any that is drifted there (from the breaking up of great antarctic masses in the latter part of summer) is carried eastward by the current of *comparatively* warm water (about 45° to 50° Fahr.) that always sets around the great southern promontory—and not to the northward till beyond the Falklands, where prevalence of south-westerly winds, and the currents, combine to drift them, melting gradually, even to as low a latitude occasionally as about the parallel of forty degrees.

In the long dark nights of an antarctic winter, when the moon is not near the full, *ice* (especially the low and less visible floes which are not many feet above the surface of the water) should be specially guarded against by a most vigilant look-out, and by keeping under manageable sail, in readiness to alter course instantly, if danger should be suddenly reported.

These quantities of ice drifting partly with the wind, but more influenced by currents of water (as so much the larger portion of each mass of ice is entirely submerged), may be thought to affect the weather near them. However unimportant may be the effects on climate by action of those *detached* icebergs, often seen by passing ships, the general influence of that enormous mass, extending all around antarctic polar regions, must be momentously important, whether unchanging, increasing gradually, or diminishing.

So little are we sensibly affected, in our inhabited portions of the globe, by polar icy regions, that their aggregate effects on climates are hardly considered, except by an effort of the mind. Yet the course, duration, and nature of air currents, with all their consequences in climatology, are mainly dependent on those cold regions, as extremes of one kind, — and on intertropical heats, as the other. Do they vary from age to age? Do they increase in their respective peculiarities? Or are they diminishing? What would be the conditions of our world's surface without accumulated ice at the poles? Was it so once, and were climates then not only more equable, but very much warmer?

Such are a few of the questions that reflection suggests, but philosophers cannot answer, except speculatively, turn to whom we may.

Reverting now to the eastern coasts of South America. We find between the tropic and the great river Plata a fine climate, less arid by far than its opposite in Africa, under the same parallels, less heated in summer and not exposed to cold, from mountains, in any part of the north-eastern side of the Plata, called 'Banda Oriental.' A finer climate is hardly to be found. Sea-winds sufficiently moistened, not injuriously charged with vapour, alternate with the anti-trade, dried by passing across the continent. But it is subject to storms of a violent character at changes of winds (tropical to polar), and to extreme alternations of temperature, at such times, even to 40° or 50° of difference, in a few hours. These storms (called 'pamperos,' because they appear to come from the 'pampas,' or plains of the level Plata district, many hundreds of miles square), are preceded by hot weather, moderate *variable* winds, lightning, and sometimes by myriads of insects. Cumulonus clouds gather in the SW., becoming gradually more massed, dark, and ominous, while distant lightning is almost incessant. Then the storm bursts, — squalls from the NW. (tropical) being overpowered and displaced by tremendously heavy rushes of wind from the SW. (polar). Once in a few years such storms are equal to hurricanes in force, but at other times are not formidable.

Another kind of storm occurs on these coasts occasionally, and is more dangerous, on account of its direction towards the land, from the Atlantic, and its accompaniments of dense clouds and rain. This is the south-easter which, although apparently different, is really part of a cyclonic circuit, extensive in expanse, and originated far south. A pampero, or SW. gale, sweeps circuitously round as it advances toward the NE. — its northern half being south-easterly, and then easterly, till expended, which is the case along the coast in question, from Patagonia, and the Falklands, to Brazil. Easterly, or south-easterly gales, at any part of that coast, are backed by southerly and south-westerly, farther to the south. Hence the weather clears up by the S. and SW., the *later* direction of the wind.

Such interruptions as these are only occasional, the general character of weather being fine, and the winds moderate, more or less on or off shore — easterly or westerly inland, according to the season.

Those who say that trade winds are not a principal cause of accumulated water in the Gulf of Mexico, and its outpour in a *stream*, should take note of what occurs in the very wide but shallow estuary of the river Plata: — where, when a pampero is blowing in the South and East, the water is raised many feet *everywhere* within the upper river, above Monte Video, and *some fathoms* at and above Buenos Ayres.

On the other hand, when tropical (northerly) winds are prevalent in the interior, the river falls proportionally below its average level. Tides there are scarcely sensible, at any time,* but these changes — of *feet* continuously—of fathoms at times, depend on the direction, strength, and duration of winds on the sea coast, and of those acting on the river *far inland.*

At the outer anchorage or roadstead, off Buenos Ayres, horses and carts have gone where, at ordinary times, ships lie at anchor in three or four fathoms water, and where, on the rare occasions above mentioned, six fathoms have been found. These changes have been caused by wind, and (in some slight degree) by diminished tension of atmosphere.

With the high lands of South Brazil the wooded districts cease—as forests. From the north bank of the Plata, or rather from the river Grande — treeless extensive plains everywhere bound the horizon, even down to Magellan Strait, excepting only low hills, and a few ranges scarcely many hundred feet elevated, though dignified relatively by being called mountains.† All is a level expanse, from the sea to the Andes; the northern districts from the river Grande to the Negro (in 40° S.) being rich — inexhaustibly — in depth of fine soil, and well-watered *generally*; but the country south of the Negro, to the Strait, is an arid desert, saline, stony, and, except near the very few rivers, without verdure.

Why are there no trees in the pampas, except a few *ombus*?‡ is often asked. Vegetation is rank. Thistles

* See TIDES, in Appendix.

† Sierra Ventana, Monte Video, Monte Negro, &c.

‡ Somewhat like a fig tree; not unlike a banian, but more resembling a baobab; peculiar to the country, and an object of religious attention among the aboriginal Indians.

spring up to a height that hides cattle. Grass is equally luxuriant. The soil is very deep.

It is a curious enquiry. Fruit trees thrive. Peach wood is grown and cut for fuel, pigs are fed with the peaches, and yet timber trees are not found till you reach the interior near Paraguay.

Can it be that the very deep soil, absolutely without a stone, or stony substance, 'tosca' being only hardened clay, is unsuitable? Have the violent and cold winds impeded the growth of trees, unsheltered, as at the Falklands, and elsewhere? or have immense numbers of grazing animals eaten off the young shoots and destroyed them as fast as they grew above ground?

Vast herds of cattle, horses, and sheep, have roamed over those almost unlimited tracts since the Spanish conquest in the fifteenth century, before which time, countless herbivorous animals, including the guanaco (now in droves about Patagonia), ranged everywhere in the open country. Perhaps no sapling tree could exist two years, exposed even to the biscacho, armadillo, hare, and other small animals which thrive in an open, earthy, arid country, where they can burrow, or hide in perfectly dry places?

Patagonia, east of the Andes and south of the river Negro, is usually swept by *dry* and strong westerly winds, warm in summer, but cooled much by the Andes in winter. They are anti-trades.

Only with rare sea-winds, or occasional northerly, is there rain in Eastern Patagonia, therefore the whole extent, excepting a very few oases, is a stony, arid desert, where, nevertheless, herds of guanaco find food and congenial country. On them the Indian regales, the condor feeds till too heavy to fly, and the puma satiates both hunger and thirst, leaving the bones to vultures and dogs.

Ostriches are numerous, and there are numbers of deer (roe) in some places. Hence it is obvious that the *climate* is healthy and fine. Salt ponds (Salinas) of the purest white salt, formed naturally, are frequent in those wild deserts.

The Falkland Islands are remarkable for their windy but very healthy climate, resembling that of *south-eastern* Patagonia. Treeless moorlands, peaty soil, and numerous small lakes, show effects of the continuous westerly winds, and frequent showers, that are usually experienced.

Some degrees eastward, and to the northward of the Falklands, is a space of sea in which driftwood, seaweed, and other floating substances, are long retained by a great central eddy caused by currents of water from Cape Horn and the Falklands, met by others from the eastward, and affected by those which set toward the south along the coast of Patagonia. On a very small scale it is another 'mare sargassum':—kelpweed (*fucus natans*), being a very substantial substitute for *Gulfweed.*

South-eastern Patagonia, and north-eastern Tierra del Fuego, are much alike in climate and character, excepting that the latter is less arid, rather more hilly, and partially wooded. It is in winds, weather, and climate, a mean between the extreme characters of Eastern and Western Patagonia, or Tierra del Fuego.

The eastern entrance of Magellan Strait is very notable on account of the strong winds without rain, or calms with fogs, and extraordinary tides.* Seven fathoms (forty-two feet) vertical rise, with a current of eight or nine miles an hour in the narrow parts, are regular each spring tide: and remarkable it is, in the Western Strait only a seventh of these amounts exist.

* See TIDES, in Appendix.

Climates are much affected by such peculiarities. A current approaches the eastern entrance of those famous Straits, which is much lower in temperature than that of the Western Ocean. Along the eastern shores of Tierra del Fuego and Staten Land, between them and the Falkland Islands, a current is impelled from the *south.* Along the western islands of Tierra del Fuego and Patagonia the constant stream is from the *north.* There are many degrees of difference in temperature (five to ten) between them all the year, the northern being always warmest. With allowance for local peculiarities, and excess of sea, the climate and meteorologic nature of those far distant lands, the southernmost by ten degrees that are inhabited, have a striking accordance with those of Orkney and the Western Islands, also particularly with that of Norway.

The Strait of Magellan is proverbially stormy, wet, and dismal. Yet, in the rare intervals of fine weather, grander scenery, more striking combinations of high, snow-covered mountains, *extensive* glaciers, forests with every tint and shade, immense precipices, numerous waterfalls, and *deep blue sea* at their base — cannot be found in all the world. In Switzerland there is not the oceanic element, though lakes are some substitute. In Norway, the glaciers are inferior, in Greenland there is much less concentrated *variety.*

Western Tierra del Fuego and Patagonia, from Cape Horn to South Chile, may be described to the mind's eye, by supposing ranges of mountains sunk lower beneath the sea as extended farther southward, until only their summits and higher ranges remained above water, as an archipelago of islands, islets, and rocks. Westerly winds (the prevalent anti-trades) almost always blowing against and between these obstacles, have swept some rocky surfaces into a barrenly desolate state,* while carrying rain and fertilisation to every less exposed valley or slope in the vicinity. The power of storms, as experienced among these intricate passages, is like that of hurricanes. The barrier opposed to regular currents of wind and water by projection of the mountainous range of the Andes into fifty-six south latitude, at Cape Horn, naturally resists, impedes, and deflects both water and wind: the results of which are tempestuous weather, and high, cross seas. But the winds, weather, and general meteorologic characteristics of these regions, about Cape Horn, are so like those of the North Atlantic in autumn and winter, between fifty and sixty north, and the instrumental notices are so similar, that we need not risk repetition, but might now proceed through the Pacific to Chiloe.

However, a few words more about climate and weather off Cape Horn, with respect to passages, and the choice of seasons, may not be unacceptable.

There is deep water everywhere close to the shores, which are bold, but rocky. Currents set always along shore south-eastward, eastward, and then, from Cape Horn, north-eastward, past Staten-land, toward the Falklands.

Icebergs do not *generally* approach the land within two degrees of latitude, they are all carried eastward, in a higher south latitude. In summer and autumn (December to May), gales are heaviest, and prevail from westward: but the days are long. In winter and spring are easterly winds, some hard gales, and short days.

* 'So desolate land to behold.'—Sir John Narbrough, 1677.

CHAPTER XII

Continuation of temperate Zone — South of Equator — Western Patagonia — Chonos Archipelago — Chiloe — South Chile — Currents — Cape Horn — South Pacific — Icebergs — Volcanoes — New Zealand — Tasmania — Southern Australia — South Sea — Indian Ocean Southward — Mauritius — Hurricanes — Bourbon — Madagascar — South-East Africa — Lagulhas Stream.

Polar Regions — Ice or Water — Animals — Early Voyagers — Modern Means — Effects of Icebergs and Fields of Ice — Second Summers and Little Winters — Summary.

BETWEEN Western Patagonia and Chiloe, the southernmost inhabited part of Chile is the Chonos archipelago, in climate and characteristics only differing from either in degrees of wetness and wind.

When the first Spanish explorers of these coasts had reached their extreme limits, they named the southern habitable port in Chiloe, 'El fin de la Christiandad,' not deeming any places farther south fit for permanent occupation. Even Chiloe was scarcely habitable, thought the men accustomed to Peru and Chile, where rain is so infrequent. Since their time, however, clearing the forest, cultivation, and fires, have altered and improved the climate so much that Chiloe is now important as a well-peopled province. There is a gradual change, from much wet and wind to a clear atmosphere, and to a tranquil beautiful climate— as the latitude diminishes, from near forty south, to about thirty — where the nightly cry of a 'Coquimbo' watchman is '*Sereno*,' from which the city itself has been often, indeed generally, so termed in Chile.

Along that part of Chile, southerly (or polar) winds prevail, except during autumn, winter, and (rarely at) other times, when the opposite or tropical current holds sway, and blows occasionally with great force. The characteristic peculiarities of these winds, and their alternations or sequences, are much the same as those of a higher latitude, though less extreme.

There is much less difference between these climates, their prevailing *winds*, and the *order* in which they *follow*, than persons would suppose who judge only by their positions geographically: and as their resemblance to those of the North Atlantic and the British Islands (substituting north for south) is strikingly corroborative of views elsewhere expressed in these pages, and has been noted, in quotations, by Professor Dové, it may be useful to repeat here what was said in 1835–8 by the present writer, and thus quoted.

North-westerly* winds prevail, bringing clouds and rain; south-westers † succeed them, and partially clear the sky; then the wind moderates, and veers into the south-east ‡ quarter, where, after an interval of fine weather, it dies away. Light airs spring up from the north-east,§ freshening as they veer round north,‖ and augmenting the moisture which they (the *tropical* currents) always bring. From the north ¶ they soon shift to the prevalent direction north-west,** and between that point and south-west they shift and back (veer and haul) for weeks sometimes before they take another round turn. Whenever the wind backs (from south-west towards north-east), bad weather and strong winds are sure to follow. Wind does not *back* suddenly, but it shifts

* Like our *south*-westerly. † Our *north*-westers. ‡ Our *north*-east. § Our *south*-east. ‖ Our south. ¶ South. ** South-west.

with the sun (in *that* hemisphere) very suddenly, sometimes flying from north-west to south-west,* or south, in a violent squall. These sudden shifts are to the left, *there* (against watch hands). While a north-wester is blowing with force, accompanied by rain, the wind may fly to the south-westward at any minute. It never blows hard from the east, rarely with force from north-east,† but occasional severe gales from south-east‡ occur, principally in winter. In the summer southerly winds last longer, and blow more frequently than in winter, and conversely.

The winds never go completely round the circle: they die away as they approach east, and, after an interval of calm, more or less in duration, spring up gradually between north-east and north.

Heavy tempests sometimes blow from north-west to south-west.§

Such are the leading and general characteristics of interfering, or prevailing polar and tropical currents of wind, between the extra-tropical calm variables and the polar regions, around the world — with local modifications.

Easily are they explicable on the basis of alternating main currents, polar and tropical, with a continuous translation of all — eastward. On no other hypothesis hitherto proposed can all the varying conditions of regular or normal winds, monsoons and storms, be reconciled.

Across the Southern Pacific Ocean, about New Zealand, along the shores of Australia, from Sydney and Bass Strait, to Swan River and Perth in West Australia,

* Like south-west to north-west in our hemisphere. † South-east.
‡ North-east and north of this our northern hemisphere.
§ South-west to north-west.

similar remarks apply generally. In the ocean there is more regularity and uniformity in the winds than has been found near land: but the principles, usual sequences, and times are reliably similar.

Passages have been made eastward from Tasmania to western Patagonia, in the anti-trade, more rapidly than from Chile to Australia, through the trade wind, while intolerable delays have occurred in the intermediate spaces of calm variables.

The *general* circulation of oceanic currents in the South Pacific ought to be here noticed, as connected with winds and climates. It is *with* the prevalent winds, as in other oceans, throughout the greater expanse; but near South America, in about 40° of latitude, a division occurs, and one stream of oceanic current moves south-eastward, along the Patagonian and Fuegian islands, toward Cape Horn. One of the effects of this separation, to the westward of America, seems to be the fact that no icebergs are carried far northward (beyond near 50° S.) between New Zealand and America, though in the South Atlantic, about the Falklands, they have been found sometimes even in a lower latitude than 40°.

There is a space of ocean in the South Pacific, between about 100° and 150° of west longitude, 50° and 60° of latitude, in which every ship, that risks a passage through, finds numerous, and some enormous — masses of ice. Immense islands, rather than bergs, have been passed thereabouts, 800 to 1,000 feet vertically above the sea, and several miles in length.* The present writer measured one trigonometrically that was at least 800 feet high and two miles in direct horizontal length. Can they be aground, or are some of them really *islands*?

* See Towson's published notices.

Considering how little the far South Pacific has been explored, how small a space has been thoroughly examined, and that the last discoverer (Ross) found an active volcano (Erebus) with its crater about 13,000 feet above the sea (in lat. 77° long. 167°), it appears probable that there are not only islands, but much continental land amongst the almost impenetrable icy barriers of Antarctic regions: and that some of those huge masses seen by Australian voyagers are, really, snow-covered islands.

Approaching New Zealand, we find a climate between that of southern Chile and Chiloe. Windy, much rain at times, comparatively equable in general temperature; warmer in the north, and everywhere healthy.

In the sheltered vallies of New Zealand a tropical character of vegetation and a moist warmth, with much bright sunshine between frequent rainy intervals, are prevalent.

On mountain summits snow lies all the year. The western and especially the southern coasts are tempestuous.

The south-easterly gales that blow with force on the eastern coasts of New Zealand, are precisely similar to those of eastern Patagonia.

The westerly, and, in a word, all the winds are likewise similar to those already described; and the same may be said presently for Tasmania.

The south-easter, is the *north-east* part of a large sweep, pressed along by a south polar current, and, at times uniting with, because meeting and deflecting, north-easterly, or northerly winds, there the tropical.

A remarkable effect has been noticed in the *large* southern Island (usually called the Middle), of New Zealand, but not elsewhere—except at sea between it and New South Wales. This is a hot wind, from the north-west, evidently a stream from Australia.

Passing now to the south-east, or extra-tropical coast of that *continental* region, we find drier weather, even with *sea-winds*, which there are polar, deflected more or less, and only *at times* combined with north-easterly (or tropical) — as at New Zealand.

With this combination, in *both* cases, there is the apparent anomaly of a high barometer, with much rain and very strong wind. But the instrument tells truth; the tension or pressure is *increased* by mutual action of opposing currents, until one is relaxed, when the barometer begins to fall, and, as the polar influence fails, the wind draws through north towards north-west, and the mercury falls. After which, and probably wind with rain, the glass rises; the wind shifts towards south-west (polar), and the weather improves, either for an interval only (the wind perhaps backing toward north), or for a considerable time.

In extra-tropical Australia, inland, as well as on the coasts, occasional hot winds, from the interior arid and heated deserts, sweep across the country, like a sirocco, or being *dry*, almost as a simoom. They are immediately met and displaced by polar winds, raising dust in clouds ('brickfielders'), and changing the temperature twenty or thirty, even to fifty degrees, almost suddenly.

As through all the extra-tropical range of Australia, extensive as it is, tropical upper currents are rainless, having passed over heated arid land only; and as the natural polar currents are not usually *moisture*-bearing —though in passing over an ocean they are slightly moistened by taking up vapour—the consequence is that dry sterility is *general.* Localities of course may differ;—fertile vallies,—near heights attracting rain, and occasional water-courses, occur often; but there are few fresh-water rivers, and fewer large lakes. Untowardly there are *many* salt streams.

Tasmania, in point of climate, winds, and weather, approaches Australia, excepting that it is less hot, arid, and saline, but windier and more rainy; therefore (being extensively wooded) shelter in extremes of temperature is available, and agriculture flourishes.

At sea, off its southern coast, the strong winds of those latitudes (forty-five) prevail. Their characteristics have already been sufficiently described. When known familiarly, as they ought to be, and their indications understood—by the skies, as well as by the instruments, advantages become available by voyagers, by agriculturists, and by gardeners, which without such (almost alphabetical) instruction are overlooked, or made detrimental by mismanagement.

What has been just said may be applicable to the space of sea reaching from Tasmania to Western Australia, where, with sudden change in the trend of the coast, and some remarkable peculiarities of the tidal currents,* alteration in climate is immediate.

Consequent on these facts, Cape Leeuwin has had a bad name as a very tempestuous promontory, but this seems to have arisen from ships passing it *from* Indian fine weather (inter-tropical) and directly encountering the strong winds with high seas of the anti-trade, in about thirty-five south, while ill-prepared, except for the smooth water and fine weather of Indian ordinary navigation.

From Cape Leeuwin, the summer winds are along shore, right into the south-east trade, or inclining

* Tidal paper in Appendix.

towards *then* heated Australia. The winter season, and occasionally, though rarely, the summer, is liable to heavy gales from tropical, and next from polar quarters, which raise a high and dangerous sea, especially on the edge of soundings, where resistance to the waves impelled by wind toward land is much felt.

Hence to the Mauritius is a space occupied, in winter by variable winds from the northward, in the summer by the south-east trade.

Hurricanes occur in it, principally nearer that island than Australia, and mostly not far from Mauritius and Bourbon. Their nature is now so well known, that they may be partly avoided.

From Dampier, Franklin, Capper, Flinders, Buist, Piddington, Thom and Reid, among the past—from Meldrum among the living—useful information about these hurricanes has been made available by publication. The last mentioned, in his later as well as earlier series of facts and inferences, has shown entire corroboration of the principles expressed in publications of the Board of Trade—accordant with those of Professor Dové and Sir John Herschel.

Madagascar, and the south-east coast of Africa, have been adverted to already. They are likewise subject to storms of a similar nature, but less regular, being more affected by the land.

At the edge of the Lagulhas Stream (like the Gulf Stream of the Atlantic) there are fogs and strong gales.

We have thus superficially viewed the general climatology of our *habitable* world, without taking into sight actual figures, although available;—and with but few words may now treat of the uninhabitable polar regions.

Whether solid ice or open water may be found at

either pole, or each, is still earnestly disputed. As neither of the magnetic poles, nor the poles of greatest *cold*, are at, or even very near, the poles of our earth's axis—as at those axial localities unceasing day lasts half a year—as fish, birds, and quadrupeds migrate toward the poles at that time—as currents set *from* them, meridionally—and, as Dutch voyagers (*say they*) went farther poleward, in open water, in the seventeenth century, than Parry did in this nineteenth, even (as they assert) not only to, but beyond the Pole*—it does seem only reasonable to think that open water at or near the poles, or one of them at least, may exist, more probably than a mass of solid ice. And if ice alone filled up those extensive central spaces, would it not have a tendency to increase in an augmenting ratio? If so, what of the fish, and the birds, and the animals, especially musk oxen and reindeer? and what of now temperate climates?

Very remarkable it is that, in Greenland, herds of white reindeer migrate toward the north (no one knows how far) every summer, from the vicinity of the most northern Danish or Esquimaux settlements in north-west Greenland.†

Whenever whalemen or sealers have penetrated beyond or within the formidable outer barriers of Antarctic ice, or have pushed well through Baffin's Bay, Davis Strait, or Spitzbergen fields and bergs, abundance of fish, seals and whales, *many* birds and bears have been seen. Could they thrive there, in *numbers*, unless open water exists to a greater extent than has yet been discovered and traced on charts?

It is highly interesting to read accounts of the early Dutch voyages, by Spitzbergen, and thence eastward,

* See Burney, Daines Barrington, Beaufoy, and others.

† M'Clintock, Allen, Young, and others.

with very inadequate means, and to reflect on what a Parry or other arctic hero *might* have effected in that direction had the course of discovery, aided by modern appliances, been so directed.

The effects of icebergs, or even floating field ice, on climate, temporarily, has been much considered. It would seem that currents of wind passing over them must be chilled, and yet take off a certain amount of vapour to be condensed against land, or by a colder current of air, into rain, or hail, or snow.

Heat absorbed in thawing ice or snow, and converting its water into invisible vapour or gas, is well known to be *very* considerable in amount.

Of a similar kind, but infinitely greater in extent, are those grand natural operations every year around arctic and antarctic circles, affecting all the circumjacent temperate zones. As either pole is turned more or less toward the sun, after the vernal equinox, the solar effect increases, in the direction of that pole, until a thawing is produced on the exterior ice, when an interval of comparatively cold weather occurs, caused by absorption of heat near polar circles, affecting more or less the contiguous regions; and thus the frequent cold of later spring months, especially after a warm early spring, may be accounted for *generally*.

As has been previously said, in effect, — If the above be a correct view, the converse should occur, namely, that a short second summer, or rather an interval of fine and comparatively warm weather, soon after the autumnal equinox, should be caused by liberation of heat (during condensation of vapour and formation of ice) and by precipitated moisture. Is not this the case, all around the world, in both temperate zones? The familiar expressions 'St. John's summer,' 'St. Martin's,' and the 'Indian' Summer, the 'red leaf,' advert to this period, which is recognised in each hemisphere, everywhere—in the middle or higher latitudes.

Having endeavoured thus to submit an extensive but generalised view of all climates, with their prevalent winds and weather—it is supposed that the reader, while attending to any one locality principally, will be less likely to overlook what may be simultaneously occurring in other parts of the world, as well as atmospheric changes more particularly in his own special zone; and near his place of local observation.

CHAPTER XIII

Utilisation of Meteorology: its Statistics and Dynamics — Simultaneous Observations — Separate Fields of Labour — Meteorologic Telegraphy — Forecasts — Storm Signals — Explanation — General Considerations — Special and Notable Conditions Explained — Brief Sketch of System now in Practice, and Method of Procedure — General Observations and Reflections — Arrangements.

Prepared by general information about instruments, observations and climatology, we may now undertake to apply ourselves beneficially to the practical utilisation of meteorology.

Having statistical facts, and understanding their dynamical relation to our atmosphere at any given time or succession of times, we know what is occurring around within a certain area of several hundred miles in diameter, in the air and clouds that may be above or passing near us: and, not only so, we can tell, with even more than probability, what will be the atmospheric conditions within and at any part of such an area during the next two or three days. To those whose attention has not been directed to the precise import of dynamical as connected with statistical facts, it may be convenient here to say that by the latter we mean the barometrical tension (pressure), the temperature of air, the direction and force of wind, and all other meteorologic data which are observed at one place, at one time. Comparison of these with other similar observations at the same place or elsewhere shows any movement, its force, and the duration of motion,—in a word the dynametry of air, in a given time. Single sets of observations show statical measures or statistical facts, and their comparison shows dynamical values, or relatives, or measures; one is instantaneous, the other is a continuance.

Until lately, meteorology had been too statical in practice to afford much benefit of an immediate and general kind. Indefinitely multiplied records only tended to make the work of their utilisation less encouraging, if not almost impossible. By less ambitious courses—by separating fields of labour, especially by treating of climates individually, and referring observations to independent centres—a prospect has been opened of immediately useful exertions. Stones may be shaped, bricks may be accumulated, but without an object in view—without an edifice to be constructed—how wearily unrewarding to the mind would be such toil, however animated (even like Schwabe's) by true scientific faith in future results.

As an example of what has been done in this direction, recently, under the auspices and by the powerful means of Government, authorised by Parliament, a brief *outline* will now be given of the practical system established at the Board of Trade with reference to Meteorologic Telegraphy; of its history, and the methods of present application; after which the more *difficult* parts of these subjects will be further treated—namely, their actual management in daily practice, the various conditions and circumstances under which the ever-changing states of atmosphere occur; and full explanation of the reasons for such decisions as are made in forecasting weather.

In meteorology some degree of increased interest has been caused not only by various discussions and publications, but by this organised system of forecasting weather and giving cautionary notice of expected storms.

In treating so complicated and extensive a subject as that of our atmosphere and its movements, it is extremely difficult to combine mathematical exactness with the results of experience obtained by practical ocular observation and much reflection; but to some extent this has been effected recently—the Board of Trade having arranged telegraphic and frequent communication between widely-separated stations and a central office in London, by which a means of *feeling*—indeed one may say *mentally seeing*—successive simultaneous states of the atmosphere over the greater extent of our islands was established, and an insight into its dynamical laws has been obtained, to which each passing month has added elucidation and value.

Possibly at this time, when extensions of our arrangements to the Continent are being established in France, in Hanover, and in Prussia (although *here* there are still persons who doubt, if they do not entirely disbelieve their utility), it may be desirable to give an explicit description of the basis, and the nature, of those forecasts and occasional warnings which have been proved useful during the past two years.

The first cautionary or storm-warning signals were made in February 1861; since which time similar notices have been given, as occasion needed.

In August 1861, the first *published* forecasts of weather were tried; and after *another* half-year had elapsed for gaining experience by varied tentative arrangements, the *present* system was established. Twenty-two reports are now received each morning (except Sundays), and ten each afternoon, besides five from the Continent. Double forecasts (*two* days in advance) are published, with the full tables (on which they *chiefly* depend), and are sent to eight *daily* papers, to one weekly, to Lloyd's, to the Admiralty, and to the Horse Guards, besides the Board of Trade.

The forecasts add almost nothing to the pecuniary expense of the system, while their usefulness, practically, is said to be more and more recognised.* Warnings of storms arise out of them, and (scarcely enough considered) the satisfaction of knowing that no very bad weather is imminent may be great to a person about to cross the sea. Thus their negative evidence may be actually little less valuable than the positive.

Prophecies or predictions they are not: the term forecast is strictly applicable to such an *opinion* as is the result of a scientific combination and calculation, liable to be occasionally, though rarely, marred by an unexpected 'downrush' † of southerly wind, or by a rapid electrical action not yet sufficiently indicated to our extremely limited sight and feeling. We shall know more and more by degrees. At present it is satisfactory to feel that the measures practised daily in these proceedings do not depend solely on *one individual*, but are the results of facts exactly recorded, and deductions from their consideration, for which rules have been given. An able assistant shares their responsibilities *now*, and others are advancing in the study of dynamical meteorology.

* At a meeting of the shareholders of the Great Western Docks at Stonehouse, Plymouth, it was stated officially that 'the deficiency (in revenue) is to be attributed chiefly to the absence of vessels requiring the use of the graving docks for the purpose of repairing the damages occasioned by storms and casualties at sea.'

† Herschel.

In order to enable a reader to judge of the basis on which rules for forecasting probable weather are founded, some degree of explanation may now be offered — as the method is new in its combinations, although depending on old or well known principles.

Repetition, to a certain extent, is unavoidable here, for two or three pages.

We have said that air-currents sometimes flow side by side, though in opposite directions, as parallel streams, for hundreds or even thousands of miles. Sometimes they are more or less superposed: occasionally, indeed *frequently*, crossing at various angles; sometimes combining, and by the *composition* of their forces and *qualities* causing those varieties of weather that are experienced as the wind veers more toward or from the equator or the nearest pole; and sometimes so antagonistic in their angular collision as to cause those large circular eddies or rotatory storms called cyclones, which are really like the greater storms in all parts of the world, although they do *not* quite assimilate to local whirlwinds, dust storms, and other commotions of atmosphere, which seem to be more *electrical* in their characteristics, if not in their origin.

Whenever a polar current prevails at any place, or is *approaching*, the air becomes heavier, and the barometer is high or rising. When the opposite (tropical) prevails or approaches, the mercury is low or falls, because the air is, or is *becoming*, specifically lighter — and these changes take place *slowly*. Whenever, from any causes—electrical, chemical, or simply mechanical—either current, or any combination of currents, ceases to press onward *without being opposed*, a *gradual* lightening of the atmosphere, through a greater or less area of hundreds or perhaps thousands of miles, occurs, not suddenly, but very gradually, and the barometer falls: there is less tension of air, in *every* direction, about the mercury.

To restore equilibrium, the nearest *disposable* body of air (so to speak), or most movable, advances first; but an impulse at the same time may be given to other and greater masses that — though later in arriving — may be stronger, last longer, and cause greater pressure mechanically as well as by combination. Air, like water, mingles *slowly*, either from above or laterally.

Taking, with Dové, north-east and south-west (*true*) as the 'wind-poles,' all intermediate directions are found to be more or less assimilated to the characteristics of those extremes, as they are nearer one or other; while all the variations of pressure or *tension* (many of those caused by temperature), and all *varieties* of winds, may be clearly and directly traced to operations of the two constant principal currents, polar and *tropical*,—*our* north-east and south-west.

It has been stated that storms — indeed all the greater circulations of atmosphere in the zone between the tropics and polar regions, have an eastward motion bodily, while circulating round a centrical area: and that within the tropics it is otherwise, or westward, till they *recurve*, moving first toward the *nearer* pole direct, and then eastward, with more or less direction toward the same pole.

Clear distinction should be made between those ever alternate and often conflicting main currents — tropical or polar, and the *local effects* of their union or antagonism — namely, mixed winds, whether westerly or easterly, with occasional eddies, or cyclones, on a larger or on a smaller scale.

The lower current does not ordinarily extend far upward (only some few thousand yards), and high lands, mountains, especially *ranges* of mountains, alter and impede its progress, so that a variety of eddy winds, or streams of wind, with local and apparently anomalous effects, are frequently caused.

Heat, electric action, or cold — condensation of *vapour* into hail, snow, rain, or fog, or its other changes, namely, evaporation, rarefaction, and expansion — absorbing heat, and therefore causing *cold*, immediately cause currents of air, in a degree proportional to such influence; inducing *horizontal* motion and dynamic *force*.

The polar current always *advances* from the polar quarter while *laterally* moving eastward (like a ship making lee-way), being pressed toward the east by the tropical flow which advances from the south-westward, usually above and at an angle with the polar stream or current of air, often mixing with it, but at times *separately* penetrating downward, sweeping and warming the earth's surface, uncombined with the polar current, even while *feeling* its approaching *influence*; and thus, as it were, forcing passages between streams of chilling polar air that at the same time are moving in opposite and nearly parallel directions.

At times, after a continuance of tropical air current, or during its general prevalence, a polar flow or separate stream of air (electric, cold, dry, and of greater pressure or tension than the prevailing body of air then next the earth) passes above, chilling or otherwise influencing the lower air through which, at some places, it penetrates completely — before it descends entirely, and (usually) displaces the tropical or south-westerly current.

These movements of air-currents are shown by clouds crossing the heavenly bodies, by the visible characteristics of those clouds, and by *simultaneous* observations of temperature, tension, force of wind, and its true direction, at *many* places.

It is very interesting as well as practically useful to mark how these inroads or mixtures of air-currents occur, and to note their beginnings or endings, at a few places considerably separated — such, for instance, as Copenhagen and Lisbon, Galway and Heligoland, Jersey and Aberdeen, Queenstown (or Valentia) and Berwick (or Yarmouth), with intermediate places. But these special features may be better treated after a few considerations have been submitted as preliminary.

Dynamic force, pressure of air in motion, is generated by disturbed equilibrium, whether electrically by heat or cold, mechanically by aqueous expansion into gas, by contraction into rain, snow, or ice, or by previously induced action of air currents among themselves which has caused inertia or, rather, momentum.

Hence it follows that no great disturbance of equable temperature, tension, dryness, or moisture can occur without a proportionate dynamical force tending to cause currents of air, or wind, however resisted, deflected, or otherwise influenced by similar and simultaneous actions, more or less in opposition, or in combination.

Sometimes their opposition is so equal, and equilibrium is so complete, that a calm is the result, no sensible movement *horizontally* along the earth's surface being perceptible.

Frequently combination occurs, and dynamic effects are produced in proportion. These are particularly evident in the *meetings* of tropical and polar winds (by the *west*), by their subsequent continuance in strength as mixed winds, and by the concurrence or combination of following cyclones.*

Successive, or rather *consecutive*, gyrations, circuits, or cyclones, often affect one another, acting as temporary

* See Diagram.

mutual checks until a combination and joint action occurs; their union causing then much *greater* effects, resemblances to which may be seen even in water-currents as well as in the atmosphere itself.

Between the tropics and the polar regions, or in *temperate* zones, the main currents are incessantly active, while more or less antagonistic, from the causes above mentioned: besides which, wherever considerable changes of temperature, development of electricity, heavy rain, or these in combination, cause temporary disturbance of atmospheric equilibrium (or a much altered *tension* of air), one or both of those grand agents of nature, the two great currents, speedily move by the *least resisting lines* to restore equilibrium, or fill the comparative void. One current arrives, probably, or acts *sooner* than the other; but invariably collision or mixture occurs of some kind or degree, usually occasioning a sweep or a circuit, a cyclonic (or *ellipsonic*) gyration, however little *noticed* when gentle or moderate in force, and while *gradual* in mutual appulse.

As there must be *resistance* to moving air (or a contest of currents) to cause gyration, and as there are no such causes on a large scale near the equator, there are no storms (except local squalls) in very low latitudes.

It is at some distance, from about 5° to 20° from the equator, that hurricanes are occasionally felt in their violence. They originate in or near those hot and densely-clouded spaces, sometimes spoken of as the '*cloud-ring*,' where aggregated aqueous vapour is at times condensed into heavy rain (with vivid electrical action), and a comparative vacuum is suddenly caused, towards which air rushes from all sides. That which arrives from a higher latitude has a westwardly, that from a lower an easterly tendency, due to the earth's rotation and to change of latitude, whence is a chief cause of the cyclone's invariable rotation in *one* direction, as above explained.

The hurricane, or cyclone, is impelled to the *west* in *low* latitudes, because the tendency of *both* currents there is to the westward along the surface, although one —the tropical—is much less so, and becomes actually easterly *near* the tropic, after which its equatorial centrifugal force becomes more and more evident, while the *westwardly* tendency of the polar current diminishes; and, therefore, at that latitude, hurricane cyclones cease to move westward (recurve), go then easterly, and onward more and more toward the polar quarter.

Great and important changes of weather and wind are invariably *preceded*, as well as accompanied, by notable alterations in the state of the atmosphere.

Such changes, being indicated at *some* places sooner than at others around the British Islands, give frequent premonitions; and therefore great *differences* of pressure (or tension) shown by barometer, of temperature, of dryness or moisture, and direction of wind, should be considered as *signs of changes likely to occur soon.*

It will be observed, on any continued comparison of weather reports, that during the stronger winds a far greater degree of uniformity and regularity is shown than during the prevalence of moderate or light breezes; and this should be remembered in forecasting weather from such publications.

When neither of the greater and more extensive atmospheric currents is sweeping across the British Islands (currents of which the *causes* are *remote*, and on a large scale), the nature or character of our winds approaches to and is rather like that of land and sea breezes in low latitudes, especially in summer; as in such cases either the cooler sea-wind is drawn in over land heated by the summer sun, or cold air from frosty heights, snow-covered land, or chilly valleys, moves toward the sea, which is so *uniform in temperature* for many weeks together, changing so *slowly* and but little, in comparison with land, during the year. These light *variables* may at such times be numerous, simultaneously, and around the compass, on the various coasts of the British Islands.

Frequently it has been asked, 'In this country, how much rise or fall of the glasses may foretell remarkable change or a dangerous storm?' To which can now be replied: 'Great changes or storms are *usually* shown by falls of barometer exceeding half an inch, and by differences of temperature exceeding about fifteen degrees. Nearly a tenth of an inch an hour is a fall presaging a storm or very heavy rain. The more rapidly such changes occur, the more risk there is of dangerous atmospheric commotion.

As all barometric instruments often, if not usually, show what may be expected, a day or even days in advance, rather than the weather of the present or next few hours—and as wind, or its *direction*, affects them much more than rain or snow, due allowance should always be made for *days* as well as for hours to come.

The general effect of storms is felt unequally in these islands, and less *inland* than on our coasts. Wind is much diminished or checked by its passage over land. The mountain ranges of Wales or Scotland, rising two to four thousand feet above the ocean level, have great power to alter the direction and probably the velocity of wind, independently of alterations caused by changes of temperature at elevations affecting moisture and tension.

Extensive changes, showing differences of pressure above or below the normal or mean level, amounting to nearly an inch, or thereabouts, are certain to be followed by marked commotion of the elements in the course of a few days. If the fall has been sudden, or the rise very rapid, swift but brief will be the resulting elementary movement; if slow or gradual, time will elapse before the change, and the altered state of weather will take place more gradually, but last longer, whether for better or for worse.

Notice may thus be obtained and given a few hours, or a day, or even some days before any important change in the weather actually occurs,—and having such knowledge, it obviously follows that telegraphic warning may be sent in any direction reached by the wires; and that occasionally, on the occurrence of very ominous signs—barometric and other, including always those of the heavens—such cautions may be given before storms as will tend to diminish the risks and loss of life, so frequent on our exposed and tempestuous shores.

Barometers show the alterations in tension—or, so to speak, the *pulsations*, on a large scale—of atmosphere; and their diagrams express to practised observers what the 'indicator-card' of a steam-cylinder shows to a skilful engineer.

Our own islands have very peculiar facilities for meteorologic communication by telegraph between outlying stations on the sea coast and a central place, all being at nearly the same level, and nearly all comparatively uninfluenced by mountain ranges.

And now the results are, that having daily knowledge

of the weather (including ordinary facts of a meteorologic nature) at the extreme limits and centre of our British Islands, we are warned of any *great change* taking place; the greater atmospheric changes being measured by days rather than by hours. Only local changes, however violent they may be *occasionally* (and *dangerous* undoubtedly in proportion to their suddenness and violence), only those changes are unfelt at a *distance*, and do not influence great breadths—such as hundreds of miles' area of atmosphere.

Some special, and to many persons entirely new, considerations should be mentioned here, as they are practically very valuable in connection with the means of forecasting weather.

When opposing currents of air meet, their masses must *continue* in motion a certain time, either rotating, or ascending, or going onward horizontally in *combination.*

Masses of air, either of polar or tropical *origin*, so to speak, returning (when driven back by stronger opposition), at first, and for a certain time, retain the characteristics of their peculiar and very different natures.

In our latitudes there is a continuous alternation of air-currents, each specifically different, and denoting approach by marked characteristics; and we have proved, by successive series of simultaneous statical observations over a wide range—embracing Scotland, Ireland, all England, and adjacent islands—that while these alternating, *or* circuitously-moving, currents are thus incessantly passing, the whole body of atmosphere filling our *temperate* zone is moving gradually *toward the east*, at an average rate of about five miles an hour (from two to eight miles).

During strong westerly winds this eastward motion is greatly increased, and in easterly gales it is proportionately diminished, as measured by its passage along a horizontal surface of earth or ocean.

Knowing these circumstances, and having accurate statical observations of these various currents at selected outlying stations, showing pressure (or tension), temperature, and relative dryness, with the direction and estimated horizontal force of wind at *each place simultaneously*, the dynamic consequences are already measurable approximately on geometric principles; and, judging by the past, there appears to be reasonable ground for expectation that meteorologic dynamics will soon be subjected to mathematical analysis and accurate formulas.

The facts now weighed and measured mentally, in what may be correctly called *forecasting* weather, are the direction and force of air-currents or wind, reported telegraphically to the central station in London from many distant stations, their respective tension and temperature, moisture or dryness, and their changes since former recent observations. These show whether any or either movement or change is on the increase or decrease; whether a polar current is moving laterally off, passing from our stations towards Europe, or approaching us from the Atlantic; whether moving direct toward the south-westward, with great velocity, or with slow progress. If moving fast in the direction of its length, it will approach England more from the east, its speed direct being twenty to fifty or eighty miles an hour; while its *constant* lateral or easterly tendency (like a ship's leeway in a current) being only five miles an hour, is then insensible to us (though clearly deducible from other facts ascertained), and is that much in alteration of actual direction, as well as of what would *otherwise* be the velocity of that polar current.

With the opposite principal current, the equatorial or south-westerly, more briefly and correctly *tropical*, similar but opposite results occur. The *direct* motion from a *south-westerly* quarter is accelerated sensibly to our perception by part of the eastward constant (about five miles hourly), and therefore a body of air approaches us sooner (other things being equal) from the westward than it does from the eastward.

To seamen accustomed to navigate in ships making leeway while in currents setting variously over the ground, such movements, complicated as they may appear, are familiar. There are the ship's headway, leeway and drift to be considered, in combination with the motion or *current-rate* of the buoyant water, and that perhaps an *upper* current, differing from one *beneath*, while each is passing across the bottom or bed of the sea beneath all.

But the *motes* circling in a beam of light across a draught of dusty air may perhaps show most simply and directly what is exactly meant by such combined and varying motions of *fluid*, *elastic*, and *mobile* air, as are here mentioned.

A very important consideration is the *subsequent* disposal or *progress* of bodies of air united, or *mixed*, or contiguous to each other, *after their meeting*, either directly opposed or at an angle, on the earth's (or ocean's) surface. They do *not vanish*. They cannot go directly upwards, against gravitation; westward they cannot (*generally*) go when there is collision or meeting, because the momentum, elasticity, and extent of the tropical 'anti-trade,'* or south-wester, usually overpowers

* Sir John Herschel's excellent term.

any direct polar current, or rises over it and more or less affects the subordinate one *below* by the friction of its eastward pressure. Downward there is no exit; eastwardly (toward the east) the accumulating air must go, and this tendency *continued* causes the *varieties* of wind from the westward; being more or less mixed, more or less purely polar or tropical, as either one prevails in *combination.*

After a body of air has passed, and gone to some distance southward or northward, it may be stopped by an advancing and more powerful mass of atmosphere which is moving in a direction contrary to or diagonally across its line of force. If their appulse be gradual and gentle, only a check occurs, and the weaker body is pushed back until its special qualities, respecting temperature and moisture, are so masked by those of its opponent as to be almost obliterated; but if these currents meet with energy at very different temperatures and tensions, rapid changes are noticed as the wind shifts, and circuitous eddies, storms, or cyclones occur.

Otherwise, when their meeting is, as first mentioned, *gradual*, there is the *return* of a portion of either current (which previously prevailed), either *direct* or deflected, deflected even through more than one quadrant of a circle, by its advancing opponent, and retaining for some considerable time its own previous characteristics. Thus we have for short times cold dry winds from the S.W. instead of the usual *warm* and *moist* ones; or winds of the *latter* kind from the north instead of cold ones.

The circuitous tendency of air in motion, and the numerous impediments to its horizontal progress, such as land, ranges of mountains, hills, or even cliffs, induce many a deviation from normal directions, extremely puzzling to the student of this subject; but so retentive is air of its tension and temperature, for a time, that, like currents in the ocean, each may be traced by its characteristics as long as within our extensive web of stations.

When the polar current is succeeded or driven back by a tropical advancing from a very southerly direction *gradually*, their action united becomes south-easterly (from the south-eastward); and as the one or other prevails, the wind blows more from one side of east or from the other. When the tropical is more from westward, their combination is a westerly wind.

Time is required to produce motion in the air, horizontally, and more *time* is indispensable for its gradual cessation from movement. *Statical* effects are noticed at observatories, or by careful observers anywhere, some hours or days before their notable dynamic consequences occur, such as strong winds.

When a body of atmosphere is moving from or toward the pole, its *impelling* force (*vis a tergo*) or its *attraction* toward a place of lessened tension, may cease, while the mass itself has a certain impetus or momentum.

Diminishing tension then results at the place of checked energy, and an upper current (*always present*) descends. At the same time there is an alteration of tension at the *farther extreme*, which is meeting and mingling with, if not resisting, while checked and deflected by, the advancing opponent.

Consequent on this, a body of air, extending perhaps across some hundred miles, becomes, as it were, *isolated*. Detached from its original source and maintenance, whether polar or tropical, and then quite surrounded by air of a different character, it is impelled in new and varying directions, still retaining for a time more or less of its characteristics, until gradually altered entirely, and totally incorporated with its conqueror.

Hence sometimes we have *cold* tropical wind, as to *direction*, with electric and other polar characteristics (for a limited time *only*) before the tropical predominates; or, on the other hand, a warm *apparently* polar air-current, in direction, with *tropical* peculiarities.

Moreover, in addition to these causes of *apparent* inconsistency, or irregularity, are the results of *circling* currents, streams of air retaining their features although changed, it may be even totally, in direction, along the earth's surface; besides a variety of merely local alterations, such as are effected by high lands, or valleys, or coast-lines. All these, and many other minor considerations, ought to be familiar and present to a forecaster of weather who would judge comprehensively — according to *observed facts* and ascertained *laws*.

At the Board of Trade from thirty to forty weather-telegrams are received *daily* (except Sundays), and forecasts, or premonitions of weather, are drawn up on the following arrangement, for publication in newspapers, as speedily as possible.

Districts are thus assumed: —

1. Scotland.
2. Ireland, around the coasts.
3. West Central (Severn to the Solway), coastwise.
4. South-West England (from the Severn to Southampton), by the coast.
5. South-East England (Wight to Thames).
6. East Coast (Thames to Tweed).

As newspaper space is very limited, and as *some* words are used in *different senses* by various persons, extreme care is taken in selecting those for such brief, general, and yet *sufficiently definite* sentences, as will suit the purposes satisfactorily.

Such words as are commonly found on *published* scales of force, or descriptions of wind and weather, being generally understood, are therefore used in preference to others, however *apparently* expressive to some persons by whom they are familiarly employed.

In saying, on any day, what the *probable* character of the weather will be *to-morrow*, or the day after, at the foot of a table showing its observed nature that very morning, a *limited* degree of information is offered, for about two days in advance,—which is as far as may be trusted *generally*, on an average: though at times a longer premonition *might* be given, with sufficient accuracy to be of *occasional* use.

Minute or special details, such as showers at particular places, or merely local squalls, are avoided; but the general, or average characteristics — those expected to be *principally* prevalent (with but few exceptions) the following day and the next after it, including the nights (not those of the weather actually *present*), are *cautiously* expressed, after careful consideration. Ordinary variations of *cloudiness*, or clear sky, or rain, of a *local* or only temporary character, are not noticed usually, because they cannot be perceived from a *distant* station.

That thus a broad *general average* or *prevalence* is kept in view, referring to a day or more in *advance*, and to a *district*, rather than only to *one* time or place, should be constantly remembered by the reader.

Although there is some practical difficulty in separating the effect on the mind of *present* states of air, weather, and clouds, from abstract considerations of what is to be *expected* on the morrow, or next following day, attention and ability may soon acquire the requisite competency.

As meteorologic instruments usually foretell important changes by at least a day, or much longer, we have to consider what wind and weather may be expected, from the morning observations, *compared* with those of the days immediately previous, as indicative of the morrow's weather, and of the day after, at *each* place; to take an *average* of those *expectations* for each district collectively, *in a group*; and then to estimate the dynamic effects which may be anticipated as the legitimate consequences of such *relative* tensions, temperatures, and dryness, occasioning more or less inequality in the atmospheric equilibrium, and thus causing greater or less horizontal motions of air-currents, or ordinary winds: and more or less *downfall* — whether hail, snow, or rain.

Comparisons of the moist and dry thermometers are *very* useful, if *well* observed, in telling the hygrometric condition of air; and thence, with *other* facts, showing how either current prevails, or has relative influence — a point of much importance in forecasting a change of wind either way, as well as the *probability* of rainy or dry weather. A good electrometer is not yet available at our out-stations, however desirable such an instrument would be, in expressing, not only relative electric states of air, but what may, perhaps, be called the relative *polarity* of atmospheric currents (*if not their polarisation*).

Whether there is a condition, or *relative position* of the particles of air, in a *tropical* current, differing from those in a *polar* current — (analogous to the polarisation of light) — and whether there is a direct connection between these principal air-currents, or winds, and those mysterious electro-magnetic *earth-currents*, are questions easy to ask — but difficult to be answered, as yet, even by philosophic authorities of the highest eminence. To such physicists, however, the writer would appeal for further particular consideration of the following facts, for which he can vouch : — *

With polar currents of air, electricity is above par, or plus ; the air is comparatively harsh, clouds in it have a hard, *oily* appearance; animal as well as vegetable life is peculiarly affected in various familiarly known ways; tension is above par ; and all these peculiarities are *constant* qualities, independent of *temperature* of night or day, and of the time of year, though, as it *usually* varies, more or less, with the winds, and may *seem* to be their direct consequence, like temperature, their correlation occasions some ambiguity.

With the opposite or tropical current, very different effects are well known to most people ; but the comparative *absence* of electrical tension (or plus electricity), the soft, *watery* aspect of clouds in *such air*, and the absence of *hard edges* or outlines, *unless* influenced in *some* degree by the polar element *then above*, and more or less mixed, have not been noticed generally, though they are properties expressive of tropical winds *solely* (west to south in *this* hemisphere) when in their *purity*, unmixed with the polar current.

In all frequented and known parts of the world, these peculiar characteristics of the so-called *easterly* and *westerly* winds have been carefully ascertained, and found to be irrespective of locality, — land or water, whether with an *ocean to the east*, or with a continent in

* By numerous specific notes, made at the *times* of remark, and by recorded observations, for which space cannot be allowed in these pages.

that direction, or the converse. It may be remarked, in passing, that *easterly* winds everywhere (*prevalent*, not merely temporary currents), either mixed or deflected, are polar — derived more or less from the nearest pole; and that so-called *westerly* winds are tropical, from a tropical direction; or they are *mixed* tropical and polar currents.

There is much to be remarked, in connection with these distinctive features, respecting atmospheric colours, clouds, auroras, and meteors, which at present must be reserved.

Outline maps, with movable windmarkers, and cyclone glasses or horn circles, are useful in forecasting weather; and full consideration should be given to the probable position, direction, extent, and degree of progress of those centrical areas, which may be termed *nodes*, around which the principal currents usually circulate, or turn, as they meet and alter, combine with, or *succeed* one another, laterally (in their lines of length, though *approaching* sideways), or at any angle.

Here dynamic considerations, with comprehensive comparisons of statical facts, become most important; and to treat them even approximately well, with such *quick dispatch* as is requisite, demands aptitude, experience, and close attention.

Those who are most concerned about approaching changes, who are going to sea, or on a journey, or even on a mere excursion; those who have gardening, agricultural, or other out-door pursuits in view, may derive useful *cautionary* notices from these published *expectations* of weather: although (from the nature of such subjects) they can be but *scanty* and imperfect under present circumstances.

Occasional objections have been taken to such forecasts,

because not always correct, for all places, in one district. It may, however, be considered by many persons, that general, comprehensive expressions, in aid of local observers, who can form independent judgments from the daily tables and *their own instruments*, respecting their immediate vicinity, *though not so well for distant places*, may be very useful as well as interesting: while to an unprovided or otherwise uninformed person, an idea of the kind of weather thought *probable* cannot be otherwise than acceptable, provided that he is in no way *bound* to act in accordance with any such views, against his own judgment.

Like the storm signals, such notices of expected bad weather should be merely *cautionary*, to denote anticipated disturbance *somewhere* over these islands, without being in the least degree compulsory, or interfering arbitrarily with the movements of vessels or individuals.

Certain it is, that although our conclusions may be incorrect, our judgment erroneous, the laws of nature and the signs afforded to man are invariably true. Accurate interpretation is the real deficiency.

Seamen know well the marked characteristics of the two great divisions of wind, in all parts of the world, and do not care to calculate the *intermediate* changes or combinations — to two or three points. They want to know the *quarter* whence a gale may be expected — whether northerly or southerly, in *general* terms: and every seaman will admit that, however useful, and therefore desirable, it would be to know exactly the *hour* of a storm's commencement — as our acquaintance with meteorology does not enable such times to be fixed — the next best thing is to have limits assigned for extra vigilance and special precaution. Such limits *are* clearly stated, in all the printed popular instructions, to be from the *time* of hoisting the signal until *two* or *three days afterwards*.

But, say some, and justly—are ships to remain waiting to avoid a gale that after all may not happen? are fishermen and coasters to wait idle and miss their opportunities? By no means. All that the cautionary signals imply is, 'Look out.' 'Be on your guard.' 'Notice glasses and signs of the weather.' 'The atmosphere is much disturbed.'

Perhaps sufficient thought has not always been given to the consideration of mere pecuniary *loss* by wear and tear, risk, accident, delay, and demurrage, caused by a gale at sea; balanced against the results of waiting for a tide or two, perhaps *once in two months*, when cautioned by a storm-signal.

Be this as it may with coasters, short traders, or even screw-colliers, the question is entirely different with ordinary over-sea or foreign-going ships; especially when starting from a southern, or from a western port. To such vessels, a gale in the Channel, or even during the first day or two after clearing the land, must always be very prejudicial. Officers and men are mutually strange; things are not in their places, often not secured, and the ship, perhaps, is untried at sea. Of course, however, these remarks are inapplicable to fine, first-class ships, and to powerful, well-managed steamers, independent of wind and weather, which start at appointed and fixed hours.

It is scarcely too much to say, even now, that if due attention be paid on the coast to cautionary signals—and, at the Central Office, to the telegraphed reports—no very dangerous storm need be anticipated without more or less notice of its approach being generally communicated around the British Islands, or to those particular coasts which probably may be most affected by its greatest strength: though this hardly yet applies to our extreme outposts, such as Jersey, Valentia, Nairn, and Heligoland, because their remoteness (invaluable as that condition is for warning other places nearer the centre) is an obvious reason why they cannot always be forewarned, themselves being as videttes. It is probable that another source of warning may be found available in natural and spontaneous *electric currents*, as the most marked indications of this kind noticed during the last two or three years have immediately preceded considerable atmospheric commotions.

In using the published daily tables it should be borne in mind that only one state of atmosphere in twenty-four hours is there recorded (excepting for rainfall); therefore it is only by comparisons and by due reference to immediately previous reports that probable consequences can be fairly inferred.

It is advisable, in considering the forecasts, to look always at the *second* as in some degree part of the first; the *time* of weather *continuing* not being a sufficiently certain or *reliable* notice, although the *nature* of a change, the force and *direction* of wind, may be generally trusted.

In *conclusion*, it may be here impressed on the reader that this system is only a tentative *experiment*. Hitherto, however, each month has added useful facts, and increased our acquaintance with the difficult, though not uncertain, dynamics of the subject.

Nothing, it should be remembered, could have been

well effected in an attempt to apply meteorology to daily practice with *confidence*, had not a foundation of facts existed in the works of scientific authorities—whose statical records and invaluable deductions afforded a sufficiently extensive basis on which to rely, while endeavouring to utilise modern powers of communication, by telegraph, from a large number of mutually remote stations, simultaneously corresponding with central Superintendence.*

* See instructions for Meteorologic Telegraphy in Appendix.

CHAPTER XIV

Method of Proceeding with Telegrams — Considerations — Comparisons — Rainfall — Tension — Temperature — Moisture — Wind Direction — Force — Clouds—Character — Sea Disturbance — Respective Changes and Indications — Reasons why — Veering and Hauling (or Backing) of Wind — Shifts (direct or retrograde) caused by Alternate Currents, acting at the same Time, or by consecutive Cyclones.

WE will proceed to show some practical working of the system now existing at the Board of Trade, and to give explanatory reasons for each step in the proceedings.

At ten o'clock in the morning, telegrams are received in Parliament Street, where they are immediately read and reduced, or corrected, for scale-errors, elevation, and temperature; then written into prepared forms, and copied several times. The first copy is passed to the Chief of the Department, or his Assistant, with all the telegrams to be studied for the day's *forecasts*, which are carefully written on the first paper, and then copied *quickly* for distribution.

At eleven—reports are sent out to the Times (for *second* edition), Lloyd's, and the Shipping Gazette; to the Board of Trade, Admiralty, and Horse Guards. Soon afterwards similar reports are sent to other afternoon papers: and, *late in the day*, copies, more or less *modified* in consequence of telegrams received in the afternoon, are sent out for the next morning's early papers.

Thus the earliest possible *distribution* of the intelligence is secured (almost insensibly to the public, respecting *expense*), the observations and their telegraphic communication to London having been authorised and paid for by Parliamentary vote, chiefly for scientific purposes, out of which these *additional* practical measures have legitimately grown—not at *great* additional charge.

Let us suppose that on a given morning the barometrical readings are nearly alike, it may be not differing more than a few hundredths of an inch from Nairn to Jersey, from Valentia to Heligoland. Imagine the temperatures also very similar *throughout*, within a few degrees (less than five) of each other, and a fair amount of evaporation, say three to six degrees. Suppose also the direction of wind nearly uniform if fresh, variable if light, the sky but little clouded, the sea undisturbed, and no fall of rain since the previous morning. Such a state of facts (such statical data) at once would show a settled state of the air, an equilibrium undisturbed, and, as statical alteration must precede dynamic motion, a probability of its continuance. *How long* in each place will depend on *previous* conditions and probable local effects, such as heated or chilled air, caused by plains or heights, by vicinity of sea, at a certain temperature, and by gradual movement of the atmospheric mass, horizontally eastward, whatever *other* motions its currents may have, *locally* northward or southward, or *from* the east. A calm at any place implies but slight motion in opposition to the *usual* movement *from* the west, a resistance to *air* advancing, but no friction or even a ripple, along the earth's or water's surface.

Calms are usually between opposing currents, but may be at their *mutual offset in contrary lines.*

In fine weather, with light or moderate winds, there

are commonly circuits around calm places, or contrary but gentle currents near them. In bad weather they are the nodes of stormy cyclonic circuits or sweeps of wind-currents.

With equilibrium undisturbed, as described above, and having been so for some time, no dynamic alteration, no general change of importance *can* occur during a day, or more, after such observations: and, if the previous interval of equilibrium has been long, proportionally long will the interval be before *much* change.*

Equilibrated conditions of atmosphere occur with either current—tropical or polar, but not during their mixtures or combinations, because then a contest is always in more or less activity above, whatever degree of tranquillity may seem evident below at the earth's surface. The barometer may be rather high, or at par, or somewhat but not much below that normal or average level,—with such an equilibrium.

And the thermometer may be high or low, provided its indications are *similar* throughout at least our islan range of stations.

Small, indeed, our range or web is on the *globe*, but it is sufficient for our practical objects, and not unmanageable. A much larger range would involve *loss of time* and too great differences of climate. These are considerations that, even now while we have continental observations, impede their considerable utilisation.

Let a case be now taken of another kind, namely,—disturbed equilibrium after two or three days of unsettled weather, with changing statical quantities, or measures. Suppose the barometer in Scotland at about twenty-nine

* 'Long notice, long last:
Short warning, soon past.'

inches, and the temperature sixty degrees, an overcast cloudy sky, little or no evaporation, sea 'getting up' (swell setting in), and diminished electricity.

Let similar indications, or extreme ones, be reported from Ireland, while on the east coast, in the south, and in the south-west of England, there is a high barometer, say thirty inches, with much the same *temperature* as in the north, or rather *lower* than in the north-west.

In this instance there is a difference in atmospheric *tension* between Scotland and Cornwall, amounting to what is indicated by an inch of the Torricellian column: and, if represented by a diagram, the curve, as a profile or sectional view, would be that of a wave, high at the south-west. Any increase of compression, or pressure, *laterally*, on a homogeneous fluid, must cause it to rise vertically, if it cannot flow away horizontally. The *first* movements must be in lines of least resistance, and they, although against gravitation, are upwards, until accumulation and gravity cause downward and horizontal force with a proportional flow *laterally*.

Here it may be expedient to pause, while considering rather closely the nature and action of atmospheric waves. While a fluid, air, or water, is in continuous equable and unchecked motion, it has no wave, vibration, oscillation, or pulsation. But the slightest check by friction, or any kind of opposition — by diminished channel, by alteration in energy, or by varied 'potential' (to adopt Green's and W. Thomson's term for a very analogous consideration in electricity), instantly causes a wave-like or pulsatory movement which, in so highly elastic and mobile a fluid as air, is speedily propagated, more or less confused by lateral (or *inductive*) waves, and is much longer in regaining a state of equilibrium than such a liquid as water, which is heavy and dull.

Hence the motion of air is seldom uniform in its whole extent or space horizontally, even for very limited areas, either in force or direction. Accurate delineations of self-registering anemometers at established observatories — the critical examinations of Whewell, Lloyd, and Robinson—and more generalised observations at sea (where even the least changes of wind are naturally more noticed, in *sailing* ships, than on land)—have universally proved the variability of even the most steady and direct winds, their fluctuating force, and, within certain limits, their actually *varying* direction, while to superficial observation they appear unchanged. There are always tendencies to stream-like, or even thread-like separations, with almost eddying curves, or even *curls*, and these tendencies are much more remarkable in squalls or *unsettled* weather — indeed, one may almost say they are nearly proportional to the irregularity or disturbed state of the atmosphere.

Waves of air thus caused ought not to be considered the same as those *apparent* waves which have been represented as traced on paper, barometrically, divided descriptively into crests and troughs, and mentioned as if *they* had *directly occasioned* changes of wind, and often with accompanying storms. Such so-called 'atmospheric waves' are correctly designated 'barometric curves,' and their real character may perhaps be explained succinctly in the following manner.

We have described in former chapters the great general circulation of air *around* our globe; and more or less *meridionally* across.

We have noticed the polar convergence of meridians, their expansion equatorially, and the relative tensions, bulk for bulk, of dry polar air and aqueous tropical; from which considerations it is obvious that, in moving from a polar region, air becomes lighter, and has diminished tension, for two reasons—its elasticity acquires more space in which to expand, and augmenting heat causes it to take up vapour. Precisely the converse action occurs in a tropical current. It is cooled, diminished, and, temporarily, has *increased* velocity, while momentum lasts, and its lateral limits (like the banks of a river, up which a tide flows) are narrowing. We have also noticed that there is a general, an universal movement of the atmosphere *eastward*, in temperate zones, while there is a constant alternation of the polar and tropical currents, either along the surfaces (of earth or sea), or more or less superposed. And now let us carry our thoughts to these actions,— *simultaneous* around either polar region and its adjacent temperate zone — to the continual ebb and flow, as it were, the *alternating* reciprocal action of great air currents (in a meridional direction), or the pulsation, so to speak, of atmosphere— and then notice that the barometric curves, as shown in diagrams, from west to east, are the faithful exponents of these grand changes, not only in direction, in time, and in character, but in the dynamic tension (or potential) of each great current.

Barometric curves in the higher latitudes show more tension, and greater extremes, than those of lower latitudes. Their direction is north-east and south-west, and they are quite distinct from the *various* curves of casual local tensions occasioned by minor atmospheric disturbances.*

Waves of air are *comparatively* free to expand *upwards* — however frictionally checked by the crossing of upper currents, and always held down by gravity.

* See diagrams in Appendix, and Espy's great collection in his Fourth Report.

At a height of about seven miles, the pressure, or tension of air, is so diminished, that the barometer would fall to less than seven or eight inches.

In the truly heroic ascent of Mr. Glaisher, on the 5th of last September — (of which an account is now before the writer) — when he and his intrepid aeronaut were so near being carried up to a height at which the balloon would have burst, and their dreadful fate must have been certain, — their greatest elevation was said to be above six miles: which is higher than the loftiest Indian mountain summit (Deodunga, about 29,000 feet — six miles being 31,680); and then the barometer's indication must have been less than eight inches. The last registration before Mr. Glaisher lost consciousness was ten inches, and this was in the extreme cold of *fifty-seven* degrees *below freezing point*, and an extraordinarily rarefied air, through which their *liberated pigeons* fell like stones. There was no moisture — there were no clouds — for they were far above both: they were nearer to heatless, airless, and mysterious space than ever mortal man had previously penetrated;— and into which their daring venture will probably deter any others from making so desperate, however meritorious, an excursion — even for the interests of science.

Reverting again to waves. So much has been written by the ablest mathematicians, in a manner which only a mathematician can read intelligently and beneficially, that it may seem futile, for those who are not so qualified, to study — much less to write about — a subject generally considered so abstruse. But the author of these remarks has gradually become convinced that, although mathematical analysis of a high order — the intellectual machinery of extensive power — is requisite for numbering, measuring, and weighing physical effects, plain common sense, and comprehensive reflection, may perceive and approximately compare material relations, as fairly as moral conditions.

Waves, as *seen* in water, are sometimes slight ripples on a quiet pond, sometimes are undulating hill-like masses more than sixty feet in *vertical* height, and distant apart about a furlong. We have been told by some authorities that waves, unopposed, never rise more than about thirty feet. So said the lamented Scoresby (among others) until, in his last voyage, on board the 'Royal Charter,' he saw, and measured, the size of waves such as he, in his previous *northern* experience, had never *seen* and therefore continued to disbelieve — (as the late Sir John Barrow denied *cannibalism*; by which both those well-known voyagers *implied* that *other* travellers told *tales* — they themselves being the only 'Simons.')

What is the actual motion, the change of *position* among particles of water in *any* wave? The *undulation* goes along, more or less swiftly in proportion to its size (the larger the faster;) but the *water* remains.

A *substance* floating on it is carried up and down chiefly; but it also goes onward and back again, for a *short distance*; and its motion is in a curve, elliptic or other, according to the circumstances of the wave — whether resisted or unconfined, small or large, urged on from behind, or expending its *previously* acquired energy. When a wave of water is unimpeded in the *onward* motion of its particles or mass, no break occurs — the particles advance and again retire in succession; but if opposed, as by a rock, or other unyielding obstacle, a *breaking* dispersion at once is made, and with an effect that is proportionate to the size of the wave. Immediately afterwards is the inevitable recoil, when all the broken-apart and disseminated particles of water are hurried back, by gravitation, to the places which would otherwise become *vacant* (in respect of *fluid*), and therefore not equilibrated, if they were not thus drawn in, or *backward*, by such a *hydraulic* suction.

To form a wave — water being *incompressible* and inelastic (in general terms) — there must be a certain actual movement, from place to place, of particles. There *cannot be* a visible change of form, without alteration in the relative position of matter. When a rising wave advances, it disturbs only a portion of the fluid below (at *considerable* depths waves are not felt *); but the *uniformly* consecutive motion of particles appears to be nearly as follows: —

The first to move are followed by those next below; others *instantly* take their places, and more follow successively, whose places are as immediately filled by particles from *before* the growing wave, where the surface of water is *falling*. Thus the *first* particles (and others similarly in unbroken close succession) rise, go onward, and, still rising, to the wave *crest*,— thence they descend — still going *onward*, through the rest of that wave's length; and, in so descending, occupying the places of other particles, which as consecutively are drawn back, under the next *advancing* wave, to supply the places of those which are then rising.

Thus each particle, or molecule, moves a small distance vertically and circuitously, but returns to its original *relative* position, if not forcibly interrupted; and as its circuit depends on the size of the wave, of course a larger wave will give its particles,—or their mass, aggregated,—greater force than a smaller, when

* Divers, diving-bells, surface of sea bottom, &c.

impelled against an obstacle (as when breaking on the shore), because they have the greater momentum (of mass multiplied by velocity). Simple as this explanation may now appear, the writer has often looked for such a one in vain, and therefore offers it, in the hope it may save a few others from being perplexed by what too long mystified himself.

Whether he may here appropriately venture a step further, as a digression, is doubtful; but the brief attempt will be risked; with hopes of pardon?

As in electric *circuits* (so called) no particle of matter can be moved, or *impelled*, in any direction, without a corresponding *induced action*, to *prevent*, rather than fill an electric vacuum — there cannot be a current through a conductor without a return in *some manner*. And, electrically, such a return can only be made from a body not in equilibrium, or, in other terms, electrified differently; and such a body is the earth. Therefore, to effect a rapid transmission of an electric current, or wave, along a wire, it is indispensable to have a ready and adequate source of other electricity to follow, *instantaneously*, its coadjutor.

Just so, though seemingly almost infinitely slower, no wave could *grow* without the rising particles having their places *succeeded* by such a supply, that their material support could be continued instantaneously, and sufficiently maintained.

But this so-called circuit does not imply a *return* of electricity from the utmost end of a long wire (perhaps more than a thousand miles), as some have imagined; it involves only a connection with the *nearest* earth.

That the electric influence through or along a wire, whatever its length, has been occasionally misunderstood or mis-stated — when an explanation has been at all attempted — may, perhaps, be thus shown: —

No conductor is *efficient* unless solid. Of a solid body, the particles or molecules are *closely* in *contact.* If *inelastic*, and adhering in a line, however long, no one particle can be moved, lengthwise, without displacing all the rest, however numerous. Push, or strike one end of a long solid rod or *inelastic* wire, however lengthened, and an equal impulse is felt, at the same instant, at the other end. An electric shock is a severe concussion.

Mathematically, it may be shown that the above view is correct — if the conductor is unyielding, *solid*, and *inelastic*. That a *line* of steel balls, rigidly confined in an inflexible tube, and struck at one end, must feel the blow at the *farthest* ball — simultaneously coincident — may be variously demonstrated. *

These views may possibly help to explain that *inductive* action of electricity which has so perplexed many of us; and to show why *substance*, sectional area, is requisite in conductors rather than *superficies* (as some authorities *used* to think); but in this place they must not be further followed, however enticing — and especially so as connected with *magnetism*.

We have digressed very far, though perhaps not entirely in a useless direction, and now would ask to be allowed to return to the *atmospheric* case and

* Perhaps one of the remarkable instances of effects produced at a distance (not to mention sound, much less light) is that of a scratch on one of a number of logs of timber, lying in contact endwise, which, touched with a pin or the nail, convey the sound or vibration to their farthest end, synchronously.

conditions under consideration in page 197. We then supposed that there was about an inch difference of barometers (south and north) with high temperature in the north, from which it should be inferred that the polar current had ceased or *failed* in the *north*—was checked in the south by an advancing tropical—and that a certain quantity of polar air was cut off from its source of supply; consequent on which an accumulation southward, from the *momentum* of that (so detached) polar mass, and from the opposition of advancing tropical, in great volume, probably, would cause a strong dynamic effect from south-west to north-eastward, and a fall of the barometer *with* it (not before), but no immediate change of temperature, no change of moment, until the mass of polar air, recently present in the south, had been driven back northward and to the eastward, *after which* the pure *tropical*, with higher temperature, would *succeed*, and last for a time.

Very strong winds, gales between south and west, would certainly follow, and their duration would be proportional to the length of immediately previous disturbances of atmospheric equilibrium, and to the *interval* between those signs and the beginning of dynamic results.

Such gales would be ultimately (if not soon) followed by polar currents setting in on the west side of these tropical winds (induced *partly* by the low tension in their vicinity, *added*, as a cause of motion, to their normal succession or alternation) and either rushing into them, from above, or deflecting, and then uniting with them, laterally. These streams or currents, of great length, and perhaps hundreds of miles in breadth, but only one, two, or three miles deep, pass on eastward over Europe — become gradually changed in nature, force, and direction, by land — mountainous ranges especially, and by temperature; and are succeeded, after the polar current only, by a combination of both currents, as a westerly wind:—or by their regular succession, if not union, through the east, till they become south-east, southerly, and south-west: unless indeed a retrogression or backing occurs (as often happens), or a complete and *sudden* change, or shift, to nearly an *opposite* quarter.

The duration, the repetition, and the force of these governing currents, is too dependent on *remote general* causes — such as polar frosts or thaws, tropical heats or rains, electrical action and *lunisolar tides* — for us to know or do much in foreseeing *their distant* changes.

CHAPTER XV.

Supposed Cases for Forecasting and Warnings of Weather — Modes of Proceeding — Currents advancing above or below — Dove's View — Notices of Contrary Conditions — Other Cases — Various Considerations — Sea Swell — Electricity — Local Storms — Earth Currents: how to be foreseen — Winds from Sea diminished by Land — Light Variables hard to trace or follow — Land and Sea Breezes — Animals' Sense of Change may be electrical.

We may next take a case of atmospheric change in the south of England, while the northern districts, Scotland and Ireland, are apparently under air undisturbed by abnormal causes.

In the Channel and along the south-west and south-east coasts, a *rapidly* falling glass, an increase of temperature, diminished evaporation, heavily-clouded sky, and variable easterly breezes; while in *North* Britain and Ireland there is cold dry air, with a barometric column above par, perhaps rising with light polar wind; such statical facts show that a rush of air will soon be felt, but first from the tropical quarter, whence there is as yet the greatest influence indicated.

If the column falls *much*, and other signs increase, probably the wind will back through east into the polar quarter, and blow, with rain, toward a cyclonic area then in formation at more or less distance in the south-west. Such an area will generally progress across France, toward the Netherlands and the Baltic; its strength, or force, and development as a storm, having commenced about the Bay of Biscay.

In such a case England would feel the northern half of a cyclone, between a polar current across Scotland, Ireland, and the north-eastern Atlantic, and a tropical current passing along Spain, West Africa and Portugal, over the Bay, and across eastern Europe; its central area occupying much of France and Germany successively; all places to the left of its course, or to the north-westward, would have the wind from south-east to north-east and north-west consecutively—strong proportionately to the dynamic potentials (of differences of pressure or tension, and of temperature), ending, if not *again* disturbed, like the winds of the south-western half, which shift direct from south-east through south, and south-west to north-west eventually.

If the central area is far west at the commencement, though with southing enough to pass southward of an observer, he will have much south-west and southerly wind, hauling or backing to the south-east and then continuing to back round, as above described. But if the growing change, cyclonic in its nature (like all eddies between currents of wind), is far south and not much to the west when first its signs are manifested, then but little or no wind from these quarters will be experienced.

In the very marked cases of the centrical area of a great cyclone passing over the middle of the British Islands, as in that well-known instance of October 1859, when the 'Royal Charter' was wrecked, there is a general lowering of the barometer, with remarkable differences of temperature and evaporation.

If these statical alterations extend throughout a wide range, as through all the British and Irish stations, extensive and considerable will be the dynamic consequences; as the corresponding excesses of tension, somewhere, in proportion always to any diminutions, must be far off, and therefore indicating a wide range of influence, with a proportionately augmented momentum, *when* the so distantly but widely affected atmosphere is once set in motion toward the locality of least tension. Hence, therefore, not only a longer duration of following commotion, but a much more violent collision of the elements.

When a disturbance of air is small, comparatively, in extent, it does not affect very distant stations, nor does it last long; though it may be very severe, even like a whirlwind, or hurricane squall, for a short time.

Frequently, such squalls (*on land*, usually called *thunder-storms*, though seamen hardly would apply to them such a term as storm), are very localised, scarcely affecting more than one or two countries; but they never happen, with any force, without well-watched barometers showing by sudden, though not great, falls of the column, or by its oscillation, that *something* of the kind *will* occur. Thermometers and camphor-glasses also contribute their indications.

Hitherto we have been considering the conditions of such changes as if they were isolated, or happened singly, which is seldom the case in reality; whence great confusion has arisen in some descriptions, and in attempting to trace storms from insufficient data.

Usually there are two, three, or more eddies, *irregular* in their curvilinear figures, between the main *currents*, while *they* are approaching or closing with force; and a day, two days, or more may elapse between these successive cyclonic *effects*. In general, at least one or two minor circuits occur, and then there may be a marked lull—a most deceitful pause happens. This comparative calm, often with apparently fine weather (to the eye without instruments), is occasioned by one cyclone overtaking and influencing another.*

Notice two eddies in a river stream (from a bridge or other elevation), see how one overtakes, stops, then mixes with, and joins force to the other. Two or three eddies may thus be seen to run together, and combine into one larger and more continuous circulation.

Similarly, atmospheric eddies act, though in a much more extensive and more gradually progressive manner.

When one approaches near another, and their dynamic energies (*potentials*) are equal in opposite directions, a calm ensues, if near their extreme outer limits; but if the appulse occurs near their strength, one having more or less overlapped the other, or descended diagonally on it, with rapidity, then the most violent and dangerous squalls, the most powerful blasts of air that are known, sometimes happen.

With the diagram it may be readily seen that a current from SW. in the SE. semicircle, or half of a cyclone, impinged on by a NE. current in the NW. half of a much larger and overlapping cyclone, must be rapidly, if not suddenly, turned (against the sun), or *backed* through SE., E., and N., to NE. These are usually the most dangerous shifts, and, in connection with *ordinary* changes from NW. to south-westerly, have occasioned the seaman's saying, 'when it backs it blows.'

Changes against the sun occur, (in the north hemisphere *against* watch hands), it should be clearly understood, from two distinct causes—one the interference of following circuits, the other a yielding of one current to the force then increasing of another.

Suppose now a north-west wind blowing. If a south-

* See diagram, 'Interfering Cyclones.'

wester is approaching, above or along the surface, with as much energy (momentum or potential) as the existing north-wester, the two will *combine* into a west wind. If the south-wester prevails, their combination will be more southerly (and the converse), in which case the wind will appear to *back* (or, if the converse, veer direct).

But as the south-westerly (or tropical) current is the moisture-bearing, and the more impulsive one (from its elastic mobility, and continuous increase of compression, as it *forces* a way north-eastward), while also it is more altered, irregularly, by influence of, or contact with, the polar, its steady opponent,—we see that unsettled, squally, rainy, or blowing weather is, on this account, more likely to follow or accompany retrograde, or backing winds, than those which veer round direct.

Of the results that accompany such shiftings of wind, of squalls and of electrical indications caused by changes of direction or force, the next chapter will treat.

Generally, such consecutive and interfering cyclones or circuitous sweeps of wind, increase in force and diameter, or area, from the first to the second, and thence to a third, if not more, the third or fourth being the *greater* and longer, though *not* the concluding one. On land, among a number of fixed stations, separated distantly, it is easy to follow and trace such phenomena; but for a sea discussion, when only one or two, or at most a very few, ships' logs can be collected, it is almost certain that errors will arise, and that effects of several storms may be treated as if they were facts, that occurred in one continuous cyclone only.

It is very rare that a single circuit, a centrical or rotatory wind of considerable force, occurs in one place only, or unaccompanied soon by another. Atmospheric currents which occasion cyclonic eddies are on far too great and prolonged a scale to cause only one such effect. Air, when extremely disturbed, takes a long time to regain its equilibrium : one disturbance inductively causes another, and so on, till inertia, friction, and counteraction of other movements, entirely check momentum, by equal action in opposition.

There are no *proved* instances of continuity in one cyclone beyond *four* days, as one storm; very few indeed that demonstrate three. Their ordinary duration is from a few hours to a day or two. But as a following one may *then* happen, and after it possibly another, we may readily perceive how it has happened that in piecing together the extracts from various logs of ships far apart, using some data, and neglecting other facts (because seemingly at variance), extraordinary courses of storms have been *supposed traced* accurately across a whole ocean — and even back again,* as if only one such meteoric gyration then existed, even in so extensive a quarter of our world, during some weeks of time.

In truth, as is now becoming known, the greater atmospheric commotions usually occur, in *many* localities, at about the same time (within a few days, or weeks), and not only so in one quarter of the world, but throughout one zone, at least, successively—if not through *other* regions, hemispherically distant.

When the sun, material mover of our atmosphere, has recently crossed the Line, when he has lately been at a solstice, or when his influence has been for a time in vertical action over any parallel of latitude, how marked, general, and notorious are the consequences!

Changes of monsoons, storms, heavy and perhaps continuing rains, everywhere, more or less (under corre-

* Redfield — Reid.

sponding conditions of physical geography), are recurring evidences of the very general accordance, similarity of action, and most extensive intercommunication always existing in our atmosphere.

In such grand disturbances as these, the Lunarist and the Astro-meteorologist should endeavour to trace influences of moon and planets. Welcome, indeed, would each proved effect of either be—duly eliminated from masking effects of other causations.

Let our attention now be again directed to the system of Meteorologic Telegraphy. We have considered some states of weather, and their resulting consequences; but as nothing has been yet said of the deduced forecasts, or of warning signals, it may be convenient to the reader that allusion to those points should be made here, before entering on the discussion of other and more varied atmospheric conditions.

The area of our islands has been supposed divided, for these purposes, into six districts, suitable for ready consideration, convenience for telegraphic communication, and respectively not very dissimilar in climate and conditions. In noticing our little islands on a *globe*, and considering their position with respect to polar and opposite currents, NE. and SW., with the *composite* advances of those principal winds, it is obvious that the western and northern stations will be first touched, *usually*, by the approaching edges, or lateral limits of air currents:—excepting when *outshoots*, or advanced streams having much onward motion, in lines of their length, are pushed or drawn off, in either direction, along the lower surface, (earth or water) or overhead above the then surface current:—in which last case *touches* (as it were) of the coming current, will be felt, here and there, some time previously.

Having these (and many other) considerations in mind, the district of Scotland is first taken by the telegrams; the data for each place are used in deducing a probable state for each locality, and then an average is struck for the whole.

This average is *subsequently* collated with the conclusions for other districts, in order to estimate, and allow duly for, dynamic effects.

Next in order is Ireland, for which similar steps are taken. Past rainfall, and existing moisture, are weighed (mentally) in connection with appearances of sky, direction and force of wind, and the way the wind is shifting, *veering* or *backing*, (on which so much depends.) The state of sea also (sea-disturbance) is a useful fact, as distant gales send undulations against shores many hours before the wind that causes them is felt, when approaching from seaward. Upper currents of air, in a direction much differing from the lower, should be taken into account, and especially if they move rapidly, as there is no more certain indication of a change of wind in the temperate zones, where, (however superposed occasionally, often indeed over *land*, where there are obstacles, such as hills or mountains), their normal condition is that of alternation, with more or less parallelism, along the surface of earth—in opposite directions.

Here another brief digression may be pardonable, on account of its importance, and relevancy to what has just been said.

Dové in his *latest* work, (only just translated and published,) adverts to the polar current as advancing along earth's surface, and to the other as approaching first from above.

As much pains have been bestowed on this subject—the approach of new currents—by the present writer, and as he has recorded many instances in writing when south-westerly or westerly winds were blowing at the surface, while northerly or north-easterly were *evident* above (by light clouds crossing heavenly bodies), and which, in some hours, or (in other cases) one or two days, displaced or succeeded previous long-continued south-westerly (or tropical) currents, he trusts that his highly-esteemed friend will reconsider this subject, though difficult to prove *readily*, as it is only on rare occasions that the polar current, when above, or superposed, has any clouds by which its presence and course can be demonstrated.

It will appear, the writer believes, in the next chapter, how satisfactorily all the variations of clouds, and their precipitations of rain, hail, or snow, may be explained on the supposition of either current being occasionally uppermost.

It *was* stated, in more than one meteorologic paper from the Board of Trade, that the polar current is the normal one of either zone, and that it always advances along the surface (not from above). This statement was erroneous, its author now believes. He has become convinced that the truly normal movement in each temperate zone is westerly, from the westward—a composite result of the constant tropical and occasionally polar currents, uniting, *generally*, in an anti-trade wind.

Thus he also thinks that the polar air often, if not usually, *advances* above, *over the tropical*, at its *first* approach to a station.

Let the circumstances of this case be more closely considered. Suppose that a south-westerly or westerly wind is blowing over a wide extent of land, that it has continued during some days, therefore has much momentum, and admit that a current of polar air may be impelled (or drawn) toward the same region. Can the *advancing* current (referred to land stations) push *under* its adversary, against not only the frictional opposition of air in motion, but the much greater resistance of earth's varied rough surface, along which it would have to force a way, while hoisting or wedging up the whole body of another current?

On the other hand, a current advancing *above* has space, unlimited space, in which to move forward, affected only by friction along the superficial (lightest) air of the current then on earth's surface, and without any weight to raise except its own, which becomes less sensible, proportionally to the weakening or diminution of the under current.

As the polar current is dry and unmixed, *generally*, it is seldom that cirrus can be seen in it; therefore its advent *above*, *first*, before reaching earth's surface, has not been notably remarked by observers in general. The effect of a powerful polar upper current, in a diagonal or contrary direction to the lower one, is to deflect, or check, or act in both these ways on the current below, which it either entirely stops, supplants, and drives away, or affects—for *a time only*,—in force, direction, and temperature, without total change; after which the lower current again acquires strength and prevalence. Similarly a polar wind, at the *surface*, is affected by an advancing tropical current above; one acting more or less on the other, as presently will be shown, by partial or total displacement, or gradual incorporation by intermixture and complete combination.

Reverting, again, to the present trial system of forecasting and warning. Electrical, auroral, and any meteoric occurrences are sedulously noticed. Hitherto their near coincidences with *changes* of wind and weather, if not premonition of storms, have been so interesting that it is contemplated to arrange some means by which earth-currents, or spontaneous electric action along telegraph wires, may be signified to the Central Meteorologic Office in London.

On a *small* scale, such changes of weather, as one *main* current succeeds another, are not dissimilar to changes of monsoons; and they shew *periodicity*.

Having collated and duly considered the Irish telegrams, the first forecast for that district is drawn; and then, successively, the West central, SW., SE., and East coasts are taken; after which are the purely dynamic questions, respecting horizontal forces and directions consequent on the respective energies exerted in specific directions, proportional to the respective differences of statical quantities at stations, to the distances between them and other stations (or groups of stations), and to the moments (or potentials) of these prevalent or approaching currents.

These comparisons being made, and the first forecasts altered as requisite, short expressive abstracts are written, copied, and forthwith sent out for immediate publication. These proceedings, seemingly tedious, only require about half an hour after the telegrams are collected and converted. The copied papers are on their way to various Offices soon after eleven o'clock, at the latest, every working day.

Should the indications be such as to require cautionary signals to be shown along any or all of the coasts, a *printed list* of places is sent, with a word or two only in addition, to the telegraph offices close at hand. Those words are simply North Cone or South Cone, Drum, or Drum and N. (or S.) Cone, as the case may require,—those districts *only* being warned, which it is believed will feel the force of the coming gale, or storm, with severity. This selection of districts implies of course a certain knowledge of the storm's course and probable *greater* force; to which we are now able to approximate tolerably near.

When first commencing these warnings, some were sent out too numerously or extensively, as at that time less knowledge of the subject was available. Now, however, the notices are found to be more accurate as to localities as well as in time. An outline chart, with wind-markers, is useful; likewise a transparent horn, or a glass, with circles; but a certain amount of practice enables one to dispense with such assistance, and work out the questions mentally (like a chess-player who need not look at the board).

Comparing the wind and weather round our coasts, on any day, by the published reports, it is seen that the East coast is usually unlike the N., the W., or the S., but approximates in its meteorologic characteristics to East Scotland. From midland districts we have no reports. Those of a very limited nature which are published for *inland* districts, are not from the meteorologic office.

The specific character of our warning signals and directions about them being given fully in the appendix, need not be here mentioned. Generally, they are obtaining much popular favour and confidence, even among those whose natural habits, if not prejudices, inclined them, at first, to indifference or opposition.

These cautionary signals are transmitted so rapidly, being shown around the coasts in about half an hour from their leaving London, at nearly two hundred stations, that their value has been proved and acknowledged; but the forecasts, which are their actual foundation, are not perhaps so generally noticed, not being yet fully appreciated.

While newspapers are printed and travel to distant towns, time escapes so fast, that the day and its forecast too often arrive at a distant place together, and then of course there is no value in such information — the day and its *weather* being *present.* For this there is yet no remedy; but in some measure the *second* day's forecasts may make up for the retardation of the first, if duly noticed and compared.

The morning forecasts are published in the afternoon papers of that same day, as well as in the 'Times' (*second* edition), which, considering that they embrace more than twenty stations—from Nairn to Jersey, and from Valentia to Heligoland, besides the central ones of London and Liverpool—is perhaps as short a process as at present can be executed.

A case may next be supposed of *very* low barometers in the W., say nearly *twenty-eight* inches, with high temperature and much moisture. Unquestionably, a violent gale or storm will follow, first from the southward and then from NW., or more northerly, and, on the eastern coasts, perhaps easterly.

The centrical area of such a coming storm may be known, and its course approximately traced, on a chart, with markers; and places which are found to lie within its probable sweep, should be forthwith warned accordingly.

Some should be warned by the S. Cone, others by a N. one, intermediate stations by the Drum, but those places at which the gale may be very heavy, dangerously violent, ought to have the extra warning of a Drum and Cone, the latter being below, or above, according to the expected first direction of the wind, southerly or northerly, the drum indicating great force either way.

Great depression of the barometer, in the W., over the Atlantic, will be *followed* by similar, though perhaps somewhat less, loss of tension across Ireland and England or Scotland. It will assuredly be near the centre of a rotary storm, which subsequently—perhaps two or three days after— will be felt heavily, first on our western— then on our east coasts, and will expand, while probably expending itself, in the North Sea.

It should be remembered that many local threatenings of storms, or actual gales, on the W., and to the SW., are not followed by very strong winds *inland*, or to the eastward. They are broken by our western heights: they there part with much rain; and their force becomes materially abated.

Sometimes the barometer falls considerably on the *eastern* coasts, with a *low* temperature — in which case — remembering that *direction* of wind *alone* causes several tenths of difference in the column of mercury, a glass near twenty-nine inches, with a *low temperature*, may be as ominous of a northerly storm as one at twenty-eight inches might be of a southerly gale. Such a statical condition, therefore, is sure to be followed by a powerful polar wind, met probably, and made rotary, by an opposing gale from southward.

Such a commotion as this might be felt on the East coast of England, in the North Sea, and on the Western coasts of Europe; but not in Scotland, Ireland, or South England.

Local storms, (whirlwinds, thunder-squalls, or very limited gun-like explosions of air,) unroof houses, scatter hay-ricks, upset waggons, destroy boats, blow down chimneys, tear off branches, uproot trees, or break them off short, and drive vast furrows, as it were, through wooded tracts. Such sudden and dangerously concentrated effects are not to be correctly foreseen from a distance, though instrumental means may say, by sudden falls, or changes, and oscillating irregularity, that there is mischief impending.

Happily, such storms or squalls are but local, however much noticed when over the *land*; and they always give warning to an *attentive* observer, by visible evidences in the sky, or instrumentally, so that he cannot easily *be taken unawares.*

Our attention has thus been drawn principally to forecasts and warnings of storms; but it should be recollected that they are only exceptional, and occur comparatively seldom — perhaps a gale once a month on a *yearly* average, and a very great storm annually.

In some months, nevertheless, they may be *frequent* — even three or four gales may occur in one week; but at other periods, a month, or two, or three months, may elapse without a single strong gale requiring warning-signals to be hoisted.

In ordinary settled weather, it is more difficult to draw correct forecasts than during strong winds.

So many minor causes then influence local air-currents, when no master-wind is sweeping across, that the Central Office cannot safely say more than *variable* on such occasions—which are frequent.

When land is colder, generally, than the sea near it, and no marked air-current is prevailing, there will be land-breezes seaward, and conversely when the land is warmer than the sea. Changes of local temperature, or breezes from cold heights, cause fogs, or rain.

Melting ice, thawing snow, heavy falls of rain, cause considerable local effects; but they are only local, and do not influence the great general atmospheric changes.

Many animals and birds, most insects — even fishes — are acutely sensitive of changes in the air, which can only be accounted for readily by considerations of temperature, moisture, perhaps tension, and *varying* degrees of electricity.

In ordinary weather, the alternation of moderate breezes between SW. and NW. is normal. A deviation northward, and towards E., is occasional, comparatively; and, when it does sweep round so far, it usually passes through SE. (or there is a calm) and S. to SW. Circuitous sweeps are always evident to a close observer, however imperfect, or broken, in light variable weather.

As the anti-trade is normally prevalent, deviations from it towards either direction are soon followed by a return, either *backing* or by a circuit *direct.*

Only a north-easter lasts long, as an exception, and that is a pure polar current, from and to a great distance.

Wind that blows along the W. coast of Scotland to Ireland, is there more from the W. than the *same* current (from *polar* regions) is on, and along the E. coasts of Scotland and England.

The mass of Scotch mountains impedes and deflects such a current (as if it were a water-stream). Urged on from behind, pressed above, and laterally limited, it blows more strongly through some places, as the various openings between islands and channels — is even stopped, apparently, at others — and eddies around high ranges, or across lower lands, *under their lee*, in various irregular directions.

CHAPTER XVI

Our Atmosphere: its usual Conditions — Evidences to the Eye — Attainable by Balloon Excursions and by Ascents of Mountains — Gay Lussac — Welsh — Green — Rush — Monck Mason — Glaisher — Clouds — Suspension — Dew — Formation — Damp — Cold of Space — Currents superposed — Electricity — Heat — Light — Agencies subordinate to Divine Power — Unsettled cloudy Weather — Squalls — Camphor Glasses — State of Electricity — Earth, as a Leyden Jar — Points as Conductors — Forecasts — Cautions — Patience in Repetition — Signalling to Stations.

OUR atmosphere has been so frequently described that it may seem unnecessary to say more about it, and yet, practically, very few have either distinct or correct ideas of its nature. Some think it extends indefinitely upwards. Some suppose it twenty miles high or deep, others fifty. Dalton held this last opinion in 1834. Aeronauts and mountain-travellers have proved, since then, that air, in which man may live, does not extend to ten miles from our ocean level, probably not to eight. Glaisher and his Aeronaut almost died at six miles or thereabouts, and no other human being had ever ascended to fully five miles. At about ten miles there can be no pressure of air, or tension equal to more than an inch of mercury: there may be *very* light gas, but there can be no atmosphere such as we feel and breathe. Those who have supposed a much more extensive body of air around our globe cannot have sufficiently estimated the effects of centrifugal force, and even the resistance of *any* ether, however imaginary some may think the so-called all pervading medium by which space is *filled*. Delicately subtile as our *outermost* air or gas must be, it is still held down, by gravitation, to a certain distance, at which either a collision and friction with ether, if there is any, (however exceedingly slight, in withstanding rotatory velocity), or a centrifugal loss, if not so held or resisted, must occur.

Our aeronauts, and travellers upward by *land*, have proved that there are, within six miles of ocean (the summit of Deodunga being half a mile less), successive currents, at least two, sometimes more;* which differ in nature, tension, temperature, moisture, direction, and force. Beds of moisture (clouds or fogs) lie at various heights, not exceeding about two miles, however, and currents of wind set, in different directions simultaneously.

Mr. Rush ascended in a *calm* at London, was carried nearly sixty miles in an hour, horizontally (on reaching an upper current), and landed again in a calm near Lewes! Mr. Coxwell lately made a *long* and *rapid* run, at a moderate elevation, with officers from Winchester, in a *very short* time.

Mr. Green, having ascended four hundred and twenty-six times into the higher regions, and now living to describe them, says that he always found a current from the westward if he went high enough, but that nearer earth, he had found more than one current before he reached the westerly. On examining the notes of his various ascents, it is evident that the upper current, which he considers constant in *summer*, is about WSW., true, corresponding to the general average of wind currents across Ireland and Great Britain, and to the *returning* current of temperate zones, so fitly termed the anti-trade.

Now considerable allowance should be made for aeronautic *estimation*, on account of their ascents being

* Gay Lussac, Glaisher, Green, Mason, Rush, Welsh.

made, not only in summer, but *usually in fine weather*. They have not ascended during a strong polar, or in a strong southerly wind (at the surface), in which cases *only* might we expect a general motion of atmosphere, perhaps through its whole depth, for a certain period.* Such — we know, from experiment — takes place at Teneriffe and on other high mountains, for a time, occasionally, though in general there are at least two distinct and contrary currents setting against them, one above the other, with variables or calms between.

We are so little accustomed to investigate common every-day appearances, that it does not often occur to anybody to enquire *much* about clouds, so familiar are they continually.

Were it not for crossing currents, with changes of air-temperature, and of their electric conditions, only stratus would appear. Squalls would be unknown, and there would be no storms. Climate and weather would be like those of Peru,† where rain never falls, and the sun is shaded by a daily extension of stratus that disappears each evening in dew, leaving a clear starlight sky.

The vapour existing in one current, chiefly the tropical, remains suspended, *invisibly*, as vapour or gas, while unchilled by a fall of temperature; a slight chill, as of an approaching cooler air, causes a *steam*-like change, or, if more, a fog; if still greater, rain, or snow, or hail. Such changes occur variously, and at different elevations, in accordance with the action or influence of adjacent or perhaps superposed air, of *cold space* itself, or of the

* Mr. Coxwell's *last* Winchester voyage having been a hazardous exception.

† In Peru there is only one current, owing to the height and position of the Andes, and that quite dried.

earth. Heat radiated upwards, and cold air in the higher regions, suspend vapour in air until one, the colder, predominates, and more or less precipitation occurs. From the mist over a river or a meadow in the evening, to the fog that obscures a street; between the low nimbus, the aggregated cumulonus, and the lightest delicate cirritus, there is no difference except density, quantity, and electric condition. All are vapour more or less condensed — all are identical in chemical constitution.

The meadow mist is, like dew, vapour held in air, invisibly, by a certain temperature during the day, but deposited or precipitated as its airy container becomes chilled in contact with, or near, earth that is radiating off its day's acquired heat, and cooling the stratum of air nearest to its surface.

Fog is the moisture of warm earth evaporating into cold air. It is like the steam of warm water exceedingly magnified, and surrounded by air too moist and cool to allow of further evaporation, but not cold enough to cause it to be condensed into rain.

Clouds are condensed vapour held *between* lower and higher temperatures, having therefore forces acting on them oppositely. Stationary and unchanged as any cloud may seem to a casual glance, close watching through a telescope shows that every part is incessantly changing—that there is a continuous succession of atoms, appearing and disappearing faster than the eye can follow, while the cloud itself remains *seemingly* unchanged.

Sometimes clouds float in one current, sometimes in another. They occasionally remain between two currents. By the sides of mountains, and by balloon ascents, depths of more than 2,000 feet of clouds have been measured vertically.* Sometimes clouds are dry, at others saturated with moisture, and this quite irrespective of the state of air elsewhere, or at earth's surface.

Temperature and dryness being so different, electric conditions must differ extremely, and various manners of combinations, attractions, or repulsions among clouds must be continually occurring. Bearing in mind that the higher and *much* colder regions are highly (plus) electrified, or have an excess of (vitreous) electricity; that air is a non-conductor, and that earth is in a state of electric deficiency, (minus) or is negatively electric; that moisture, especially water, conducts electricity well, and that every collision of clouds, or fall of rain, aids in transferring from plus to minus, a view is caught of many most interesting electric questions, which we are not now free to treat of, or say more about than that they are inseparable from higher meteorologic studies.

In the previous chapter we mentioned that bad weather usually follows what seamen call 'backing' wind, and we gave two reasons for it, while alluding to further remarks *to follow* in this chapter respecting its consequences.

Now, therefore, it may be opportune to notice how the alternation, or mutual counteraction, or approaching *influence* of air currents causes clouds, squalls, hail, rain, snow, thunder or lightning, or some of these phenomena, and why, without them, there would be invariably tranquil uniform weather, partly clouded, with stratus only, but without more *downfall* than a dewy mist.

In a homogeneous stratum of air, unaffected by change of temperature (and therefore by electricity), aqueous vapour remains suspended, invisibly, as such, or in foggy cloudiness. Warmth (heat) from *below* causes

* Humboldt, Glaisher, Green, Gay Lussac, Rush, Welsh.

diminution of cloud, if not counteracted by cold *above*, and conversely. Hence, as temperature rises at the surface of earth, cloudiness diminishes, *if unaffected* by cold air above; and the contrary, as may be seen on many mornings. The *cold* of earth's surface about daybreak, or before, causes extensive visibility of stratus, all of which vanishes soon after a considerable increase of temperature has been felt. There is an apparent anomaly, however, about evening, which, unexplained, might seem contradictory. It is this: often after sunset light clouds which had overspread the sky, and threatened to become nimbus (or rain cloud), with at least some showers, swiftly disappear, and a clear sky, with a fine night, follows, till toward the cold of early morning. This light stratus is but vapour that was held in air, invisibly, during the warmer hours, and it is soon absorbed by, or (as dew) deposited on the earth's surface. This scarcely visible vapour—visible indeed only when one looks at a quantity of it (as when cloud-like, or a mist along low places)—is but too well known to sensitive persons, who may not be exposed to the (so-called) 'falling dew' with impunity.

By persons acquainted with the real nature of *dew*,* this distinction between a gradual lowering of vapour, *approaching* the condition of water, as temperature slowly falls, by which a *dampness* is diffused without *visible* moisture, and an actual formation of fluid (water) on certain surfaces exposed to the sky, radiating off their heat, and therefore condensing *adjacent* aqueous vapour, will be fully appreciated. But to others, who may not have given attention to the subject, we may add — that the effect on paper, exposed to damp air, although under cover, and in a room, is similar to that

* See Wells on Dew, Maude, and others.

of evening dampness, usually *called* 'dew,' while that on a decanter of *iced water* is the *genuine* deposition.

What is called the 'pride of the morning' (a sign of fine weather) is the *sudden* effect on rising vapour of a cool breeze, usually from the *northward*, drying (although *first* causing precipitation), and generally with a clear sky. A slight shower exhausts the supply, and the air is cleared. There is no nimbus or other cloud then advancing over a place so circumstanced.

Sometimes very light rain occurs, similarly, in the evening, after which there is a clear sky, and usually a fine night.

This effect is caused by a *more rapid* action of *cold* on previously invisible vapour than that which causes only dampness. It may be from a cool breeze, along the surface, or a cold current above, or from earth's radiation.

A fog is exactly the same as a cloud. A traveller on a mountain is sensible of no difference. A certain antagonism of temperatures, or continuance of one alone, maintains each variety of vaporous exhibition, in a visible state, until a change of heat affects the balance, and more or less speedily precipitates or evaporates that gaseous element, the steam or vapour of water.

Remembering that the usual condition of our air is a mixture of currents between about half a mile and five miles from earth (or, rather, from the *sea level*); that these currents vary in temperature, tension, electricity, direction, force, and moisture; that the heat near earth does not extend beyond the range upward of tropical currents, which may, at times, be three or four miles, though generally not more than two or three; that above, below, or between those warmer currents are, or may be, cool, if not cold, polar winds; and that, above all, in space, is excessive cold, with proportionate electrical tension—abundant cause appears for every atmospheric change that is witnessed, or has been faithfully described.

Clouds or cloudiness of every kind and degree result from temperature acting on vapour in air. Very distant from its effects *may* be the cause—or, on the other hand, it may be contiguous.

Sometimes extensive layers of clouds hang or float in the lower current, or wind, then blowing along the surface: sometimes there are no clouds in the lower current, but there are more or less above it in the next, or in a third stratum of air.

Balloon ascents made for the British Association, at considerable expense, and at extreme personal hazard, by Welsh and Glaisher, have demonstrated the facts of temperatures varying with the *currents*, *besides* with increase of elevation *nominally*; also of degrees of moisture, and *dew-points* above, very different from those below, whether on earth or in intermediate air, and *irregularly differing*. They have also proved that depths, or thicknesses of clouds, may exceed two thousand feet (a third of a mile) continuously, without any other clouds above those masses. But no cloudy trace, even the faintest cirritus, has been observed at a *greater* height (estimated) than seven miles.

We are not generally in the habit of considering earnestly how intensely cold is *space*—that the diffusion of heat is only terrestrial, and for a short distance, its *average* diminution, with height, being about one degree for each hundred yards, or sixty degrees for six miles (in round numbers, as an approximation, not in excess of observed facts *).

* Glaisher, four to six miles high.

We look at the sun, feel *his* warmth *apparently*, and with difficulty realise the conviction, that by going towards him—our great luminary, visible centre of our system, we should be frozen.

What are heat, light, and electricity—three words for perhaps only one power or influence, under various forms or conditions—intimately *correlated*.

All-pervading, ubiquitous, incomprehensible *now* to man, almost infinite in power, rapidity, and extent, though but an agent of the Almighty. Marvellous, indeed, are the effects of this subordinate influence as studied in these forms, and in other combinations, such as magnetism and gravitation. They indicate the power of Divine will *looming* through the mist of man's materialistic philosophy.

Returning to the condition and connection of clouds, with especial reference to weather and its changes — it may now be stated with more evidence for the assertion than in a previous chapter, that unsettled weather, squalls, and all the other results of air in commotion, however grand in scale, or small in effect, are results of at least two antagonistic currents. Therefore, while such causes are actively present in any region or locality, their effects must follow proportionally.

Hence, in forecasting the weather, the presence or vicinity of more than one air current is most important to be known, and in the following manner their relation may always be ascertained. *Temperature*, especially in the morning—directions, in which *uppermost* clouds are seen to be moving, and their nature (whether hard-edged and oily-looking, or soft, indefinite, and watery), with the degree of electrical tension—as shown by electrometers or camphor glasses, indicate unfailingly the *relative* presence of plus or vitreous electricity.

Minus (resinous or negative) indications, *subsiding* camphor—falling rain, or snow, and the look of the sky, assure one of a *lessened* tension. Increase of either characteristic implies action, or alteration, in the upper air, or at a distance horizontally, but within influential causation. Camphor glasses, in proper positions and duly attended, are most useful to a quick eye and skilled perception.

There is a clear analogy between the relations of earth,—atmosphere,—with space beyond—and those of a Leyden jar. Air, a non-conductor, representing the glass dielectric. Communication between overcharged space and under-tensioned or negative earth, is impracticable except by means of moisture, aqueous vapour, rain, or *forced* collision of elements;—such as happens in a thunder-squall, or when lightning *breaks* a way through even dry air, usually downward, but sometimes upward.

Considering this resistance of air to electric action, a purely mechanical reason may be suggested for the very remarkable effect of *points* in aiding the passage of electricity, which is—that a close aggregation of particles (atoms or molecules), whether polarised or not, may be separated, or divided, more readily along a wedge-like insertion than by a broad mass.

Wherever a flash of lightning has passed through a body not a perfect conductor, though far from being merely dielectric, the smallest possible hole or mark has been made visible; although, in other parts of its course, that same flash may have shivered a tree or a mast. Through a perfect conductor, such a stroke passes without a *trace*, even though powder, the *most explo-*

sive gunpowder, is placed in absolute contact around the metallic rod.*

When air is highly electric, or indicates much excess of electricity, a collision of clouds (from opposing air-currents), a fall of rain or hail, at once changes its state, and electrometers alter instantly. In unsettled, squally, or stormy weather, such alterations are frequent.

While *librations* of wind, between polar and tropical quarters, and corresponding electric indications, are prevalent, there can be no settled weather. Squalls, if not gales — at all events showers — will be frequent, and the term *changeable* may then be used in preference to any other word.

During such variable conditions of atmosphere, a *Forecaster* may not use the term 'fine,' or 'settled,' or 'steady'—he should only employ words indicative of probable extent of variability, and amount of rain or snow, while expressing the expected degrees of wind's force, and its anticipated directions.

Repetition — even though it may be day after day as well as place after place — should not be shunned in forecasting, if it seems to be correct. In nature there is much repetition: 'One day telleth another;' we must not be weary of successive similarities. Accurate truthfulness will have its reward (for the negative evidences daily recorded) by the real *attention obtained*, and due interest occasioned, when important alterations are actually about to occur, for then *premonition* becomes an object of general importance.

Forecasters should always remember that a table of the tamest nature, even having only indications of the quietest and dullest character, has much absolute value in declaring, expressively, *No bad weather.*

* Snow, Harris, — Franklin — Powder Magazines — Beagle's Voyage, &c.

A few more words, on the subject of districts to be cautioned by signal, may be advisable before ending this chapter.

Against signalling too frequently, as well as too extensively, caution should be urged, lest 'Wolf' should come while unprepared; but, on the other hand, it is better to risk occasional error in excess, than to let danger arrive without a warning, by which mistake *lives* may be sacrificed.

It is not the centrical area of a storm, but the course of strongest wind around such a space, that should be most considered; and as this circuitous sweep of a gale is irregularly altered by configurations of land, such local circumstances and conditions should be always intimately known by personal acquaintance or accurate description. For example—Dover, under Shakespeare Cliff, and in a narrow strait; Valentia, at a point projecting into the Atlantic; Galway, in an inlet under heights; Portrush, Nairn, Aberdeen, Scarborough, Yarmouth, each so *very* different from others in local circumstances require corresponding *special* consideration.

CHAPTER XVII

Diagrams illustrative of Polar and Tropical Air-Currents — Eastwardly Progression or Translation — Royal Charter Storm — Forecasts of Weather — Appulse of Wind-Currents — Veering Winds — Diagrams — Interfering Cyclones — Ominous and Treacherous Intervals — Retrograde or backing Winds — Changes consequent on veering (*direct*) or backing — Atmospheric Waves — Tides in the Atmosphere as well as in the Ocean.

THE diagrams first adverted to in this chapter (VI. and VII.) may assist in explaining how the northerly currents of our atmosphere stream from arctic circles toward the south, and diverge or are deflected toward the west, while their entire mass, as a combination, or singly (as specially shown here) progresses eastward, gradually and almost uniformly. A *following* illustrative figure (VIII.) will show how polar currents are deflected *toward the east generally*.

Often as explanations have been given of the movements of polar or tropical currents of air toward or from either direction of their length, their constant translation *meanwhile*, to the eastward, has not been noticed distinctly enough for general understanding, though very important.

The first diagram (VI.) is intended to express a polar stream (gray) of moderate and *diminishing* force, just sweeping across the British Islands, but checked by an approaching tropical current of considerable width and *supposed* momentum (light red).

The next (VII.) shows them in violent collision, as during the Charter storm of 1859.

The lateral *translation* of currents in an extensive expanse, *within which* they stream and circulate variously, had never been elucidated by any one before the present writer, who was struck by their evidences soon after those earliest inter-comparisons of simultaneous observations in 1857, for which the means were afforded through the Board of Trade. By combining the effects of such constant local *translation*, horizontally, with those of Dové's parallel currents, and the eddies, cyclonic or *ellipsonic*, between them, all the movements of air-currents which we feel on earth's surface as winds, may be satisfactorily followed out and completely explained.

It is this new combination which now enables forecasts of weather to be drawn by any person of fair ability, who will take the trouble of qualifying himself for such an undertaking by a reasonable study of the subject. They are strictly scientific conclusions, modified by practical acquaintance with the physical geography of localities affected.

While looking at the diagram (VI.) an *imaginary* movement of *all* the land, towards the *west*, while the atmosphere over it continues its several motions as if unattached to it (partly shown by the drawing), may illustrate the translating movement. Whether the *whole body* of atmosphere, as shown here, moves *eastward* together, over the land and water, or whether *they* are supposed to be in motion westward (with respect to the aeriform mass above), the effects produced at any given points between them are the same.

The polar air is insufficient in quantity to fill so

great a breadth as opens to it, in moving toward the tropic. It divides, diverges, or splits into streams, interspersing with those advancing from more or less opposite directions as 'parallel currents.' Hence in middle latitudes or temperate zones, the continuous alternation or succession of polar and tropical currents, which in their innumerable modes and degrees of opposition, or combination, occasion every variety of mixed wind, easterly or westerly, with more or less polarisation.

In this first diagram (VI.) we may repeat that the gray tint represents polar currents solely, and the red, advancing tropical. First touches of the polar are felt on the W. coast of Ireland, or also in Scotland—possibly sometimes even at Penzance or Jersey (observations have proved): hence we may here suppose this gray representative tint to have been so placed first, and to have been pressed toward the South as it spread *both* ways like a wedge, and diverged towards the west, partly from earth's rotation, but more, in this case, from opposition and consequent deflection.

Somewhere in the temperate zones, the two principal currents must often *meet* in varying latitudes, when either does not occupy the whole space in latitude between arctic and tropical zones, as sometimes is the case, though not frequently. In this diagram their first appulse is supposed to be about the British Channel, and its consequences are deflections of the real polar current into an E., then ESE., next SE., and eventually a southerly wind. Gradually this body of air is incorporated or driven back, and the tropical wind prevails over its opponent.

Thus the longitudinally* extensive and overpowering

* Having great breadth in longitude, or E. and W.

advance of tropical wind drives the polar current *toward the west*, when its direction has been normal or north-easterly, by which combined action easterly, or south-easterly, winds are caused.

But when the polar current is, or has recently been, mixed with tropical wind, by combination from the westward, being felt at the surface as north-westerly, then an increased pressure of a southerly wind tends to deflect the polar towards N. and E., as the 'veering winds' (VIII.) and their explanation will show.

Turning now to the diagram (VII.), which shows tropical currents advancing with force, and rapidly gaining ground, to be yet more speedily driven back by polar, as in the instance of the Charter storm. The features of this illustration are not throughout exactly according to the facts of that well-known tempest, but their general characteristics are similar, as may be proved by comparing it with another diagram (XIII.)

The features selected correspond to those observed about nine o'clock in the morning of that day on which the Royal Charter was driven by polar wind against the N. side of Anglesea. The cyclone, of which some idea respecting relative form, position, and force, is here essayed, had then advanced from near the entrance of the Channel, where it was the *previous* morning (as shown in XII.), and the following day, the 27th, its circuitous sweep was in the North Sea, having crossed Lincolnshire.

After the 27th, it was still traceable, though less strongly, toward Norway and the Baltic, expanding, and diminishing in force. Through three days and nights, that rotary storm was traced by indisputable evidence. Earlier than the 24th, or later than the 28th, there are proofs of its *non-existence*, but none of its having travelled farther; yet the facts show that a more extensively powerful cyclone has seldom passed across the British Islands. Nevertheless, in all its extent and power, it was only an eddy between opposing currents of wind, which diminished in force as their respective moments and tension decreased. Moreover (and this point should be well estimated), as there were preceding and simultaneous eddies, smaller, generally, less strong, entirely distinct from, however influenced by, the great sweep, and, as similar groups of circuits are usual, it is evident that when only a few observations are obtained, from ships changing their localities, and during successive days, they may appertain to different circuits.

In VIII. (Interfering cyclones), the smallest circle A, is supposed to represent the first of three circuits, succeeding and affecting each other in passing toward the NE. over a fixed station.

Although shown thus by *circles*, such regularity of form or curve is by no means accordant to facts observed: it is used here as a kind of average, or mean, for simplicity. The actual curvatures, or sweeps, of cyclonic gyrations of wind are *very irregular*, between approximations to circles, long ovals or ellipses, in which, as *they* move *bodily* along, their particles describe *spirals*. In open ocean, no doubt, their configuration is somewhat less irregular than over land; but even there at sea, when no mountainous ranges of land, no arid deserts, or extensive fields of ice, are near enough to be influential, it is proved (by inter-comparisons of reliable observations) that the dimensions, irregularly waving curvatures, figures and forces, of such atmospheric eddies, are very variable, though within certain limits, and according to regular principles or laws.

In the diagram, cyclones A, B, and C, are shown as if

increasing in area, which, in fact, is usually, if not invariably, the case: the third or fourth circuits being not only larger, but the more powerful, in the *strongest* portions, which are usually those near, though not in the (varying) centrical area, round which the currents of wind circulate.

In each circuit the winds gyrate similarly as to direction, and successively they are influenced, or are impinged upon by a contiguous cyclone, and become checked for a time (as it were, locked), till overpowered or absorbed, when augmented effects follow, from continuing and elastic action of the conflicting great currents which caused these eddies. Between absolute check (occasioning calms, probably with rain, but sometimes treacherously fine), and the violence of combined forces, every kind of squall, more or less accompanied by rain, hail, lightning, and thunder, occurs at times.

Consideration of the diagram will show that slight effects only would be caused at *d*, if no closer approach followed the contiguity of A and B, but that a more or less slight check only would occur till they separated, or became exhausted and failed. At *f*, from *f* to *g*, and throughout the south-westerly half of B, as C overpowered it, in advancing north-eastward, there would be all gradations of change successively, until the two cyclones acted together with united force, owing to the greater absorbing, and being strengthened by the smaller one.

Meanwhile, it should be remembered, all these gyrations are in progress, as it were *translated* along the surface, toward the north-eastward, more or less toward the one or other cardinal point, as the polar or tropical current of wind at the time may prevail more or less than usual, their normal relation being considerable preponderance of the tropical, or anti-trade, which, however forcibly at times, is only temporarily driven back, opposed, or otherwise influenced by purely polar winds.*

In these cases of interfering cyclones, or even partial circuits of wind, the change, shift, or veering, apparent to a fixed or stationary observer, is retrograde, against watch hands, or backing (N—W—S—E. in N. latitude), as inspection of the diagram, and some thought of the usual *direct* apparent veering, when a single circuit passes over any fixed station, will soon convince a reader, however paradoxical or contrary to fact it may at first seem to most persons.

We have said that similar though greater effects follow the appulse and overpowering succession of a third or fourth and greater, probably the greatest, of several successive cyclonic circuits (C).

After more or less duration of check (or stoppage of the sweep), an ominous calm, perhaps a seemingly fine interval, occurs; although more frequently there is rain, sometimes very heavy. Or there may be violent squalls, even hurricane squalls like tornadoes, with lightning, thunder, and, in places, waterspouts.

These concluding cyclones expand, after expending their redoubled force, and in a day or two after the greatest tempest appear to be deprived of the qualities so formidable only a few hours previously, and to become ordinary winds, generally of a polar character.

These facts show some, but by no means all, of the reasons, why bad, or 'worse' weather usually follows shifts of wind *against* watch hands † (retrograde or backing), either during gales or in intervals of circuits.

Other causes for the saying, proverbial among seamen,

* Considerations of meridional convergence, rotation, and other primary relations, need not be here repeated.

† *With* them in S. latitude.

'when the wind backs, it will blow,' may be thus explained with the aid of Diagram VIII.

Suppose an observer at O (to the right-hand), and that wind is blowing over him, from W. to E., which is caused by a combination or joint action of polar and tropical currents. Now imagine the polar impulse shown by P *h* to be so far augmented by great atmospheric changes, however remote, as to deflect the tropical air-current southward to *l*, along the line T *l*; O would then be in a *north*-west wind. Conversely, a tropical increase relatively to the polar, from T *l* to T *h*, so far pressing back, or deflecting the polar, would cause a *south*-west wind to be felt at O. This would be a retrograde change, the former a *direct* one, thus shifting, or veering. The northerly or polar winds being usually *much* drier, and with finer weather than the southerly, whether with westing or easting; and the tropical winds between SE. and SW. generally bringing much *wet*, with excess of warmth, and often great force; besides which, squalls being caused by the condensation from polar opposition, and still stronger winds speedily following — the seaman's saying quoted above is amply verified, and another, equally true, though trite, may here be added — namely, 'A north-wester is seldom long in debt to a south-easter.'

An important question, often asked, may here be repeated, and possibly answered in rather more detail than hitherto. What *are* 'atmospheric waves,' and how can they *cause* storms?

Objections have been made by the writer of these words to an application of the term 'atmospheric wave,' in its sense of alternate trough and crest, to curves showing a series of barometric columnar heights; but not *necessarily* corresponding atmospheric *depths*. He has also adverted to waves of pulsation, rather than undulation, meaning impulses extending through a mass not necessarily causing altered dimensions, either vertically or horizontally, nor, while *unopposed* by a resisting medium, either direct or lateral translation of particles beyond a very limited space. Now such waves, in their progress, can *immediately* cause no more sensible *horizontal* motion of air (or wind) than is felt in the ocean, remote from land, when a tide wave passes. But there are other modes of action, also well illustrated by tidal analogies, which may be described in the succeeding chapter.

Previously, however, to their attempted explanation according to views of a new and possibly unsubstantial character, resting as yet very much on hypothesis, it is earnestly requested, by their originator, that his paper on *Tides* (of the *ocean*) in the Appendix, may be *glanced* through for the *principles* (not details) first submitted to consideration, in 1839, which, if sound, ought to be likewise applicable to the atmosphere.

CHAPTER XVIII

Tidal Effects of Moon and Sun — Difference between Oceans of Water and an uninterrupted Aerial Ocean — Newtonian View of Tidal Action — Direct Observations — New Hypothesis — Lunar and Solar Tides — Periods — Peculiar Effects hitherto overlooked — Harmony with Halley, Herschel, Dové, and others' Theory of ascending and overflowing Air-Currents — Semilunar recurring Periods — Horizontal Impulses — Increase and Diminution — Diurnal Six-hourly Periods — Casually frequent Coincidences — Synchronous Changes or Extremes — Origin of popular Views respecting Weather Changes and Phases of the Moon — Sun's Action — Intertropic Oscillation of Barometer Semi-diurnally — Hazardous Speculation — Espy's and Webster's Collections of Facts — Masking Occurrences — Central Tides affect all Regions — Comparisons of Facts with Theory — Causes of Equinoctial Commotions — Solstitial extreme Periods — Modifications —Crucial Trials — Storms — Lunar Temperatures— Dispersion of Clouds.

Irrespective of, and in addition to, the sun's action on our atmosphere, rarefying, expanding, and therefore raising it, inter-tropically, there may be a tidal effect caused; — and very much greater, really, than that evident in our oceanic tides,—because air is so very much more mobile and expansible than water, while it is unfettered, unimpeded *horizontally* (speaking generally), by barriers of land.

The moon also acts on every particle of air, as on water and earth, by universal gravitation. Tidal effects must therefore be caused by the moon and by the sun, in earth's atmosphere, and their scales may be *large* (it is submitted), in proportion to its depth and extreme mobility.

Such tidal effects in a horizontally unbounded aerial ocean, to whose onward inclination no real barrier exists (although the higher ranges of mountains may be small local impediments), should *continue* round the world, as in an ocean around a smooth circular globe without terrestrial projections. These tidal effects of lunar and solar influence would be felt around the world, and from equator to pole, but chiefly tropically, where the greatest actions would be nearly under the sun (sub-solar) and sub-lunar. In such a case, the high tide waves, according to Newton, should be nearly under, and nearly opposite, to those influencing luminaries—the low tide at quadrantal points. Syzygial tides should be greatest, quadrature tides (neaps) the least, as in ocean. But their greatest effects should be not only thus in accordance with the Newtonian theory (supposing earth entirely smooth and covered by an ocean), but all the lunar and solar periodicities, of apogee, perigee, and declination, would have proportionate effects, and the extremes of all actions combined together, would be when sun and moon, in perigee and in syzygy, are in or near the equator.

Next in importance to these would be the actions, extra-tropically, of both luminaries in extreme similar declination, and likewise in perigee. Now what are the facts as hitherto observed?

Such observations as have been made, *barometrically*, would *appear* to have almost demonstrated the absence of any direct solar tide that causes more than a few inches (less than a foot) of vertical effect, and of any lunar tide that occasions a rise of more than a few feet of air—quantities seemingly almost insensible, and quite inoperative, one might consider, as principal agents, much less as prime motors of atmospheric currents.

Statical measures, however, the writer ventures to submit (with much deference to those authorities who will judge these remarks), cannot *alone* elicit all the facts of this important case, if the following views are based on tenable grounds: —

Let the moon's action, *alone*, be first considered, and suppose her in the equator.

As the earth rotates, a wave is attracted by the moon, and drawn toward the west. Similar waves follow; none are impeded; and as successively repeated impulses are given continuously, all in one direction, their aggregate result would *appear*, at first thought, to be a constant tidal current around the world (generated by wave impulses *solely* westward), and—a level of the ocean, under the moon's path, *above* its level of normal gravitation, or *equilibrium*, caused by the *lateral*, as well as following, horizontal movements of air, which, when once set in motion, continue, and tend to prevent a *return* of the tidal wave, which, it should be fully remarked, is not a wave of *vibration*, or *undulation*, but direct attraction, in *effect* like expansion of air, and its rising toward the sun. Now what follows? Surely a *continuous* overflow of air, like that described by Dové, and others, which not only prevents much sensible increase of statical pressure or tension, but augments the dynamic forces of the tropical currents of air *periodically* by lunar periods, and diurnally also. It is admitted that the overflow of inter-tropical air occasions those perennial *upper* currents seen (by the clouds) *over* the trade winds; and we know that those currents are very variable in force, by their effects as anti-trades in the temperate zones, and otherwise.

Recurring periods of about fourteen days (semilunar), of seven, and of three or four days, have been traced, however masked and irregular, more or less synchronous with the moon's phases, *occasionally*, and then, for a few times, rather correspondent—therefore evidencing some kind of connection:—but a *vera causa* seemed to be wanting for an explanation.

One *might* say, indeed, after entering a little farther into the apparent consequences and connected relations of this entirely new, and even to the writer *still* almost startling view (so satisfactorily does it *seem* to elucidate some of the greatest difficulties of meteorology)—*se non è vero, è ben trovato.*

From such consecutive raising, and subsequent *overflow*, instead of falling or returning, all around the world, impulses or pulsations should be given, of which the effects, at a distance, would be more or less periodical, in certain times, however interfered with or masked: and such effects *are traceable.*

Consecutive impulses, in one direction only, given to masses, or particles, cause motion, and motion given does not cease suddenly, *momentum* (product of weight, and velocity) continuing a certain time: hence currents should be generated.

As the world turns on its axis, successive waves are raised, and drawn on; so that before the effect of one is lost another advances, and the result is *continual* motion: constant *elevation* of atmosphere being avoided by overflow toward each side, in *augmentation* of the solar heat action.

Such *lateral* impulses, so caused by waves having a totally different *direction* and nature (like tide-waves advancing up the British Channel, and causing tidal currents, in harbours, *successively*) — such offsets (so to speak) vary diurnally and weekly or fortnightly, one may say by semilunar periods (or *semilunes*?). They also vary with the declination and distance of the moon.

During the moon's passage, in her orbit, from quadrature to syzygy, her action on air-currents should increase, and conversely. When she has great north declination, it ought to be greater *here* than when she is far south, and when in perigee greater than in apogee. Tabular records show that such are the facts.

Owing to these varying reinforcements of tropical currents, and proportionate augmentations of their *supplies*, or feeders, the *generally* infraposed polar streams usually increase through about a week, and then decrease; so that from one maximum to another, or one minimum to another, is about a fortnight (a *semilune*), but irregularly, and so often *masked*, by causes as yet untraced with accuracy, that one cannot expect so much value to be *generally* attached to this theory as may be by the few persons who have *yet* studied it.

We suppose that during the moon's passage from conjunction to opposition, and again to conjunction, or from syzygy to syzygy, there is *about* a week's diminution of current impetus, and a week's increase, due to the central lunitidal wave, of which the greatest impetus is soon after each syzygy.

These successive *alternations* of impulses seem to be connected with the successions of polar and tropical currents, in force as well as period. They are made up of *daily* pulsations, or tidal impulses, unnoticed barometrically because of the *overflow*, but distinctly traceable in the *daily* four changes of force of wind that may be noticed everywhere, at *about* six hourly intervals; not regularly nor synchronously, but *averaging* six hourly periods: so that if *for a time*, at any place, these intervals should agree with particular hours, it is probable they will *recur* similarly for a few days.

One seldom observes a strong wind with rain or snow continue more than six hours without any change. Most storms, and indeed *general* weather and winds, have noticeably marked changes, or alternations, at about six hourly intervals. Often these times synchronise with noon or midnight, evening or morning, for some days together; and hence probably has arisen the common belief in changes, at those times particularly: the facts being that—such intervals *average* six hours, but do not occur regularly, just as the semilunar periods are *about* two weeks, but variously affected so irregularly as not to recur uniformly with the moon's phases, although corresponding *frequently*, and therefore giving fair reason for the general, however fallible, belief, that weather is affected by, or changes, with the moon's phases.

Tidal action of the sun is, of course, similar in nature, though very much smaller in degree, and only *diurnal* (excepting the slight changes, consequent on apogee or perigee).

Such slight effects are hardly distinguishable in general, and may be passed over, in practical consideration, at present.

The regular *diurnal* atmospheric tides of inter-tropical latitudes are due to another cause entirely, which should be here described in passing. Solar heat expands and lightens air, vaporising its watery particles, and drawing their combined volumes upward; therefore lessening downward pressure and tension.

This action is greatest during the morning, and till

about two or three o'clock in the afternoon, during which time the barometer falls. From three to nine opposite causes—namely, a return of vapour to sensible moisture, and condensation or cooling of air—occasion slight increase of local tension, and a corresponding rise of the barometer.

On Newtonian principles, such six-hourly waves or expansions and contractions, must have similar waves opposite to them, at the other side of the world: hence the *fall* of a barometer within the tropics, from about nine in the evening to near three the next morning, and its rise from that time till about nine, with clock-like regularity.

The manner in which that grand motor, the Sun, principally affects our whole atmosphere, has been repeatedly shown elsewhere. It may be here remarked, however, as illustrative of the inexpressibly beautiful and marvellous system, order, and harmony of this sublime universe in which 'we move and have our being,' that the ascending tropical currents which Halley, Hadley, Dové, and Herschel, have considered as facts demonstrated, should accord (in their *overflowing* action, and subsequent motions toward the poles) so entirely with *similar* effects of lunar, and solar, tidal action—as to produce only beneficial variations, not injurious interference, among those ever alternating main currents, to whose conflicting opposition are due our minor variations of temperature, our rain or snow, and generally those remarkable changes of weather which, on the whole, make the temperate zone so suitable for Man, so favourable for his supplies.

Probably (if one may presume to hazard such a merely speculative idea), were there no moon to cause varying impulses in our air, it would tend toward such equilibrated and regular movements, occasioned by the sun *only*, that circulation would prevail so uniformly between tropical and polar regions, as to cause *general* approximation to weather and winds similar to those of regular trades, or settled polar currents, almost without downfall of condensed vapour, and without any '*down-rush*' of the genial south-wester.

Existing extreme variations in periodical force of main air-currents seem to *recur* (as has been briefly said above) at intervals of which the numbers *average* about twenty-six in a year (semilunar), as deduced from Espy's, Webster's,* and later records.†

Espy's collections are immense (in his Fourth Report), but require certain allowances for character (reliability), instruments, and *localities* of which *elevations* above the sea were unknown, and *normal levels* had not been ascertained sufficiently, if indeed at all considered. In these numerous and extensively varied documents, *evidence* is obvious of a continual succession of alternate currents, all in lateral progression or translation eastward, while their rapid *principal* motions are in meridional directions. There are also very remarkable expositions of comparatively regular *successions* of extremes (however varying in amounts) which, when taken in large groups, average semilunar intervals, or periods. These extremes show *nearly the middle* of each current, tropical and polar, when the barometer is about the lowest, or the highest. And that there are *always* such 'recurring periods' of atmospheric changes as happen *between* the extremes of high and low barometer, varying usually

* Recurring Monthly Periods. Webster, 1857.

† Six months' observations, collected for *another* object, in 1856-7, but illustrative of this subject, are shown in Diagrams XIV. and XV.

from a week to a fortnight, however interfered with, or masked, appears to be fully demonstrated by the collections of facts above mentioned, registered without any special object in view.

To the frequent casual coincidences of these partly varying periods, agreeing with lunar phases in *time*, although not taking place regularly, nor reliably (in accordance with *present* knowledge?), as scientific facts, —owing to far greater masking occurrences,—indeed may well be attributed the popular belief in a connection between weather and the moon.

How periodical actions of great central or tropical atmospheric tides may affect the winds and weather of all regions, shall now be submitted to the reader in rather more detail.

That there is always an alternation, or change and circulation of polar and tropical currents, has been often repeated, but perhaps *sufficient* notice has *not* been hitherto taken of the irregularity with which these continuous currents flow, as to time, force, and direction.

Hitherto their anomalies have been attributed to the very various circumstances of geographical localities, more or less affected by the sun and elements operating as he influences them: but why there is a constant, however irregular *alternation* of the two great or main currents, in temperate zones, while the average action of the sun is so uniform, and while other general conditions seem to be so little changing, has *not* been demonstrated, and consequently there has been a sense of insufficient facts, and deficient theory.

The *variations* of lunitidal impulse are correspondent, *in times*, with *average* periods of recurring extremes, or changes of main air-currents, and with the *intervals* occupied by their consecutive *translations* towards the east, as following parallel currents.

The moon's greatest tidal action being syzygial, and the least at quadrature, should cause maximum impulse about the former, and minimum near the latter, period: besides which, general effects should be augmented considerably at or soon after the equinoxes.

In our hemisphere such effects should be found to last, or prevail longest from a *tropical* direction, when the sun and moon are near the Tropic of Cancer; and the contrary, a prevalence of polar currents, extensive and lasting long, should happen when those luminaries are near the Tropic of Capricorn.

Now the facts observed, to whatever cause attributed, do correspond exactly to these postulates.

Great atmospheric commotions do occur, over all the world (except where no disturbances ever happen), soon after the equinoxes.

In summer and autumn tropical winds *prevail* over extra-tropical or temperate zones.

In winter and spring polar currents extend widely and last long — on an average.

What causes such equinoctial disturbances? Not the mere fact of the sun's astronomical position?

No: the united tidal action of moon and sun upon the *whole atmosphere*, which *then* is a maximum force. *Lateral offsets*, streams overflowing toward each pole, and, as they go, preserving more or less momentum, are at those times more powerful, and their effects are more felt everywhere.

Greatly, however, are such atmospheric currents affected, modified, or varied by the peculiar nature of regions over or through which they pass.

Crossing over an ocean — or above an African desert

—deflected by the Alps, by the Andes, or the huge Himalayas—extreme deviations are occasioned from ordinary or normal movements, although through even those anomalies a radical line of *periodicity* may be traced, in connection with semilunar periods.

The manner in which such lunitidal effects accord with *apparent* atmospheric waves, supposed to move from west to east, and by some persons said to *cause* storms,* seems to the writer satisfactory, because it appears to unite facts and reasonings (of the highest meteorologic authorities) about tides, waves of air, and storms,—by a chain of theory, *deduced from observations*, sufficiently strong to bear even a crucial strain.

With more or less horizontal action, induced, meridionally, by great central tide waves, each main current, of all regions, is affected by propagations of periodic and varying impulses, or surges: sometimes effects of solar *heat* waves principally, sometimes of heat and compound tidal action—occasionally affected by hurricanes, and extensive *electrical* changes in Nature—reacting on the very forces originating such elemental operations.

Inter-tropical grand movements should thus, apparently, be sought and traced as the real origin, next to the moon and sun, of *derivative* atmospheric waves of air-currents, or winds, and storms.

It may have already occurred to the reader, that if great tidal action attracts and draws to the westward all our atmosphere so continuously as to cause horizontal impulses, or currents, how is it that there is not a *rapid* equatorial air-current always toward the west?

The earth rotates in a *contrary* direction. There may then be a beautiful opposition and compensation of

* *How caused*, has not been explained satisfactorily.

forces. Every particle of matter, air included, certainly tends toward the east, with earth's surface, attracted to it vertically, and having rotatory momentum. As the earth's gravity diminishes and that of the moon increases, the rotatory *velocity* (in opposition to the moon's attraction tending to cause direct horizontal motion of air toward the west) augments, and there may be a balance between them, which perhaps is the limiting boundary of our atmosphere.

Whether *all* atmospheric circulation, including the trade winds, may not be primarily caused by such lunar and solar tidal action, however much increased or affected by solar influence also in *heating*, as usually understood — and whether lunar as well as solar *periodicity* may be traceable through the *correlated* forces of attraction (however caused), heat, light, electricity, and magnetism — are overwhelming questions into which the writer is not qualified to enter, but earnestly submits to philosophers.

Before closing this chapter (already too long), perhaps an allusion may be *briefly* made to *lunar temperatures* and dispersion of clouds.

Are not the *first*, direct consequences of mistaking temperatures of *air-currents*, having periodicity, for supposed effects of the moon's rays (in which no heat has yet been *felt*); and may not the *supposed dispersion* of clouds by the moon be partly an effect of seeing them in profile, when at a *distance* — near the horizon — or, in plan, when *overhead*? — and in *some* degree owing to the *general* diminution of cloudiness, in a rather fine night, when there is radiation from earth and consequent deposition of dew? Vapour from air adjacent to earth, condensed into dew, cannot leave *dry* air remaining *above*. Immediate and extensive *devaporisation* must continue *upward*, while dew is forming below, and the result must be disappearance of light *stratus*, such as the moon has been said to disperse.

So likewise *nimbus* escapes from sight, as *rain* is precipitated.

In the morning a converse action occurs. Solar heat draws up expanding aqueous vapour from below to a certain height, where it is visibly condensed by colder air and held in a *middle* or *transition* state between invisible gas and actual water. Such clouds — as indeed *all* clouds — are in constant motion, incessantly changing form and actual substance (as may be seen through a telescope). Action and reaction, absorption and condensation, continual and rapid motions, are distinguishable in what may be *apparently* almost motionless masses. In fine weather—*at night*—whether the moon is visible or not, whether full, or near any other period, there is a *general* tendency (as many a *night-watcher* knows) toward a disappearance of clouds soon *after* evening.

Sometimes *slight* rain falls, and not a cloud is seen afterwards for some hours. Oftener dew is deposited, but in either case clouds soon vanish in *still weather*.

Such effects *may* have been unnoticed, when no moon appeared, and consequently no person was watching for them particularly.

CHAPTER XIX

Extracts from various Accounts quoted by Sir William Reid illustrating Force of Hurricanes — Repetition of similar Storms at about the same Periods and in the same Region not necessarily continuous or even directly connected, but consecutive — Instances in point, from which to form Opinions.

Having attained a position at which one may pause, to interpose doubts and queries,—this appears to be a suitable time for adverting to a few remarkable instances of occurrences, exceedingly well known, which may illustrate our arguments.

Many storms having been described as if continuous, although really not so, but consecutive, the following well-authenticated descriptions are selected as examples, from which the reader may judge. In Sir William Reid's work, a storm in the West Indies, in 1831, is thus described: —

The distance between Barbadoes and St. Vincent is nearly 80 miles. This storm began at Barbadoes a little before midnight on August 10, 1831; but it did not reach St. Vincent until 7 o'clock next morning; its rate of progress, therefore, was about ten miles an hour.

A gentleman who had resided for forty years in St. Vincent, had ridden out at daylight, and was about a mile from his house, when he observed a cloud to the N. of him, so threatening in appearance, that he had never seen any so alarming during his long residence in the tropics; and he described it as appearing of an olive-green colour. In expectation of terrific weather, he hastened home to nail up his doors and windows; and to this precaution attributed the safety of his house.

The centre of this hurricane, coming from the eastward, seems to have passed a little to the N. of Barbadoes and St. Vincent; and Mr. Redfield has traced its course to the southern United States of America.

On August 10, 1831, the sun rose without a cloud, and shone resplendently. At 10 A.M. a gentle breeze which had been blowing died away. After a temporary calm, high winds sprung up from the ENE., which in their turn subsided. For the most part calms prevailed, interrupted by occasional sudden puffs from between the N. and NE.

At noon the heat increased to 87°, and at 2 P.M. to 88°, at which time the weather was uncommonly sultry and oppressive.

At 4 the thermometer sunk again to 86°. At 5 the clouds seemed gathering densely from the N., the wind commencing to blow freshly from that point: then a shower of rain fell, followed by a sudden stillness; but there was a dismal blackness all around. Toward the zenith there was an obscure circle of imperfect light, subtending about 35° or 40°.

From 6 to 7 the weather was fair, and wind moderate, with occasional slight puffs from the N.; the lower and principal stratum of clouds passing fleetly toward the S., the higher strata mere scud, rapidly flying to various points.

At 7 the sky was clear and the air calm: tranquillity reigned until a little after 9, when the wind again blew from the N.

At 9.30 it freshened, and moderate showers of rain fell at intervals for the next hour.

Distant lightning was observed at 10.30 in the NE.

and NW. Squalls of wind and rain from the NNE. with intermediate calms succeeding each other until midnight. The thermometer meantime varied with remarkable activity: during the calms it rose as high as 86°, and at other times it fluctuated from 83° to 85°. It is necessary to be thus explanatory, for the time the storm commenced and the manner of its approach varied considerably in different situations. Some houses were actually levelled to the earth, when the residents of others, scarcely a mile apart, were not sensible that the weather was unusually boisterous.

After midnight the continued flashing of the lightning was awfully grand, and a gale blew fiercely from the N. and NE.; but at 1 A.M., on August 11, the tempestuous rage of the wind increased, the storm, which at one time blew from the NE., suddenly shifted from that quarter, and burst from the NW. *and intermediate points.* The upper regions were from this time illuminated by incessant lightning; but the quivering sheet of blaze was surpassed in brilliancy by the darts of electric fire which were exploded in every direction. At a little after 2, the astounding roar of the hurricane, which rushed from the NNW. and NW., cannot be described by language. About 3 the wind occasionally abated, but intervening gusts proceeded from the SW., the W., and WNW., with accumulated fury.

When the lightning also ceased, for a few moments only at a time, the blackness in which the town was enveloped was inexpressibly awful. Fiery meteors were presently seen falling from the heavens; one in particular, of a globular form, and a deep red hue, was specially observed to descend perpendicularly from a vast height. It evidently fell by its specific gravity, and was not shot or propelled by any extraneous force,

On approaching the earth with accelerated motion, it assumed a dazzling whiteness and an elongated form, and dashing to the ground in Beckwith Square, it splashed around in the same manner as melted metal would have done, and was instantly extinct. In shape and size it appeared much like a common barrel-shade;* its brilliancy and the spattering of its particles on meeting the earth gave it the resemblance of a body of quicksilver of equal bulk. A few minutes after the appearance of this phenomenon, the deafening noise of the wind sank to a solemn murmur, or, more correctly expressed, a distant roar; and the lightning which from midnight had flashed and darted forkedly with few and but momentary intermissions, now, for a space of nearly half a minute, played frightfully between the clouds and the earth with novel and surprising action. The vast body of vapour appeared to touch the houses, and issued downward flaming blazes which were nimbly returned from the earth upward.

The moment after this singular alternation of lightning, the hurricane again burst from the western points with violence prodigious beyond description, hurling before it thousands of missiles — the fragments of every unsheltered structure of human art. The strongest houses were caused to vibrate to their foundations, and the surface of the very earth trembled as the destroyer raged over it. No thunder was at any time distinctly heard. The horrible roar and yelling of the wind, the noise of the ocean — whose frightful waves threatened the town with the destruction of all that the other elements might spare — the clattering of tiles, the falling of roofs and walls, and the combination of a

* The glass cylinder put round candles in the tropics.

thousand other sounds, formed a hideous and appalling din. No adequate idea of the sensations which then distracted and confounded the faculties, can possibly be conveyed to those who were distant from the scene of terror.

After 5 o'clock, during short moments (the storm, now and then, abating), the falling of tiles and building materials, *which by the last sweep had probably been carried to a lofty height*, became clearly audible.

At 6 A.M. the wind was at S., and at 7 SE.; at 8 ESE., and at 9 there was again clear weather.

* * * * * *

As soon as dawn rendered outward objects visible, the narrator, anxious to ascertain the situation of the shipping, proceeded, but with difficulty, to the wharf. The rain at the time was driven with such force as to injure the skin, and was so thick as to prevent a view of any object much beyond the head of the pier. The prospect was majestic beyond description. The gigantic waves rolling onwards, seemed as if they would defy all obstruction; yet as they broke over the careenage, they seemed to be lost, the surface of it being entirely covered with floating wreck of every description. It was an undulating body of lumber * — shingles, staves, barrels, trusses of hay, and every kind of merchandise of a buoyant nature. Two vessels only were afloat within the pier; but numbers could be seen which had been capsized, or thrown on their beam ends in shallow water.

On reaching the summit of the cathedral tower, to whichever point of the compass the eye was directed, a grand but distressing picture of ruin presented itself.

* The American term for timber. *Shingles* are made of split blocks of wood, and are used instead of tiles or slates for roofs.

The whole face of the country was laid waste; no sign of vegetation was apparent, except here and there small patches of a sickly green. The surface of the ground appeared as if fire had run through the land, scorching and burning up the productions of the earth. The few remaining trees, stripped of their boughs and foliage, wore a cold and wintry aspect; and the numerous seats in the environs of Bridgetown, formerly concealed amid thick groves, were now exposed and in ruins.

From the direction in which the cocoa-nut and other trees were prostrated next to the earth, the first that fell must have been blown down by a NNE. wind; but far the greater number were rooted up by the blast from the NW.

The centre of this storm appears to have passed a little to the N. of Barbadoes, and over the southern extremity of St. Lucia.

On the evening of the 10th no unusual appearance had been observed at St. Lucia; but as early as 4 or 5 o'clock next morning, the garrison, stationed near the northern extremity of the island, began to be alarmed, as some hut-barracks blew down. The wind was then nearly *north*.

The storm was at its greatest height between 8 and 10 o'clock in the morning; but from that time the wind gradually veered round to the *east*, diminishing in force and dwindling as it were to nothing in the *south-east*, when it was succeeded by a beautiful evening, with scarcely a breath of wind.

At the southern extremity of the island, the most violent part of the storm is reported to have been from the *south-west*.

At St. Vincent, the garrison was at Fort Charlotte, near the SW. point of the island; and there the wind first set in from *north-west*, veering to *west* and to *south-west*, raising the water of the sea in Kingston Bay so as to flood the streets. It unroofed several of the buildings in the fort, and blew down others. At Martinique the wind was *easterly* during the gale.

A great part of the island of St. Vincent is covered with forest, and a large portion of the trees at its northern extremity were *killed without being blown down*. These were frequently examined (in 1832), and they appeared to have been killed, not by the wind, but by the extraordinary quantity of *electric* matter rendered active during the storm.

Most accounts of great hurricanes represent the quantity of electric matter exhibited to be remarkable; and the description given of a great storm, which occurred at Barbadoes during the night of August 31, 1675, is nearly the same as that of 1831. The lightning darted, not with its usual short-lived flashes, but in rapid flames, skimming over the surface of the earth, as well as mounting to the upper regions.

During the severest period of the hurricane at Barbadoes, on the night of August 10, 1831, two *negroes were greatly terrified by sparks passing off from one of them.* This took place in the garden of Codrington College; and it was related on the spot where it happened, by the Rev. Mr. Pindar, the Principal of that College. Their hut in the garden had just been blown down, and in the dark they were supporting each other, while endeavouring to reach the main building.

In the work quoted on this Barbadoes hurricane, allusions are made to the declarations of some persons, that they felt shocks of earthquakes during the storm. But after attentively listening to the opinions of different people on this disputed point, and careful examination of the ruins with reference to it, we feel persuaded there are no sufficient reasons for believing that any earthquake occurred at this period: and it is very material that the phenomena of hurricanes and earthquakes should not be connected together without proof.

A very curious fact seems to have been almost overlooked, viz. the raining of salt water in all parts of the country. We shall give below a passage from the account of the Barbadoes hurricane of 1831, which alludes to this; and it will be found, when enquiry is pursued into the storms of the Indian seas and of S. latitudes, that there also are reports of salt-water rain.

At the N. point, the sea broke continually over the cliff, a height of more than seventy feet, and the spray being carried inland by the wind for many miles, *the rain of salt water in all parts of the country* is thus accounted for. Fresh-water fish in the ponds were killed: and at Bright Hall, about two miles SSE. of the point, the water in the ponds was salt for many days after the storm.

About 2 P.M. of August 10, a Mr. Gittens observed indications of approaching bad weather; and at 4, intimated to his negroes that a hurricane might be expected. At 6 he bid them not quit their homes, as a dreadful storm was approaching, and if they went abroad they would probably be seen no more. At 9, the indications which caused his apprehensions were less apparent, and he retired to rest. It is well known that this gentleman foretold the storm of 1819, some hours previous to any other person suspecting such an event. The indications observed by him were — 1st. The darting forward of the clouds in divided portions, and with fleet irregular motion, not borne by the wind, but driven as it were before it. 2ndly. The distant roar of the elements, as of wind rushing through a hollow vault. 3rdly. The motion of the branches of trees, not bent forward as by a stream of air, but constantly whirled about.

At Antigua a hurricane happened on August 12, 1835; the wind during the first part blowing from the N., and during the latter part from the S., with a calm of twenty minutes in the middle of it. From this account, the centre probably passed over Antigua.

The barometer was observed to fall 1·4 inch; the oil sympiesometer was much agitated, and fell proportionably.

Trees were blown down, *as if forming lanes*, an effect which has been remarked in many other descriptions of hurricanes; and at its commencement the wind was described as coming in gusts.

It has been said that hurricanes are not met with to the eastward of the West India islands; but this is not correct. A ship met the Barbadoes hurricane of 1831 to the eastward of that island. Two of the hurricanes of 1837 I have traced to the eastward of the West Indies; and there seems no reason to believe that they are caused by the islands, as some persons imagine.

Whatever their cause may be, that cause seems to act with very different degrees of intensity at different periods; for the usual atmospheric current, or trade wind, is sometimes disturbed, the veering and changes indicating a rotatory movement of part of the atmosphere, without proving destructive. Such an instance occurred on July 9 and 10, 1837; and this is also another instance in proof that storms come from the eastward of the West India islands — occasionally.

The gale about to be mentioned was met to the eastward of Barbadoes: all the crew and passengers appear to have taken one of the squalls for *land*; and it seems to have passed very nearly over St. Lucia. At St. Vincent the wind became *west.*

On July 9 the Castries (Mondel), from Liverpool to St. Lucia, in lat. 15° 4′, long. 54° 58′, having the wind then at ESE., the master being confident in his reckoning, his mate suddenly reported, 'Land on the lee bow!' the man at the helm pointing it out at the same time: it had all the appearance of the broken outline of the West India islands, and looked as if within a mile and a half from them. Never doubting that it was land, the captain trimmed his sails, that he might alter his course: and when he had finished, he again looked for the land, when nothing like it was visible. On reaching St. Lucia, and hearing that there had been a hurricane there on the 10th, he concluded that what he had seen was this storm. The Castries had no barometer on board.

Of the hurricanes in 1837, four were traced (on charts) which followed each other with only the interval of a few days. The investigation into these is connected with a fifth storm, not drawn on the charts. An attentive examination of the details of these, strengthens the probability, that all such storms are rotatory, if it does not actually confirm it: and by tracing and connecting so many in close succession, the subject opens in yet another form, altogether new and of fresh interest, for it leads us to an explanation of the variable winds.

But it is necessary to examine each storm with attention and to follow the details, in order to ascertain whether or not they were really rotatory.

The Spey packet brought to England the account of two severe hurricanes in the West Indies in 1837. These have been traced, and are laid down on charts. The earlier of the two passed over Barbadoes on the morning of July 26; at 10 the same night it was at Martinique, by which hour it was all over at Barbadoes; at midnight on the 26th, and morning of the 27th, it reached Santa Cruz. By July 30 it reached the Gulf of Florida, where some vessels were wrecked by it, and many damaged; it then took a more northerly direction, being on August 1 at Jacksonville, in Florida.

From Jacksonville, it passed over Savannah and Charleston, going in a direction to the eastward of N.

The other hurricane was at Antigua on August 2; by the 5th and 6th it was also on the coasts of Georgia and Florida, crossed the line of the other hurricane, nearly meeting it; and it seems to have touched Pensacola on August 8.

The reports of these two storms are arranged in the order of their progress, and are as follow:—

Barbadoes, July 26, A.M.—At 2 o'clock, light showers of rain, wind shifting from S. to NW., the sky dark and gloomy, with flashes of lightning in the SE. and SW.: at 4, calm, with a heavy swell rolling into the bay; lightning and thunder, sky assuming a blue-black appearance, with a red glare at the verge of the horizon; every flash of lightning was accompanied with an unusual whizzing noise, like that of a red-hot iron plunged in water: at 6, the barometer fell rapidly, the sympiesometer much agitated and unsettled, and fell at length to 28·45; hoisted in the boats, sent down top-gallant masts, struck lower yards and topmasts, let go both bower anchors, veered out a long scope of cable on the moorings and both bowers: at 7·30 the hurricane burst on us in all its dreadful fury: at 8, it shifted *from ESE. to S.*, and blew for half an hour, so that we could scarcely stand on the deck; made preparations for battening the hatches down and cutting away the masts; the sea came rolling into the bay like heavy breakers, the ship pitching deep, bowsprit and forecastle sometimes under water; the wind shifting to the *west-south-west*: at 9 the barometer began to rise, and to our great joy we observed a change in the sky for the better. As the haze cleared away, we counted twenty-one sail of merchantmen driven on shore, and perfect wrecks. Her Majesty's ship Gannet drove, with four anchors down, but fortunately brought up and rode out the gale. Her Majesty's steamer Alban went on shore. One brig foundered at her anchors, and sunk. Thank God we rode it out so well! The Spey, the Gannet, and Fortitude merchant ship, were all that rode out the hurricane. The city of Kingston steamer put to sea, and returned next day.

On July 30, the Spey left Barbadoes to run along the islands and pick up the mails for England. Found that the hurricane had scarcely been felt at St. Lucia, but at Martinique several ships were wrecked.

The barque Clydesdale, from Barbadoes to Antigua, encountered a severe hurricane ten miles north of Barbadoes on July 26, 1837.

Granada and the neighbouring islands were visited by a violent gale on July 26, 1837.

The gale of July 26 was severely felt at St. Vincent, the wind being from the *west* and the *south*, with a heavy swell of the sea.

St. Lucia, July 30, 1837. — There was a severe gale from the *north-west*, which blew very violently for several hours.

Martinique suffered a severe gale on July 26th, from the *south-east*. The brig Blayais went on shore, with forty-three persons on board, and only six were saved.

The storm of July 26 was felt severely at Martinique. The tempest raged there with great violence at 10 at night, at which hour all was calm at Barbadoes. The Blayais was driven on shore at St. Pierre, a harbour much exposed to the SW. An American vessel was driven on shore at Fort Royal, which is an unusual occurrence, as that harbour has always been considered a safe anchorage in any weather.

At Dominica one of the most violent gales of wind, which at that season are so alarming to these colonies, occurred on July 26, 1837. The wind blew *from south-east all day*, and about 8 in the evening, a violent swell set in from the SW., which occasioned a tremendous surf. The barque Jane Lockhart was obliged to slip her cables, and stand to sea. The Venus sloop was washed up into Kew Street. The sloop Dolphin, from St. Bartholomew's to Barbadoes, was forced back to this island, after having got within twelve miles of Barbadoes.

At St. Croix about midnight on Wednesday, July 26, it came on to blow smartly *from the east-south-east*, shifting by Thursday morning, July 27, *to south-east*, blowing a gale of wind until towards noon, when it began to moderate.

Le Navire Bonne Aimée a péri à Porto Rico dans un coup de vent, 26, 27 Juillet, 1837.

A Spanish brig was totally dismasted on July 28, off St. Domingo, in a hurricane, and had to throw overboard a quantity of flour.

St. Domingo. — *Two hurricanes* were experienced here, during which the Edward (French ship) was wrecked in the outer roads, and three of the crew drowned: three Haytian vessels were also lost on the coast, and only one man saved.

The gale on July 29, at Nassau, was *from the east and the east-south-east*, as reported by the master of the sloop Humming-bird.

There was a violent gale at Nassau, New Providence, from the *east and south-east*, on July 29, which continued until 2 P.M. on Monday, July 31.

H.M. packet Sea-gull arrived at Falmouth on the 8th from Mexico and Havannah; had the wind for twenty days from the E. and ENE., with four days calm. In coming through the Gulf of Florida, and in the narrow part of the Channel, on the night of July 30, experienced a very heavy gale of wind from the *north-west*, which increased on the morning of the 31st, with thick weather, lightning and rain in torrents. At about 10 A. M. discovered discoloured water on the lee-beam, having had no observation on the 30th. At this time the wind was *west*, which made the Bahama bank a lee-shore; and in carrying a press of sail to clear it, all of them were split and blown out of the bolt-ropes: we were therefore under the necessity of anchoring in five-fathoms water; and by the time we had veered out 100 fathoms of chain, the vessel's stern was in 4½ fathoms. We did not let go the other anchor, fearing she might founder, as the sea was making a fair breach, and rolling aft to the wheel on the quarter deck; and if we parted, we had still a chance of getting into the Old Bahama Channel. With great difficulty we tried to get another jib and trysail set.

On the morning of August 1 the wind increased, and blew a perfect hurricane for about four hours, when it moderated a little, and veered to the SW., which enabled us to bend another topsail. At noon we began to weigh, and in three hours we were able to make sail off the reef.

The barque Baltimore, from Havannah, experienced

heavy gales from the *westward* on July 31, which continued until August 1. She was over the reef on the Bahama Banks by the Cat Keys, and compelled to anchor and ride out the gale. When the weather cleared on the 2nd she saw three vessels on the reef wrecked, but she was unable to lend them assistance.

The barque Cossack, on August 1, encountered a violent gale forty miles S. of St. Augustine. Met a ship supposed to be the Emily of Liverpool, dismasted, and making for a port.

The ship Providence, on August 1, in lat. 29° 30′, experienced a heavy gale.

Extract of a letter from St. Simon Island.

(Lat. 31° 2′, long. 31° 28′.)

On August 1 and 2 we had a very severe gale here.

The brig Monument (Fisher) experienced a severe gale on August 1 off Cape Florida.

The barque Josephine, on August 1, experienced a severe gale from *north-east*, lat. 27° 50′, long. 79° 20′, and had some of her sails blown from the yards, though they were furled.

The brig Moses, on August 1, off Cape Carnaveral, lat. 28° 16′, long. 80° 24′, experienced a severe hurricane, commencing at *north-east* and veering round to *south*, which hove the brig on her beam ends, and obliged her to cut away her mast. She was in fourteen feet water, and was saved by the wind coming from the *south*.

The schooner A. Brook, on August 2, lat. 29° 38′, long. 80° 41′, experienced a severe gale of wind *from east-north-east to south-south-east*.

A severe gale of wind at Jacksonville, on Tuesday, August 1, which continued until Sunday, August 6,*

* This was owing to the second hurricane nearly overtaking the first one.

when it blew a hurricane from the *north-east* and *south-east.* Two government warehouses were blown down at Jacksonville, and the crops of cotton destroyed.

The barque Mablehead, of Boston, was lost on the western reef of the little Bahama bank on August 2.

The brig Howell anchored on the little Bahama bank on August 2, 1837. Obliged to cut away both masts to prevent her going ashore in a violent gale.

The Ida experienced a severe gale in the gulf on August 3. All her sails were blown to pieces. The boats and twenty of the crew were washed overboard. The captain brought her into port with five men.

The Georgia steam packet left Charleston on Saturday, August 5, 1837, in the morning, and arrived at Norfolk in the Chesapeake, on Monday, August 7. Had rough weather and *north-east winds.*

Greenock, Dec. 5, 1837.—Thursday, 27 (26 P.M. *civil time*) July, in lat. 14° 28′ N. and long. 56° 12′ W.,* wind veered from ENE. to WSW., with a tremendous swell from the southward; the sky clouded, with thunder and lightning and heavy rain, with all the appearance of a coming hurricane; furled all sails but the main topsail. At 1 P.M. a heavy squall took the ship, and laid the sail under water, which continued for the space of half an hour; at 3 P.M. the wind veered to the northward, and cleared up to the southward, but a very bad appearance to the SW.; had no barometer or sympiesometer; at 6 o'clock fine clear weather; made all sail for Demerara, where the Balclutha arrived on August 3.

The Spey packet, which had been at anchor in Carlisle Bay, Barbadoes, during the hurricane of July 26, sailed from that island on the 30th for St. Thomas, delivered

* About 1 P. M. the S. portion of the storm must have been about WSW. of the Balclutha. This squall reaching her is a remarkable circumstance.

mails at the northern islands as she went along; and was very nearly sailing into the second hurricane.

New York, August 23, 1837. — During a violent gale at Pensacola, on the 8th inst., the brigs Alvira, Rondout, and Lion, were driven on shore, and much damage done to the shipping in port. Most of the small vessels were driven on shore.

The brigantine Judith and Esther sailed from Cork, bound to Kingston, Jamaica, on July 2, 1837. A fair wind prevailed until August 1, on which day was experienced a most dreadful hurricane, of which the following are particulars: —

On the night of July 31, at 8 P.M., in lat. 17° 19′ N., and long. 52° 10′ W., the wind blowing fresh from the NE., and all possible sail set, *a white appearance of a round form, nearly vertical, was observed*, and while looking steadfastly at it, *a sudden gust of wind carried away the topmast and lower studding-sails.* At 8.30 P.M. the atmosphere became very cloudy, and the wind increasing we took in our small sails and one reef in the top-sail, *not observing at this time any swell* but what would have risen from such a breeze. The wind continued after this time quite steady from the NE., and not increasing until the hour of 1 A.M. on the following morning (August 1), when the wind increased and the sea rose very fast, so that it caused the vessel to labour hard. At 6.30 A.M. on the same day, close-reefed the topsail, reefed the foresail and furled it, and close-reefed the mainsail; sent top-gallant yards down, and housed the main-topmast; the sea at this time very high and regular from the NE. Seven A.M. *the wind gradually increasing*: took in the mainsail and topsail, and let the vessel run under bare poles, all hands being of opinion that she would do better running than if hove-to; the sea at this time very high, the vessel labouring and straining much, and shipping great quantities of water — the pumps being particularly attended to. At about 8 A.M. very heavy rain, and the wind increasing to a hurricane, so that it was impossible to hear each other speak on deck, or yet do anything for our safety. She broached-to, and was hove on her larboard beam ends, by a tremendously heavy sea, which took nearly all the bulwark away from the larboard side. She had been for some time on her larboard beam ends before she rose, and when she did, the wind veered suddenly to the *southward of east*. After running a short time before the wind, she was hove again on her beam ends, which, when she righted, took all the bulwark away on the other side except a few planks; she then became again manageable for about fifteen minutes, which time was about noon. After the short time she was manageable, it fell calm for about fifteen minutes, and the hurricane suddenly veered to about *south*, when we gave up all hopes of safety. A sea, owing to the sudden shift of wind, had struck her on the starboard side, and hove the vessel the third time on her beam ends. *She had remained some time so*, the cabin and forecastle nearly filled with water (though as much precaution as possible was taken against it); all the boats (3), the cookhouse, water-casks, spare spars, sails, a quantity of spare rope, in fact everything of any value, was gone; the mate, who was attending (as well as *possible*) to the wheel, was washed from it — the wheel was carried away. All the stanchions on the starboard side were broken, and every sail, except the mainsail, blown away into rags, though furled properly; the foretop, while on her beam ends, nearly smashed to pieces; when to our cheering surprise we observed her again righting, and could not account for the manner in which we were saved, but through the powerful hand of an Almighty Protector. *For nearly an hour we could not observe each other, or anything but merely the light; and, most astonishing, every one of our finger-nails turned quite black, and remained so nearly five weeks afterwards!* After she had righted, we observed the clouds break (which were from the commencement of the gale in a body, with heavy rain); the wind also abated a little. One hand managed to get below and procured a handspike, which we shipped as a tiller, and managed to get her again before the sea, which was then running tremendously high; the pumps were again got at, and kept going. This time we considered about 3 P.M.; the gale then began to abate, and the sea did not break so furiously, so that we managed to set a balance-reefed mainsail, and hove her to. The gale still abating, we went below, and found every article, that could be damaged by salt water, injured. The pumps were still attended to; and we found she did not make any water except what got from the cabin and forecastle. At 6 P.M. the gale greatly abated and the sea fell fast. The appearance of the sky at this time was most remarkable, being of a deep red colour to the N., and looking very dark to the W., as if the gale was moving in that direction. At midnight the gale considerably abated and the weather appeared much better, the vessel not making any water. At 4 A.M. on the following morning, being August 2, the weather appeared as before the gale (a steady breeze from NE.), the atmosphere at this time being a dark red, and the clouds *not moving*. We at this time bent the second topsail and ran under it single-reefed, and a close-reefed mainsail. At 10 A.M. on the same day, the wind remaining quite steady, ran under a whole topsail and single-reefed mainsail; the crew being quite exhausted, gave them the remainder of the day for rest. The wind was at first *north-east*, and veered *easterly* to *south*, or *south-south-west*. No swell preceded the storm. Our barometer was broken ; but that of the barque Laidmans, of Liverpool, Capt. Hughes, which arrived in Kingston four days afterwards, was very unsteady, rising and falling during three days, while a very heavy sea was running, though without increase of wind (in the lat. and long. in which we experienced the gale).

Our sufferings were *very* great, more so than any person could easily imagine.

The blast of wind which first alarmed us on the night commencing the hurricane came from a *north-east* direction, and remained so without changing until the time mentioned.

The third time the vessel was on her beam ends, some of the crew were in the main rigging, and the others were standing on the weather side, holding on the weather rail.

Why we were not able to see each other, it is impossible now to tell; but while running, before the vessel was hove the third time on her beam ends; and while on her beam ends, the atmosphere had quite a different appearance; much darker, but not so dark as to hinder one from seeing the other, or from seeing a greater distance, were it not that our eyes were affected. It was about this time our finger-nails had turned black :— whether it was from the firm grasp we had on the rigging or rails, we could not tell, but our opinion is, that the whole was caused by an *electric* body in the elements. *Every one of the crew was affected in the same way.*

Probably the first storm, the Barbadoes one, was proceeding toward Cape Hatteras, on August 6, at the time the second hurricane, from Antigua, was arriving on the coasts of Florida and Georgia. It will be easily understood with a little consideration, that if these storms were rotatory, where their tracks approached each other, the wind, as it blew in the first, would be reversed by the approach of the second; and thus we have a clue toward explanation of the *variable* winds.*

On August 15, at noon, the Calypso was, by observation, in lat. 26° 47′ N., and long. 75° 5′ W.; the wind was from the eastward, about *east-north-east*; she had royals and fore-topmast studding-sail set: shortly after we got a heavy swell from the north-eastward, and the wind freshened gradually till 9 o'clock, when only the double-reefed topsails, reefed foresail and mizen, could be carried. During the night the wind increased, and daylight (the moon about full) found the vessel under a close-reefed main-topsail, with royal and top-gallant yards on deck, and prepared for a gale of wind. At 10 A.M. the wind about *north-east*, the lee-rail under water, and the masts bending like canes; got a tarpaulin on the main rigging, and took the main-topsail in; the ship labouring much, obliged main and bilge-pumps to be kept constantly going. At 6 P.M. the wind *north-west*, the lat. probably about 27°, and long. 77°. At midnight the wind was *west*, when a sea took the quarter-boat away. At day-dawn — or rather, I might have said, the time when the day should have dawned — the wind was *south-west*, and a sea stove the fore-scuttle; all attempts to stop this leak were useless, for when the ship pitched the scuttle was considerably under water. The gaskets and lines then were cut from the reefed-foresail, which

* Sir William Reid (from whose work these passages are taken *freely* might have said here — *varying* or *shifting* of *these* winds. — R. F.

blew away; a new fore-topmast studding-sail was got up and down the fore-rigging, but in a few seconds the bolt-rope only remained ; the masts were then to be cut away. My chief mate had a small axe in his berth, which he had made very sharp a few days previous ; that was immediately procured; and while the men were employed cutting away the mizenmast, the lower yard-arms went in the water. It is human nature to struggle hard for life; so fourteen men and myself got over the rail between the main and mizen rigging, *as the mast-heads went in the water*: the ship was sinking fast; while some men were employed cutting the weather-lanyards of the rigging, some were calling to God for mercy; some were stupified with despair; and two poor fellows who had gone from the afterhold over the cargo to get to the forecastle to try to stop the leak, were swimming in the ship's hold. In about three minutes after getting on the bends, the weather-lanyards were cut fore and aft, and the mizen, main, and foremasts went one after the other, just as the vessel was going down head foremost.

She then righted very slowly. On getting on board again, found the three masts had gone close off by the deck: the boats were gone, the main hatches stove in, the planks of the deck had started in many places, the water was up to the beams, and the puncheons of rum *sending* about the hold with great violence; the starboard gunwale was about a foot from the level of the sea, and the larboard about five feet; the main and mizen-masts were held on the starboard side by the lee-rigging; and the foremast was kept from floating from the starboard side by the stay. The sea was breaking over the ship as it would have done over a log. You will, perhaps, say it could not have been worse, and any lives spared to tell the tale. It *was* worse; and although the main and bilge-pumps were broken, yet, by Divine Providence, every man was suffered to walk from that ship to the quay at Wilmington! The wind, from about noon of the 16th till about 10, or noon of the 17th, blew with nearly the same violence. There was no lull; neither did it fly from one quarter of the compass to the other, but backed from *east-north-east* to *south-west*, and then died away gradually. On Sunday, while beating off Rum Key, the wind was variable and squally. On Monday, in lat. 24° 40′, long. 74° 45′, had fine steady winds from the eastward. Tuesday has been described. Had no barometer; but from the *appearance* of the weather on Monday and Tuesday morning, we did not apprehend any bad weather.

On August 31, we sighted the land, about thirty miles to the southward of Cape Fear, but *the wind coming more from the eastward*, had to bring up in five-fathoms water. During the night *the wind increased*, but fortunately *backed into the northward* (which was off the land), and at noon on the following day *blew a very heavy gale of wind*, and continued until the *morning of the* 2nd, when it *backed to the west-north-west*, and moderated; we then slipped the cable, sailed along the land for Baldhead lighthouse, at noon got a pilot on board, and anchored once more in port. We were kindly received by the good people at Smithville and Wilmington, who complained bitterly of the late storm, for many of their houses were unroofed, and trees blown down.

The *shifting of the wind to the eastward, and its increasing*, are adverted to, in illustration of our subject. This was the fifth storm, and came from the *west.*

The Calypso appears to have been upset just after half the storm had passed over, and to have been very nearly, although not quite, in the centre of its course.

The brig Cumberland put into Nassau, having experienced a hurricane on August 15.

The Mary, Sharp, from New Orleans to Barbadoes, was abandoned on September 5, lat. 32°, long. 80°, having been dismasted and thrown on her beam ends, with six-feet water in her hold, in a gale on August 16, in lat. 27° 30′, long. 73° 53′.

The Neptune, from Jamaica to London, was dismasted in this storm.

The Jennet, Gibson, from Honduras to London, was capsized in a gale on August 21. On September 3, the crew arrived at Rhode Island.

The Emerald saw the Rosebud, of Glasgow, on August 23, in lat. 34°, long. 75°, a wreck; stood for her, and found her *derelict*.

The Duke of Manchester was thrown on her beam ends, and lost her mainmast in a gale on August 18 and 19, lat. 32°, long. 77°.

The brig Yankee, on August 16, in lat. 24° 30′, long. 70° 30′, experienced a severe gale of wind from NE. to SSW., which lasted until the 20th.

The packet ship Sheridan, Russell, arrived at New York on August 28, from Liverpool. August 22, in lat. 39° 45′, long. 68° 33′, experienced a hurricane, which took away the fore and main-topsails (double-reefed) entirely from the yards, leaving nothing but the bolt-rope standing.

The Mecklenburg brig Harmonie, Galle, from New York to Alexandria, was driven on shore fifty miles to the southward of the Capes in the gale above mentioned.

The Hindley, Turner, from Laguna for Liverpool, was off Sandy Hook on the 16th, dismasted.

The New York packet, encountered in September, homeward bound, to the northward of Bermuda, a heavy gale from SE., which continued for two days, *when it suddenly became calm.* A small clear spot appeared in the opposite quarter, NW.; and in a very short time the ship was on her beam ends, with lower yards in the water, from the action of the wind *upon spars and rigging alone.* We were obliged to cut away some of the masts, or she must have foundered.

Between the Havannah and Matanzas, in the Sophia, in company with several other Jamaica ships, occurred a similar storm to this last one. Having paid close attention to the *barometer, and other signs of a change of weather*; and having prepared accordingly, we suffered little or nothing in spars or rigging, when some of those in company were dismasted. On that occasion, ships not thirty miles off were not aware of this storm. *It began at south-east, and going round the compass, westward*, ended where it began in six hours.

Narrative from the ship Rawlins, Macqueen, from Jamaica to London. Latitude, commencement, N. 30° 30′; latitude, termination, N. 30° 40′. Longitude, commencement, W. 77° 40′; longitude, termination, W. 77° 18′. Dates — 17th, 18th, 19th August.

Wind commenced at *north-east by east*, blowing strong from that quarter, about twelve hours, then suddenly veered to *north*, continuing with unabated vigour until midnight of 18th; in an instant a perfect calm ensued for one hour; then quick as thought the hurricane sprung up, with tremendous force from *south-west*, not again shifting from that point. No swell whatever preceded the convulsion. *The barometer gave every notice of the coming gale for many previous hours.* Two days antecedent the weather beautifully serene, but oppressively hot, with light shifting airs; barometer during that time standing at 'set-fair,' during the gale as low as *almost to be invisible*, in the tube, above the *framework* of the instrument. The force subsided at midnight, August 19; the sea tremendous, and rising in every direction; from the *force of wind* — no tops to the waves, being dispersed in *one sheet of white foam*; the decks tenanted by many sea-birds, in an exhausted state, seeking shelter in the vessel: — impossible to discern, even during the day, anything at fifty yards' distance; the wind representing numberless voices, elevated to the shrillest tone of screaming;—but few flashes of lightning, and those in the SW. A very heavy sea continued for some days after.

In the log of the Rawlins, on August 20, A.M., there is this remarkable expression, after saying —

'The wind and sea much abated.—A dismal appearance to the *north-west.*' This was the direction in which the centre of the storm had moved.

Witton Castle, Canney, Jamaica to London, experienced a tremendous gale August 21, in lat. 40°, long. 70°.

Catherine, Potter, arrived at Greenock, September 11, from Grenada, having experienced the tail of a hurricane 22nd and 23rd ultimo, in lat. 39°, long. 58°.

Columbus, Burgess, from Plymouth to Turk Island, experienced a gale August 21, lat. 37°, long. 71°.

Dunlop, Gifney, Campeachy to Liverpool, in a gale on August 24, lat. 33°, long. 76°.

Cicero, Watts, at Baltimore, from Jamaica, in a gale, August 18, lat. 32°, long. 76°.

Margaret, Marson, for Martinique, in a hurricane August 14, lat. 21°, long. 59°.

The Duke of Manchester and another vessel, the Palambam, were to the S. of the two first hurricanes, but they were in the heart of the third one, and the Palambam foundered. When last seen she was under a close-reefed topsail, near the centre of the storm.

An extraordinarily *black squall* mentioned in their narrative, was described as the most appalling sight ever witnessed on the ocean.

The Victoria, Dunn, from Lunenburg to Dominica, was upset and dismasted in a hurricane, on August 24, 1837, in lat. 33°, long. 58°, — and abandoned on September 12.

The barque Clydesdale, from Barbadoes and Antigua, encountered a severe hurricane ten miles N. of Barbadoes, on July 26, 1837. On August 24, encountered a hurricane more severe than the former, in lat. 32° 30′, long. 59° 30′, in which the vessel was hove on her beam ends, and remained in that position for two hours. She righted after the whole of her top-gallant masts and rigging had been cut away. On August 23, 1837, lat. 30° 21′, about noon, it came on to blow fresh breezes from the ESE., accompanied with a heavy confused swell. At 4 P.M. sent down royal yards: — at midnight atmosphere dark, and wind *south-east.* Close-reefed at 5 A.M. on the 24th; took in all sail; at noon blew a complete hurricane; ship lying over very low, sea washing over; at 4 P.M. top-gallant masts and yards cut away to save the vessel; at midnight gale moderated. At 4 A.M. of the 25th kept away; at 8 moderate, but still a confused swell.

The greater storm had passed over the same part of the

ocean on August 22, where the Castries was lying-to on the 24th and 25th, at which last date that greater storm was beyond the place of the Wanstead. Here therefore we have an explanation of the *variable* winds; for the great storm would cause a *westerly* gale on the 22nd, over the same part of the ocean, where the smaller storm, coming from the S. (and bringing up the Castries along with it in the right hand semicircle), changed the wind to *east.**

A hurricane swept over the town of Apolachicola, August 31, 1837, and half destroyed it. Nearly every house was unroofed; a number of the upper stories were blown down, and many houses levelled. The storm commenced on the afternoon of August 30, but was not severe until 4 A.M. on the morning of the 31st, when it became very violent until 7 P.M. The wind was from the *south-east to north.*

This terrible tempest completely destroyed the town of St. Mark. The lighthouse was almost the only building left standing, yet the town of St. Joseph suffered very little in the gale.

At St. Mark it commenced about sunrise on the morning of August 31, 1837, the wind being from *north-east.* At 8 A.M. the wind was N., and it had increased in violence. Only one wharf has been left standing. At the lighthouse the sea rose eight feet higher than usual. *At Pensacola there was no wind.* The schooner Lady Washington was *becalmed* at the same time at Key West. The wind was off shore at the time of the storm, which makes it difficult to account for the high tide; but it is supposed, *while the north-east wind was blowing on shore,*

* Surely Sir William Reid *implied,* or intended to advert to, *varying* (shifting, veering, or backing) winds.—R. F.

a south-easter prevailed at sea. This is frequently the case, and invariably produces a high tide.

Another storm commenced about the middle of the night (of August 31), and at 10 A.M. next morning was blowing with violence from the *north-west.* It continued with increased violence until noon, when the wind veered to about *west.* At 2 o'clock, was still blowing a severe gale.

The ship Florence experienced a severe hurricane on September 2, 1837, fifty miles ESE. of Cape Hatteras. It commenced blowing at *east-north-east,* and veered *round the compass.*

The Danish brig Maria, on September 2, in lat. 36° 6′, long. 73° 40′, was scudding in a gale from the *south.*

The brig Stranger, on September 2, from Port Plata (in St. Domingo) to Philadelphia, experienced a severe gale from *south,* changing suddenly to *north.*

CHAPTER XX

Hurricanes in Pacific — At Mauritius — In the Indian Ocean — Bay of Bengal — China Sea — Typhoons — Royal Charter Storm — Previous Occurrences in Apparent Relation — Seasons — Auroras — Electric Incidents — Principal Facts — Meteors and Contemporary Gales — Similarity to Hurricanes, or Cyclones, in other Oceans.

It may be useful to notice two or three instances of severe storms in the southern hemisphere, by way of caution to inexperienced voyagers, especially in the so-called Pacific Ocean.

Mr. Williams, the well known missionary martyr, witnessed a hurricane at Rarotonga, one of the Hervey Islands (19° S. lat., 160° W. long.), Dec. 21 and 22, 1831: —

The vessel belonging to the missionaries was at the time hauled up on shore to be lengthened. By Mr. Williams's account, it appears that a 'ground swell' *preceded* the 'coming tempest,' and the sea was raised so high that his vessel was carried some distance inland from the shore. When the east end of their chapel was blown in, we may conclude that the wind was easterly, and it is stated that the gale ended in the west.

The morning of December 21 Mr. Williams received information that a very heavy sea was rolling into the harbour, and if it increased (of which there was every probability) the vessel must sustain damage. He set out for Avarua, and was alarmed, on arriving, by the threatening appearance of the atmosphere, and agitated state of the ocean. He instantly employed natives to carry stones, and raise a sort of breakwater round the vessel. One end of the chain cable was then fastened to the ship, and the other attached to the main post of their large school-house, which stood on a bank ten feet high, forty or fifty yards from the sea; and having removed all the timber and ship's stores to what he conceived a place of safety, and taken every precaution to secure the ship and property from the coming tempest, he returned to Ngatangiia. As he was leaving Avarua, he saw a heavy sea rolling in lift the vessel several feet; she fell again, however, to her place gently. Next day (Sunday) was one of gloom and distress; the wind blew most furiously, and rain descended in torrents from morning to night. Nevertheless they held their religious services as usual. Toward evening the storm increased; trees were rent and houses began to fall: among the latter was a large shed used as a temporary school-house, which buried their best boat in its ruins.

About 9 P.M. notice came that the sea had risen to an alarming height; that the vessel had been thumping all day on the stones; and that at 6, the roof which covered her was blown down and washed away: to complete the evil tidings, the messenger told them the sea had gone over the bank, and reached the school-house, which contained the rigging, coppers, and stores of their vessel; and that if it continued, all the settlement would be endangered.

As the distance was eight miles, the night terrifically dark, and the rain pouring down like a deluge, Mr. Williams determined to wait till morning.

Before daylight he set out for Avarua; and in order to avoid walking knee-deep in water all the way, and to escape the falling limbs of trees which were being torn with violence from their trunks, he attempted to take the sea-side path; but the wind and rain were so violent, he found it impossible to make any progress. He was obliged to take the inland road; and by watching opportunities, and running between the falling trees, escaped without injury. Half-way he was met by some of his workmen, who informed him that the sea had risen to a great height, and swept away the store-house with its contents. The vessel was driven in against the bank, upon which she was lifted with every wave, and fell off again when it receded. On reaching the settlement, it presented a scene of fearful desolation: its beautiful groves, broad pathway, and neat white cottages, were one mass of ruins, among which scarcely a house or tree was standing. The poor women were running wildly with their children, seeking a place of shelter, and the men dragging their property from the ruins of the prostrated houses. . . . On reaching the chapel, he was rejoiced to see it standing; but, as he was passing, a resistless gust burst in the *east* end, and proved the premonitory symptom of its destruction. The new school-house was lying in ruins by its side; Mr. Buzacott's excellent house, which stood on a stone foundation, was unroofed and rent: the inmates had fled.

Shortly after his arrival a heavy sea burst in with devastating vengeance, and tore away the foundation of the chapel, which fell with a frightful crash. The same wave rolled on till it dashed on Mr. Buzacott's already mutilated house, and laid it prostrate with the ground. The Chief's wife had conducted Mrs. Buzacott to her habitation; but shortly after they reached it the sea dashed against it, and the wind tore off the roof, so that they were obliged to take refuge in the mountains. They waded nearly a mile through water, in some places several feet deep, to reach a temporary shelter, and found that a huge tree had fallen and crushed the hut. Again they pursued their way, and found a hut standing, crowded with women and children taking refuge, where they were however gladly welcomed.

The rain was still descending in deluging torrents; the angry lightning was darting its fiery streams along the dense black clouds, which shrouded us in their gloom. The thunder, deep and loud, rolled and pealed through the heavens, and the whole island trembled to its very centre as the infuriated billows burst upon its shores The crisis had arrived—this was the hour of ou greatest anxiety; but 'man's extremity is God's opportunity.' Never was this sentence more signally illustrated than at this moment—the wind shifted suddenly a few points *to the west*, which was a signal to the sea to cease its ravages, and retire within its wonted limits. The storm was hushed; the lowering clouds began to disperse; and the sun, as a prisoner, burst forth from its dark dungeon and smiled upon us. * * * * *

As soon as possible I sent a messenger to obtain some information respecting my poor vessel, expecting she had been shivered to a thousand pieces; but, to our astonishment, he returned with the intelligence, that although the bank, the schoolhouse, and the vessel, were all washed away together, the latter had been carried over a swamp and lodged among a grove of large chesnut trees, several hundred yards inland, and yet appeared to have sustained no injury whatever. As soon as practicable I went myself, and was truly gratified at finding that the report was correct, and that the trees had stopped her wild progress; otherwise she would have driven several hundred yards farther, and have sunk in a bog.

One among many very remarkable storms in the *south-western* part of the Indian Ocean may be here mentioned.

On February 28 and March 1, 1818, the Magicienne frigate was lying at Mauritius, moored in the harbour of Port Louis: and on that occasion, this frigate and forty other vessels went on shore, or were sunk; the American brig Jason being the only vessel out of forty-one that rode out this storm — which was felt at Bourbon Isle, though not so severely as at Mauritius.

In the accounts given of it, we find that, as was observed at Barbadoes in 1831, '*the rain tasted salt*;' and it is added, that next day, '*the rivers ran with brackish water.*'

'Ouragan à Maurice :
'du 28 Février au soir, au 1 Mars, 1818.

'Les signes auxquel on reconnait à Maurice l'approche des grandes tempêtes n'ont point annoncé celle-ci. Dans les jours précédens le mercure des baromètres de la ville était descendu deux fois au dessous de 28 pouces (29·8 English), mais le 28 Février, il avait repris son niveau ordinaire. Seulement dans l'après-midi, le vent se mit à souffler par rafallés variant de l'est-sud-est au sud-est et au sud-sud-est. La force des grains augmenta progressivement jusques à la nuit et cependant peu de personnes conçurent des inquiétudes. Plusieurs fois dans cette saison, des menaces de tempêtes plus caractérisées n'avaient eu aucun résultat fâcheux. Aussi les marins du port, et les habitans des campagnes négligèrent-ils également les précautions que l'on prend d'ordinaire lorsqu'on craint un coup de vent. Peu de navires renforcèrent leurs amarres; aucun habitant ne songea à couper les tiges des maniocs pour en sauver les racines. La nuit survint et l'ouragan commença ses ravages. La force du vent toujours croissante, et la descente rapide du mercure dans le baromêtre, ne laissèrent plus de doute sur le fléau dont on allait éprouver les terribles effets.

'Jusques au milieu de la nuit les vents soufflèrent du *sud-sud-est, au sud* avec une extrême violence. Vers une heure après minuit, ils commencèrent *à tourner vers l'est*; au point du jour, ils étaient *au nord-nord-est* et *au nord*; le mercure était descendu à 26 pouces 4 lignes (28·00 English), hauteur réduite à celle du niveau de la mer. Jamais on ne l'avait vu aussi bas. Plusieurs personnes crurent que leurs baromêtres etaient dérangé, celles qui ne pouvaient se méprendre sur la cause de cette dépression, s'attendaient à une grande catastrophe. Heureusement pour la colonie que cet état de l'atmosphère, n'eut qu'une courte durée. En effet on peut juger, par le mal qu'a fait l'ouragan, de celui qu'il aurait produit si sa violence, telle qu'elle était, de 4 heures ½ à 6 heures du matin, se fût prolongée de quelques heures. En passant au *nord-ouest*, le vent se calma assez promptement; le mercure remontà avec toute la rapidité qu'il avait mise à descendre, et dans le journée même du premier Mars, on parvint à communiquer avec la plupart des vaisseaux échoués dans la rade, et l'on put s'occuper de porter quelque remède aux accidens causés par la tempête, à ceux du moins qui en étaient susceptibles.

'On à observé le lendemain du coup de vent que *les eaux avaient partout un goût saumatre. La pluie, pendant sa durée, avait elle-même une saveur très-salée.*

'La salle de spectacle est un très-grand édifice. Sa forme est celle d'un T dont la tête est un avant-corps considérable, puisque la partie postérieure, formant la queue du T, a seule 53 pieds de largeur sur 82 de long. Si cet édifice eût été brisé par la tempête on aurait pu attribuer cet événement à la manière dont il était construit; mais, ce qui est à-peine croyable, cet immense arrière-corps de 34 pieds et surmonté d'un comble en charpente, lié en outre avec l'avant-corps qui forme la façade, a cependant chassé de près de cinq pieds sur son soubassement. Quelle force prodigieuse que celle qui a pu produire, le déplacement horizontal d'une telle masse! son renversement eut été un phénomène ordinaire; sa translation, si l'on peut employer ce terme, ne se conçoit pas.

'Toutes les maisons couvertes en bardeaux (*shingles*) et c'est la presque totalité de celles de la colonie, ont été inondées intérieurement par la pluie. On n'imagine point la violence et l'abondance avec laquelle elle est lancée horizontalement pendant nos tempêtes. Alors les couvertures imbriquées sont inutiles et dangereuses même car elles donnent au vent une grande prise, et contribuent à la destruction des édifices. Si l'ouragan eut duré jusques à midi seulement avec la méme-force la ville n'eut été qu'un monçeau de ruines. Déjà, au moment où il a cessé beaucoup be belles maisons, intactes en apparence, étaiént entamées par le toit. Celles qui n'auraient pas été renversées, eussent été emportées pièce à pièce.

'Les maisons couvertes en terrasses ou argamasses, à la manière de l'Inde, ont résisté à la tempête, et on y a été à l'abri de la pluie. Mais aucune sorte de couverture n'a mieux soutenu cette épreuve décisive que celle construite suivant le procédé de M. Chaix, c'est-à-dire en briques unies par *un ciment résineaux de sa composition.*

'Les couvertures en *ardoises* ont été enlevées. La plupart de celles en cuivre et en fer-blanc ont été enlevées aussi, et cependant les toîts de cette dernière sorte ont sur les bardeaux l'avantage inappréciable de ne point donner de gouttières et d'être facile à réparer. Le mal est venu de ce qu'on n'avait pris pas les moyens convenables pour les fixer sur le lattis des combles.

'Autrefois les habitans aisés construisaient une petite maison servant habituellement de dépendance, mais destinée surtout à leur servir de réfuge pendant les coups de vent. Quoiqu'il soit probable qu'un fléau pareil à celui du 1 Mars, ne se reproduira pas de longtemps, on ferait bien de revenir à cette sage précaution. Un petit pavillon en pierre soigneusement bâti, peu élevé sur le sol, et couvert d'un toit plat étroitement lié à la maçonnerîe, ne coute pas beaucoup plus, que construit à la manière ordinaire, et il a le double avantage d'une durée indéfinie, et d'être un lieu de sureté pour les familles, lorsque l'ouragan se déclare.'

Extract from the Log of H.M.S. Magicienne, Mauritius, February 28, 1818:*—

* Written by the present Admiral George Evans.

'March 1, 1818.—Wind SSE.; A.M. 2.10 strong gale, heavy squalls, and rain, blowing excessively hard; the best bower bent to a mooring-anchor; ship driving slowly; got the spars out of the rigging; SE. at 2.40 a merchant ship drove athwart us, and carried away the jib and flying-jib-boom, with gear, then went clear and upset; at 3 a schooner drove athwart us, remained some time, and then drove on shore; at 4 blowing a complete hurricane, ship still driving; drove on board the Prince Regent, merchant ship; carried away the ensign staff, and cut the stern down to the cabin windows; carried away her jib-boom, and sprung her bowsprit; jolly-boat swamped and went down; the barge went adrift, and stove her broadside in with the Prince Regent's anchor; made fast a cable to the careening hulk; ship aground, heeling very much to port; ESE. at 5 a brig drove athwart us; carried away her mainmast, and went on shore; daylight, hurricane still unabated; observed all the ships in harbour (except the American brig Jason), forty-one in number, were either on shore or sunk; found the main and mizen channels shifted with the violence of the wind, and the hammock-cloths, rails, and boards blown away; at 6 parted the sheet cable; the hulk parted her mooring-chains, and we drove on shore at the point of the entrance to the fort; NE. ship heeling very much to starboard; sounded round the ship, and found 10 feet of water from the fore to the main chains, 17 feet under the stern, and 18 feet under the larboard bow; at 8 a hard gale with heavy squalls and rain; issued a gill of spirits to ship's company; at 9 more moderate; noon, strong wind and squally; found as the weather moderated *the water shoaled* fast; under starboard fore-chains only 7 feet, a-stern 14, and on the larboard bow 15 feet; NE. between 2 and 3 P.M. fresh gale and squally with rain; at 4 fresh breeze and rainy weather; attempted to heave the ship off by the single bower, fast to mooring-anchor; at 4.30 found anchor coming home; ENE. at 7 and 8 fresh breeze, and cloudy weather; easterly at 10.30; midnight moderate with rain.'

Extract from the Asiatic Journal:—The frigate Magicienne, Captain Purvis, is on shore, and many houses of the town are in ruins. On the plantations the buildings have suffered as much as the fields: many planters have lost their all, and the distress is general. The barometer sunk lower than ever was known, and most of those who observed it were unable to account for the notice it gave in so extraordinary a manner.

It appears that the most violent blast was from the north-east, but with a force very unequal, as we could see small vessels withstand it, whilst others of the greatest strength were destroyed at a small distance from them.

Many persons observed that *the rain water was salt*; and on the day after the storm the water which flows near the town was found *brackish.*

The Magicienne suffered greatly while on this station from the effects of hurricanes; she experienced two storms in 1819, though less severe than those in 1818.

The first one, like that of the previous year, began with the wind at SSE. and ended with the wind about NW.

In a hurricane on February 23, 1824, at Mauritius, upwards of thirty vessels were wrecked.

The following remarks relate to the manner in which the wind appears to blow in veins differing in degrees of strength:—Il parait qu'une trombe, ou tourbillon (de ceux qui ont fait donner aux ouragans le nom de typhon), a parcouru une ligne sur laquelle se sont trouvées plusieurs maisons du Champ-de-Lort, et particulièrement le Collége Royal.

C'est contre ce terrible phénomène, qu'il faut se précautionner dans les ouragans: aussi n'est il pas prudent en pareil cas, de demeurer dans les maisons élevées; dans celles surtout qui sont posées sur de hauts soubassemens en pierre formant le rez-de-chaussée. C'est tres mal raisonner que de dire, qu'une maison a résisté à tel ouragan ou à tel autre. Elle ne s'est pas trouvée sur le *chemin d'un tourbillon*, voilà ce qui l'a preservée. Telle est aussi la cause d'un fait observé dans tous les ouragans, celui de la préservation d'une maison tombante de vétusté, étroite, élevée, qui n'est pas même ébranlée à peu de distance d'un édifice neuf, qui est renversé ou mis en pièces.

La météorologie est encore dans son enfance. Tout-ce-que nous savons c'est que, dans ce qu'on appelle les mauvais tems, la pesanteur des colonnes atmosphériques decroit plus ou moins; mais les proportions entre ce décroissement, et l'action de l'air à la surface de notre planête, demeureront probablement longtemps ignorées. Probablement aussi ce n'est pas nous qui verrons construire l'anémomêtre capable de mesurer la force acquise par l'air, lorsqu'il *réduit en filamens*, et qu'il tord comme un cordage le tronc d'un arbre vigoureux, ou qu'il fait tourner sur sa base, une édifice en pierre comme la Maison Laffargue. Aussi les diverses denominations données récemment aux différens dégrés de la tempête, en raison de l'espace que le vent parcourt dans une seconde, nous semblent elles fort insignificantes. C'est le tort de beaucoup de savans. Ils ont la fureur de réduire prématurément en théories certains points des sciences naturelles, sur lesquelles on est entièrement dépourvu de faits suffisamment observés.

The Commandant of the Island of Bourbon wrote relative to a hurricane of February 23, 1824:—Nous avons ressenti à Bourbon, le contre coup de votre tempête. Il est à remarquer, que le 22 Février, nous eûmes aussi des apparences de mauvais tems; qui s'accruèrent jusqu'au lendemain, au point de me déterminer à donner le signal d'appareillage à nos batimens. Mais ces deux jours, les vents restèrent à l'est et au sud-est ils s'appaisèrent dans la journée même du 23. Le lendemain le tems fut magnifique, et se maintint en cet état, jusque dans l'après midi du 25, que le vent s'étant déclaré au nord, amena des nuages, et une simple apparence de pluie. L'indication barométrique, n'était nullement défavorable. Par malheur les batimens étoient revenues sur la rade; dans la nuit la mer devint affreuse, et contribua surtout, à en pousser neuf d'entre eux, sur la côte. Le vent souffla alternativement du nord, et du nord-ouest; mais sans une extrême violence. Le baromètre etoit descendu alors à 27·7 (or 28·2 English).

Among records of storms in south latitude, two, very disastrous in their consequences, left a deep impression on the minds of many persons, from the great loss of life as well as property they occasioned. These were the storms of 1808 and 1809, encountered by the fleets of the East India Company, under convoy of H.M.S. Albion, Captain John Farrer, and of the Culloden, with the flag of Rear-Admiral Sir Edward Pellew, the first Lord Exmouth. The East India Company's ships Glory, Lord Nelson, and Experiment, foundered in the storm of 1808. The Lady Jane Dundas, Jane Duchess of Gordon, the Calcutta, and the Bengal, with H.M. brig of war Harrier, foundered in the hurricane of the year 1809.

The Jane Duchess of Gordon was last seen on the 14th, by the Inglis, with her fore and main-topsails close-reefed and set: it was then blowing a storm, and she lost sight of her at 3 o'clock in the afternoon.

The Lady Jane Dundas was also last seen that day, with close-reefed fore and main-topsails set.

Each ship had on board from 5,000 to 7,000 bags of saltpetre; and in hurricanes, when water gets into a ship's hold, such cargoes as saltpetre and sugar are well known to melt; the trim of a vessel becoming deranged. She is, consequently, in danger of oversetting. In the Calypso and H.M.S. Raleigh we have instances of ships blowing over when under bare poles.

The orders of the Dutch East India Company would appear to have had reference to ships encountering rotatory gales. When the wind, at SE. or ESE., shifted to north-eastward, the Dutch commanders were directed to take in the main-sail. If lightning appeared in the NW. quarter, they were to wear and shorten sail. In the first case, they expected a hard gale at NW.; and if lightning was seen in that direction, they thought the gale would commence by a sudden shift or whirlwind, which might be fatal to a ship taken aback.

In a succession of hurricanes on March 6, 7, and 8, 1836, the barometer at Mauritius ranged through one inch and seven-tenths.

Typhoons in the China Sea correspond, in their extraordinary violence and gyrations, to West India hurricanes, and the worst of North Atlantic cyclones. That in which H.M.S. Camilla was lost, exactly resembled the storm at St. Kilda—and both happened in the same month—October 1860.

In 1835, H.M.S. Raleigh sailed from Macao. The barometer (in a typhoon) fell to 28·20, soon after which the ship upset. The crew were on that vessel's broadside, while 'keel out,' twenty minutes.

In the Bay of Bengal, during a hurricane in October 1832, the London's barometer fell *about two inches*, and was *recorded* at 27·8 inches.

In the various works, already mentioned, are such numerous and striking instances of great storms and their results, that a reader who wishes for ample information should do their authors the justice of attentive perusal.

British Storms.

It is well known that no year passes in which the British Islands are not visited by storms, and that they vary, in degree of force, from what is usually called a gale, to a hurricane almost irresistible in violence. Only of late years, however, has it been supposed, and but recently proved, that nearly all, if not indeed the whole of these remarkable tempests, by which such excessive injury has been done, have been so much alike in character, and have been preceded by such similar warnings, as to warrant our reasoning inductively from their well-ascertained facts, and thence deducing laws. Every one looks back to some extraordinary storms as exceeding all others in a lifetime; but a tempest that is severely felt in one part of a country is not always extensive, it is usually the reverse, more or less limited in area, varying in range, direction, and force. It would be inexpedient to refer to many of even the most devastating tempests in much detail; therefore we propose to allude only to a few, and glance but summarily over their most marked features.

The first storm to which we would advert is that so well and so fully described by De Foe, 1703.* He calls it 'the greatest, the longest in duration, the widest in extent of all the tempests and storms that history gives any account of since the beginning of time.' 'Our

* The 'Storm,' 1704. A most striking collection of the then recorded tempests in England, *said* to have been written by De Foe.

barometers,' he continues, 'informed us that the night would be very tempestuous; the mercury sank lower than ever I had observed it on any occasion;' it fell to 28·47.* This storm began at south and veered through the west towards the north, round to the south, and continued (chiefly between SW. and NW.) with more or less strength, for a whole week!

Very remarkable it is that not only did De Foe *suppose* this storm began near the southern coast of North America, but that it traversed England, Denmark, the Baltic, and lost itself in the Arctic regions. He recurs afterwards to its shifting from SW. to NW., and coming from the west *like other storms in the south of England*, but does not advert to any *corresponding* north-easterly wind, nor had he evidently any idea of a rotatory or circulating atmospheric current. Probably, accounts from the north of England were less inquired for then: it is noted, however, that the north of England escaped the violence of that storm, which seems to have been one of a succession of cyclones.

Among other storms, two alone will probably suffice as types. The Royal Charter gale, so remarkable in its features, and so complete in its illustrations, we may say (from the fact of its having been noted at so many parts of our coast, and because the storm passed over the middle of the country), is one of the very best to examine which has occurred for some length of time. It commenced on October 25, in 1859. The *lowest* barometer and a corresponding or simultaneous central *lull* prevailed over areas of from ten to twenty miles across

* In the Orkneys, Mr. Clouston has recorded 27·45. Perhaps De Foe's mercury could not fall more for want of space in the cistern, a defect common in the earlier barometers, and not unknown now occasionally.

successively. But at the time that this comparative lull existed, there were violent winds around the centrical space (by some called a vortex, but which can hardly be thus *appropriately* termed, because there was no central disturbance), while there were only variable winds, or calms, with rain, in the middle of the area. The wind attained a *maximum* velocity of from sixty to one hundred miles an hour, at a distance of twenty to fifty miles from the middle of this comparatively quiet space, and in successive spiral eddyings seemed to cross England toward the NE., the wind blowing from all points of the compass consecutively around the lull; so that while at Anglesea the storm came from the NNE., in the Irish Channel it was northerly, and on the E. of Ireland it was from the NW.; in the Straits of Dover it was from the SW.; and on the east coast it was easterly—all at the *same minute*.*

Thus there was an apparent circulation, or cyclonic commotion, passing northward, from the 25th to the 27th, being two complete days from its first appearance in the Channel; while outside of this circuit the wind became less and less violent; and it is very remarkable that, even so near as on the west coast of Ireland, there was fine weather, with light breezes, while in the Bristol Channel it blew a northerly and westerly gale. At Galway and at Limerick, on that occasion, there were moderate breezes only, while over England the wind was passing in a tempest, blowing from all points of the compass, in irregular succession, around a central variable area.

As it is the *NW.* half (from NE. to SW., true), which seems to be principally influenced by the cold,

* See Diagrams XII. and XIII.

dry, heavy, and positively electrified polar current; and the SE. half of the cyclone that apparently shows effects of tropical air — (*warm, moist, light, and negatively or less sensibly electrified*), places over which one half of a cyclone passes are affected differently from others over which the other part of the very same atmospheric eddy passes, the sweep itself being caused by the meeting of very extensive bodies of atmosphere moving in nearly, but not exactly, opposite directions, one of which gradually overpowers, or combines with the other.

On the polar side of a cyclone, continually *supplied* from that side, the sensible effects are chilling, drying up, and clearing the air — with a rising barometer and falling thermometer; while on the tropical (or equatorial) side, overpowering quantities of warm, moist air, rushing from comparatively inexhaustible supplies, push toward the NE. as long as their impetus lasts, and are successively chilled, dried, and intermingled with the conflicting polar currents.*

Another storm that occurred a few days after was similar in its nature, though it came from a slightly different direction. This one was on the 1st and 2nd of November, and its character was in most respects like that just mentioned. Its centre came more from the westward, passed across the north of Ireland, the Isle of Man, and the north of England; then went over the North Sea toward Denmark.

The general effect of these storms was felt unequally on our islands, and less inland than on the coasts. Lord Wrottesley has shown, by the anemometer at his observatory in Staffordshire, that wind is diminished or checked by its passage over land. The mountain ranges of Wales and Scotland, rising two to four

* See Diagram VII.

thousand feet above the ocean level, must have great power to alter the direction, and probably the velocity of wind, independently of alterations caused by changes of temperature (and Wrottesley *trees* show *their* shelter by Wales).

Very remarkable were the similarities of the storms of the 1st and 2nd of November — the 25th and 26th of October — the series of storms investigated by Dr. Lloyd during ten years; and the observations of Mr. William Stevenson in Berwickshire.* There is no discrepancy between the results of ten years' investigation published by Dr. Lloyd in 'Transactions of the Royal Irish Academy,' the three years' enquiries published by Mr. W. Stevenson, and other investigations which have been brought together during the last few years. They all tell the same story. Gales from the S. and W. are followed by dangerous storms from the N. and E.; and those from the N. and E. do most damage on our coasts. By tracing the facts it is shown that storms which come from the W. and S. come on gradually; but that those from the N. and E. begin suddenly, and often with extraordinary force. The barometer, with these north-eastern storms, does not give direct warning upon this coast, because it ranges higher than with the wind from the opposite quarter. But though the barometer does not give much indication of a NE. storm, the thermometer does; and the known average temperature of every morning in the year affords the means (from the temperature being much above or below the average of the time of the year) of knowing, by comparisons, whether the wind will be northerly or southerly (thanks

* On the Storms which pass over the British Isles, 1853.

to Mr. Glaisher's deductions from more than eighty years' Greenwich observations).*

For a few days before the 'Royal Charter Gale' came on, the thermometer was exceedingly low in most parts of the country: there were northerly winds in some places; also a good deal of snow; with low barometers. There had been a great deal of exceedingly dry and hot weather previously, which made the sudden change to unusually cold weather, with snow, more remarkable (for the season). In the north of Ireland, especially, at that time, thermometers were very low (on the 22nd and 23rd of October). Many days preceding the storm an extraordinary clearness in the atmosphere was noticed in the north of Ireland—the mountains of Scotland were never seen more prominently than they were in the few days preceding those on which it took place. The summer had been remarkable for its warmth; it was exceedingly dry and hot. All over the world, not only in the Arctic but in the Antarctic regions, in Australia, South America, in the West Indies, Bermuda, and elsewhere, auroras and meteors had been unusually prevalent, and they were more remarkable in their features and appearances than had been noticed for many years. There were also extraordinary disturbances of the currents along telegraphic wires, which were so disturbed at times that it was evident there were great electric or magnetic commotions in the atmosphere which could then be traced to no apparent cause. Perhaps these electric disturbances were connected with a peculiar action of the sun upon our atmosphere. Certainly electric wires above ground, and *also submarine wires*, were greatly disturbed, and those disturbances were followed within a

* Electrical indications by telegraph wires, are also becoming available.

few days by great commotions in the atmosphere, and by some remarkable change of weather.*

Instances of singular exceptions to the force of these particular storms occurred. At some places there was little or no wind, though much rain; the barometer fell much, but there was no storm; the wind apparently circulating around those districts did not affect them, while at other places, only a few miles off, the tempest was tremendous.

Many other special atmospheric peculiarities were noticed from 1857 to 1859. The summer of 1859 was hot and dry, the two previous years were similar, and the intervening winters comparatively mild. In 1858 a severe drought prevailed in Africa, America, the West Indies and Australia; and a mild winter followed in Western Europe, but without a sufficiency of rain, so that during spring and summer of 1859, drought was severely felt, especially in England.

Some violent local thunder-storms occurred, in summer, but not till September was there any important rainfall.

In Africa, however, at this time, the rains were excessive, and the rivers swollen greatly; so much that in even the sea entrance of the Bonny there were three feet more water than usual, and other rivers were

* 'Moorgate Street: London, March 28, 1860.

'*Last autumn* we had very remarkable weather. The changes on that occasion were preceded by tremendous "magnetic storms." Very powerful electric currents flew about the earth, and frequently paralysed our circuits, submarine and land.

'*To-day* we have had notable deflections, but not nearly so strong as those of last autumn.

'As these probably indicate a change, I have thought it would be interesting to you to be informed.

'C. F. Varley.'

similarly flooded by heavy rains in the interior of the country.*

Turning to the Arctic Regions, as on one side affecting our temperate zone, while influenced by varying tropical conditions on the other, it was found that in 1860 great quantities of icebergs had accumulated on the coasts of Greenland, to an extent not previously known for about thirty-six years.†

Those masses of ice must have been moved by some abnormal cause, perhaps by the successive heats of 1857–8 and 1859: and such immense quantities — displaced from more northerly localities, indicated an unusual action in the arctic zone, near Iceland and Greenland, if not around the polar region.

Some eminent men of the first authority on such subjects, do not think that 'magnetic storms,'—or even auroras, are directly connected with atmospheric currents, or have any special relation to storms of wind, but there are many facts on record that seem to point toward a different conclusion.

We have adverted to auroral exhibitions as preliminary to those sensibly felt changes which occur subsequently, because, whether really connected or not, their approximate coincidence seems to many persons at least deserving of record. Among the more experienced seamen who have visited many climates, an opinion prevails that lightning, the aurora, meteors, or shooting stars — are indicative of disturbance in the air — and foretell wind or rain, if not both, in no long interval of days.

But as this *may be* like faith in change of weather at the moon's quartering (a mere illusory deduction from

* From the late W. Laird, Esq., of Liverpool.

† From Sir Leopold M'Clintock and Captain Allen Young.

coincidences, many of which must occur within a day or two of limits bounding only one week), it is mentioned now, merely with the view of inducing further notice and information.

That lightning in *high* latitudes, antarctic or arctic, is a certain indication of marked atmospheric disturbance—has been proved.

Besides several auroral, and some meteoric occurrences observed during September and October, 1859, the following are particularly worthy of notice, as having been witnessed at Holyhead, and near Athlone, the evening of the Charter storm.

Sir W. Snow Harris wrote from Plymouth (Nov. 10, 1859),—

'My son, who is on the Holyhead works as a civil engineer, under Mr. Hawkshaw, observed, on the evening of the late great storm, a very interesting phenomenon, which should, I think, be noticed. Here is an extract from his letter: — "Since Wednesday, October 19, heavy winds NNE. to NNW., with bitter storms of hail, sleet, and rain. In the evenings, brilliant lightning, with distant thunder; Welsh hills covered with snow. Monday, October 24, this weather seemed breaking up; wind moderated; weather becoming mild. Tuesday morning, 25th, preceding the gale, fine, with sunshine; light easterly wind, with a thick dirty-looking sky to leeward, as if working up against the wind. The wind freshening a little, but not very much; by and by, during the forenoon, the sky became overcast, with a uniform dull mass of vapour; at 6 P.M. very heavy and dark; breeze had freshened to a strong wind. At 7, a strong gale from east; night *very dark. I was then walking into the town, and was startled by what appeared to be a bright ball of fire directly over my head; the light of it was intense; it pierced* through the heavy mass of vapour which obscured the heavens, and illuminated the whole bay and land with the light of day. This meteor lasted from two to three seconds. *Very soon after* this appearance, the *wind increased to a hurricane*, and the rain came down like a deluge."

'This was the evening and night just before the wreck of the Royal Charter. When we consider that for a week or two previous to this northern hurricane we have had *blood-red streamers* of aurora crossing the sky, and other electrical exhibitions, such a phenomenon is important, and should be recorded.

'I observed, on the 12th, at about 7 to 9 P.M., within a fortnight of the storm, blood-red streamers reaching quite across the zenith, from the western to the eastern horizon — most magnificent.

'This is worthy of remark, as connecting electrical action with the source of such a storm.'

'Holyhead Harbour Works,
'November 20, 1859.

'It is with much pleasure that I send a brief account of the occurrence of a meteor of great brilliancy on the evening of Tuesday, October 25, understanding that a description of the circumstances attending this phenomenon will be acceptable to you. I have heard of other meteors having been seen, both in this country and on the other side of the channel, at about the time of the late heavy gale on October 25 and 26; but having been much engaged lately, I have not been able to make proper enquiries respecting their appearance.

'On Tuesday evening, October 25, at about 7.15 P.M., my attention was suddenly arrested by the appearance, directly over head, of a bright ball of fire, the light of which rapidly diffused itself and illumined the dense mass of vapour then filling the sky to such an extent that objects for a considerable distance around me became visible as by day. At this time it was blowing a rather fresh gale from E., but the wind now began to increase so rapidly that by 9 P.M. a complete hurricane was raging, accompanied by a deluge of rain; the wind continued increasing until it appeared to have reached its climax some time between 2 and 3 A.M. of October 26, flying then into NE., soon after sunrise going into N., and by 10 A.M. to NNW., from which point it blew, if possible, harder than ever until 11 A.M., when the weather began to moderate — the wind, in the afternoon getting round to NW. For about a week, previous to the gale, we had very heavy cold winds varying from NNE. to NNW., attended by bitter squalls of sleet, hail, and rain, varied in the evenings by displays of most dazzling lightning, although the thunder was slight. On Monday, October 24, this weather seemed to be breaking up: the day was fine, with light breezes, and much warmer. The morning of Tuesday, 25, was also fine, with sunshine, and a light breeze from east; but by noon the sky was completely overcast; the wind then gradually freshened, but not much until 6 P.M., when the sky became very dense, and it began to blow fresh, the night setting in pitchy dark. About an hour from this time I observed the meteor I have mentioned.'

That this meteor may have been seen, at the same time, in Ireland, the following letter seems to show: —

'Dublin, November 9, 1859.

'As I understand that any information respecting the storm of the 25th and 26th ultimo is acceptable, I beg to offer the following: —

'I was at Belmullet, in the north-west part of the county of Mayo, in October. There had been several days of beautifully mild weather up to Wednesday, the 19th; on the 20th, there was a change in the weather—some cold showers, and in the evening hail and snow storms, with wind, of short duration. This state of things continued getting worse, the mountains in the neighbourhood being covered with snow; and on Sunday night the roads were two inches deep in snow where they pass through the Erris mountains. On that evening I saw two balls of fire fall to the earth from one of the snow-clouds. I left that part of the county on the 24th, Monday, and proceeded to Castlebar and Ballinrobe, where, though there had been, as I was informed, some snow, there was none on the ground, but the air was very cold. On Tuesday, 25th, I could perceive nothing at all unusual in the appearance of the weather, till, at half-past seven, when in the neighbourhood of Ballinamar and Ballyporeen, about, I should say, twelve or fourteen English miles W. of Athlone, the sky being free from clouds, I saw, in the direction of the Pleiades, a meteor. At first, when I saw it, it was about the size of a star of the first magnitude; it advanced swiftly towards me for about four or five seconds, rapidly increasing in size, and appeared to be coming so straight towards where I was that it created alarm; the colour was an intense white light, similar to the electric spark. At the end of the first four or five seconds it changed colour to a bright ruby red, and it seemed then (but of this I could not speak positively) both to change its course and to lose its velocity. While the red colour remained was not more than one-and-a-half to two seconds. It then burst into about, I should suppose, fifteen or sixteen bright emerald green particles, which, after remaining visible for about two more seconds, disappeared altogether. I saw nothing more that night. I arrived at Athlone about twelve o clock, and up to that period the sky was quite clear and calm, and there was not the slightest appearance of storm. I was much astonished to hear, on my arrival in Dublin, on the night of Wednesday 26th, of the violent storm that had taken place on the coast of Wales.

'From the fact of the meteor appearing to come so directly towards me at first, I should find great difficulty in giving a correct sketch of it. I think after it changed its colour it seemed to have decreased in diameter, and to have taken more the form of a *current* than a solid substance. I am sure the whole duration was not more than ten seconds, or less than seven.

'I should say the direction from where I was — some twelve English miles, as a crow would fly, west of Athlone — was about NW. to NNW.

'Of course it is impossible for me to say at what distance it was from me; but if any other of your correspondents observed it, some idea of its distance from the earth might be arrived at. It was the most beautiful meteor I ever saw, and, with the exception of one I witnessed in the day-time, a few years ago, in Oxfordshire, which passed S. over Southampton, and I believe the whole of France, I have never seen one so large as it appeared toward the period of white light.

'I could not but think that the fall of that meteor had some connection with the storm.

'THOS. T. CARTER.'

Numerous other instances of a similar kind have been mentioned; but none so marked and definitely recorded have as yet reached the writer of these pages.

Few Londoners have yet forgotten the state of the Thames in 1859. Deficiency of water supply during 1858 and 1859, and great evaporation (often to *fourteen* degrees of thermometric difference in Mason's hygrometer), caused a condition of its liquid excessively disagreeable to eye and nose, if not actually pestiferous.

Everywhere a want of water was felt, and this had been of considerable duration. In August the heat reached 92° (in places where usually summer heat is not above 80°), and the temperature of evaporation was 78°, by the same hygrometer.

Hail and snow in the N., clouds and rain in the S., prevailed before the Charter gale; and this wintry weather, on October 21, seems the more remarkable as so rapidly following very warm if not hot weather.

It happened that the late Mr. Laird, who made several notes of this and following days, was in the N. of Ireland, near Garron Tower, on the 21st. It was exceedingly cold, the air remarkably transparent, and the Scotch mountains so distinct that every one noticed their extraordinary visibility. There was much vivid lightning to the southward.

Writing about these same days, the lamented Captain Boyd said,—'On the 19th I was at Belfast, oppressed with heat, in close weather, with small rain. It was like a muggy May day. The next three days I was travelling along the E. coast, cut to the vitals by a piercing N. wind, with snow and hail squalls.'

The barometer continued to fall. Near London that night the temperature was only 22°,* a degree of cold

* In Onslow Square.

not often exceeded during a whole winter, and, on this occasion, the more remarkable, from its sudden succession to very mild, if not warm weather.

On the 22nd there were northerly, mixed with westerly winds — great variations of temperature — within narrow geographic limits—and barometers still low.

On this day a friend said his barometer had fallen very much, and asked what it could be for, as the weather seemed fine. 'We shall hear of much wind and snow in the N. the thermometer is so low,' was replied. That very evening some relations arrived from Yorkshire, whose journey had been delayed on the railway by a very heavy fall of snow, with a strong NE. gale.

On the 23rd much mixture, or contest of air currents was evident, the temperature being even lower (only 18° that night near London), and the barometer remaining low, but unsteady,

The differences of temperature between the E. and W. coasts of England were very remarkable on these days.

On October 24, with a low barometer and excessive differences of temperature (in very limited spaces), there was not much wind, or horizontal movement of air currents. The barometer was low, and almost equally low, therefore generally expressive of an extensive 'area of depression,' a *comparative* vacuity, or diminution of *tension*, necessarily to be filled, or equilibrated, by supplies, or by pressure, from other regions. If this were considered as an extensive, but shallow basin — a lagoon, as it were, on a vast scale, into which two streams were admitted from opposite directions — one having the start of the other — their effects and motions might be rather analogous to the recorded movements of the truly *fluid*, however highly *elastic*, air.

On this day, the 24th, it blew hard along the coast of Portugal, from the southward, but no evidence has been obtained of any storm, or cyclonic commotion at that time in the Atlantic, to the southward or westward of the British Islands,—no proof of a cyclone having originated considerably to the south-westward, and having travelled across much of the ocean.

It was blowing strongly, from the northward, to the W. of Ireland, on the same day (24th), but no ship reported a storm on that or the previous two days.

The gale of October 25 and 26 appears to have had its commencement near the Bay of Biscay, and its conclusion about Norway or the Baltic.

During the night of the 24th and in the morning of October 25, there was no evidence of a storm moving towards England. During the previous days there was a preponderance of northerly wind (polar currents) over and near the British Islands. There was no cyclonic commotion of any kind to the westward or southward. It is very important to mark these facts, because ideas have prevailed that all cyclones crossing our islands have travelled far, even across the Atlantic, from the SW. Plausible theories, and elaborate diagrams have been published, intended to show how cyclones had travelled, not only across the Atlantic Ocean from near the West Indies — but (having there altered their course, or recurved) actually all the way from the coast of Africa.*

That such storms do travel, like eddies in water, a considerable distance, during two, three, or four days, has been demonstrated; but any further extension of

* Redfield's track of the storm of September 1853, and other tracks shown by Sir William Reid, in his invaluable works.

their continuous progress has not hitherto been satisfactorily proved.

Consecutive storms, at the meetings of main currents in zones of latitude, at certain periods, have had appearances of continuity. The familiar instance of the Charles Heddle has so often been adduced as proof of continuing circuitous action or gyration, that it may seem injudicious to doubt the *evidence* ; but knowing how frequently circuits, or cyclones, succeed each other *rapidly*, and how unreliable are some of the earlier logs of events in a storm, written after its cessation: especially respecting directions of wind and courses steered, when waves and storm blasts were the guides, not the oscillating compass (if indeed *that* had not been washed away, as in the Charles Heddle's case)—it does not appear accordant to experience, and enlarged acquaintance with the subject, to imagine that such atmospheric eddies are, *sui generis*, erratic, and so considerably independent as to cross a wide ocean.

At midnight of the 24th and very early on the 25th, a ship named Alipore* was between 46° and 47° N. lat., 13° and 14° W. long. crossing the Bay of Biscay, and, therefore, to the SW. of the British Channel. She had the barometer *then* at 28·98 with the wind at NNE. (true) blowing hard. Clearly (by our charts) there was no storm to the *westward* of her. It was on the other side, though near. Its central part was at the entrance of the Channel, not far from the Land's End. The Alipore had come from the SW. No cyclone or strong wind had passed her from the southward. She *met* a NE. gale. The Alipore could not have overtaken a cyclone, supposing it moving only fifteen miles an hour

* Belonging to Mr. Lindsay, M.P.

to the north-eastward, bodily. Had it travelled from far westward, or south-westward, it must have overtaken and passed that ship. Another ship, the Neikar, passed down Channel to sea, on the day immediately preceding the 25th. She met no storm. A ship belonging to Mr. Laird met none.* More 'crucial' instances could not be desired.

In the morning of the 25th, there was a strong gale from between SW. and SE., over Portugal, Spain, France, and England. This was a warm and very wet wind, which did not raise the then low barometer. Fog, dense clouds, or heavy rain prevailed. At this time a northerly and cold wind was blowing in the Atlantic, and soon it contended against the warm wet, southerly wind, from which its chilling influence caused the precipitation or deposit of vapour, in fog or rain. Both these winds were then blowing toward (afterward around) that area of the region near, in which the barometric depression was greatest.

At this time in Ireland, at Kingstown, there was a very dense fog—so dense that (said Captain Boyd), 'although I fired full charges from guns on the seaward side, the packet (for whose guidance into port I intended them), though not more than a mile distant, heard but a few. The fog-bell was heard by her *only* as the fog 'lifted' for a time, when she was about half a mile from the bell. In the afternoon it cleared to a fresh NE. wind. Not till near midnight had we the gale, fierce and startling, at the ship. The tide was unusually high. The weather had been singularly ominous and threatening

* See p. 319.

some days; so baffling also as to perplex the oldest and most weatherwise pilots.' *

The Channel squadron, under Admiral Elliot, not far from the Eddystone, had a strong SE. gale all the earlier part of the 25th, but about three in the afternoon the wind ceased and the sun shone, though the sea continued 'towering up and breaking.' The barometer on board was then 28·50. Suddenly, after less than half an hour (the barometer *having* begun to rise), a blast swept furiously over the ships, from NW.; and during the next three hours it blew with the force of a hurricane. *There*, then, at three o'clock, was a lull or vortex of the storm, occasioned by an opposition of contrary currents of wind.

At half-past five that afternoon, Mr. Laird was in a railway train, near Reigate, which was struck so forcibly by a violent squall from *south-east*, that he 'thought the train would be capsized. It was so very sudden and heavy, that every one was alarmed.'

* Captain Boyd adverts to a very dense fog. Sir W. Snow Harris quoted —

> 'When morning mists come *from* the hills,
> And the huntsman's horn is free,
> Fine weather reigns : but, woe the time,
> When the mists are *from the sea*.'

Pressure of westerly winds, with a low barometer, raise the sea level, temporarily, round the British Islands. North-easterly winds, with high barometer, have a contrary effect, driving the surface water bodily, seaward, toward the ocean, from comparatively shallow 'soundings.'

Before a gale is felt, its advent is often signified on the shore, or at Light-ships (such as that of the Kish, Cockle Gat, &c.), by the undulation or swell that sets in, caused by the then distant gale. From Valentia we have been telegraphically warned of a coming gale, by heavy swell on the shore, a day before the wind reached even that projecting point.

According to the most reliable accounts the centrical area, where the barometer fell lowest, — *toward* which the winds blew, while distant, and *around* when near, was over Cornwall at about three o'clock in the afternoon of the 25th, and over Lincolnshire at nine next morning, having thus advanced about 250 miles toward the NE. (true) in eighteen hours, *averaging*, therefore, fourteen miles an hour *over land*.

During the advance of this centrical area (a varying space, in which there was heavy rain but very little wind), from Cornwall to Lincolnshire, all places south-eastward of the *line between them* (axial line of the progression shown by charts, or axis of the cyclone) had a storm veering from south-eastward, through the S. to SW., W., and NW.; while all those places NW. of the axial line of progress found the same storm veer round from south-eastward, through E., NE., and N., to the north-westward.

This is beautifully proved by facts, as to general limits and direction; but no proof is given of the contour outline of that area, which, probably, varied considerably as it passed over Cornwall, near the Welsh mountains, or across the Midland counties. Excessive quantities of rain fell on the SE. side of, and within the area, as it progressed north-eastward: but comparatively little or none on the NW. side of that *centrical space*.

So limited was the actual gyration, that it only extended to Kingstown, hardly to Dublin, and did not affect France, beyond a few miles inland. Thus its diameter scarcely reached 400 miles at the utmost, but often was nearer 300 (as the charts show), and therefore while there was a storm from every point of the compass around the progressive vortex above mentioned, the greater part of Ireland, especially its W. coast, and the W. of Scotland, had but little wind. The weather at those places was actually fine.

While there was an area of extreme barometric depression about Cornwall, the Channel, and the 'edge of soundings' toward the Bay of Biscay,—there were two strong currents of wind advancing toward that place, one from the northward, and another, *then* strongest, along Portugal and across France from southward. Their encounter occurred near the Channel entrance, and from that time, on the 25th, the two bodies of atmosphere that had been drawn toward the same place, to restore due equilibrium, mutually pressed on to maintain advance, while their place of gyration, an immense eddy, was forced north-eastward by the overpowering mass and momentum of the southerly (or tropical) current. But this eddy, or cyclone, commenced only on the 25th, and had almost expended its energy on the 27th, near the coast of Norway, having lasted between two and three days, as a definite and (mathematically proved) continuous circulation, or circuit. While the centrical area was moving north-eastward, from 10 to 20 miles an hour, the sensible velocity of wind, estimated (by comparison with measured pressures — and *practical experience* not only then but at other times), could not have been less than 60 nor much more than 100 miles an hour. Probably at the strongest part, in the SE. half of the circuit (which had winds from SE., S., SW., W., and NW.), the velocity was about 80 miles, which, added to near 20 for the cyclone's advance, would make 100;— while on the other side about 60 would be the utmost.*

* With many *exceptions*, caused by local circumstances, and by the very *varying* forces of heavy gales; owing to the great *elasticity* of air, to its

It has been observed that places in Scotland had no remarkable wind during the night of the 25th. When it blew hardest on the northern coasts of Britain, from the eastward, on the 26th, there was but little wind in the British Channel or Ireland. This shows, in connexion with the facts immediately preceding the circular or gyratory movement which commenced near Cornwall, that the nearest quantities of air were pressed by ordinary dynamic laws towards the place of deficiency, and that the two great normal movements of atmosphere, from and towards the pole, were immediately affected by the local and temporary disturbance of equilibrium.

It may be useful to reconsider the progress of this storm with reference to the condition and circumstances of surrounding regions.

It has been noted that the W. coast of Ireland, and a large proportion of that island, were not affected at all. Scotland was not reached on the 25th, but was so subsequently. Neither the Alipore, nor a ship sailing *from* the Channel* (on the 23rd), nor any other vessel, felt its influence *before* the 25th.

As the Neikar left Channel soundings on the 23rd, having been off Scilly on the 21st, she must have crossed any cyclone advancing from the south-westward, or from the Atlantic Ocean.

One of Mr. Laird's African vessels sailed from Liverpool on the 24th. No storm was encountered. Only strong northerly winds were found, as she went southerly

eddyings, and to numerous obstacles to the wind's swift advance horizontally. Remarkable streams, thread-lines, or veins of force have been noticed at Observatories, especially by Dr. Robinson of Armagh, whose anemometric investigations, in conjunction with those of Dr. Lloyd, have been so valuable to their followers.

* Neikar, of Hamburgh, Captain Brolin.

and to the westward. But the barometer was *generally* low, over at least a thousand square miles of sea and land, and had become so *gradually* during many previous days—about a week, indeed.

The *lowest* point then reached, however, was not nearly so low as has been *known*, nor was it even equal in depression, to that caused by the subsequent storm of November 1, which apparent anomaly may have been caused by the rapid shift to the *northward*, and by so much polar current resisting the southerly mass.*

On board the Alipore 28·98 inches was the lowest registered pressure. The Channel squadron noted 28·50. In London, the mercury was rather below 29 inches (reduced to sea level and 32°), rain being incessantly heavy, and wind violent from southward all the earlier part of the night.

At this time the Royal Charter was making way round Anglesea, close in shore, to her fatal anchorage, on the N. side of that island; where the full force of next day's tempest, from the northward, was felt,—and that *doubly*-powered ship, of iron, which had circumnavigated the globe, was destroyed, with nearly all on board, in one short hour, near 7 in the morning. With her power of steam, in addition to that of sails in perfect order, a few hours on the starboard tack, with but little way, would have saved her. So much, at such a time, depends on individual judgment. Another ship but a few miles off, a wooden *sailing* ship, not a *steamer*, the Cumming, and several smaller vessels, acted thus

* Daniell, Chiswick, 28·60 inches. Howard, London, 27·73 inches. Clouston, Orkneys, 27·45 inches. Reid, West Indies, 27·00 inches. Piddington, India, 26·47 inches (?). *Recent* observations in the North Atlantic, in 48° lat., with Kew barometers, have been as low as 28 inches.

— stood to the westward — and not one was wrecked; nor even injured materially.

Unfortunately many cases might be cited of a similar nature, in other storms, where accidents, heavy expenses, or great losses, have been traced to similar errors of judgment.

It has been supposed by many persons, and asserted authoritatively in public prints, that if warnings had been given from lighthouses, or salient points on the coast, the Royal Charter might have been saved.

Now, it is extremely desirable to separate what is practicable, and may be accomplished, under any or some conditions, from that which is only supposed to be so, yet so much wished for, that the means of effecting the object are over-estimated.

The Royal Charter could not have made (seen) the land in time, or sufficiently plain, to make out a signal. It was raining and dark on that afternoon and evening. Holyhead, the high mass of land behind it, and bright lighthouse lights, were distinguishable, but nothing more.

No warning signal from the land could *then* have averted the consequences of erroneous management.

That ship had excellent instruments on board when she left her last port—they *should* have given sufficient notice—but had they not been there, or had their indications been unheeded, those of the heavens should not have been disregarded — overlooked they *could* not have been from any ship — and *were* not by the Cumming, or by numerous coasters.

While the storm was most violent against Anglesea Island, its force was not excessive at Liverpool. The strongest part of the NW. side of the cyclonic circulation did not sweep over that town till shortly before noon of the 26th. Mr. Hartnup wrote thus, 'The storm on October 25 and 26, did not reach Liverpool till about twelve hours subsequent to the wreck of the Royal Charter.

'We had at the Observatory, Liverpool, light winds until 9 A.M. on the 26th, when the gale first reached us. At 11.45 A.M. the extreme pressure was 28lbs. on a square foot, and the greatest horizontal motion, measured hourly, was fifty-seven miles between noon and 1 P.M. The direction of the wind being NNW.' (true).*

The greatest force recorded at Liverpool, was 42 lbs. on the square foot, in December 1852, when the velocity was seventy miles an hour. At Lloyd's, a pressure of thirty-eight has been noted by a similar instrument (in February, 1860), and during the St. Kilda storm of October 1860, the force was 28 lbs. At Lord Wrottesley's observatory, on the summit of a rising ground in Staffordshire, no pressure has been noted exceeding 16 lbs on the square foot, since his lordship first placed an anemometer there; being a remarkable instance of the modifying effect of certain local circumstances, or an inland position. That generally speaking (allowing such *exceptions* as those of local storms or whirlwinds, as, for example, those of Calne,† and Clifton,‡ in 1859), there is much less strength of wind, continuously, in inland places, is shown by the full regular growth and rich foliage of trees, in contrast to the stunted, inclined, and scantily leaved trees of a sea coast, exposed to prevailing winds.

A letter from Dublin said, 'In England you have had

* At the Liverpool Observatory, on one of the northern quays of the Mersey, there are local circumstances common to valleys or low places near heights, influencing the direction as well as strength of wind.

† See Mr. Rowell's very interesting statement.—Oxford, 1860.

‡ Mr. Burder's account.

a tremendous gale (October 25-26). *Here* it was not felt. The barometer fell much, but nothing followed.'

Captain McKillop, R.N., informed us that 'during the gale which swept the coast of England and Wales, when the Royal Charter was lost, a dead calm, and a sharp frost of unusual severity for the country (Ireland), was experienced along the coast, from Westport to Galway, the wind going round from NE. to SE.—when the frost ceased, and a most unusual quantity of rain fell, with light variable winds from S. to W.'

A vessel returning from Iceland* had heavy gales from ENE. (true) between October 23 and 28. This was in latitude 64° to 61°, and longitude 28° to 23°. On the 24th, 25th, 26th, the wind's force was stated at 10 to 11.† During the *whole* of the time when variable or southerly winds prevailed, eastward of Ireland, *as well as* while the polar current alone was felt between Ireland and the Baltic, across France to Spain, and in the Eastern Atlantic—during the whole of this time, the expeditionary vessel Wyman, employed by Colonel Shaffner to explore a submarine track for his intended telegraphic communication, was in northerly (or polar) winds, on four days extremely strong, with a high barometer.

On the 28th the barometer had risen considerably in general, but not to its normal or par height.‡ Winds were variable, and temperatures extremely so. Much rain fell.

On the 29th there was a local cyclone apparently at the meeting of northerly and southerly currents of wind, near the E. coast of Scotland in the North Sea. This had not travelled. It grew and then diminished in one

* The bark Wyman, Captain Baker, with Colonel Shaffner.

† In her log, kept carefully.

‡ Near thirty inches (29·90 to 30·00).

locality. There was much variation in the temperatures of even neighbouring places, showing great mixture of air currents. There was little wind, and that very variable — in many places from the *land to the sea*—the land having been considerably chilled by previous northerly winds, by rain and evaporation, while the sea retained nearly uniform, and, at that time of year, rather high comparative temperature (October 30).* With barometers everywhere low, and falling, ominous skies and increasing warmth, with SE. winds, approaching toward NE., it was seen that another gale might be expected immediately; and next day, 31st, it commenced in Ireland, having been felt heavily in the Atlantic, at a considerable distance, previously.

On November 1, this storm's centre crossed Ireland, the N. of England, and then, on November 2, appeared to diminish rapidly in its strength as it overspread the North Sea, progressing toward Denmark. A more distinctly marked cyclone than this as it appears demonstrated on our charts, it is hard to imagine. That it existed three days is proved, and that its centrical area progressed eastward about fifteen miles an hour, on an average, cannot be far from the truth. The barometer fell before this storm, considerably lower than it did before its more generally remarked precursor, and the thermometer was much higher. These indications showed preponderance of the southerly (tropical) element over that from the polar direction ; and that the meeting place of gyration, or node, was therefore further toward the North.

That its direction of progress should have been nearer eastward, across the British Isles, instead of more

* Averaging then 48°.

northerly (in consequence of such southern predominance), may have been a consequence of the Scottish mountains, three to four thousand feet high, impeding such a course as *would* have been taken across open sea. Probably Norway had influence, similarly.

At the Board of Trade, at Kew, and at Brompton, the lowest barometrical reading in the night of October 31, or morning of November 1, was 28·80, the thermometer in open air being then 50. It *has* been stated already that *there* the lowest on the night of the 25th was 29·00 (sea level and 32°), and the temperature then 25°. Two aneroid barometers, considered to be good instruments, near Lake Windemere, fell to 28·09 and 27·70 (approximately reduced to sea level) the night of the 31st. The first of these showed 28·77, nearly (reduced) the night of October 25.*

On the 29th, Colonel Rogers' barometer had fallen to 28·42, and at 11 P.M. on the 31st to 28·27; but nothing of consequence followed besides rain; no strong wind. At 8 next morning his barometer showed 28·09, and at 3 P.M. the sky had cleared—the glass was rising; Windermere had felt no storm, and did not experience any strength of wind afterwards. This is by no means a singular case, but is quoted here as one of the well-marked exceptional anomalies that occurred during this storm of November 1, as well as that of October 25, on which occasion also, Lake Windermere escaped undisturbed. Colonel Rogers said of that time (Tuesday night, October 25):—'My aneroid fell to 28·60 † at

* From Captain Hemming, H.I.C.S., Colonel Rogers, and Captain Crowe. Reduced to sea level and 32°; 156 and 200 feet having been estimated as their respective elevations.

† 28·77 reduced to mean sea level, or *half-tide* height, and to the freezing point of Fahrenheit.

night. Rain fell, but no remarkable wind occurred. It was fresh and gusty, but at no time severe.' Similar exceptions occurred in Ireland, Wales, and Scotland; in some degree resulting, probably, from sheltering or deflecting effects of high land, but chiefly from the very diversified action of violent winds, expanding and expended, in some places, but so extremely compressed (as it were) and elastic at others, that heavy weights are lifted, large trees snapped asunder, or laid prostrate, and strong buildings unroofed.

Of this other heavy gale which followed on October 31 and November 1, it was recorded that on October 31, there was a circulation of wind around a place about 200 miles W. of Ireland; barometers indicating very diminished pressure everywhere, but particularly to the south-westward of Ireland, and thermometers showing great differences of temperature. Extreme cloudiness, much fog, and a good deal of rain prevailed during the 30th and 31st. It became evident that a southerly gale was impending. Barometers near London fell to 28·76 at midnight of the 31st, the thermometer, exposed, being then 50°. (Near Lake Windermere 28·09 was the reduced height soon after that time.)

A steamer, in the Channel, on her passage to Cork, during this night (31st) and the following day, thus describes the weather:—

'On Monday (31st) and Tuesday following, we had a very severe gale in the English Channel:—Noon, October 31, wind SE. fresh, dark gloomy weather, barometer 29·0 falling. At 4 P.M. increasing wind with rain at times. Barometer falling, dark and cloudy weather at 9 P.M. In a heavy arched squall of both wind and rain, attended with vivid flashes of lightning, the wind changed to WNW. Midnight, blowing severe gale from W., with low white haze, over which showed a clear sky. At 1.30 A.M. the appearance of the western horizon was like thick smoke, the stars visible to the eye like balls of fire through the black haze, very vivid lightning from the same quarter.

'Barometer then down to 28·50. There was at this moment a lull, and the wind felt quite warm (we had felt similar heated wind in West India hurricanes, also in the tropical belt of calms during heavy squalls, more particularly when accompanied by lightning, near the Line). A fierce gale then commenced, the ship could not be steered, and fell off broadside to wind and sea (then running very high), and rolling the lee paddlebox nearly under water; the gale so continued unabated till daylight of Tuesday, with fierce gusts. On the horizon a white haze was visible about masthead high, partly drift or water blown up from the surface. With this appearance the gale lasted all the day, till at 4 P.M. we perceived a lull, and found the barometer inclined to rise. At 6 P.M. between fierce squalls, and lulls at intervals, the gale moderated to a strong wind, with sea decreasing.'

A letter from Bute Docks, Cardiff, stated:—'The gale of November 1, began here at noon of the 31st. The wind was then E. (magnetic). It veered round to the SSW. blowing heavily. At midnight it was WSW. (SW. true) with loud thunder and lightning, and terrific squalls, with heavy rain; and so it continued till after noon of the 1st, when the gale abated *here*. The heaviest of it was from WSW. (SW. true).'*

At Dublin and at Kingstown, at 10 A.M, on the 31st, it was blowing strong from the NE., at sunset a gale

* Cardiff is sheltered from NW. by Welsh mountains.

from ESE. with rain,* at 11 P.M, from NW., with a great deal of lightning, and at 10 A.M. on the first from W.

It blew hard all the morning of the 1st; a good barometer in Dublin fell to 28·010, at 8 A.M, while the wind was W.†

At Liverpool the extreme pressure shown by the Observatory wind plate was only 14lbs. on a square foot. This was at 8 A.M., the wind being then WSW. true, (west magnetic). The utmost hourly horizontal motion that day was but forty miles, showing that the greatest force of that gale did not reach the entrance of the Mersey.

At this time the Wyman (already mentioned as chartered for exploring a northern submarine line) was near 62° latitude, and 18° longitude, in a very heavy south-east gale.

The much-lamented Captain Boyd wrote that the night of the 29th was fine at Kingstown; on the 30th the weather was gloomy and threatening, on the 31st a strong gale was blowing from NE., while at Cork he heard it was SE. (magnetic). Between 3 and 4 P.M. on that day the barometer fell, at Kingstown, from 29·30 to 29·00 in less than one hour, the wind being *then* south-westward. The tides were much affected.

On November 1, at 2 P.M. the barometer afloat at Kingstown showed 28·50. Heavy NW. gales followed at Cork, likewise thunder, with lightning and rain. Our charts show a very remarkable rotation of wind around the Solway Firth and the 'Merse' of Berwick. That Circuit or gyration had progressed across the north of Ireland from at least two hundred miles to the west-

* More probably ENE. (?)

† If a hundred feet above the sea level, this would be about 28·10 inches.

ward (as several ships' logs prove), and diminished or dispersed toward the Baltic, apparently; but with respect to its exact direction and condition, after reaching the North Sea, facts are yet wanting to demonstrate all the particulars accurately: though no information has been obtained of its continuance beyond Denmark and Norway.

The great range of Norwegian mountains, seven to eight thousand feet above the sea, and always capped with snow, must have much influence over adjacent areas of atmosphere.

CHAPTER XXI

A few Extreme Cases witnessed by the Author — River Plata — Brazil — Remarkable Effects of Lightning — Pampero — Magellan Strait — Harbour of Mercy — Want of Common Precautions — Extraordinary Escape — Force and effect of very large Waves in Open Oceans.

A FEW instances of force, effect, and nature of heavily tempestuous winds, of lightning, and of waves, *personally* observed by the author, shall now be offered, in concluding this fragmentary weather book.

At Buenos Ayres, in 1820, a storm from the SE. drove ashore all the smaller vessels anchored in the inner roads,—and among the trees in adjacent low grounds many coasting craft (bilandras) were found irrecoverably fixed next day. The water of the river (Plata) having risen two fathoms above its usual level, small vessels were floated nearly a mile inland, over low level tracts.

In the outer roads (*excellent* holding ground), H.M.S. Owen Glendower, with topmasts and lower yards down, brought four anchors ahead — and H.M.S. Icarus drove about a mile, notwithstanding similar precautions. In Buenos Ayres, it was difficult to cross the street, so furious was the wind. Not many years before, a violent wind from northward drove the inner waters of Uruguay and Paraguay so much outward that all the vessels off Buenos Ayres grounded (or stuck on the mud), and carts were driven out alongside ships, stranded at their anchorages.

These effects happened in the roads where usually there are from four to two fathoms of water. A northerly wind always lowers the river, a southerly raises its level at least one or two fathoms. All the country near that extensively wide and very long river being low, without hills, near the water, every wind that blows is felt to the utmost, and in so broad yet shallow an estuary, atmospheric pressure has great influence, so much indeed that the *height* of water is always noticed by the seafaring people, pilots and others, as indicative of the coming wind and weather.

In no part of the world, perhaps, is there more lightning at times. In H.M.S. Thetis, at sea off the Plata, the whole heavens seemed (on one occasion) like an immense metal foundry, so incessant and diversified were the lightning flashes in every direction, even *from the sea* upward. Repeatedly lightning struck the *water* between that ship and another vessel about a mile distant. Indeed the whole vault above was illumined, in every direction, though black clouds shut out every star. So grand a sight the writer never witnessed. Much rain, at times, poured down. Neither ship was struck, though forked lightning was seen to strike the water in every direction, during about three hours of illuminated darkness, from 9 o'clock till midnight.

Ascending lightning has but seldom been seen, but there is evidence of its occurrence at times. The writer *witnessed one* instance, among many he has heard of, besides the above described. H.M.S. Hind was at single anchor off Corfu, in the Mediterranean, in 1823. The day was fine, but cloudy and hot. All was quiet till a shock startled every one, an explosion, and a smell of sulphur, which seemed to be from a gun burst. But nothing was visibly changed, though two men, who had been sitting on the chain cable where it passed along the deck, were thrown off numbed, and a strong smell of sulphur came from the main hatchway out of the chain cable locker. The conclusion *seemed* to be irresistible that lightning had entered by the chain cable, *from* the earth below the sea. No trace of it was evident on the masts or bowsprit, but it *was felt* along the chain.

Neither the Hind nor the Thetis had any kind of conductors then *fixed*, though there were copper chains in boxes *below — as usual*.

In 1827, that frigate was struck in Rio de Janeiro harbour, when the fore-topmast, and foremast were ruined. In an instant the topmast was like a faggot of reeds — so shivered was it throughout.

Not long after this happened, H.M.S. Heron (then commanded by the Hon. Frederick W. Grey*) lost foremast and other spars, by lightning, in the river Plata.

It was not till 1829 that any ship was secured against that destructive element by fixed and efficient conductors. In 1831, the writer of this account was thought very unwise in applying for, and retaining Snow Harris's conductors in all the masts, bowsprit, and even the flying jibboom of the Beagle, a gunbrig of 235 tons. The result, however, was, that during ten subsequent years, in all quarters of the world, though repeatedly struck by lightning, no damage was ever done by it, not a mark even was ever left.

On one occasion, at night (also in the Plata), a violent stroke shook the little vessel, with startling force. Up flew the purser, out of a sound sleep, asking what *had*

* Now senior Sea Lord of the Admiralty.

happened. The lightning conductor passed *close to his head*, as he lay asleep in his fixed bed place. The *shock* had waked him, but not a trace of it was *visible*. To those on deck, the main-mast had seemed in a *blaze*.

To show how even a common want of experience, or how *incautiousness* from want of thought, may cause not only destruction of property, delay, and expense, but loss of life—while, on the other hand, due precaution and acquired knowledge, may, humanly speaking, be the means of great saving — two instances shall here be briefly mentioned.

In 1829, the writer was approaching Maldonado harbour, in the Plata, when a *Pampero* was threatening. Signs in the sky, barometric evidence, and temperatures shewed what was coming, but want of faith in such indications, and the impatience of a very young commander, in sight of his admiral's flagship, induced disregard, and too *late* an attempt to shorten sail sufficiently. Topmasts and jib-boom were blown away, the vessel just saved from foundering (being almost on her beam ends) by cutting away both anchors, and letting the cables run out to the clinch (which brought her head to wind and righted), while two fine fellows, blown from aloft, swam hard for their lives, but were immediately overwhelmed by the sea which was torn along, not in 'spoondrift' or spray, but in a dense cloud of broken water.

An instance of a contrary kind happened to the same person, then comparatively experienced, in 1846. He was in a merchant ship — the David Malcolm, anchored in the harbour of Mercy,* at the westernmost end of Magellan Strait. Land-locked in a small and smooth water

* *Separation* harbour — of Wallis and Carteret.

harbour, under very lofty and steep ranges of heights, the captain of that ship (then homeward bound from New Zealand) thought the shortest scope of cable, and the lightest anchor quite sufficient. He neither had, nor cared for, a barometer. This man had kept no log going while crossing the ocean, *if at any time*, but navigated by one indifferent chronometer, which his steward noted, *below*, when this character *stamped* on the deck—*twice* to look out, and then *once* for a *single sight* (observation) of the sun; no more!

Anchored thus, with all yards and masts aloft, as arrived from sea, he would have gone to sleep, as usual, on April 11, though the writer's two sympiesometers then told *him* a storm approached, and by *great* exertion he did induce this Captain, *Cable* by name, to send down light spars, point yards, and veer chain; besides getting a second anchor ready. Then the skipper made himself happy, in his own peculiar way, below—and was soon too sound asleep, to be seen again that night.

Fast, and to a low degree, the monitors sunk, till at midnight they were very low, twenty-eight inches and a fraction. Aided by a good officer and a few willing hands, the writer (whose family were on board) got the second anchor let go, cable veered, and then waited. The night was beautiful, clear and still moonlight. Every one thought him mistaken. At about two o'clock, as he was watching, in confidence, a roar was heard on the western heights:* and in a few minutes that ship was nearer on her beam ends than at any time, when under sail, on her passages. A white dense cloud of driven water, as high as the lower yards, came with the

* 1,200 to 2,000 feet above the sea, and very precipitous—closely land-locking three sides of the small harbour.

torrent of wind, and nothing could be seen — or heard but the roar, till the ship righted as she swung to her anchors, dragging them both across the harbour, but *just* holding on, within a stone's throw of sharp granite rocks astern, at some distance from land, at the most exposed outer point near the harbour. Had that ship been taken unprepared, not a soul would have been saved, in human probability; only God's providence could have rescued any one in so desolate, wild, and savage a country.

When the chain cables were hove in, after the *first* storm, it was discovered that the chain by which that ship was held against the first blast had parted close to the bows, whirled around the other chain, then *straitened out*, slipped along, and so jammed its bare end, with a hitch, on the then *dragging* second anchor, that during the heaviest weight of wind that ship was held by *two* chain cables '*an end*' — the best anchor in the ground, and a lighter one hanging as a *weight* between it and the ship — probably (with the action of a *spring*) giving the chain something like the elasticity of a hempen cable. By one half hitch only was that first cable nipped to the wooden anchor stock. And as it was hove to the bows — so *slight* was its hold — that a *sudden* exclamation of 'avast heaving,' and *instantly* passing a rope through the *then slipping* chain, saved that ship from being *adrift* — close to rocks. In another *moment* — the then lifted anchor — holding up the *half*-hitched chain — and swinging round — would have *dropped* it — and the other anchor must have been *lost* — with a chain cable then holding the ship, in alternate lulls and squalls.

We all gave *earnest* thanks for our Providential preservation. For many days afterward it was impossible to move out of that harbour — to us, as to others of former time, indeed one 'of Mercy.'

Moored close under high steep land, in still water, so powerful were the hurricane squalls that blew down from those ridges which alone separated us from the fury of a tempestuous ocean, that sometimes the ship—though then made as snug as possible — was hove over to one side — and then again, as she swung suddenly round, *down* on the other — as if a light boat, instead of being a heavy, *deeply laden*, *teak-built*, and very stiff ship of six hundred tons.

From that time, stormy weather, a succession of heavy gales, prevailed during many days—after which the David Malcolm passed through the Strait of Magellan, and continued a very tediously slow passage to England.

Instances enough have been now given of the force of wind. Perhaps a few words should be added about the power of *water*, as a sea, or swell.

Ordinary passages, across Oceans, even to India or Australia, are so frequently made without encountering any *remarkably* high seas, that many persons, even many of those who have, nominally, been seafarers a long time, have never seen really great seas, in very heavy storms. Such huge waves as those make the very largest ships seem small, and jeopardised, as they are tossed about like great boats. When a three-decker is in a gale of wind with a very high and large sea (such as the St. Vincent was in with Sir Charles Napier in the Bay of Biscay, or the Great Eastern, off Cape Clear, in the Atlantic), even such a huge ship is hidden between two seas, from other ships near her. Only mast-heads are mutually visible, at times, of ships not half a mile distant. When such seas strike a ship forcibly they sweep her along (like a boat by a common wave), if freely yielding and lurching over, with the sea, not rising *against*, or *resisting* it;—as when this occurs, heavy *shocks* are received, and great damage is often done.

In such a sea the writer witnessed chain-plates started, in a very fine, *easy sea-boat*— the Thetis, and a main deck bow gun, then lashed abreast of the mainmast (having been run in, and well secured there), turned round in the lashings, carriage upwards, by the shock of a great sea, one among many that were *at least* sixty feet, vertically, from crest to lowest trough level.

In such movements, there is not only the heel or lurch, but a great *send*, with the wave, that gives *momentum*, not only to the ship but to everything on board: and, of course anything *free to move*, will *continue* to do so, *after* the impelling force has ceased, or is become contrary;— whence the difficulty of *checking* motions, and preventing injuries, or inconvenience on board ship, in a *seaway*: when there are the rolling, pitching, *'scending* and *yawing*, besides *sending* motions due to *momentum*.

APPENDIX.

A

ARRANGEMENTS FOR METEOROLOGIC TELEGRAPHY.

METEOROLOGIC OFFICE:
2 Parliament Street, London, S.W.

SIR,

I send the Meteorologic instruments specified, with directions for their use.

Will you have the goodness to read the cautionary instructions about *placing* these instruments very carefully;—before unpacking and suspending them (see 'Extracts from Barometer Manual' in page 25).

The aid of an optician may be serviceable in fixing and first reading the barometers, two of which should be suspended near each other, for comparisons.

A third is intended as a reserve, in case of an accident occurring to one of the others.

The thermometers should be taken *carefully** from their cases, and suspended, singly, near each other.

Reductions and corrections will be made in this office (except in a few *special* cases).

You will be expected to send the Observations *as read off* without alteration. We have the scale corrections of each instrument, and shall have *your elevation above the sea,* in accordance with instructions now transmitted.

I am faithfully,

————————
Station.

* To do this easily, press on the circular guard and strap of metal, while pulling out the thermometer.

Instructions.

1. Two barometers should be suspended in a room; one being a check on the other.*

2. Two thermometers should be fixed *outside* the house, at the north side, and a third near them, with its bulb wet, or, rather, *moistened* (as explained in the Barometer Manual).

3. Once a day, at eight in the morning, or as soon after as possible, the rainfall (R), the highest or lowest extreme of the mercury in the barometer, and in the *exposed* thermometer, since last report (as far as may have been noticed or can be ascertained by the reporter), the reading of one barometer (B), and its attached thermometer, the general character of the weather since the *last* report; the reading of the exposed dry thermometer (E), the difference of the damp or moistened thermometer (D), the wind direction at that time (W), its estimated force (F), the character of the weather at that time (I), and the state of the sea (S); should be telegraphed to the Meteorologic Office, in accordance with the following explanations:—

4. Each telegram will usually consist of five or six groups of figures (each group containing five figures), and perhaps a few words.

5. No alterations or reductions are to be made by the observer, who will transmit them as 'read off' (except in a few *special* cases).

Rainfall (if any).

6. The first group will be 'rainfall' (R), omitting decimal points. (See 12, in p. 4.)

With each morning report, when rain enough has fallen to be *measurable*, its duration, in hours, from 1 to 24 (or to 48, after Sunday or a holiday), should be in the two first places of a group, or word, of five figures; a cypher being before 1 to 9. Quantity of rain, &c., should be shown, by the three last figures of five, as inches and two places of decimals. Thus, if rain has prevailed about eight hours since last report, and an inch

* The distinguishing number of whichever is used, and its estimated height above high water, should be made known, by telegraph, the first day: and *occasionally* afterwards, when requisite.

and half of water is in the gage, the group should be 08150; if thirteen hours, with two inches and five hundredths, the group should be 13205; if three hours and thirteen hundredths, then 03013.*

Highest or lowest Extreme.

7. The second group will show the highest or lowest extreme (the *most* remarkable) of the mercury in barometer (B), and in *exposed* thermometer (E), since *last* report by telegraph, whether recent or otherwise.

B will have the three *first* places for *last* integer and two first decimals; E will have the *two* last figures for degrees (only) of exposed dry thermometer. Thus, supposing B=30·142 and E=59, the telegraphic group should be 01459; or if B=30·147 and E=59·8, it should be 01560 (7 and also 8 being more than half).

Barometer (B), *omitting points.*

8. The third group will be the height of the barometer (B), read to two places of decimals, but omitting first figure, and adding two figures for the temperature of the attached thermometer, to degrees only; thus, 90462.

9. The fourth group should express the *extreme*, not general character of wind and weather (D, F, I) *only*, *since* the last report, or during the whole time elapsed since the *last* hour of reporting (as far as may have been noticed or can be ascertained by the reporter).

The first two figures will show direction of wind (D); the third and fourth figures, force (F); and the last figure, character (I). Thus, supposing D=10, F=6, and I=6 (overcast), the telegraphic group should be 10066.

Thermometers E *and* D *with Direction of Wind* (W).

10. In the fifth group the first three figures will show the readings of the exposed thermometer (E) and its difference above the damp one (D), and the two last figures the direction of wind (W) given by the *true* meridian (by the sun or pole star, by a chart, or by the world).

* See additional explanation, under 'Rain and Fog,' in page 6.

The direction of the wind will always be given in figures—1 to 32—North being 32, East 8, South 16, West 24, and so, proportionally, for the intermediate points (a cypher being placed *before* the figure indicating the direction when *less than* 10 (=N. by E. to E. by S.). Thus, supposing E=54, M=51, and D=8, the telegraphic word will be 54308.

Force of Wind (F).

11. In the sixth group, the first two figures will show the estimated force of the wind (F) from 1 to 12, supposing 1 to represent the lightest breeze, and 12 a hurricane (a cypher being placed *before* the figure indicating force when it is less than 10).

Amount of Cloud (C).

The third figure giving the estimated amount of cloud (C) from 1 to 9.

Character of Weather—Initial I.

The fourth figure indicating the character of the weather (I), according to the abridged 'Beaufort scale.'

Sea-Disturbance (S).

And the fifth figure the amount of 'sea disturbance' (S) from 1 to 9. Thus, supposing F=2, C=3, I=1, and S=4, the telegraphic word will be 02314.

12. *No decimal points* should be noted in the telegrams. Using the method just described, they are unnecessary: while each decimal point *might* be counted as a word or figure, and thus increase expense.

13. *Five* figures should be placed invariably for *each word*, cyphers being used to keep the figures in their proper relative places; the cypher being very carefully placed, and always *before* the unit, or *other cypher, to which it refers*, when used for this purpose.

14. Special occasional information, when necessary, should be transmitted in the common manner by actual words, in addition to the above described groups; but *abbreviations* should be made, by substituting such letters, for words, as

are used in the scales to which reference is made in these directions.

15. No regular Meteorologic *Telegram* is required to be forwarded on *Sundays* or official holidays, but one reading of instruments, and a regular notice of the previous weather, &c., should be taken on such occasions, and recorded, with other daily ordinary observations, in a telegram, which should be sent by next post.

16. It will be understood that telegrams should be *despatched* from their *starting* points (if practicable) at eight o'clock in the morning, and from selected *special* stations at two in the afternoon. To effect this, the observations should be made, and the summaries of recent weather well considered, before those hours arrive. The *slight* change that *may* occur, in about a quarter of an hour, is of little importance compared with the real advantage to the public of *early* and *sufficiently* precise information.

17. Reporters should send *extra* telegrams, *at times*, on their own responsibility, when the barometer is falling much or rapidly;—say, *having* fallen *nearly* one-tenth of an inch, *hourly*, for more than two hours, since the last weather report was sent to London.

18. All telegrams, from *all* stations, should have five or *six* groups of figures in the morning; but in the afternoon, from the *special* stations, fewer may be transmitted.

19. It should be clearly understood that the first and second groups of figures refer to the *whole interval* of time (whether only a *few hours*, or one or two days and nights, as from Saturday to Monday) elapsed since the *last* official telegram, whether a regular or an *extra* report.

20. The reports of weather just recently prevailing, and the extreme ranges between the last two *transmitted* records, are very valuable; and it is earnestly hoped that not only individual abilities and judgement will be exercised, but also that conclusions may be drawn from the opinions of others, especially seafaring persons, shepherds, fishermen, gardeners, or agriculturists.

21. *When reports are delayed* beyond such a time as would enable them to be published in their proper order, they should

be sent by the next post: *not* by telegraph, as in such cases they can be used only for record, and subsequent inter-comparison.

22. Although reporters are not on duty beyond a certain time of the day, it is hoped that *general*, and occasionally *special*, information will be obtained by them from other persons, which may much enhance the value of their communications, and will be duly estimated in future arrangements, as well as in recommendations to favourable consideration.

Rain and Fog.

23. Portable rain gages should be placed on the ground, or any position exposed to a free fall of rain, snow, or hail, where neither buildings, nor walls, nor trees shelter, or cause eddies of wind. They should be supported by a frame, or other means, admitting daily *emptying*, but preventing their being blown down.

24. Generally, on or near the ground is preferable to an artificial elevation; but, if so raised, height above ground should be registered and officially reported.

25. From day to day, in the morning, the quantity of water from rain, snow, or hail (melted) should be measured very carefully and recorded.

26. It is not expected that exact *duration* of rain, snow, hail, or fog can be *usually* registered, but very near approximations may be made by collecting the notices of various persons. When fog continues for an hour or more, its duration and character should be registered and telegraphed with the next usual *morning* report, thus:—'Five hours of very thick fog* till seven p.m.;' or, 'Three hours of light fog still continuing,'† &c.

27. The measuring glass or tube should be kept apart from the gage, which should not be opened oftener than once a day (except on special occasions of heavy rain, thick snow, or much hail, in a comparatively short time).

The glass tube (supplied in duplicate) is graduated to inches

* Or, 5 ff till 7 p.m.

† Or, 3 f continuing.

and decimals. The marks are fixed by actual trial, and comparison with another kind of rain gage duly verified. They are artificial inches. This tube should be placed upright in the gage, with its upper end open; then a thumb or finger *pressed* on the upper aperture, while the tube is lifted gently out, holding in the lower part a small quantity of water, the upper edge of which is at the mark to be read off, and registered. Smaller decimals of an inch may be estimated by eye. The rain gage should then be completely emptied, and carefully refixed.

Storm-Warning Signals.

28. A staff and two canvass shapes being provided, the following use may be made of them occasionally; perhaps once or twice in a month, on a yearly average.

One shape, that of a drum (or cylinder), has the appearance of a black square of (not less than) three feet (seen from any point of view) when suspended.

The other shape, a cone (not less than) three feet high, appears triangular (from any point of view) when suspended.

A cone, with the point upwards, shows that a gale is *probable*; at first from the *northward.* North Cone.

A cone, with the point downwards, shows that a gale is *probable*; at first from the *southward.* South Cone.

A drum, alone, shows that stormy winds may be expected, from more than one quarter, successively.

A cone *and* drum give warning of *dangerous* winds, the probable *first* direction being shown by the position of the cone—point up, above the drum, for northerly (or polar) wind, WNW. by the N., to ESE.; point down, and below the drum, for southerly (or tropical) ESE. by the S., to WNW.

29. A conspicuous place should be selected for signalling; near the telegraph station; whence other places may repeat the signal, or be warned; and, if practicable, the signal staff or pole should be in view of seafaring persons, besides the nearest Coast-guard Station.

When both these objects cannot be attained without too great distance from the telegraph station, one only—that of visibility to some of the seafaring community—should be secured; and in this case a *message* should be sent to the nearest Coast-guard.

30. Whenever such a signal is shown (in consequence of a telegram from London) it should be kept up, distinctly, till dusk of *that day only*, unless otherwise specially directed.

31. These cautionary signals advert to winds during some part of the next night and two or three days; therefore due *vigilance* should prevail (until the weather is again settled), but without deferring *departures*, or any other operations, *unnecessarily*.

32. More extended notice may be given by *local interests* and *authorities*, as London can only warn principal outports. The Coast-guard will repeat the warning as far as means allow, and *extension* of such cautionary notices can be effected by *private* assistance along the most *frequented* shores, where alone they are required.

33. When a cautionary telegram is *received* at any place *after* three o'clock p.m., it should be followed by a NIGHT SIGNAL, which should be hoisted at dusk, and kept up till about nine o'clock, or even later, till towards midnight.

NIGHT SIGNALS.

34. Three, or four, signal lanterns are intended to be hoisted, as shown in the following diagram.

35. They should be kept up from dusk, or the time of receiving a warning telegram, until late the same evening; even till near *midnight*, if thought advisable on the spot, but not after that time.

36. A person should be employed to clean, trim, hoist, keep alight, take care of, and return these signal lanterns, for which service payment for each night of actual use will be made. This payment is intended to be an *average*, whether three or four lanterns are hoisted, and for whatever time shown lighted.

37. Spreaders, or yards, not less than four or five feet long, should be provided at each station, with good durable rope fittings.

38. Larger signal shapes, and better lanterns, masts *with yards*, and greater distances between the lights of a signal, would be desirable—though, at present, too expensive for general establishment.

39. Telegrams will not be sent on Sundays, except on *emer-*

gencies (seldom occurring), and then, of course, only to those stations open at the time; but as vigilance will always prevail, by night as well as by day, on the part of those officers who are interested in the Meteorologic Department, no *extensive* change of weather, or *generally* dangerous atmospheric commotion, ought to be unforeseen by them, nor should delay occur *at any time* in telegraphing to the coasts threatened, since attempting to prevent unnecessary risk of human life is the important object of these measures.

40. It should be remembered that only the greater and more *general* disturbances of the atmosphere can be made known by this method, not *merely local* or sudden changes which are not felt at a certain distance, and do not, therefore, affect other localities. Local changes should be indicated to observers at such places, by their own instruments, by signs of the weather, —and by due attention to the published Weather Reports.

41. Much *inequality* of electricity, atmospheric pressure (*tension*), or temperature; great fall or rise of the barometer; sudden or rapid alternations; great falls of rain or snow, foretell more or less *strong* wind, with its usual accompaniments, either in some places only, or throughout an extensive area of hundreds, if not thousands, of miles: some tracts, however, remaining almost unaffected, unless by rain.

42. Speaking *generally*, there is less occasion to give warning of *southerly* gales, by signals, than of northerly; because those from the southward are preceded by notable signs of the atmosphere, such as a falling barometer, and a temperature higher than usual *at the season*: whereas, on the contrary, dangerous storms from a polar quarter (NW. to N. and easterly) are *sometimes* sudden, and preceded by a *rising* barometer, which may mislead persons, especially if accompanied by a temporary lull of a day or two, with a fallacious appearance of fine weather. This fallacy is caused by a circuitous movement of wind following (influencing by checking and then overpowering), or uniting with a preceding similar cyclonic sweep.

43. It should be kept in mind that these signals are merely *cautionary*, to give notice of much atmospheric disturbance over some considerable part of the British Islands; and that they are not in the least degree *compulsory*, or intended to interfere with individual judgement on any occasion.

North Cone. South Cone. Drum. *Probable Heavy Gale or Storm*

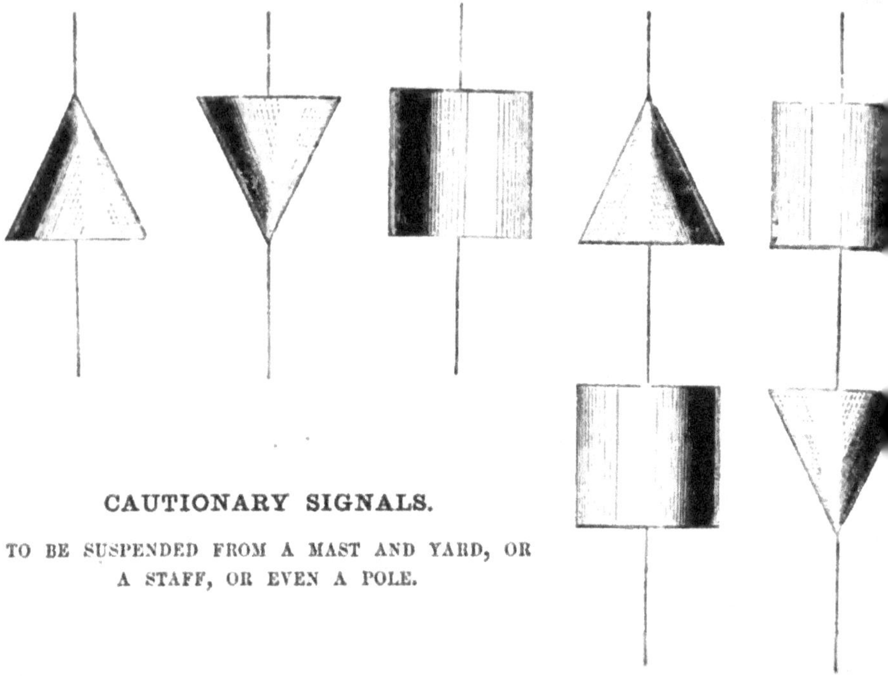

CAUTIONARY SIGNALS.

TO BE SUSPENDED FROM A MAST AND YARD, OR A STAFF, OR EVEN A POLE.

Gale probably from the Northward. — Gale probably from the Southward. — Gales successively. — Dangerous Winds probably at first from the Northward. — Dangerous Win[ds] probably at fir[st] from the Southw[ard].

NIGHT SIGNALS.

(instead of the above)

LIGHTS IN TRIANGLE OR SQUARE.

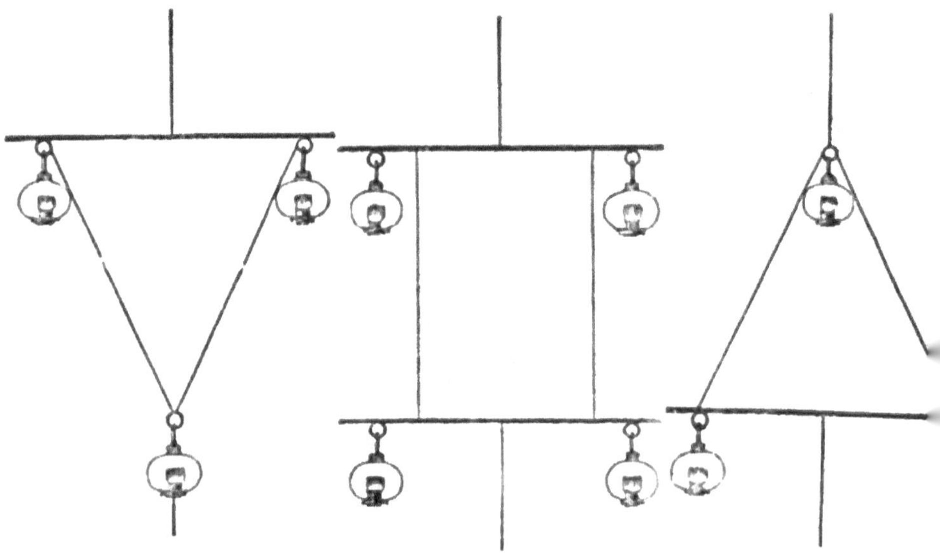

Four lanterns and two yards, each not less than four feet long, will be sufficient — as only one signal will be used at nigh[t].
These signals may be made with any lanterns, showing either white, or any colour, but *alike*.
Red is most eligible. Lamps are preferable to candles. The halyards should be good rope, and protected from chafi[ng].
The lanterns should hang *at least* three feet apart.

WEATHER REPORT, 1862.

28th July 8 A.M. Monday.	B	E	D	W	F	X	C	I	H	R	S
Nairn	29·84	55	1	SW.	5	7	1	b	2	0·23	2
Aberdeen	29·77	56	6	SW.	5	7	4	c	—	—	2
Leith	29·83	59	5	SW.	6	6	4	m	—	—	3
Berwick	30·00	54	3	SE.	4	3	4	b	—	—	1
Ardrossan	29·99	55	2	NW.	5	6	7	o	2	0·13	4
Portrush	30·03	54	2	SW.	4	1	2	b	—	—	3
Galway	30·16	56	2	Z.	0	6	3	b	—	—	1
Valentia	30·22	63	7	WNW.	1	4	2	b	—	—	4
Queenstown	30·18	58	3	NW.	1	3	1	b	—	—	1
Holyhead	30·11	57	4	WSW.	3	3	3	c	—	—	3
Liverpool	30·15	57	1	WSW.	3	3	6	c	—	—	2
Pembroke	30·18	57	4	NW.	1	2	5	b	—	—	1
Penzance	30·22	60	1	NNE.	2	4	4	c	—	—	2
Plymouth	30·17	58	5	NW.	1	5	3	b	—	—	1
Jersey	30·20	61	4	N.	3	1	4	c	—	—	2
Weymouth	30·18	61	3	WSW.	1	3	5	c	—	—	3
Portsmouth	30·16	60	5	NNE.	3	4	3	c	—	—	3
Dover	30·15	63	1	E.	2	3	1	b	—	—	1
London	30·18	57	4	NNW.	2	4	2	b	—	—	—
Yarmouth	30·14	61	5	N.	2	4	1	b	—	—	1
Scarborough	30·11	57	3	W.	2	3	5	b	—	—	2
Shields	30·07	55	5	W.	4	4	5	o	—	—	2
Heligoland	30·12	59	2	WSW.	2	3	1	b	—	—	1

PROBABLE.

Tuesday.		*Wednesday.*
	SCOTLAND.	
W. to N. and E., fresh to moderate. Generally fine.		W. to N. and E., moderate. Fine.
	IRELAND.	
W. to N. and E., light to moderate. Fine.		NE. to SE. and SW., light to fresh.
	WEST CENTRAL.	
W. to NNE., moderate. Fine.		As next above. Generally fine.
	SW. ENGLAND.	
NW. to N. and E., variable, light to moderate. Fine.		NE. to SE. and SW., moderate. Fine.
	SE. ENGLAND.	
As next above.		NE. to SE., moderate to light. Fine.
	EAST COAST.	
Similar to above.		NW. to E., moderate. Fine.

Explanation.

B.—Barometer corrected and reduced to 32° at mean sea level; each ten feet, of vertical rise, causing about one hundredth of an inch *diminution*; and each ten degrees, above 32°, causing nearly three hundredths *increase*. E.—Exposed thermometer in shade. D.—Difference of moistened bulb (for evaporation and dew point). W.—Wind direction (true—two points *left* of magnetic). F.—Force (1 to 12—estimated). X.—Extreme Force since last report. C.—Cloud (1 to 9). I.—Initials: b.—blue sky; c.—clouds (detached); f.—fog; h.—hail; l.—lightning; m.—misty (hazy); o.—overcast (dull); r.—rain; s.—snow; t.—thunder. H.—Hours of R = Rainfall, or snow or hail (melted), since last report. S.—Sea-disturbance (1 to 9). Z.—Calm.

Extract from Beaufort Scale; with additions.

1 = b = blue (sky).
2 = c = clouds (detached).
3 = f = fog, foggy.
4 = h = hail.
5 = m = misty (haze).
6 = o = overcast.
7 = r = rain, rainy.
8 = s = snow.
9 = t = thunder. Lightning.
And a line under, or a dash, or a dot, or repetition (as r r) is for MUCH of either character.

Examples.

ABERDEEN TO LONDON, 25th July, 1862, 8 A.M., received at 10.

South-west — very strong wind.*

06041 93453 94663 21072
60420 05628

Conversion in Report.

1862	B	E	D	W	F	X	C	I	H	R	S
Friday, 25th July, 8 A.M. Aberdeen .	29·39†	60	6	SW.	5	8	6	r	6	0·46†	8

PORTRUSH TO LONDON, 25th July, 1862.

Blowing a hurricane from South-west.†

92958 94055 20126 52828
12968

Conversion in Report.

1862	B	E	D	W	F	X	C	I	H	R	S
Friday, 25th July Portrush .	29·39†	52	4	NW.	12	12	9	0	—	—	8

VALENTIA TO LONDON, 25th July, 1862.

West-north-west — very strong, with heavy squalls.†

99751 01565 26072 59528
04217

Conversion in Report.

1862	B	E	D	W	F	X	C	I	H	R	S
Friday, 25th July Valentia .	30·07†	59	4	NW.	4	9	2	b	—	—	7

* Cautionary Drum hoisted on the 24th, the previous day.

† Corrected and reduced. (Scale errors, elevation, and temperature.)

LIVERPOOL TO LONDON, 25th July, 1862.

South-west. At 6 A.M. it blew with a force of 18 lbs. on the sq. foot.*

97568 98964
20052 61424 07526

Conversion in Report.

1862	B	E	D	W	F	X	C	I	H	R	S
Friday, 25th July Liverpool . .	29·89†	61	7	W.	7	9	5	C	—	—	6

JERSEY TO LONDON, 25th July, 1862.

South-west — moderate.

03042 02258 02363 20032
63920 03862

Conversion in Report.

1862	B	E	D	W	F	X	C	I	H	R	S
Friday, 25th July Jersey . .	30·21†	63	4	SW.	3	5	8	r	3	0·47†	2

YARMOUTH TO LONDON, 25th July, 1862.

South-west — strong.

99864 99863 20061 64724
06323

Conversion in Report.

1862	B	E	D	W	F	X	C	I	H	R	S
Friday, 25th July Yarmouth .	29·92†	64	7	W.	6	8	3	C	—	—	3

* Cautionary Drum was shown on the previous day.

† Corrected and reduced. (Scale errors, elevation, and temperature.)

Meteorologic Telegraphy with the Continent.

In telegraphing with the Continent, some modification of these arrangements is indispensable, on account of variety of scales and expressions.

The metric scale may be easily substituted for that of inches on the barometer, as three figures of either are sufficient to express equivalent measures; but as the Centigrade and Reaumur thermometers are graduated both ways from freezing point (thirty-two of Fahrenheit), and as *minus* quantities are inconvenient in telegraphing figures, it is expedient to use a *constant* quantity, say *twenty* degrees, with the reading of a Centigrade, or Reaumur division. Thus, +9° would be *telegraphed* as 29°, +13° as 33°, −7° as 13°, −11° as 9°; from which the numbers to be used may be immediately obtained by duly applying 20, the constant.

A harmonious system may then be general, each observer reading as accustomed, and telegraphing on a uniform method of five or six groups of five figures each. The recipient may convert and reduce as requisite, being informed of the necessary corrections, or supplied with observations already corrected, if not also reduced, for inter-comparison.

As for some time past there has been a regular interchange of observations between Paris and London, besides Greenwich, with many other places, and as arrangements are now in progress for communicating similarly with the NW. and SW. coasts of France, with Hamburg, and to the northeastward, it would be desirable to arrange all these intercommunications on one principle, to which an approximation might be effected in the following manner:—

The metric and centrigrade scales being in general continental use, difficulty of using them in cooperation with ours, and on similar principles, may be obviated by omitting the first barometric figure, and, as above mentioned, by applying a constant to the actual reading of the thermometer.

The moistened thermometer reading may be telegraphed by the difference between it and the dry one, which is never lower than the moistened, nor more than nine degrees different from it, near the sea, in the morning.

Names of places may be indicated by figures:—a blank, or cyphers, being used to preserve due *position* for reference when there is a casual deficiency of a report from any station.

On these principles, two, three, four, five, or six groups of five figures each, may be used with facility, the reporter reading and telegraphing his own measures, and the recipient converting them, if requisite.*

Corrections for error of scale, reductions for temperature, and elevation above *mean* sea level, may be made as specially arranged between authorities at the respective central stations.

Communications with France may pass through Calais; those for the north-eastern coasts through Cuxhaven; from which two stations any branching arrangements can be organised to spread.

To convey our forecasts and cautionary storm signals speedily and effectively, requires special words, because their varying order and character prevent figures from being substituted without a risk of sacrificing security.

A sweep of five hundred geographical miles around London includes Bayonne, Valentia, Nairn, Copenhagen, Heligoland, Berlin, Munich, and Geneva, with all their nearest coasts.

Forecasts can be drawn here for South-west and North-west France, Belgium, Holland, and Denmark respectively, which may be telegraphed daily; and cautionary storm warnings can be given occasionally.

November, 1862. R. FITZ ROY.

* On the Continent *five* figures are counted and paid for as *one* word. In England each *figure*, even a decimal *point*, is charged as a *word*.

CAUTIONARY STORM SIGNALS

SENT BY ELECTRIC AND INTERNATIONAL TELEGRAPH TO PLACES AND PERSONS SPECIFIED, BESIDES RESPECTIVE TELEGRAPHERS.

LLOYD'S . . . . Secretary.

SOUTH-EAST ENGLAND.

HURST CASTLE .
COWES . . . . Secretary, R.Y.S. Mr. White, Docks.
RYDE . . . . . Victoria Yacht Club.
SOUTHAMPTON . .
PORTSMOUTH . . Commander-in-Chief.
SHOREHAM . . .
BRIGHTON . . .
NEWHAVEN . . .
EASTBOURNE . .
HASTINGS . . . H. Stevenson, jun.
RYE . . . . .
FOLKESTONE . . Collector of Customs.
RAMSGATE . . . Mr. Whitehead.

EAST COAST.

HARWICH . . .
ALDBOROUGH . .
LOWESTOFT . . . Harbour Master.
YARMOUTH . . . Collector of Customs. Sailors' Home.
LYNN . . . . . Collector of Customs.
HULL . . . . . Collector of Customs, Trinity House (warns Spurn).
BRIDLINGTON . . Flamborough Head.
SCARBOROUGH . . Collector of Customs.
WHITBY . . . .
HARTLEPOOL . . Collector of Customs.
SOUTH SHIELDS. . Sunderland.
NORTH SHIELDS . Collector of Customs, and Tynemouth.
BELFORD. . . . Budle.

SCOTLAND.

NAIRN. . . . . Mr. Penny.
ABERDEEN . . . Collector of Customs, and at Peterhead. Montrose, Harbour Master.
DUNDEE . . . . Collector of Customs. Chamber of Commerce. Broughty Ferry.
GLASGOW . . . Exchange Rooms.
GREENOCK . . . Collector of Customs.
BERWICK. . . .

IRELAND.

ROCHE POINT (*Cork*)
PASSAGE EAST (*Waterford*)
WEXFORD . . .

WEST CENTRAL.

ILFRACOMBE. . .
NEWPORT . . .
CARDIFF. . . . Harbour Master. Penarth.
SWANSEA. . . . Mr. Sydney Hall, and Collector of Customs.
LLANELLY . . . Harbour Master. Lloyd's Agent. Pembrey.
PEMBROKE . . . Superintendent Dockyard.
HOLYHEAD . . . Admiralty Office.
CARNARVON . . Bangor.
CHESTER. . . . Queensferry, Connolis Quay.
GREENFIELD. . . Bagilt.
BARROW . . . . Mr. Ramsden.
WHITEHAVEN . . Collector of Customs.
WORKINGTON . . Collector of Customs. Harbour Office.
MARYPORT . . . Collector of Customs.
DOUGLAS—MAN .

SOUTH-WEST ENGLAND.

ILFRACOMBE . .
PENZANCE . . . Collector of Customs. Hayle.
FALMOUTH . . . Collector of Customs. Mr. Duckham.
PLYMOUTH . . . Commander-in-Chief. Collector of Customs.
DARTMOUTH . .
TORQUAY. . . .
WEYMOUTH . . . Senior Naval Officer at Portland.

Telegraphers also warn nearest Coast Guard.

CAUTIONARY STORM SIGNALS

SENT BY BRITISH AND IRISH MAGNETIC TELEGRAPH TO PLACES AND PERSONS SPECIFIED, BESIDES RESPECTIVE TELEGRAPHERS.

LLOYD'S . . . . Secretary.

WEST CENTRAL.

LIVERPOOL . . . Observatory. Exchange. Collector of Customs. Mersey Yacht Club.
RUNCORN . . . Bridgewater Agent.
PRESTON . . . . Lytham.
FLEETWOOD . . . Harbour Master. Collector of Customs.

SOUTH ENGLAND.

JERSEY . . . . Gorey.
DOVER . . . . Harbour Master. Collector of Customs.
DEAL . . . . . Collector of Customs.

EAST COAST.

MIDDLESBOROUGH. Mr. Tallows, Dock Office.
REDCAR . . . . Mr. Joseph Dove.
HELIGOLAND . . The Governor.

SCOTLAND.

LEITH . . . . . Collector of Customs. Edinburgh.
GRANTON . . . Harbour Master.
ARDROSSAN . . . Greenock.

IRELAND.

PORTRUSH . . . Ballycastle.
GALWAY . . . . Collector of Customs.
TRALEE . . . . Harbour Office.
VALENTIA . . . Knightstown.
QUEENSTOWN . . Commander-in-Chief. Collector of Customs.
WATERFORD . .
KINGSTOWN . . . Harbour Master. Howth. Dublin. Wicklow.
DROGHEDA . . .
DUNDALK . . . . Collector of Customs.
SOLDIER'S POINT . Giles Quay.
CARRICKFERGUS . Culton.
BELFAST . . . . Collector of Customs. Harbour Master.

Telegraphers also warn nearest Coast Guard.

EXISTING ARRANGEMENTS FOR METEOROLOGIC TELEGRAPHY BETWEEN LONDON AND PARIS.

Seven or eight places are represented numerically, thus: —

1. GALWAY.	4. YARMOUTH.	7. QUEENSTOWN.
2. SCARBOROUGH.	5. WEYMOUTH.	8. ———.
3. VALENTIA.	6. PENZANCE.	

— numbers being used to indicate the names of the places.

Meteorologic data are comprised in three groups of figures; for example: —

Meteorologic	To	Observatoire—Paris.
12975	58110	06864
23002	55418	02562
32969	60130	01731
43004	58510	04112
52990	60208	04974
62981	60112	08876
72970	60116	06976
8——	——	——

The first figure in the first group on each line gives the name of the place; the next four figures show the reading of the barometer to the nearest hundreth of an inch.

The two first figures of the *second* group give the reading of the exposed thermometer to the nearest degree (Fahrenheit), the third figure the *difference* between the readings of the dry and moistened thermometers, and the last two figures the true direction of wind; North being 32, NNE. 2, East 8, and similarly for the other points.

The first two figures of the *third* group give the force of the wind, from 1 to 12 (a cypher being put before the figure when below ten to keep relative position), the third figure gives the amount of cloud from 1 to 9, the fourth the character of the weather, and the fifth the amount of sea disturbance.

The addresses used are the shortest possible, because each word of the addresses is paid for on Continental lines, which is not the case in England. Each group of five figures is counted as one word, on the Continent; but *each figure* as a *word* in England.

EXAMPLE.

Paris To Meteorologic Office,
London.

Brest 753·8 p* 19·2 p 15·7 très nuageux O.S.O. zero, calme. Bayonne p. 18·2 nuageux pluvieux S.S.O. 2 houleuse. Copenhague 762·7 p 13·5 vent calme pluie mer pas de vue. Helder 758·73 S.O. 1·3 17·4 nuageux beau temps calme. Lisbonne 759·15 p 20·4 S.S.O. 2 très nuageux mer belle.

* In the above, p = plus.

COMMUNICATION WITH NORTH-WEST FRANCE AND HAMBURG.

In meteorologic communication with North and West France, through Calais, of course such information ought to be given, in the smallest compass, as may be most useful along the sea coasts to which it is sent by telegraph.

As at times southerly winds indicate their *approach*, in Scotland and Ireland, before they are felt over North-west France (strange as it may seem until explained) and as northerly winds are always felt over England *first*,—London can *sometimes* send useful notices, even of approaching *southerly* gales,—and, generally, of those which come from north-west to north-east, the polar quarter.

For what is requisite at present, forecasts will be drawn for North-west France, and transmitted *with daily reports* from Penzance, Queenstown, and Valentia (or Galway), to Calais, whence these telegrams may be sent on, as authorised by the French Government.

Cautionary notices for storm-warning signals will be transmitted, as to places in South England.

On similar principles, daily reports from a few places, and occasional cautions, can be sent through Heligoland to Cuxhaven for Hamburg, whence they may be forwarded alongshore *both ways*.

Aberdeen, Scarborough, Yarmouth, and Dover, reports — with a special forecast for the *eastern* side of the North Sea, would inform those coasts without much additional expenditure of money or time.

Equivalents for French Words descriptive of Weather.

Beau	Fine	b *	1†
Belle	Smooth, still	—	—
Brouillard	Fog	f	3
Brumeux-se	Foggy	g	—
Calme	Calm	—	—
Ciel	Sky	—	—
Claire-e	Clear	b	1
Couvert-e	Overcast	o	6
Coup (de vent)	Heavy squall	q q or q	—
Eclair	Lightning	l	4
Éclaireux-se	Lightning around	l l or l	—
Faible	Light, slight	—	—
Fort-e	Much, strong	(— or • or repetition)	—
Grains	Squalls	q or q	—
Grand-e	Great, much	(— or • or repeated letter)	—
Humide-ité	Damp, humidity	—	—
Intense-ité	Intense-ity	(— or • or repetition)	—
Legèr-e-ment	Lightly	—	—
Mauvais-e	Bad, threatening	u	—
Nébuleux-se	Misty, hazy, obscure	m	5
Neige-ant	Snow-ing	s	8
Nuage-s-eux-se	Cloud-s-y	c	2
Orage-ux	Storm-y	qww	—
Pluie-s	Rain-s	rr	7
Pluvieux-se	Rainy	r	—
Presque	Almost, slight	—	—
Rafales	Sudden squalls	q	—
Serein-e	Serene, settled	b c	1
Sombre	Gloomy, dark	g or g g	6
Tempête	Tempest	w w q q	—
Tempestueux-se	Tempestuous	—	—
Tonnerre	Thunder	t	9
Tonnant-e	Thundery	t t	—
Très	Very, excessively	(or • or a repetition)	—

* Beaufort Letters, with additions. † Telegraphing Numbers 1 to 9.

TABLE of FRENCH and ENGLISH WORDS for the STATE of the SEA, or 'SEA-DISTURBANCE;' corresponding with their equivalent numbers, for telegraphing by groups of figures, instead of words.

État de la Mer	State of Sea, or Sea-Disturbance	Equivalents
Calme	Dead calm	0
Assez calme	Calm	1
Très belle	Very smooth	1
Belle	Smooth	2
Tranquille	Still	2
Faible houle	Slight swell	3
Petite houle	Do.	3
Un peu houleuse	Some swell	3
Un peu de mer	Rather rough	4
Risée	Ruffled, broken, or curled	4
Agitée	Disturbed irregularly	4
Houleuse	Considerable swell	5
Très houleuse	Much swell or sea	6
Moutonneuse	Crested waves	7
Creussée	Cross sea	7
Grosse houle	Great swell	8
Haute mer	High sea	8
Très-gros mer	Very large and high sea	9

WIND SCALES.

SEA SCALE.		WIND.		LAND SCALE.
1 to 3	=	Light	=	0 to 1
3 „ 5	=	Moderate	=	1 „ 2
5 „ 7	=	Fresh	=	2 „ 3
7 „ 8	=	Strong	=	3 „ 4
8 „ 10	=	Heavy	=	4 „ 5
10 „ 12	=	Violent	=	5 „ 6

Pressure in Pounds (Avoirdupois).		(Land Scale.)		Velocity in Miles (Hourly).
1	=	1	=	10
4	=	2	=	25
9	=	3	=	40
16	=	4	=	55
25	=	5	=	70
36	=	6	=	85

BAROMETER.

MILLIMETRES AND ENGLISH INCHES.

Mil.	Inches	Mil.	Inches	Mil.	Inches	Mil.	Inches
712	28·032	731	28·780	750	29·528	769	30·276
3	·071	2	·819	1	·568	770	·316
4	·111	3	·859	2	·607	1	·355
5	·150	4	·898	3	·646	2	·394
6	·190	5	·938	4	·686	3	·434
7	·229	6	28·977	5	·725	4	·473
8	·268	7	29·016	6	·764	5	·512
9	·308	8	·056	7	·804	6	·552
720	28·347	9	·095	8	·843	7	·591
1	·386	740	29·134	9	·882	8	·631
2	·426	1	·174	760	·922	9	·670
3	·465	2	·213	1	29·961	780	30·709
4	·505	3	·253	2	30·001	1	·749
5	·544	4	·292	3	·040	2	·788
6	·583	5	·331	4	·079	3	·827
7	·623	6	·371	5	·119	4	·867
8	·662	7	·410	6	·158	5	·906
9	·701	8	·449	7	·197	6	·945
730	28·741	749	29·489	768	30·237	787	30·985

Proportional Parts.

Mil.	Inch
0·1	0·008
0·2	·008
0·3	·012
0·4	·016
0·5	·020
0·6	·024
0·7	·028
0·8	·032
0·8	0·035
0·9	

ENGLISH INCHES—AND MILIMETRES.

Inches	·00	·01	·02	·03	·04	·05	·06	·07	·08	·09	Inches
	mm.	mm.	mm.	mm.	mm.	mm.	mm.	mm.	mm.	mm.	mm.
28·0	711·2	711·4	711·7	712·0	712·2	712·5	712·7	713·0	713·2	713·5	28·0
·1	13·7	14·0	14·2	14·5	14·7	15·0	15·3	15·5	15·8	16·0	·1
·2	16·3	16·5	16·8	17·0	17·3	17·5	17·8	18·0	18·3	18·6	·2
·3	18·8	19·1	19·3	19·6	19·8	20·1	20·3	20·6	20·8	21·1	·3
·4	21·3	21·6	21·9	22·1	22·4	22·6	22·9	23·1	23·4	23·6	·4
·5	23·9	24·1	24·4	24·7	24·9	25·2	25·4	25·7	25·9	26·2	·5
·6	26·4	26·7	26·9	27·2	27·4	27·7	28·0	28·2	28·5	28·7	·6
·7	29·0	29·2	29·5	29·7	30·0	30·2	30·5	30·7	31·0	31·3	·7
·8	31·5	31·8	33·0	32·3	32·5	32·8	33·0	33·3	33·5	33·8	·8
·9	34·0	34·3	34·6	34·8	35·1	35·3	35·6	35·8	36·1	36·3	·9
29·0	736·6	736·8	737·1	737·4	737·6	737·9	738·1	738·4	738·6	738·9	29·0
·1	39·1	39·4	39·6	39·9	40·1	40·4	40·7	40·9	41·3	41·2	·1
·2	41·7	41·9	42·2	42·4	42·7	42·9	43·2	43·4	43·7	44·0	·2
·3	44·2	44·5	44·7	45·0	45·2	45·5	45·7	46·0	46·2	46·5	·3
·4	46·7	47·0	47·3	47·5	47·8	48·0	48·3	48·5	48·8	49·0	·4
·5	49·3	49·5	49·8	50·1	50·3	50·6	50·8	51·1	51·3	51·6	·5
·6	51·8	52·1	52·3	52·6	52·8	53·1	53·4	53·6	53·9	54·1	·6
·7	54·4	54·6	54·9	55·1	55·4	55·6	55·9	56·1	56·4	56·7	·7
·8	56·9	57·2	57·4	57·7	57·9	58·2	58·4	58·7	58·9	59·2	·8
·9	59·4	59·7	60·0	60·2	60·5	60·7	61·0	61·2	61·5	61·7	·9
30·0	762·0	762·2	762·5	762·8	763·0	763·3	763·5	763·8	764·0	764·3	30·0
·1	64·5	64·8	65·0	65·3	65·5	65·8	66·1	66·3	66·6	66·8	·1
·2	67·1	67·3	67·6	67·8	68·1	68·3	68·6	68·8	69·1	69·4	·2
·3	69·6	69·9	70·1	70·4	70·6	70·9	71·1	71·4	71·6	71·9	·3
·4	72·1	72·4	72·7	72·9	73·2	73·4	73·7	73·9	74·2	74·4	·4
·5	74·7	74·9	75·2	75·5	75·7	76·0	76·2	76·5	76·7	76·0	·5
·6	77·2	77·5	77·7	78·0	78·2	78·5	78·8	79·0	79·3	79·5	·6
·7	79·8	80·0	80·3	80·5	80·8	81·0	81·3	81·5	81·8	82·1	·7
·8	82·3	82·6	82·8	83·1	83·3	83·6	83·8	84·1	84·3	84·6	·8
30·9	784·8	785·1	785·4	785·6	785·9	786·1	786·4	786·6	786·9	787·1	·9
	·00	·01	·02	·03	·04	·05	·06	·07	·08	·09	

Proportional Parts.

Inch	Mil.
0·001	0·03
·002	·05
·003	·08
·004	·10
·005	·13
·006	·14
·007	·18
·008	·20
0·009	0·23

THERMOMETER.

FAHRENHEIT					
Fahrenheit	Centigrade	Reaumur	Fahrenheit	Centigrade	Reaumur
°	°	°	°	°	°
1	−17·2	−13·8	51	10·6	8·4
2	16·7	13·3	52	11·1	8·9
3	16·1	12·9	53	11·7	9·3
4	15·6	12·4	54	12·2	9·8
5	15·0	12·0	55	12·8	10·2
6	14·4	11·6	56	13·3	10·7
7	13·9	11·1	57	13·9	11·1
8	13·3	10·7	58	14·4	11·6
9	12·8	10·2	59	15·0	12·0
10	12·2	9·8	60	15·6	12·4
				16·1	12·9
				16·7	13·3
11	−11·7	−9·3	61	17·2	13·8
12	11·1	8·9	62	17·8	14·2
13	10·6	8·4	63	18·3	14·7
14	10·0	8·0	64	18·9	15·1
15	9·4	7·6	65	19·4	15·6
16	8·9	7·1	66	20·0	16·0
17	8·3	6·7	67		
18	7·8	6·2	68		
19	7·2	5·8	69		
20	6·7	5·3	70		
				20·6	16·4
				21·1	16·9
21	−6·1	−4·9	71	21·7	17·3
22	5·6	4·4	72	22·2	17·8
23	5·0	4·0	73	22·8	18·2
24	4·4	3·6	74	23·3	18·7
25	3·9	3·1	75	23·9	19·1
26	3·3	2·7	76	24·4	19·6
27	2·8	2·2	77	25·0	20·0
28	2·2	1·8	78	25·6	20·4
29	1·7	1·3	79	26·1	20·9
30	1·1	0·9	80	26·7	21·3
				27·2	21·8
				27·8	22·2
31	0·6	−0·4	81	28·3	22·7
32	−0·0	0·0	82	28·9	23·1
33	0·6	+0·4	83	29·4	23·6
34	+1·1	0·9	84	30·0	24·0
35	1·7	1·3	85		
36	2·2	1·8	86		
37	2·8	2·2	87		
38	3·3	2·7	88		
39	3·9	3·1	89	30·6	24·4
40	4·4	3·6	90	31·1	24·9
				31·7	25·3
				32·2	25·8
41	+5·0	+4·0	91	32·8	26·2
42	5·6	4·4	92	33·3	26·7
43	6·1	4·9	93	33·9	27·1
44	6·7	5·3	94	34·4	27·6
45	7·2	5·8	95	35·0	28·0
46	7·8	6·2	96	35·6	28·4
47	8·3	6·7	97	36·1	28·9
48	8·9	7·1	98	36·7	29·3
49	9·4	7·6	99	37·2	29·8
50	+10·0	+8·0	100	37·8	30·2

CENTIGRADE					
Centigrade	Fahrenheit	Reaumur	Centigrade	Fahrenheit	Reaumur
°	°	°	°	°	°
−17	1·4	−13·6	11	51·8	8·8
16	3·2	12·8	12	53·6	9·6
15	5·0	12·0	13	55·4	10·4
14	6·8	11·2	14	57·2	11·2
13	8·6	10·4	15	59·0	12·0
12	10·4	9·6	16	60·8	12·8
11	12·2	8·8	17	62·6	13·6
−10	14·0	− 8·0	18	64·4	14·4
9	15·8	7·2	19	66·2	15·2
8	17·6	6·4	20	68·0	16·0
7	19·4	5·6	21	69·8	16·8
6	21·2	4·8	22	71·6	17·6
5	23·0	4·0	23	73·4	18·4
4	24·8	3·2	24	75·2	19·2
3	26·6	2·4	25	77·0	20·0
2	28·4	1·6	26	78·8	20·8
− 1	30·2	− 0·8	27	80·6	21·6
0	32·0	0·0	28	82·4	22·4
+ 1	33·8	+ 0·8	29	84·2	23·2
2	35·6	1·6	30	86·0	24·0
3	37·4	2·4	31	87·8	24·8
4	39·2	3·2	32	89·6	25·6
5	41·0	4·0	33	91·4	26·4
6	42·8	4·8	34	93·2	27·2
7	44·6	5·6	35	95·0	28·0
8	46·4	6·4	36	96·8	28·8
9	48·2	7·2	37	98·6	29·6
+10	50·0	+ 8·0	38	100·4	30·4

Reaumur.	Fahrenheit.	Centigrade	Reaumur.	Fahrenheit.	Centigrade
°	°	°	°	°	°
−14	0·5	−17·5	9	52·3	11.3
13	2·8	16·3	10	54·5	12·5
12	5·0	15·0	11	56·8	13·8
11	7·3	13·8	12	59·0	15·0
−10	9·5	−12·5	13	61·3	16·3
9	11·8	11·3	14	63·5	17·5
8	14·0	10·0	15	65·8	18·8
7	16·3	8·8	16	68·0	20·0
6	18·5	7·5	17	70·3	21·3
5	20·8	6·3	18	72·5	22·5
4	23·0	5·0	19	74·8	23·8
3	25·3	3·8	20	77·0	25·0
2	27·5	2·5	21	79·3	26·3
− 1	29·8	− 1·3	22	81·5	27·5
0	32·0	0·0	23	83·8	28·8
+ 1	34·3	+ 1·3	24	86·0	30·0
2	36·5	2·5	25	88·3	31·3
3	38·8	3·8	26	90·5	32·5
4	41·0	5·0	27	92·8	33·8
5	43·3	6·3	28	95·0	35·0
6	45·5	7·5	29	97·3	36·3
7	47·8	8·8	30	99·5	37·5
+ 8	50·0	+10·0	31	101·8	38·8

THERMOMETRIC COMPARISONS.

In Fahrenheit's thermometer, generally used in England, the space between the points of freezing and boiling is divided into 180 parts; and as it *was supposed* that the greatest cold was produced by mixing snow and muriate of soda (or common salt), this point was made zero; the point of freezing is therefore 32, and of boiling 212 degrees (at the sea level).

In the thermometer of Reaumur, formerly used in France, the freezing point was made zero, and the scale between it and the boiling point is divided into eighty degrees.

In the thermometer of Celsius, or the Centigrade, first used in Sweden, the scale between the points of congelation, or zero, and ebullition, is divided into 100 degrees.

In Delisle's thermometer, formerly used in Russia, the graduation commenced at the boiling point, and increased to that of freezing, which was 150 degrees. (A very inferior method.)

To convert degrees of Reaumur to those of Fahrenheit, multiply by 9, divide by 4, and add 32 to the quotient.

To convert degrees of Celsius to those of Fahrenheit, multiply by 2, divide by 4, and to the quotient add 32.

To convert degrees of Delisle, *below* the boiling point, to those of Fahrenheit, multiply by 6, divide by 5, and from the quotient subtract 212.

To convert the degrees of Delisle *above* the boiling point, multiply by 6, divide by 5, and to the quotient add 212.

Memorandum respecting a Moistened Thermometer (Damp or Wet Bulb), used in comparison with a Dry one, as a Hygrometer, on Mason's Principle.

The two thermometers should be without cases, or guards, hung in the shade, in still air, near each other, but not within a less distance than two or three inches. They should be as free from radiation as possible (from walls,* &c.).

* House walls, heated ground or stones, windows of warm rooms, areas near kitchens, or upward draughts from them, heated air at hatchways in a ship, &c.

Rain should be kept off the dry bulb. The cup, or glass, or other small holder of water for moistening the damp bulb, ought not to be under or too near the dry one, lest it should be affected. This little reservoir should be on one side of the damp bulb—that furthest from the dry thermometer.

A small *strip* of linen or cotton rag, or 'book muslin,' tied slightly round, or half round the bulb; or common cotton wick opened and tied loosely round the glass stem, close to the bulb, so as to lie on it, and reaching two or three inches from its lower part, should dip and remain in the water—which may be any water, fresh or salt, at the temperature of the atmosphere. Observations are incorrect if made while the water is either colder or warmer than the air, therefore the water holder should be replenished *after*, or some little time *before* observing.

Sometimes, at sea, when the water has been many degrees warmer than the air (as in the Gulf Stream for instance), a thermometer bulb has been moistened with it, and an observation incorrectly made almost immediately, by which the temperature of evaporation appeared to be higher than that of the air at the time; the moistened thermometer reading higher than the dry one — (of course a fallacy).

If one were to use hot, or iced water, such effects would be shown in extreme degrees. Water or wine is often cooled similarly by evaporation — a wet cloth being tied round the bottle, placed in a draught of air; or the bottle (*earthern* jar preferably) being porous, and allowing evaporation.

But as the objects of observing the temperature of evaporation are special, and have *intercomparison* as a principal one, these thermometers should be in *still* air. Draughts or currents of wind hasten evaporation, and therefore *lower* temperature, more or less rapidly, according to their velocity, or strength, which may vary considerably. (Hence the idea of *swinging* a moistened bulb is fallacious, as it cannot be done uniformly.)

The writer has had four *pairs* of such thermometers in use during a considerable time, and has found them accord perfectly, ranging in external air from a difference of fifteen degrees, during the summer, to one degree, in very damp weather — in and near London. He has seldom found a pair agree nearer than 1° in their reading (however exactly in accordance when both dry) unless the bulb which should have been dry was affected by rain, or dew, or the damp of the other when *too near*; in short, by *moisture*, when the bulb ought to have been perfectly dry.

The muslin, cotton, or other rag, should be washed frequently (once or twice a week), by pouring water over it (as it hangs), and should be changed occasionally (once or twice a month), according to its quality, and exposure to *dust* or *blacks*. Accuracy depends much on this care for cleanliness and water.

Cotton wick is as good a material, for conveying the moisture (by capillary action) to the bulb, as muslin or linen, — when opened out a little, kept clean, and renewed frequently, by simply tying it round the bulb neck.

In our climate, the *usual* difference between the thermometer readings ranges from two to twelve degrees (when the arrangement is good) in *outer* air; and from five to eight degrees in doors, in a *frequented* room, or passage, *without much fire*.

In hot and dry climates, the range out of doors has been found as much as even thirty degrees. (In Africa, India, and Australia.)

The difference between the dry and the moist, taken from the moist reading, gives the Dew-point,* *nearly* (when the air temperature is between freezing point and eighty degrees).

When the moistened thermometer is frozen, no reading need be taken for ordinary purposes; as, although *evaporation* continues, and may be noted, if the bulb be wetted beforehand, and an observation made before the moisture is frozen — it is *slower* afterwards, although continuing, and may much mislead.

In frost, therefore, it is scarcely worth noting, except as an experiment; but this signifies less, because at such a time the air is very dry; and for ordinary purposes, its state then will be known sufficiently.

* The temperature at which air first gives up its aqueous vapour (invisible while gas) in dew. Greater or more rapid condensation of vapour appears in rain, snow, or hail.

B

TIDES.

There is so striking a resemblance between the general movements of atmospheric currents and those of oceans, that a reprint of the following original paper, although written a quarter of a century ago, may now be useful, if not interesting.

Dr. Whewell expressed a favourable opinion of it (as the annexed passages show) which he has *since* repeated *recently*.

In August 1839, at a meeting of the British Association, in Birmingham, 'Professor Whewell made some observations on Captain Fitzroy's views of the *Tides*. In the account of the voyages of H. M. ships Adventure and Beagle, just published, there is an article in the Appendix containing remarks on the Tides.

'Captain Fitzroy observes, that facts had led him to doubt several of the assertions made in Mr. Whewell's Memoir, published in the "Philosophical Transactions," 1833, and entitled, "Essay towards a First Approximation to a Map of Cotidal Lines."

'Professor Whewell stated, that he conceived *doubts*—such as Captain Fitzroy's—are reasonable till the assertions are fully substantiated by facts. Captain Fitzroy has further offered a hypothesis of the nature of the tidal motion of the waters of wide oceans, different from the hypothesis of a progressive wave, which is the basis of Professor Whewell's researches.

'Captain Fitzroy conceives that in the Atlantic, and the Pacific, the masses of water librate, and oscillate, *laterally*, from east to west and back, between the eastern and western shores of these oceans, and thus produce tides.

'This supposition would explain such facts as these—that the tides take place along the whole west coast of South America at the same time: and the supposition might be so modified as to account for the absence of tides in the central part of the ocean. Professor Whewell stated, that he was not at all disposed to deny that such a mode of oscillation of the waters of the oceans is possible. Whether such a motion be consistent with the forces exerted by the sun and moon, is a problem of hydrodynamics hitherto unsolved—and probably very difficult.

'No demonstrative reason, however, has yet been published, to show that such a motion of the ocean waters may not approach more nearly to their actual motion, than the equilibrium theory, as usually applied, does.

'When the actual phenomena of the Tides of the Atlantic and Pacific have been fully explored, if it appears that they are of the kind supposed by Captain Fitzroy, it will be very necessary to call on mathematicians to attempt the solution of the hydrodynamical problem, either in a rigorous, or in an approximate shape.'—('Athenæum,' No. 618, 1839, August, page 655.)

At the end of the year 1833, I received from Mr. Whewell a copy of a work for which Seamen in general are deeply indebted to him. It bore the unpretending title of an 'Essay towards a First Approximation to a Map of Cotidal Lines;' but however lightly the author might esteem it, there can be no doubt that it tended to remove a cloud which hung over numerous difficulties; and to enable us not only to take a general view of them, but to see how we should direct our course in order to attain some knowledge of their intricacies.

In 1831 Mr. Lubbock called the attention of mathematicians, as well as of practical seamen, to the subject of Tides; but it was Mr. Whewell who aroused general interest; and, assisted by the Admiralty, engaged the cooperation of observers in all quarters of the globe.

At the first perusal of Mr. Whewell's essay, I was particularly struck by the following passages: — 'But in the meantime no one appears to have attempted to trace the nature of the connection among the tides of the different parts of the world. We are, perhaps, not even yet able to answer decisively the inquiry which Bacon suggests to the philosophers of his time, whether the high water extends across the Atlantic so as to affect, contemporaneously, the shores of America and Africa? or, whether it is high on one side of this ocean, when it is low on the other? At any rate, such observations have not been extended and generalized.'* Also: †

'If the time of high water at Plymouth be five, and at the Eddystone eight (as formerly stated), the water must be falling for three hours on the shore, while it is rising at the same time at ten or twelve miles' distance; and this through a height of several feet. We can hardly imagine that any elevation in one of the situations, should not be transferred to the other in a much shorter time than this.

'There is, in fact, no doubt that most, or all the statements of such discrepancies, are founded in a mistake arising from the comparison of two different phenomena; namely, the time of high-water, and the time of the change from the flow to the ebb-current. In some cases the one, and in some the other of these times, has been observed as the time of the tide; and in this manner have arisen such anomalies as have been mentioned.' And again: ‡

'The persuasion that, in waters affected by tides, the water rises while it runs one way, and falls while it runs the opposite way, though wholly erroneous, is very general.'

These, and other valuable remarks, showed me what indistinct or erroneous ideas I had entertained; and that many other seamen had been similarly perplexed, I could have little doubt, having often talked to experienced practical men on the subject. Perhaps the expressions 'tide and half-tide,' 'tide and quarter-tide,' &c., conveyed more distinct ideas to their minds than to mine; for to me they were unsatisfactory, and although quite aware of their meaning, I never liked them. From 1833, I and my companions on board the Beagle paid more attention to the subject, and made observations in the manner suggested

* Philosophical Transactions, 1833, p. 148. † Ibid. 157. ‡ Ibid.

by Mr. Whewell, as often as our other avocations allowed. It was, however, impossible to take interest in the subject, and discover difficulties, facts irreconcilable to theory, without trying to think how to account for them — unqualified even as I knew myself to be for such a task.* Perhaps I was encouraged to meditate by Mr. Whewell's concluding paragraph;† and, separated from assistance, I tried to reason my way out of the dilemma, by the help of such few data as I could dwell upon with certainty.

Some of the facts which seem to stand most in opposition to the theory that deduces tides in the northern Atlantic from the movement of a tide-wave originated in the great southern ocean are: — the comparative narrowness of the space between Africa and America; with the certainty that the sea is neither uni-

* Among the points which I could not establish in my own mind, by appeal to facts, were—'the tides of the Atlantic are, at least in their main features, of a derivative kind, and are propagated from south to north.' (p. 164.) 'That the tide-wave travels from the Cape of Good Hope to the bottom of the Gulf of Guinea in something less than four hours.' (p. 167.) 'That the tide-wave travels along this coast (American) from north to south, employing about twelve hours in its motion from Acapulco to the Strait of Magellan.' (p. 194.) 'From the comparative narrowness of the passage to the north (of Australia), it is almost certain that these tides must come from the southern side of the continent.' (p. 200.) 'The derivative tide which enters such oceans (North and South Pacific) from the south-east, is diffused over so wide a space, that its amount is also greatly reduced.' (p. 217.) &c.

† 'I cannot conclude this memoir without again expressing my entire conviction of its very imperfect character. I should regret its publication, if I supposed it likely that any intelligent person could consider it otherwise than as an attempt to combine such information as we have, and to point out the want and the use of more. I shall neither be surprised nor mortified, if the lines which I have drawn shall turn out to be, in many instances, widely erroneous: I offer them only as the simplest mode which I can now discover of grouping the facts which we possess. The lines which occupy the Atlantic, and those which are near the coasts of Europe, appear to have the greatest degree of probability. The tides on the coasts of New Zealand and New Holland, have also a consistency which makes them very probable. The Indian Ocean is less certain; though it is not easy to see how the course of the lines can be very widely different from that which we have taken. The course of these lines in the Pacific appears to be altogether problematical; and though those which are drawn in the neighbourhood of the west coast of America connect most of the best observations, they can hardly be considered as more than conjecture: in the middle of the Pacific I have not even ventured to conjecture. It only remains to add, that I shall be most glad to profit by every opportunity of improving this map, and will endeavour to employ for this purpose any information with which I may be supplied.'—pp. 234-5.

formly nor excessively deep in that space,* and the trifling rise of tide; not only upon either nearest shore (where it does not exceed four or five feet at the utmost), but at Ascension Island, where the highest rise is not two feet.† Secondly, the absence of any regular tide about the wide estuary of the River Plata, the situation and shape of which seem so well disposed for receiving an immense tide.‡ Thirdly, the flood-tide moving toward the west and south along the coast of Brazil, from near Pernambuco to the vicinity of the River Plata; and lastly, the almost uniformity of the time of high water along that extent of the coast of Africa which reaches from near the Cape of Good Hope to the neighbourhood of the Congo.

Against the supposition that a tide-wave travels along the west coast of America, from north to south, are the facts — that the flood tide impinges upon Chilóe and the adjacent outer coast, from the southward of west; that it is high water at Cape Pillar and at Chilóe, including the intermediate coast, almost at one time;§ that from Valdivia to the Bay of Mexillones (differing eighteen degrees in latitude), there is not an hour's difference in the time of high-water; that from Arica to Payta the times vary gradually as the coast trends westward; that from Panama to California, the times also change gradually

* Besides the 'Roccas,' Fernando de Noronha, and St. Paul rocks, various accounts have been received, from time to time, of shoals near the equator, between the meridians of fifteen and twenty-four degrees west. There can be no doubt, from the descriptions, that many alarms have been caused in that neighbourhood by earthquakes; which are, to my apprehension, indications of no very great depth of water. In 1761, a small sandy island was said to have been seen by Captain Bouvet, of Le Vaillant. This, if seen, has probably sunk down since. Krusenstern saw a volcanic eruption thereabout in 1806. In 1816, Captain Proudfoot, in the ship Triton, from Calcutta to Gibraltar, passed over a bank, in latitude 0° 32′ S. and longitude 17° 46′ W. It appeared to extend in an east and west direction three miles, and in a north and south direction one mile. They sounded in twenty-three fathoms, brown sand; but saw no appearance of breakers.

† At St. Helena it is not three feet: while at Tristan d'Acunha there is a rise of eight or nine feet under ordinary circumstances.

‡ I have passed months in that river without being able to detect any periodical rise of water, which I could attribute to tide; though it is said, that when the weather is very settled, some indications of a tide may be perceived.

§ Within about half an hour; an irregularity easily accounted for, and to which any one place is subject.

as the coast trends westward; and that from forty to sixty north, high water takes place at one time.

Having thus stated a few of the difficulties to be encountered by a theory which supposes such important tide-waves to move in the direction of a meridian, rather than in that of a parallel, I will venture to bring forward the results of much anxious meditation on the subject, trusting that they will be received by the reader — not as assertions — not as conclusions to which assent is asked without a reason for acquiescence being given — but as the very fallible opinion of one individual, who is anxious to contribute a mite, however small, toward the information of those for whom this work is more particularly written — namely, seafaring men; and who, if his ideas are fallacious, will rejoice at their refutation by the voice of truth.

Resting in confidence upon the Newtonian theory — which assigns as the primary causes of the tides the attractions of the moon and sun — I will make a few remarks, and then state some facts from which to reason.

Some persons seem to view the tidal phenomena more in connection with what would have happened had the globe been covered with water, than with reference to what actually happens, now that the oceans are nearly separated by tracts of land. They appear to consider that the effects of the moon's attraction (leaving the sun's out of the question at present, as it is similar though smaller) are felt only in vertical lines; and they do not allow for the lateral action of the moon upon a body of water, by which any portion is attracted towards her before she is vertically over it, as well as after she has passed to the westward of the meridian of that portion.

But little attention appears to have been paid to a consideration of the momentum acquired by any great body of water moved from the position it would occupy if undisturbed, and to the consequences of that momentum, when the water returns from a temporary displacement. And there seems to be a difficulty in altogether reconciling the statement that 'tides are diminished by diffusion,* with the manner in which the great tides of the Northern Atlantic are supposed to be caused

* Whewell's Essay, p. 217.

— a supposition which is mainly dependent upon the principle of forced vibrations or oscillations.' *

In consequence of similar ideas, induced by the facts previously mentioned, the following questions were inserted in the published 'Geographical Journal' for 1836: —

'It may appear presumption in a plain sailor attempting to offer an idea or two on the difficult questions of 'Tides;' yet, with the utmost deference to those who are competent to reason upon the subject, I will venture to ask whether the supposition of Atlantic tides being principally caused by a great tide-wave coming from the Southern Ocean, is not very difficult to reconcile with the facts that there is so little tide upon the coasts of Brazil, Ascension, and Guinea, and that in the mouth of the great river Plata there is little or no tide?

'May not each ocean have its own tides, though affecting, and being affected by the neighbouring waters?

'Has not the mass of an ocean a tendency to move westward as well as upward, after and toward the moon as she passes? If so, after the moon has passed, will not the mass of that ocean have an easterly inclination to regain the equilibrium (with respect to earth alone) from which the moon disturbed it (sun's then action not being considered)?

'In regaining its equilibrium, would not its own momentum carry it too far eastward; and would not the moon's action be then again approaching?

'May not one part of an ocean have a westward tendency, while another part, which is wider or narrower, from east to west, has an eastward movement?' If so, many difficulties would vanish; among them those which were first mentioned, and many perplexing anomalies on the south coast of New Holland. ('Jour. Roy. Geog. Soc.' vol. vi. part. II. p. 336.)

In a work subsequently published (in 1837) by a most eminent mathematician,† is the following passage: —

'Suppose several high, narrow strips of land were now to encircle the globe, passing through the opposite poles, and dividing the earth's surface into several great, unequal oceans; a separate tide would be raised in each. When the tidal wave had

* Herschel's Astronomy, Cab. Cyc. p. 334.

† Charles Babbage, F.R.S.

reached the farthest shore of one of them, conceive the causes that produced it to cease; then the wave thus raised would recede to the opposite shore, and continue to oscillate until destroyed by the friction of its bed. But if instead of ceasing to act, the cause which produced the tide were to re-appear at the opposite shore of the ocean, at the very moment when the reflected tide had returned to the place of its origin, then the second tide would act in augmentation of the first; and if this continued, tides of great height might be produced for ages. The result might be, that the narrow ridge dividing the adjacent oceans would be broken through, and the tidal wave traverse a broader tract than in the former ocean. Let us imagine the new ocean to be just so much broader than the old, that the reflected tide would return to the origin of the tidal movement half a tide later than before; then instead of those two superimposed tides, we should have a tide arising from the subtraction of one from the other. The alterations of the height of the tides on shores so circumstanced might be very small, and this might again continue for ages, thus causing beaches to be raised at very different elevations, without any real alteration in the level, either of the sea or land.' (Babbage's 'Ninth Bridgewater Treatise,' pp. 248, 249.)

Additional data, and leisure to reflect upon them, have tended to confirm the view taken previously to asking those questions in the 'Geographical Journal;' but before stating this view more explicitly, it is necessary to lay facts before my readers, from which they may judge for themselves.

In the greatest expanse of ocean, that which meets with only partial interruption to free tidal movements — the zone, if it may be so called, near fifty-five degrees of south latitude — there is high water at opposite sides, and low water at the other opposite sides of the globe nearly at the same time.

At the eastern part of the Falkland Islands, exposed to the tide of this zone, it is high water, or full sea, at about nine o'clock on the day of new, or full moon, by Greenwich time;* and on the southern shore of Van Diemen Land it is high-water at about ten. This is not a point *exactly* opposite, it is true, but it is the nearest so at which we have yet observed.

* To which all the times are here reduced for easy comparison.

At each of these places the tide rises six hours and falls six hours, alternately; therefore when it is low water at one, it is also low water at the other. There is no intermediate place in this zone, rather distant from these points, at which I know of a tide observation deserving confidence; but those above-mentioned are certain, and seem to corroborate the Newtonian theory in a satisfactory manner.

This is, however, the only zone of ocean which is at all able to follow the law which would govern its undulations if the globe were covered with water. In other zones (taking about ten degrees in latitude as a zone) it is high water, generally speaking, at one side of an ocean, near the time that it is low on the other.

In oceans about ninety degrees wide, this happens very nearly; but as the width diminishes, so do the times of high water at each side approach; and as the width increases beyond ninety degrees, as in the case of zones of the Pacific, the times of high water still approach (in consequence of the tendency to high water at opposite points), and appear to confirm further the Newtonian theory.

For examples (on the day of full moon): — In the Pacific, at Port Henry, in 50° S. it is higher water at 5h., at which time it is near low water at Auckland Island, where the time of high tide is 12h. 30m. In this case, the interval between one high water, and the other on the opposite side of the ocean, is 7h. 30m. or 4·30; and the width of that ocean is nearly eight hours (measured in time).

At Valdivia, in lat. 40° S. it is high water at 3h. 30m., and at New Zealand, on that parallel, at 9h. 50m. The space of ocean between is seven hours nearly: the differences are 6.20 and 5.40.

In 30° S., at Coquimbo, it is high water at 2h., and at Norfolk Island it is high at about 9h. The intermediate space of ocean is nearly eight hours wide.*

In 20° S., at Iquique, it is high water at 1h. 30m., and at New Caledonia, in the same parallel, it is high water at 9h. 15m. The space between them is about eight hours wide: the least difference 4·15.

Near 10°, or 12°, at Callao, it is high water about ten; but

* A *derivative* tide may act here.

as on this parallel a multitude of islands spread across half the Pacific, no comparison of times can be trusted.

On the equator — at the Galapagos Islands — it is high water at 8h. 20m.; and at New Ireland it is high water at 3h. 00m. — a difference of seven hours nearly. The ocean is here eight hours wide; but at New Ireland there is only one tide in twenty-four hours — an anomaly to be considered presently.

The parallel of 10° N. is similar to that of the equator — however, we may as well examine it. At the little Isle of Cocos, and at Nicoya, on the main, it is high water at about 8h.; and at the Philippine Islands, in the same latitude, at 4h.; the difference, eight hours, is not far from the meridian distance, which is about ten hours; but the Philippines also feel the effects of causes which influence the tides at New Ireland, and, generally, those of the Indian Archipelago.

In 20° N., at St. Blas, it is high water at 3h.; and at Leu Chu, the nearest known point of comparison at the other side of the ocean, at 10h. The difference, 7 hours, is about an hour less than the meridian distance. In 30° N., on the coast of California, it is high water at 4h., and at Nangasaki, in Japan, in lat. 33, at 11·12. The difference, 7·12, is nearly half an hour less than the meridian distance. In 40° N. it is high water at about 8h. on the American coast, but for the opposite shore I have no data. In 50° N. it is high water at Vancouver Island at 9h., and at the south extreme of Kamschatka it is *said* to be high water at about 6h.; the difference, 9 or 3 hours, is anomalous — made so probably by a derivative tide; or by a mistake.

Having examined the Pacific, let us proceed in a similar manner with the Atlantic and the Indian Ocean: —

In 40° S., off Blanco Bay, the time of high water is 9h.; the *same* as at the Falklands.

At Amsterdam Island, one says 6h., another 12h., for the time of high water. Both cannot be right: but having reason to think the latter correct, I have preferred it. In Bass Strait it is high water about ten. Between the two extremes there are thirteen hours, and between the times of tide there are eleven or thirteen hours. At Amsterdam Island, high water is taken as two hours after that of Bass Strait, but the difference of meridians is about four hours. The difference between high water at Amsterdam and Blanco Bay is nine hours.

In 30 S. it is high water on the African coast at 2h., and on the American coast at 6h. There are about four hours' difference of meridian between them in that parallel.

In 20° S. it is high water at 3h. on the African shore, and 6h. on the Brazilian; the meridian distance is about three hours and three quarters.

In 10° S., at 3h. 15m. on the east side, and 7h. on the west: the distance is about three hours and a quarter.

On the equator we have 4h. 30m. at the eastern limit, and nearly 8h. at the western; the distance being about three hours and a half.

In 10° N., 7h. and 10h.,—the distance being three hours.

In 20° N., at Cape Blanco, at about 1h.; and on the north coast of San Domingo, nearly at 11h. The interval is about 3·40: but there are interfering derivative tides, probably, as well as local peculiarities, among the West-India Islands.

In 30° N., about 4h. on the east and 1h. 30m. on the west. The distance is nearly five hours. This *seems* anomalous.

In 40° N., 3h. on the coast of Spain, and at about 1h. on the coast of America. This is another anomaly: but easy of explanation — considering the geography.

In 50° N. it is high water at 4h. 36m., in the mouth of the Channel; and at 10h. 45m. on the coast of Newfoundland. Their meridian distance is about 3·20.

On the west coasts of Ireland and Scotland, from 5h. to 6h. is the hour of high water; on the coast of Labrador, it is from 10h. to 11h., in the same parallels. The meridian distances are from three to four hours; but as we approach the parallel of 60° N. the North Sea and Davis Strait open, which probably affect the tide between Ireland and Labrador.

The Indian Ocean appears to have high water on all sides at once, though not in the central parts at the same time. Thus, it is high water at the north west extremity of Australia; on the coast of Java; on that of Sumatra; at Ceylon; at the Laccadiva Islands; at the Seychelles; on the coast of Madagascar; and at Amsterdam Island, at twelve; but at the Chagos Islands and Mauritius it is high water at about nine, and at the Keeling Isles about eleven. Here, then, it would seem that there is cause for much perplexity.

Having now stated the principal facts which occur to my mind, I will mention the conclusions drawn from them, and then attempt to explain the anomalies.

Let E G (fig. 1*) represent a section of our globe, of which A B C D is supposed to be land, and E F G H water. Let H M show the direction in which the moon's attraction would operate. The effect of her attraction, according to Newton's demonstration, would be to raise the water at F by positive attraction of the water, and at H by attracting the earth more than the water:—let the dotted line represent the consequent figure of the ocean.

In fig. 2, let the ocean be supposed 90° or six hours wide; let the moon act in the direction M F; and let the dotted line represent the altered position of the water when moved out of its natural position (with respect to the earth) by the moon's attraction.

Again, in fig. 3, supposing the moon acting in the line M K, and the dotted line representing the figure taken in that case by the ocean.

It will occur to the reader that very little water can rise at F and H (fig. 1), at F (fig. 2), or at K (fig. 3), unless water falls or sinks, at E and G (fig. 1), G (fig. 2), F and G (fig. 3), because water is but slightly compressible, except under extraordinary pressure, and because it is incapable of being stretched; therefore, if at any place the sea is raised above its natural level, the excess must be supplied by a sinking taking place elsewhere. There cannot be a void space left under the sea between the water and its bed; and there is no lateral movement of the particles at the surface only of the ocean sufficient to cause high tides on either shore:—therefore the conclusion may be drawn, that the whole mass oscillates or librates.

By librating I mean such a movement as that which a large jelly would have, if its *upper* part were pushed on one side, and then allowed to vibrate while the base remained fixed: and by oscillating I mean a movement like that of water in a basin, after the basin is gently tilted and let down again.

That such a motion would be imperceptible, except by its *effects*, there can be little doubt, after reflecting how small a late-

* See Diagram XI.

ral movement of an ocean would cause immense commotion at its boundary, in consequence of the inelasticity of water, free to move and impelled horizontally.

Now let the moon be supposed changed from M in fig. 2 to M in fig. 3. The highest point of the water would then be transferred from F to K, during which transfer the water must fall at F and rise at G: and so of other points. In this manner, when the moon causes a tide by her direct attraction, a wave or swelling, whose crest is above the natural level of the sea, moves westward, until it is stopped by a barrier of land. But when it recedes from that barrier, how is the excess of the wave above the height of the sea (when uninfluenced by the moon) transferred to the other side of the same ocean? There is no return wave; if there were, islands intermediate would have an ebb, and a flood tide, every six hours; four floods in twenty-four hours; but they usually have, on the contrary, six hour tides, alternate ebb and flow, twice in twenty-four hours, like those of the shores of continents, though generally smaller in amount.

Water cannot rise in one place unless it falls in another — it does fall on one side of an ocean, while it rises on the other — how then is the fluid transferred? There is only one way — which is by the mass oscillating. In the former case, when the moon passed over, it was a libratory movement, in this latter it appears to be an oscillation.

If it is shown, as I believe, that the ocean oscillates, we see that there are two principal causes of tides — one the direct raising of water by the moon: and the other, oscillation excited by that temporary derangement of the natural level of the sea.

From the preceding facts and deductions, combined with the commonly received laws of fluids and gravitation, the following conclusions may be drawn: —

1. Every large body of water is affected by the attraction of the moon, and sun, and has tides caused by their action.

2. Bodies of water are not only raised, or accumulated, vertically, by the attraction of the moon and sun; but they are also drawn laterally by them.

3. When a large body of water is prevented from continuing a horizontal movement, it rises until whatever momentum it had acquired ceases; and then it sinks gradually.

4. The momentum acquired by a body of water in thus sinking back to the position it *should* occupy, with reference to the earth's attraction only, carries it beyond that position to one from which it has a *tendency* to return again — and so to keep up an oscillation until brought to rest by the friction of its bed. (Attraction of the moon and sun not here included.)

5. The recurring influences of the moon and sun are checks on these oscillations, and prevent their taking place more than once between each separate *raising* of the water in consequence of their attractions.

6. Different zones (or widths measured by latitude) of an ocean may move differently, each having waves and oscillations at times differing from those of an adjoining zone, in consequence of one having more or less longitude, depth, or freedom from obstacles than another.

7. Original waves and oscillations combine with, and modify one another, according to their relative magnitude, momentum, and direction.

8. The natural tendency of tide-waves (so called), or oceanic librations, is from east to west; and of oscillations, from west to east, and east to west also; but derivative waves or oscillations move in various directions according to primary impulse, varied by local configuration of the bed of an ocean.

Conformably to these conclusions, I will now try to explain a few of the more remarkable anomalies of tides, in various parts of the world; taking it for granted that the reader is acquainted with existing works on the subject, especially those of Mr. Whewell,* and the brief but comprehensive and explanatory view taken by Sir John Herschel in his treatise on astronomy.†

I mentioned that between Callao and the western shores of the Pacific, in the parallel of about 12° south, no comparison of times can be trusted? Why not? may be asked. Four or five hours west of Callao, there is a multitude of islands which check the libration of the ocean. Another tide wave forms westward of them, on a small scale, and it is by this second tide, altered by derivative tides from each side, that the western

* Published in the Philosophical Transactions.

† Cabinet Cyclopædia. A Treatise on Astronomy, chap. xi., pp. 334, 5, 6, 7, 8, 9.

portion of this zone is affected. Tahiti is thus at the edge, or limit, of four tides — one east, another west, a third to the north, and a fourth to the south, and as these tides are moving with different impulses, and at different times, it is not at all surprising that they should almost neutralize each other at Tahiti. As we go west or east of that island, we find the tides augmenting gradually in height. At the Friendly Islands they rise five feet, and at the Gambier Islands three feet.

Respecting the twelve hour tide at New Ireland, and at other places in the Indian Archipelago — appeal to facts, so far as we can trace the tides at present, tends to confirm the explanation of Sir Isaac Newton, which consisted in supposing that such tides are compounded of two tides, which arrive by different paths, one six hours later than the other. 'When the moon is in the equator, the morning and evening tides of each component tide are equal, and tides obliterate each other by interference, which takes place about the equinoxes. At other periods the higher tides of each component daily pair are compounded into a tide which takes place at the intermediate time, that is, once a day; and this time will be after noon or before, according to the time of year.' (Whewell, in 'Phil. Trans.' 1833, p. 224.)

At New Ireland, the time of high water is about 3; but at New Caledonia it is 9. Again, at the north-west coast of Australia, it is 12; and at the eastern approach to Torres Strait, 10; at the Philippine Islands it is 4; and at Leu Chu 10. Now here are various times of tide, and different impulses, crowded together into a comparatively small space, sufficient to perplex any theorist of the present day. Owing to local configurations, and a variety of incidental circumstances, we find every kind of tide in this region, in a space sixty degrees square. Although tidal impulses, waves, and resulting currents are checked and altered by the broken land of the Indian archipelago, they cannot be suddenly destroyed, or prevented from influencing each other, while communications, more or less open, exist in so many directions.

At the Sandwich Islands there is said to be very little tide. As it is high water in 40° N., on the American coast, at 8; at which time it is also high water at the Galapagos, it appears that the two zones of the ocean — one about the equator, and the other near 40° N. — have high water, in the meridian of the Sandwich Islands, at two very different times; and that the high water of the northern zone will have passed that meridian about three hours before the equatorial wave. Impulses derived from them may succeed one another at an intermediate point, such as the Sandwich Islands. Besides which, there is the tide of their own zone to be considered; in consequence of which alone it might be high water at about 6: thus these islands are so situated as to receive at least three tides — one primary and two derivative — whose respective times of high water are 1, 6, and 10, a succession which may well be supposed to neutralize any ebb, and maintain the water thereabout above its natural level, independent of tide.

About the Strait of Magellan, and along the eastern coast of Patagonia, there are very high tides; apparently complicated, but perhaps less so than is usually believed.

A powerful tide arrives at the Falklands, and at the east end of Staten Land, at about 9; which is opposed by another powerful tide arriving from the west. The union of these two accumulates the water between Tierra del Fuego and the Falklands, and on the east coast of Patagonia.

Within the Strait of Magellan, westward of the Second Narrow, it is high water at about 4·40, and the tide rises only six feet; but eastward of the First Narrow it is high at 1·30, and the tide rises about forty feet (six or seven fathoms).

Now, as in one case the sea only rises three feet, and in the other twenty, above its mean level, every one would expect to find a rush of water through the Narrows, from the high sea to the low, and such is the fact. From ten to four the water runs westward with great velocity, and from four till ten it rushes eastward. During the first interval, from ten to four, the eastern body of water, between Tierra del Fuego and the Falklands, is above the mean level; and during the latter interval, from four till ten, it is below the mean level — that which it would have if there were no tides.

From 50° S. to near Blanco Bay in 40° S. the tide-wave certainly travels along the coast to the north; but this is a derivative from the meeting of tides above-mentioned, combined with the primary tides on the coast traversed. In this way, principally, we may account for a high tide in one place on this coast, and a low one at another (similarly situated, though differing in latitude); and, again, a high tide at another place. During the twenty-four hours that the derivative wave occupies in moving from Cape Virgins to the Colorado, it alternately augments or diminishes two floods and two ebbs of the great ocean. Perhaps, indeed, it reaches farther and affects the water about the Plata.

The extraordinary 'races' about the Peninsula of San José, and the apparent absence of currents about the straight coast extending eastward from Blanco Bay, may be attributed to conflicting tidal impulses.

Why there should be no tide in the River Plata, situated and shaped as it is, seems extraordinary: but as it is high water at 6h. on the coast of Brazil, and at 9h. about Blanco Bay; and as a derivative wave from this neighbourhood must move eastward and northward, there is a filling up, from the southward, as an ebbing takes place in consequence of a regular six-hour tide; and conversely.

Tristan d'Acunha has a considerable rise of tide, about eight feet, though Ascension and St. Helena have only about two feet. The former place is affected by a great southern tide; the two latter are influenced by the comparatively small tide which traverses the space between Africa and Brazil.

In the West Indies there are varieties of tides, caused by primary and derivative impulses, exceedingly modified by local circumstances; none, however, are large, while some are as small as those of Tahiti, about a foot at the utmost. There are places also in that archipelago where there is only one tide in twenty-four hours. In considering the West-India tides, those of the east coast of North America, and the exceedingly high ones of Fundy Bay, the Gulf stream ought not to be overlooked, as it may affect the tides on the coasts it traverses even more than those on the Patagonian coast are altered by the current driven along it from near Tierra del Fuego.

I may here remark that some persons have been misled by inaccurate data respecting several *times* of high water, of material consequence to theories of cotidal lines.

Looking at the Atlantic, as represented on a globe, we see that Newfoundland and the adjacent coasts are so placed as to receive tidal impulses from the Arctic Sea, North Atlantic Ocean, the tropical part of the North Atlantic, and the Gulf stream: besides which, no doubt, a derivative from the equatorial zone is felt there.

It is high water at the east side of the Atlantic, from the Canary Islands to Scotland, within an hour or two of the same time, on the salient points of the coast, namely, at about 4h.; and if the opposite coast were straight, like that of Chile, and uninfluenced by derivative tides or by currents, we might expect that it would be high water there at about 7h., allowing that the tide-wave moved as it is found to do generally. But it is high water at about 1h., from 30° to 40°, the times increasing northward from 40° N. to the Bay of Fundy, and also increasing southward from 50° N. to that bay, where, as every sailor knows, the tides rise higher than in any other part of the world. This sequence of times, each ending in about 43° N., the adjacent Gulf stream (an immense river in the ocean), and an accumulation of water in that corner higher than is known anywhere else, show that we cannot there expect to find data for tidal rules. In that quarter is evidently a marked exception, caused by the conflux of at least two primary tides, two derivatives, and a powerful current, aided by the peculiar configuration of the land.

In the Mediterranean it is supposed by many persons that there is no ebb and flow; but Captain Smyth, who surveyed so much of its shores, informs me that he found a tide, small certainly, and apparently not governed by the moon, but regular. I have myself noticed a small rise and fall there; and the current, caused by tide, in the Faro of Messina, is well known.

As the moon passes over the Indian Ocean, the natural effect of her attraction must be to accumulate the waters, and draw the wave so caused after her, as in other places: but while that ocean is obeying her power, and the wave is travelling toward the west, another wave is approaching from the Pacific — a wave which has been retarded in its passage—and its crest passes through the Indian archipelago, while the water would otherwise be falling at the western part of Torres Strait. At the same time, a derivative* wave moving northward along the West Australian coast, combines with the Pacific wave to raise a high tide about the north-west coast of Australia, where, if it were not for these auxiliaries, there would be low water at that time. Six hours afterwards, one body has ebbed toward the Pacific—the other southward, toward the then comparatively low ocean, south of Australia, and what—if Torres Strait were blocked up, and the water prevented from falling away toward the south—would be a high tide—is, in fact, *low water*. The tides in the two northern bays are derivatives, and move northward.

High water taking place at one time—within an hour—all along the east coast of Africa, shows that the rise of sea, or tide-wave, there moves westward or eastward, and the times of high water at the islands are farther confirmations; for the wave is at Chagos and at the Mauritius three or four hours before it is high water on the African coast. The Keeling time shows that there the water rises longer, in consequence of that part of the ocean being affected by the advancing swell of the Pacific.

The only remaining particular case is that of the south coast of Australia—from King George Sound to Spencer Gulf—a large space of sea in which there is very little rise of tide, and even that little very irregular.

As the high water moves westward from the meridians of that great bay, a tide moves southward from the Indian archipelago, where it is high water just as it should be low in the bay mentioned; hence there is a filling, or flowing, from one wave, while another is retreating. In this wide expanse, affected by derivative tides from three adjoining oceans, we cannot but expect irregularities—either very high tides, caused by combination; or little or no tide, in consequence of mutual destruction—one tide ebbing from—while another is flowing toward the same place.

Throughout these remarks I have intentionally omitted to say much of the sun's action, because, though very inferior, it is similar to that of the moon. Perhaps the Tahiti tide may be purely solar; this, however, is uncertain.

It appears probable, that many important currents are caused

* Derived from a great southern wave passing westward.

or augmented, by such a tidal libration and oscillation of the sea. As the earth turns only one way, the moon is continually pulling, as it were, in one direction, and to this cause much of the greater currents may be traced. Wind, evaporation, and the variable weight of the atmosphere may each have a share in moving the waters horizontally; but there are many facts which appear to lead to a conclusion that the moon and sun are principal agents in causing currents* (and therefore geologic changes likewise).

Having alluded to the effect of atmospheric pressure on the ocean, I will take this opportunity of mentioning that one cause of water rising on the shore before hurricanes, or gales of wind, is lightened pressure on the surface of the sea, as indicated by the mercury being low in a barometer. This is very remarkable at the Mauritius and in the River Plata, at both which places the water rises unusually before a storm, while at the same time the mercury falls. As the column rises, so the water falls again. I have instanced those places as being well known, and affected very little by tide: but the fact has been observed by me in many places.

These causes may materially affect the height of tides, as well as the strength of currents. In the wide but shallow Plata, the depth of water and nature of current vary in remarkable accordance with the barometric changes.

Another cause of the water rising before a high wind, or storm, as well as of a ground swell, of rollers, or of that disturbed *tumultuous heaving* of the sea, sometimes observed while there is little or no wind at a place, is the action of wind on a remote part of that sea; an action, or pressure, which is rapidly transmitted, through a non-elastic fluid, to regions at a distance.

I have collected many instances of rollers, or a heavy swell, or a confused ground swell being felt at places where not only was there no wind at the time, but to which the wind that caused those movements of water never reached. That they *were* caused by wind, I proved by the logs of ships which were in the

* A continued stream may be produced by a succession of impulses, as a rotatory system of waves may 'be kept in constant circulation by impulses received from the adjacent tides.'—Whewell in Phil. Trans. 1836, p. 299.

respective gales at the time their effects on the sea were thus felt at a great distance. The places to which I particularly allude are the Cape Verde Islands, Ascension, St. Helena, Tristan d'Acunha, Cape Frio, Tierra del Fuego, Chilóe, the coast of Chile, the Galapagos Islands, Tahiti, the Keeling Islands, Mauritius, and the Cape of Good Hope.

Waves, or rollers, caused by earthquakes, or volcanic eruptions, or electric discharges, are, of course, unconnected with wind or atmospheric pressure.

But in accounting for currents, as occasioned in some, if not many instances, by tidal pressure, or a succession of tidal impulses, we must not overlook the well known power of wind in giving horizontal motion to water, as well as in elevating or depressing it.

Wind blowing almost always in one direction is known to communicate a movement to waters, and it is remarkable that the general movements of the North Pacific as well as the North Atlantic are from west by the north to east, or, as a sailor would say, 'with the sun;' while in the southern oceans, Pacific, Atlantic, and Indian, they are generally 'against the sun,' or from west to east by the south — both corresponding to the general turn of winds in respective hemispheres.*

The Chile current, after coasting Peru, preserves a temperature of about 60° up to the Galapagos, and there it meets a warm stream out of the Gulf of Panama, at a temperature of about 80°. The two unite together, and turn westward along the equatorial zone. There is a remarkable exception on the east coast of Patagonia, where the current sets northward along the land (not far in the offing), owing probably to tides.

There may be circulations of water in a vertical direction, or in a plane inclined to the horizon, as well as horizontally. Bodies of water differing in temperature, as well as in chemical composition, do not hastily blend together. Their reluctance to mix is observable at sea, when we sail out of one current, or body of water, into another — differing perhaps in temperature, chemical composition, and colour. At the meeting, or

* Against the sun, in seaman's phrase—left handed, or contrary to the movement of watch hands.

edges of such bodies, there is usually a well defined line, often considerable ripplings, which indicate some degree of mutual horizontal pressure—as of separate masses.

At the mouths of large rivers it frequently happens that salt water is actually running up the river, underneath a stream of fresh water, which still continues to run down. This has often been witnessed in the river Santa Cruz. Of course intermixture takes place gradually, though by slow degrees.

The height of waves may be here mentioned, with reference to rollers or other undulations of water however caused. Large waves are seldom seen except where the sea is deep and extensive. The highest I have ever witnessed myself were not less than sixty feet in height, reckoning from the hollow between, perpendicularly to the level of two adjacent waves; but from twenty to thirty feet is a common height in the open ocean during a storm.

I am quite aware of, and have long been amused by the assertion of some persons, whose good fortune it has been not to witness really large waves—that the sea never rises above twelve or fifteen feet—or, that no wave exceeds thirty feet in height, reckoning in a vertical line from the level of the hollow to that of the crest.

In H. M. S. Thetis, during an unusually heavy gale of wind in the Atlantic, not far from the Bay of Biscay, while between two waves, her storm try-sails were *totally* becalmed, the crest of each wave being above the level of the centre of her main-yard, when she was upright between the two seas. Her main-yard was sixty feet from the water-line. At that time I was standing near her taffrail, holding by a rope.* I never saw such seas before, and have never seen any equal to them since, either off Cape Horn or the Cape of Good Hope, during two circumnavigations; and many years of foreign service.

Calculations of tides, adopted by Mr. Whewell and most persons whose opinions on this subject all men respect, are

* Captain B. J. Sulivan, C.B., was then a midshipman, and in the main-top.

equally applicable to the view here taken. In either case the time of high water, and rise of tide on a certain day, is ascertained at a given place experimentally; and, as the causes of that tide are the moon and the sun, changes in their position with respect to the earth will operate changes in the tides, which, as to time and quantity, will depend upon the above data, and the positions of earth, moon, and sun.

The *variation* of tide is what we have to deal with in ordinary calculation, not the original movement.

It may be added here, that although tidal waves are too broad and too nearly flat to be visibly noticed, such views as these which the writer has ventured to publish (repeatedly) do accord with facts observed *most recently*, as well as with old authentic observations (such as those of Flinders, Cook, and Dampier), throughout all explored parts of the whole world.

C

CLOUDS.

Clouds were divided, by Howard, into four classes, called—

Cirrus, Stratus, Nimbus, or Cumulus.*

Cirrus is the first light cloud that forms in the sky after fine clear weather. It is very light and delicate in its appearance; and generally curling or waving, like feathers, hair, or horses' tails (commonly called 'mares tails'). It may also be called the 'Curl Cloud.'

Stratus is the shapeless smoke-like cloud that is most common, and of all sizes: sometimes it is small, and at a distance like spots of inky or dirty water; its edges appearing faint or ill-defined; sometimes it rises in fog-banks from water or land; sometimes it overspreads and hides the sky. Rain does not fall from it. Its exact resemblance cannot be traced upon paper, because the edges are so ill-defined.

Nimbus is the heavy-looking, soft, shapeless cloud, from which rain is falling. Whatever shape a cloud may have retained previous to rain falling from it, at the moment of its change, from vapour to water, it softens in appearance, and becomes the 'Nimbus,' or 'Rain Cloud.'

Cumulus is the hard-edged cloud, or cloud with well-defined edges, whose resemblance can be accurately traced on paper. This cloud is not, generally speaking, so large as the Stratus or Nimbus.

These four classifications will not, however, suffice to describe exactly the appearance of the clouds at all times. More minute

* See Diagrams IX. X.

distinctions are required, for which the following may be used:—

Cirro-stratus— signifying a mixture of Cirrus and Stratus.

Cirro-cumulus—Cirrus and Cumulus.

Cumulo-stratus —a mixture of Cumulus and Stratus.

Which terms may be rendered more explanatory of the precise kind of cloud by using the augmentative termination onus, or the diminutive, itus. Thus:—Cirronus, Cirritus; Cirrono-stratus, Cirrito-stratus; Cirrono-cumulus, Cirrito-cumulus; Stratonus, Stratitus; Cumulonus, Cumulitus; Cumulono-stratus, Cumulito-stratus; which are sufficient to convey distinct ideas of every variety of clouds.

These terms may be abbreviated for common use by writing only the first letters of each word; allowing one letter to represent the diminutive, two letters the ordinary or middle degree, and three letters the augmentative. As Cirrus and Cumulus begin with the same letter, it will be necessary to make a distinction between them by taking two, three, and four letters, respectively, of Cumulus: thus, C., Ci., Cir.,; S., St., Str.; N., Ni., Nim.; Cu., Cum., Cumu. Suppose it were desired to express Cumulito-stratus, C.-Str. would be sufficient,—and similarly for the other combinations.

D

LETTER FROM THE ROYAL SOCIETY.

REPLY OF THE PRESIDENT AND COUNCIL OF THE ROYAL SOCIETY TO A LETTER FROM THE BOARD OF TRADE, DATED JANUARY 15, 1854.

Royal Society, Somerset House:
February 22, 1855.

SIR,—In the month of June last, the Lords of the Committee of the Privy Council for Trade caused a letter to be addressed to the President and Council of the Royal Society, acquainting them that their Lordships were about to submit to Parliament an estimate for an Office for the discussion of the observations on Meteorology to be made at sea in all parts of the globe, in conformity with the recommendation of a conference held at Brussels in 1853; and that they were about to construct a set of forms for the use of that office, in which they proposed to publish, from time to time, and to circulate such statistical results, obtained by means of the observations referred to, as might be considered most desirable by men learned in the science of meteorology, in addition to such other information as might be required for the purposes of navigation.

Before doing so, however, their Lordships were desirous of having the opinion of the Royal Society, as to what were the great desiderata in meteorological science, and as to the forms which may be best calculated to exhibit the great atmospheric laws which it may be most desirable to develope.

Their Lordships further state, that as it may possibly happen that observations on land upon an extended scale may hereafter be made and discussed in the same office, it is desirable that the reply of the Royal Society should keep in view, and provide for, such a contingency.

Deeply impressed with a sense of the magnitude and importance of the work which has been thus undertaken by Her Majesty's Government and confided to the Board of Trade, and fully appreciating the honour of being consulted, and the responsibility of the reply which they are called upon to make — considering also that by including the contingency of *land* observations, the enquiry is, in fact, co-extensive with the requirements of meteorology, over all accessible parts of the earth's surface — the President and Council of the Royal Society deemed it advisable, before making their reply, to obtain the opinion of those amongst their foreign members who are known as distinguished cultivators of meteorological science, as well as of others in foreign countries, who either hold offices connected with the advancement of meteorology, or have otherwise devoted themselves to this branch of science.

A circular was accordingly addressed to several gentlemen, whose names were transmitted to the Board of Trade in June last, containing a copy of the communication from the Board of Trade, and a request to be favoured with any suggestions which might aid Her Majesty's Government in an undertaking which was obviously one of general concernment.

Replies in some degree of detail have been received from five of these gentlemen,* copies of which are herewith transmitted.

The President and Council are glad to avail themselves of this opportunity of expressing their acknowledgements to these gentlemen, and more particularly to Professor Dové, Director of the meteorological establishments and institutions in Prussia, whose zeal for the advancement of meteorology induced him to repair personally to England, and to join himself to the Committee by whom the present reply has been prepared. Those who are most familiar with the labours and writings of this eminent meteorologist will best be able to appreciate the value of his cooperation.

The President and Council have considered it as the most

* Dr. Erman of Berlin, Dr. Heis of Münster, Prof. Kreil of Vienna, Lieut. Maury of Washington, and M. Quetelet of Brussels.

convenient course to divide their reply under the different heads into which the subject naturally branches. But before they proceed to treat of these, they wish to remark generally, that one of the chief impediments to the advancement of meteorology consists in the very slow progress which is made in the transmission from one country to another of the observations and discussions on which, under the fostering aid of different governments, so much labour is bestowed in Europe and America; and they would therefore recommend that such steps as may appear desirable should be taken by Her Majesty's Government to promote and facilitate the mutual interchange of meteorological publications emanating from the governments of different countries.

Barometer.

It is known that considerable differences, apparently of a permanent character, are found to exist in the mean barometric pressure in different places; and that the periodical variations in the pressure in different months and seasons at the same place are very different in different parts of the globe, both as respects period and amount; insomuch that in extreme cases the variations have even opposite features in regard to period, in places situated in the same hemisphere and at equal distances from the equator.

For the purpose of extending our knowledge of the facts of these departures from the state of equilibrium, and of more fully investigating the causes thereof, it is desirable to obtain, by means of barometric observations strictly comparable with each other, and extending over all parts of the globe accessible by land or sea, *tables*, showing the mean barometric pressure *in the year*, *in each month of the year*, and *in the four meteorological seasons* — on land, at all stations of observation — and at sea, corresponding to the middle points of spaces bounded by geographical latitudes and longitudes, not far distant from each other.

The manner of forming such tables from the marine observations which are now proposed to be made, by collecting together observations of the same month in separate ledgers, each of which should correspond to a *geographical space* comprised between specified meridians and parallels, and to a *particular month*, is too obvious to require to be further dwelt upon. The distances apart of the meridians and parallels will require to be varied in different parts of the globe, so that the magnitude of the spaces which they enclose, and for each of which a table will be formed, may be more circumscribed, when the rapidity of the variation of the particular phenomena to be elucidated is greatest in regard to geographical space. Their magnitude will also necessarily vary with the number of observations which it may be possible to collect in each space, inasmuch as it is well known that there are extensive portions of the ocean which are scarcely ever traversed by ships, whilst other portions may be viewed as the highways of a constant traffic.

The strict comparability of observations made in different ships may perhaps be best assured, by limiting the examination of the instruments to comparisons which it is proposed to make at the Kew Observatory, before and after their employment in particular ships. From the nature of their construction, the barometers with which Her Majesty's navy and the mercantile marine are to be supplied are not very liable to derangement, except from such accidents as would destroy them altogether. Under present arrangements they will all be carefully compared at Kew before they are sent to the Admiralty or to the Board of Trade; and similar arrangements may easily be made by which they may be returned to Kew for re-examination at the expiration of each tour of service. The comparison of barometers, when embarked and in use, with standards, or supposed standards, at ports which the vessels may visit, entails many inconveniences, and is in many respects a far less satisfactory method. The limitation here recommended is not, however, to be understood as applicable in the case of other establishments than Kew, where a special provision may be made for an equally careful and correct examination.

At land stations, in addition to proper measures to assure the correctness of the barometer and consequent comparability of the observations, care should be taken to ascertain by the best possible means (independently of the barometer itself) the height of the station above the level of the sea at some stated locality. For this purpose the extension of levels for the construction of railroads will often afford facilities.

It may be desirable to indicate some of the localities where the data, which tables such as those which have been spoken of would exhibit, are required for the solution of problems of immediate interest.

1°. It is known, that over the Atlantic Ocean a low mean annual pressure exists near the equator, and a high pressure at the N. and S. borders of the torrid zone (23° to 30° N. and S. latitudes); and it is probable that from similar causes similar phenomena exist over the corresponding latitudes in the Pacific Ocean: the few observations which we possess are in accord with this supposition; but the extent of space covered by the Pacific is large and the observations are few; they may be expected to be greatly increased by the means now contemplated. But it is particularly over the Indian Ocean, both at the equator and at the borders of the torrid zone, that the phenomena of the barometric pressure, not only annual but also monthly, require elucidation by observations. The trade winds which would prevail generally round the globe if it were wholly covered by a surface of water, are interrupted by the large continental spaces in Asia and Australia, and give place to the phenomena of monsoons, which are the indirect results of the heating action of the sun's rays on those continental spaces. These are the causes of that displacement of the trade winds, and substitution of a current flowing in another direction, which occasion the atmospheric phenomena over the Indian Ocean, and on the N. and S. sides of that ocean, to be different from those in corresponding localities over and on either side of the equator in the Atlantic Ocean, and (probably generally also) in the Pacific Ocean.

It is important alike to navigation and to general science to know the limits where the phenomena of the trade winds give place to those of the monsoons; and whether any and what variations take place in those limits in different parts of the year. *The barometric variations are intimately connected with the causes of these variations, and require to be known for their more perfect elucidation.*

The importance, indeed, of a full and complete knowledge of

the variations which take place in the limits of the trade winds generally in both hemispheres, at different seasons of the year, has long been recognised. On this account, although the present section is headed 'Barometer,' it may be well to remark here, that it is desirable that the forms supplied to ships should contain headings, calling forth a special record of the latitude and longitude where the trade wind is first met with, and where it is first found to fail.

2°. The great extent of continental space in Northern Asia causes, by reason of the great heat of the summer and the ascending current produced thereby, a remarkable diminution of atmospheric pressure in the summer months, extending in the N. to the Polar Sea, and on the European side as far as Moscow. Towards the E. it is known to include the coast of China and Japan, but the extent of this great diminution of summer pressure beyond the coast thus named is not known. A determination of the monthly variation of the pressure over the adjacent parts of the Pacific Ocean is therefore a desideratum; and for the same object it is desirable to have a more accurate knowledge than we now possess of the prevailing direction of the wind in different seasons in the vicinity of the coasts of China and Japan.

3°. With reference to regions or districts of increased or diminished *mean annual* pressure, it is known that in certain districts in the temperate and polar zones, such as in the vicinity of Cape Horn extending into the Antarctic polar ocean, and in the vicinity of Iceland, the mean annual barometric pressure is *considerably* less than the average pressure on the surface of the globe generally; and that anomalous differences, also of considerable amount, exist in the mean pressure in different parts of the Arctic ocean. These all require special attention, with a view to obtain a more perfect knowledge of the facts, in regard to their amount, geographical extension, and variation with the change of seasons, as well as to the elucidation of their causes.

Dry Air and Aqueous Vapour.

The apparently anomalous variations which have been noticed to exist in the mean annual barometric pressure, and in its distribution in the different seasons and months of the year, are also found to exist in each of the two constituent pressures which conjointly constitute the barometric pressure. In order to study the problems connected with these departures from a state of equilibrium under their most simple forms — and generally for the true understanding of almost all the great laws of atmospheric change,— it is necessary to have a separate knowledge of the two constituents (viz., the pressures of the dry air and of the aqueous vapour) which we are accustomed to measure together by the barometer. This separate knowledge is obtained by means of the hygrometer, which determines the elasticity of the vapour, and leads to the determination of that of the dry air, by enabling us to deduct the elasticity of the vapour from that of the whole barometric pressure. It is therefore extremely desirable that tables, similar to those recommended under the preceding head of the barometer, should be formed at every land station, and over the ocean at the centres of geographical spaces bounded by certain values of latitude and longitude, for the *annual*, *monthly*, and *season* pressures, — 1. Of the aqueous vapour; and 2. Of the dry air; each considered separately. Each of the said geographical spaces will require its appropriate ledger for each of the twelve months.

It may be desirable to notice one or two of the problems connected with extensive and important atmospherical laws, which may be materially assisted by such tables.

1°. By the operation of causes which are too well known to require explanation here, the dry air should always have a minimum pressure in the hottest months of the year. But we know that there are places where the contrary prevails—namely, that the pressure of the dry air is greater in summer than in winter. We also know that when comparison is made between places in the same latitude, and having the same, or very nearly the same, differences of temperature in summer and in winter, the differences between the summer and winter pressures of the dry air are found to be subject to many remarkable anomalies. The variations in the pressure of the dry air do not therefore, as might be at first imagined, depend altogether on the differences between the summer and winter temperatures at the places where the variations themselves occur. The increased pressure in the hottest months appears rather to point to the existence of an overflow of air in the higher regions of the atmosphere from *lateral sources* ; the statical pressure at the base of the column being increased by the augmentation of the superincumbent mass of air arising from an influx in the upper portion. Such lateral sources may well be supposed to be due to *excessive ascensional currents* caused by *excessive summer heats* in certain places of the globe (as, for example, in Central Asia). Now the lateral overflow from such sources, traversing in the shape of currents the higher regions of the atmosphere, and encountering the well-known general current flowing from the equator towards the pole, has been recently assigned with considerable probability (derived from its correspondence with many otherwise anomalous phenomena already known, and which all receive an explanation from such supposition) to be the original source or primary cause of the *rotating storms* or *cyclones*, so well known in the West Indies and in China under the names of hurricanes and typhoons. A single illustration may be desirable. Let it be supposed that such an excessive ascensional current exists over the greatly heated parts of Asia and Africa in the northern tropical zone — giving rise, in the continuation of the same zone over the Atlantic Ocean, to a lateral current in the upper regions; this would then be a current prevailing in those regions from E. to W.; and it would encounter over the Atlantic Ocean the well-known upper current proceeding from the equator towards the pole, which is a current from the SW. An easterly current impinging on a SW. current may give rise, by well-known laws, to a rotatory motion in the atmosphere, of which the direction may be the same as that which characterises the cyclones of the northern hemisphere. To test the accuracy of this explanation, we desire to be acquainted with the variations which the *mean pressure of the dry air undergoes in the different seasons* in the part of the globe, where, according to this explanation, considerable variations having particular characters ought to be found.

2°. We have named one of the explanations which have been recently offered of the primary cause of the northern cyclones. Another mode of explanation has been proposed, by assuming the condensation of large quantities of vapour, and the consequent influx of air to supply the place. In such case the phenomena are to be tested in considerable measure by the variations which the *other constituent* of the barometric pressure — namely, the *aqueous vapour* — undergoes.

3°. The surface of sea in the southern hemisphere *much* exceeds that in the northern hemisphere. It is, therefore, probable that at the season when the sun is over the southern hemisphere, evaporation over the whole surface of the globe is more considerable than in the opposite season, when the sun is over the northern hemisphere. Supposing the pressure of the dry air to be a constant, the difference of evaporation in the two seasons may thus produce for the whole globe an *annual barometric variation*, the aggregate barometric pressure over the *whole* surface being highest during the northern winter. The separation of the barometric pressure into its two constituent pressures would give direct and conclusive evidence of the cause to which such a barometric variation should be ascribed. It would also follow that evaporation being greatest in the S., and condensation greatest in the N., the water which proceeds from S. to N. in a state of vapour would have to return to the S. in a liquid state, and might possibly exert some discernible influence on the currents of the ocean. The tests by which the truth of the suppositions thus advanced may be determined are the variations of the meteorological elements in different seasons and months, determined by methods and instruments strictly comparable with each other, and arranged in such tables as have been suggested. A still more direct test would indeed be furnished by the fact (if it could be ascertained), that the quantity of rain which falls in the northern is greater than that which falls in the southern hemisphere, and by examining its distribution into the different months and seasons of its occurrence. Data for such conclusions are as yet very insufficient: they should always, however, form a part of the record at all land stations where registers are kept.

In order that all observations of the elasticity of the aqueous vapour may be strictly comparable, it is desirable that all should be computed by the same tables; those founded upon the experiments of MM. Regnault and Magnus may be most suitably recommended for this purpose, not only on their general merits, but also as being likely to be most generally adopted by observers in other countries.

Temperature of the Air.

Tables of the mean temperature of the air in the year, and in the different months and seasons of the year, at above 1,000 stations on the globe, have recently been computed by Professor Dové, and published under the auspices of the Royal Academy of Sciences at Berlin. This work, which is a true model of the method in which a great body of meteorological facts, collected by different observers and at different times, should be brought together and coordinated, has conducted, as is well known, to conclusions of very considerable importance in their bearing on climatology, and on the general laws of the distribution of heat on the surface of the globe. These tables have, however, been formed exclusively from observations made *on land*. For the completion of this great work of physical geography, there is yet wanting a similar investigation for the *oceanic* portion: and this we may hopefully anticipate as likely to be now accomplished by means of the marine observations about to be undertaken. In the case of the temperature of the air, as in that of the atmospheric pressure previously adverted to, the centres of geographical spaces bounded by certain latitudes and longitudes will form points of concentration, for observations which may be made within those spaces, not only by the same but also by different ships; provided that the system be steadily maintained of employing only instruments which shall have been examined, and their intercomparability ascertained, by a competent and responsible authority; and provided that no observations be used but those in which careful attention shall have been given to the precautions which it will be necessary to adopt, for the purpose of obtaining the correct knowledge of the temperature of the external air, amidst the many disturbing influences from heat and moisture so difficult to escape on board ship. In this respect additional precautions must be used, if *night observations* are to be required, since the ordinary difficulties are necessarily much enhanced by the employment of artificial light. Amongst the instructions which will be required perhaps there will be none which will need to be more carefully drawn than those for obtaining the correct temperature of the external air under the continually varying circumstances that present themselves on board ship.

In regard to *land stations*, Professor Dové's tables have shown that data are still pressingly required from the British North American possessions intermediate between the stations of the Arctic expeditions and those of the United States; and that the deficiency extends across the whole North American continent in those latitudes from the Atlantic to the Pacific. Professor Dové has also indicated as desiderata observations at the British military stations in the Mediterranean (Gibraltar, Malta, and Corfu), and around the coasts of Australia and New Zealand: also that *hourly* observations, continued for at least one year, are particularly required at some one station in the West Indies, to supply the diurnal corrections for existing observations.

Whilst the study of the distribution of heat at the surface of the globe has thus been making progress, in respect to the *mean annual temperature* in different places, and to its *periodical variations* in different parts of the year at the same place, the attention of physical geographers has recently been directed (and with great promise of important results to the material interests of men as well as to general science) to the causes of those fluctuations in the temperature, or departures from its mean or normal state at the same place and at the same period of the year, which have received the name of 'non-periodic variations.' It is known that these frequently affect extensive portions of the globe at the same time; and are generally, if not always, accompanied by a fluctuation of an opposite character, prevailing at the same time in some adjoining, but distant region; so that by the comparison of synchronous observations a progression is traceable, from a locality of maximum increased heat in one region, to one of maximum diminished heat in another region. For the elucidation of the non-periodic variations even *monthly* means are insufficient; and the necessity has been felt of computing the mean temperatures for periods of much shorter duration. The Meteorological Institutions of those of the

European states which have taken the foremost part in the prosecution of meteorology, have in consequence adopted *five-day means*, as the most suitable intermediate gradation between daily and monthly means; and as an evidence of the conviction which is entertained of the value of the conclusions to which this investigation is likely to lead, it has been considered worth while to undertake the prodigious labour of calculating the five-day means of the most reliable existing observations during a century past. This work is already far advanced; and it cannot be too strongly recommended, that at all fixed stations, where observations shall hereafter be made with sufficient care to be worth recording, five-days means may invariably be added to the daily, monthly, and annual means into which the observations are usually collected. The five-day means should always commence with January 1, for the purpose of preserving the uniformity at different stations, which is essential for comparison: in leap years, the period which includes February 29 will be of six days.

In treating climatology as a *science*, it is desirable that some correct and convenient mode should be adopted for computing and expressing the *comparative variability* to which the temperature in different parts of the globe, and in different parts of the year in the same place, is subject from non-periodic causes. The *probable variability*, computed on the same principle as the *probable error* of each of a number of independent observations, has recently been suggested as furnishing an index 'of the probable daily non-periodic variation' at the different seasons of the year; and its use in this respect had been exemplified by calculations of the 'index' from the five-day means of twelve years of observations at Toronto, in Canada (Phil. Trans. 1853, Art. V.). An index of this description is of course of absolute and general application; supplying the means of comparing the probable variability of the temperature in different seasons at *different places* (where the same method of computation is adopted) as well as at the *same place*. It is desirable that this (or some preferable method, if such can be devised for obtaining the same object) should be adopted by those who may desire to make their observations practically useful for sanitary or agricultural purposes, or for any of the great variety of objects for which climatic peculiarities are required to be known. Having these three data, viz. the mean annual temperature—its periodical changes in respect to days, months, and seasons—and the measure of its liability to non-periodic (or what would commonly be called irregular) variations—we may consider that we possess as complete a representation of the climate of any particular place (so far as temperature is concerned) as the present state of our knowledge permits.

It is obvious that much of what has been said under this article is more applicable to land than to sea observations; but the letter of the Board of Trade, to which this is a reply, requests that both should be contemplated.

Temperature of the Sea, and Investigations regarding Currents.

It is unnecessary to dwell on the practical importance to *navigation* of a correct knowledge of the currents of the ocean; their direction, extent, velocity, and the temperature of the surface water relatively to the ordinary ocean temperature in the same latitude; together with the variations in all these respects which currents experience in different parts of the year, and in different parts of their course. As the information on these points, which may be expected to follow from the measures adopted by the Board of Trade, must necessarily depend in great degree on the *intelligence*, as well as the *interest* taken in them by the observers, it is desirable that the instructions to be supplied with the meteorological instruments should contain a brief summary of what is already known in regard to the principal oceanic currents; accompanied by charts on which their supposed limits in different seasons, and the variations in those limits which may have been observed in particular years, may be indicated, with notices of the particularities of the temperature of the surface-water by which the presence of the current may be recognised. Forms will also be required for use in such localities, in which the surface temperatures may be recorded at hourly or half-hourly intervals, with the corresponding geographical positions of the ship, as they may be best inferred from observation and reckoning. For such localities also it will be necessary that the tables, into which the observations of different ships at different seasons are collected, should have their bounding lines of latitude and longitude brought nearer together than may be required for the ocean at large.

In looking forward to the results which are likely to be obtained by the contemplated marine observations, it is reasonable that those which may bear practically on the interests of navigation should occupy the first place; but on the other hand, it would not be easy to over-estimate the advantages to physical geography, of general tables of the surface temperature of the ocean in the different months of the year, exhibiting, as they would do, its normal and its abnormal states, the mean temperature of the different parallels, and the deviations therefrom, whether permanent, periodical, or occasional. The knowledge which such tables would convey is essentially required for the study of climatology *as a science.*

The degree in which climatic variations extending over large portions of the earth's surface may be influenced by the variable phenomena of oceanic currents in different years, may perhaps be illustrated by circumstances of known occurrence in the vicinity of our own coasts. The admirable researches of Major Rennell have shown that in ordinary years the warm water of the great current known by the name of the Gulf Stream is not found to the E. of the meridian of the Azores; the sea being of ordinary ocean temperature for its latitude at all seasons, and in every direction, in the great space comprised between the Azores and the coasts of Europe and North Africa: but Major Rennell has also shown that on two occasions, viz. in 1776 and in 1821–1822, the warm water by which the Gulf Stream is characterised throughout its whole course (*being several degrees* above the ordinary ocean temperature in the same latitude), was found to extend across this great expanse of ocean, and in 1776 (in particular) was traced (by Dr. Franklin) quite home to the coast of Europe. The presence of a body of unusually heated water, extending for several hundred miles both in latitude and in longitude, and continuing for several weeks, at a season of the year when the prevailing winds blow from that quarter on the coasts of England and France, can scarcely be imagined to be without a considerable influence on the relations of temperature and moisture in those countries. In accordance with this supposition, we find in the Meteorological Journals of the more recent period (which are more easily accessible), that the state of the weather in November and December 1821 and January 1822 was so unusual in the southern parts of Great Britain and in France, as to have excited general observation; we find it characterised as 'most extraordinarily hot, damp, stormy, and oppressive, that 'the gales from the W. and SW. were almost without intermission,' 'the fall of rain was excessive,' and 'the barometer lower than it had ever been known for *thirty-five* years before.

There can be little doubt that Major Rennell was right in ascribing the unusual extension of the Gulf Stream in particular years to its greater initial velocity, occasioned by a more than ordinary difference in the levels of the Gulf of Mexico and of the Atlantic in the preceding summer. An unusual height of the Gulf of Mexico at the head of the stream, or an unusual velocity of the stream at its outset in the Strait of Florida, are facts which may admit of being recognised by properly directed attention; and as these must precede, by many weeks, the arrival of the warm water of the stream at above 3,000 miles distant from its outset, and the climatic effects thence resulting, it might be possible to anticipate the occurrence of such unusual seasons upon our coasts.

Much, indeed, may undoubtedly be done towards the increase of our partial acquaintance with the phenomena of the Gulf Stream, and of its counter currents, by the collection and co-ordination of observations made by casual passages of ships in different years and different seasons across different parts of its course; but for that full and complete knowledge of all its particulars, which should meet the maritime and scientific requirements of the period in which we live, we must await the disposition of Government to accede to the recommendation, so frequently made to them by the most eminent hydrographical authorities, of a specific survey of the stream by vessels employed for that special service. What has been recently accomplished by the Government of the United States in this respect shows both the importance of the enquiry and the great extent of the research, and lends great weight to the proposition which has been made to Her Majesty's Government on the part of the United States, for a joint survey of the whole stream by vessels of the two countries. The establishment of an office under the Board of Trade specially charged with the reduction and co-ordination of such data may materially facilitate such an undertaking.

Storms or Gales.

It is much to be desired, both for the purposes of navigation and for those of general science, that the captains of Her Majesty's ships and masters of merchant vessels should be correctly and thoroughly instructed in the methods of distinguishing *in all cases* between the rotatory storms or gales, which are properly called *cyclones*, and gales of a more ordinary character, but which are frequently accompanied by a veering of the wind, which under certain circumstances might easily be confounded with the phenomena of cyclones, though due to a very different cause. It is recommended, therefore, that the instructions proposed to be given to ships supplied with meteorological instruments should contain clear and simple directions for distinguishing *in all cases* and *under all circumstances* between these two kinds of storms; and that the forms to be issued for recording the meteorological phenomena during great atmospheric disturbances should comprehend a notice of all the particulars which are required for forming a correct judgement in this respect.

Thunder-storms.

It is known that in the high latitudes of the northern and southern hemispheres thunder-storms are almost wholly unknown; and it is believed that they are of very rare occurrence over the ocean in the middle latitudes when distant from continents. By a suitable classification and arrangement of the documents which will be henceforward received by the Board of Trade, statistical tables may in process of time be formed, showing the comparative frequency of these phenomena in different parts of the ocean and in different months of the year.

It is known that there are localities on the globe where, during certain months of the year, thunder-storms may be considered as a periodical phenomenon of daily occurrence. In the Port Royal Mountains in Jamaica, for example, thunder-storms are said to take place *daily* about the hour of noon from the middle of November to the middle of April. It is much to be desired that a full and precise account of such thunder-storms, and of the circumstances in which they appear to originate, should be obtained.

In recording the phenomena of thunder and lightning, it is desirable to state the duration of the interval between the flashes of lightning and the thunder which follows. This may be done by means of a seconds-hand watch, by which the time of the apparition of the flash, and of the commencement (and of the conclusion also) of the thunder may be noted. The interval between the flash and the commencement of the thunder has been known to vary in different cases, from less than a single second to between forty and fifty seconds, and even on very rare occasions to exceed fifty seconds. The two forms of ordinary lightning, viz. zigzag (or forked) lightning and sheet lightning, should always be distinguished apart; and particular attention should be given both to the observation and to the record, in the rare cases when zigzag lightning either bifurcates, or returns upwards. A special notice should not fail to be made when thunder and lightning, or either separately, occur in a perfectly cloudless sky. When globular lightning (balls of fire) are seen, a particular record should be made of all the attendant circumstances. These phenomena are known to be of the nature of lightning, from the injury they have occasioned in ships and buildings that have been struck by them; but they differ from ordinary lightning, not only by their globular shape, but by the length of time they continue visible, and by their slow motion. They are said to occur sometimes without the usual accompaniments of a storm, and even with a perfectly serene sky. Conductors are now so universally employed in ships that it may seem almost superfluous to remark that, should a ship be struck by lightning, the most circumstantial account will be desirable of the course which the lightning took, and of the injuries it occasioned; or to remind the seaman that it is always prudent after such an accident has befallen a ship, to distrust her compasses until it has been ascertained that their direction has not been altered. Accidents occurring *on land* from lightning will, of course, receive the fullest attention from meteorologists who may be within convenient distance of the spot.

Auroras and Falling Stars.

Auroras are of such rare occurrence in seas frequented by ships engaged in commerce, that it may seem superfluous to give any particular directions for their observation *at sea*; and land observatories are already abundantly furnished with such. It is, of course, desirable that the meteorological reports received from ships should always contain a notice of the time and place where auroras may be seen, and of any remarkable features that may attract attention.

The letter from Professor Heis, which is one of the foreign communications, indicates the principal points to be attended to in the instructions which it may be desirable to draw up for the observation of 'Falling Stars.' For directions concerning Haloes and Parhelia, a paper by Monsieur Bravais in the 'Annuaire Météorologique de la France' for 1851, contains suggestions which will be found of much value.

Charts of the Magnetic Variation.

Although the variation of the compass does not belong in strictness to the domain of meteorology, it has been included, with great propriety, amongst the subjects treated of by the Brussels Conference, and therefore should not be omitted here. It is scarcely necessary to remark, that whatever may have been the practice in times past, when the phenomena of the earth's magnetism were less understood than at present, it should in future be regarded as indispensable, that variation charts should always be constructed for a *particular epoch*, and that *all parts* of the chart should show *the variation corresponding to the epoch for which it is constructed.* Such charts should also have, either engraved on the face or attached in some convenient manner, a table, showing the approximate annual rate of the secular change of the variation in the different latitudes and longitudes comprised: so that by means of this table, the variation taken from the chart for any particular latitude and longitude may be corrected to the year for which it is required, if that should happen to be different from the epoch for which the chart is constructed.

A valuable service would be rendered to this very important branch of hydrography if, under the authority of the new department of the Board of Trade, variation charts for the North and South Atlantic Oceans, for the North and South Pacific Oceans, for the Indian Ocean, and for any other locality in which the requirements of navigation might call for them, were published at *stated intervals*, corrected for the secular change that had taken place since the preceding publication. Materials would be furnished for this purpose by the observations which are now intended to be made, supposing them to be collected and suitably arranged, with proper references to date and to geographical position, and to the original reports in which the results and the data on which they were founded were communicated. By means of these observations, the tables of approximate correction for secular change might also be altered from time to time as occasion should require, since the rate of secular change itself is not constant.

All observed variations, communicated or employed as data upon which variation charts may be either constructed or corrected, should be accompanied by other observational data (the nature of which ought now to be well understood) for correcting the observed variation for the error of the compass occasioned by the ship's iron. It is also strongly recommended that no observations be received as data for the formation or correction of variation charts, but such as are accompanied by a detailed statement of the principal elements both of observation and of calculation. Proper forms should be supplied for this purpose; or, what is still better, books of blank forms may be supplied, in which the observations themselves may be entered, and the calculation performed by which the results are obtained. Such books of blank forms would be found extremely useful both for the variation of the needle, and for the chronometrical longitude (as well as for lunar observations, if the practice of lunar observations be not, as there is too much reason to fear it is, almost wholly discontinued). By preparing and issuing books of blank forms suitable for these purposes, and by requesting their return in accompaniment with the other reports to be transmitted to the Board of Trade at the conclusion of a voyage, the groundwork would be laid for the attainment of greatly improved habits of accuracy, in practical navigation in the British mercantile marine.

The President and Council are aware that they have not exhausted the subject of this reply in what they have thus directed me to address to you; but they think that perhaps they have noticed as many points as may be desirable for *present* attention; and they desire me to add, that they will be at all times ready to resume the consideration if required, and to supply any further suggestions which may appear likely to be useful.

I have the honour to be, Sir,
Your obedient Servant,
W. Sharpey, *Sec.*

To the Secretary of the Lords of the Committee
of Privy Council for Trade.

A subsequent correspondence passed, in May and June 1856, from which the following extract may be here given, being the only part of that correspondence which related to the meteorologic desiderata referred to in the communication from the Board of Trade.

Extract.

It cannot be doubted that one of the most important objects of the Meteorological Department, both in a practical and theoretical view, is the procurement of the statistics of the direction and force of the wind in different seasons of the year over those parts of the Atlantic Ocean which are most usually traversed by ships. The records kept by the vessels themselves, suitably coordinated, may be expected in the course of time to do much towards this very important purpose; but the Committee are desirous of bringing under the consideration of the Board of Trade the advisability of aiding and expediting the enquiry by establishing, as far as may be found convenient, self-recording anemometrical instruments on some of the islands of the Atlantic. Detached observations of the wind, taken at intervals on board ship, may be most valuable in filling up the spaces between fixed and unerring self-recording instruments, but are scarcely sufficient to procure such exact knowledge of the variations as is required, not less for the purposes and improvement of navigation than for the complete theory of the laws which regulate these variations. The Azores, Madeira, Bermuda, Ascension, and St. Helena, are all stations where continuous and exact anemometrical records might be obtained, probably with very little inconvenience and at a comparatively small cost, and would be most valuable in the relation above stated. A self-recording anemometer quite suitable for this purpose is now under construction at the Kew Observatory; and instruments on the same model might be procured complete, it is believed, at a cost of less than 50*l.*, requiring no other alteration than the change, once in twenty-four hours, of the paper on which the instrument itself records the direction and force of the wind.

Signed officially by the Secretary.

[N.B. — These admirably suggestive and directing Instructions,—a basis on which to act in the Meteorologic Office of the Board of Trade, were written by General Sabine, now President of the Royal Society. R. F.]

E

WIND CHART DETAILS

Square 375.

Subdivided into *a*, *b*, *c*, *d*, which subdivision may be continued by quartering and lettering *a*, *b*, *c*, *d*, as *e*, *f*, *g*, *h*, &c.

South Atlantic.

Brazilian Coast (near Rio de Janeiro).
For Three Months — January, February, March.

Four Windroses are condensed into this Diagram; namely, those for—

	a	*b*	*c*	*d*
Lats. and	20° + 25° S.	20° + 25° S.	25° + 30° S.	25° + 30° S.
Longs.	30° + 35° W.	35° + 40° W.	30° + 35° W.	35° + 40° W.

OBSNS 3671.
WINDS 3567.
CALMS 104.
UNIT OF SCALE 0.0041.
(+0.1 FOR CALMS AND RAIN SCALE.)
DAILY CURRENT

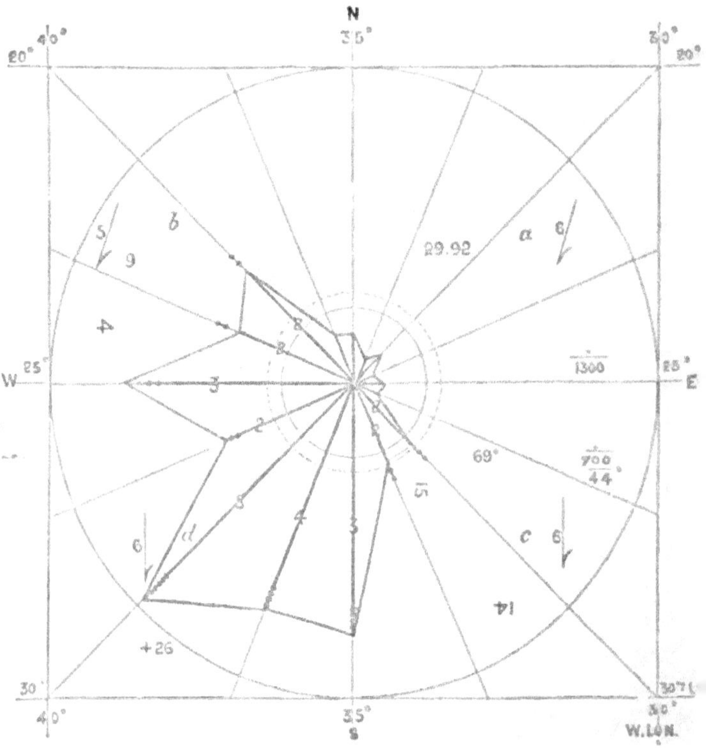

Scale of Wind:				
Beaufort . 1–12 and Land . 1–6	1 = 2 = Light	Temp. sea surf. 69°	Var. (¼ turn)
	2 = 4 = Moderate	Depth . . 1,500	Dip (½ turn)
	3 = 6 = Fresh	No ground at . 1300	Sp. Gr. + 26
	4 = 8 = Strong	Temp. at . 1500/44°	(1,000 + ?)
	5 = 10 = Heavy	Variation .	
	6 = 12 = Violent	Dip . .	

SQUARE 338.

SOUTH ATLANTIC.

Brazilian Coast (near Bahia).

For Three Months—January, February, March.

Five-inch Square: half one side (= radius of inscribed circle) has 2,500-thousandths of an inch, in which measure the *unit for scale* is taken.

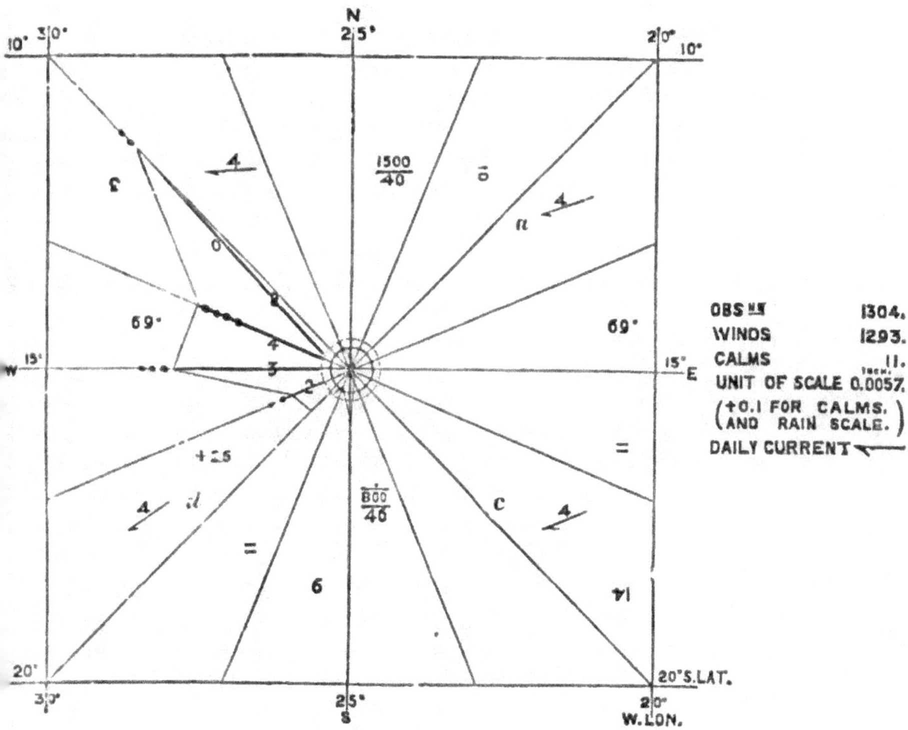

et n = number of parts in *radius* (=2,500)
n' = " " longest point (*radius*)
l = length of *one* part of radius = (·001)
l' = length of unit of scale;
en $n' : n :: l : l'$

$$\therefore \frac{n \times l}{n'} = l' = \textit{unit of scale}$$

Log. n (2,500)	$= 3{\cdot}3979$
Log. l (·001)	$= \bar{3}{\cdot}0000$
	0·3979
Log. $n' = (439)$	2·6425
Unit of Scale $= l' =$ ·0057	$= \bar{3}{\cdot}7554$

Specimen of Method adopted in Subdivision of Squares of Ten Degrees into which the Surface of the Globe is supposed to be divided.

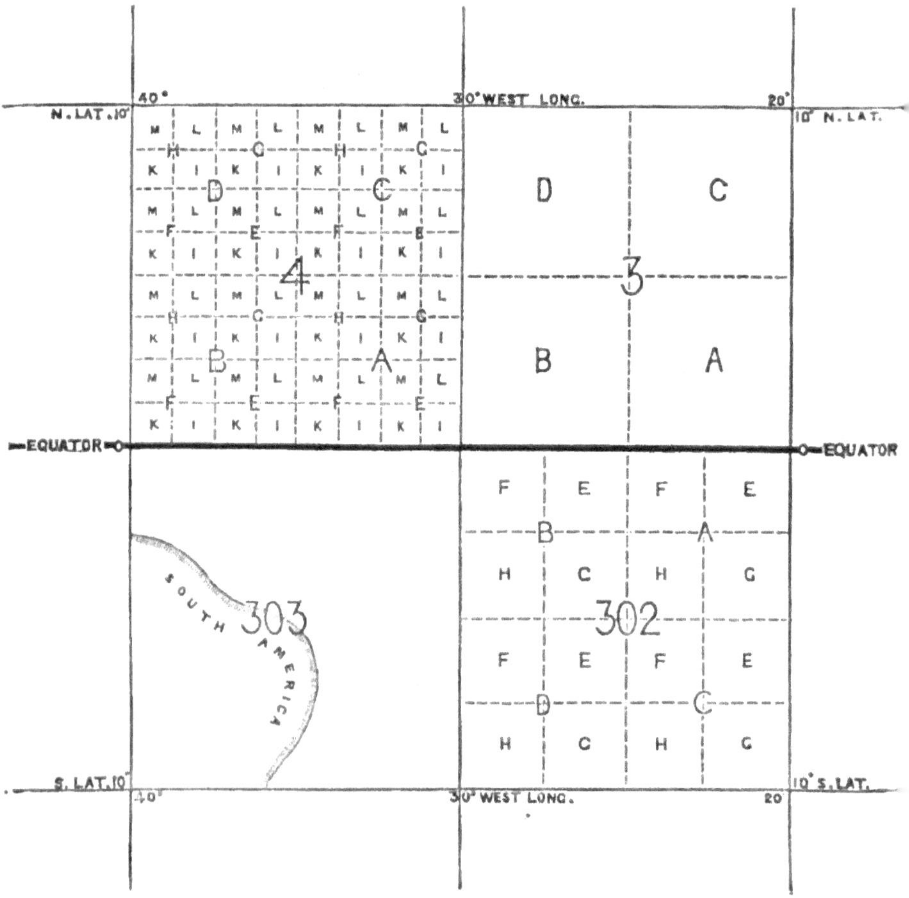

N.B. The letters in the above diagram may be of any character.

DIVISIONS OF THE GLOBE AND CONSTRUCTION OF WIND CHARTS.

Divisions of the Globe.

The mode of exhibiting barometric and thermometric oscillations by diagrams is familiar to most persons; but, as the method here adopted to show the results of observations of wind, weather, and some other matters graphically, is new, it may require explanation.

The surface of the globe is supposed to be divided into squares of ten degrees each. Beginning at the meridian of Greenwich, on the Equator, the numbers go westward until the same meridian is regained; then, on the next circle, northward, between the parallels of 10 and 20 degrees of latitude; and so on, omitting the 10 degrees' space of latitude around the pole.

From the first meridian the squares S. of the Equator are numbered from 300 in a similar manner, but *southward* to the eightieth southern parallel. Thus distinguished by numbers not exceeding 600, all those below 300 being N. of the Equator, the locality of each frequented square may soon become fixed in the memory of a navigator, and serve (like provinces on land) to recall *spaces* to the mind, rather than points indicated only by latitude and longitude.

Observations made in any square may be referred to the centre of that square, as to an Observatory at which observations are made regularly.

In such spaces it is supposed that meteorologic occurrences will not generally be very dissimilar; and that, if all are referred to the centre of that square, or subdivision of it, in which they occur, the mean result of a great number of observations will give a reliable and approximately correct general average for practical use.

If between each time of observation eight hours elapse, three winds (or calms) may be noted for one day.

During a certain interval of weeks, months, seasons, or years, a number of observations are collected. These are classified and totalled under points of the compass. A circle being inscribed in a square of so many degrees, the greatest number of observations under any point governs the scale of equal parts according to which the numbers of winds under each point are laid down, from the centre of the circle *leewardly* toward its circumference, the longest point being always equal to the radius. Through the extremities of these lines, on points or alternate points of the compass, a line is drawn, as a curve is drawn through ordinates, and the resulting diagram (a wind star) shows the *proportion* of winds.

The greater area of the figure being to leeward of the centre indicates, at a glance, the *relative* prevalence of wind from particular points, and its relative duration.

As a circle is said to be generated by the revolution of its radius, so a wind star may be said to result from the motion of a vane; and persistence in any direction may be supposed to increase the length of the corresponding line or point (like the growth of crystals).

The average strength of wind may be shown by parallel lines, or numerically, or by dots; the per-centage of calms by a circle of which the radius equals their number (according to the scale of the diagram); the per-centage of rain by a dotted circle, on a similar principle; and oceanic currents by the usual arrows and numbers. In addition may be given, without overloading the paper, confusing the eye, or using colours,* the per-centage of gales or storms (by marks on the point lines), deep-sea soundings, temperature, atmospheric pressure, and the specific gravity of sea water; besides variation of the magnetic needle, and perhaps other information.

Many wind charts for the principal oceans have been published, but they show part only of what may be given at a future time.

* Colours increase the expense of printing.

F

SIMULTANEOUS OBSERVATIONS.

It has been desired that a great many observations should be compared throughout the British Islands (with their neighbouring coasts and seas), at certain remarkable periods, to obtain the means of delineating or mapping the atmosphere at successive times; and thence to deduce the order of those changes of wind and weather which affect navigation and fisheries especially, besides agriculture, health, and all out-door occupations.

Such maps or charts should show the various horizontal or other currents of wind (existing within such an area) at one time, to which all other corresponding times should be reduced by allowing for the *difference of longitude.*

They should show the pressure and temperature of those currents — and other facts, such as the presence of clouds, rain, lightning, &c., at their respective localities.

A sequence of such maps, compiled for special periods when changes have been most marked, would enable meteorologists to trace atmospheric waves as well as currents, both in plan and section, and would throw much light on meteorology.

Means should be taken, by circular letters, accompanied by a form for details, or otherwise, to request copies of such particular observations, made between certain limits and dates, as might be specified in a general manner.

LETTER—FIRST CIRCULATED IN 1857.

Probably all persons who are interested in meteorology as a science, or in changes of wind and weather as practical matters affecting every-day life, have more or less noticed the remarkable changes of the last winter season (1856–57).

The meteorologic department of the Board of Trade is collecting facts in connection with such changes of weather and violent winds, with the view of ascertaining exactly where and when they occurred throughout a considerable area, including the British Islands and adjacent localities.

This last winter has been selected as a portion of time within which certain sequences of simultaneous observations at a great many places may be collected, and their results arranged for publication, with particular advantage.

The direction and force of wind, nature and changes of weather, height of barometer, temperature of air, and moisture, are particularly desired, at whatever time actually observed, at sea or on land, between the meridians of thirty degrees W. and thirty of E. longitude, and between the parallels of forty degrees and sixty-seven of N. latitude.

In all cases, the peculiarities and errors or corrections of instruments should be given, with the known or estimated height (saying which) of the barometer, above the mean level of the sea, besides expressing whether the observations are given exactly as made, or whether any and what corrections have been applied toward their reduction.

The more numerous the exact observations and details that may be transmitted, the more valuable will be the communication.

Captains of ships within the specified area, during the months selected, are particularly requested to send in as many observations as their logs or registers contain, for comparison made with those at lighthouses, and with the numerous records now kept by private observers, besides those of established Observatories.

[N.B. These, and subsequent arrangements, enabled us to compile and construct many hundred wind charts—to be lithographically multiplied into very many thousand.]

G

DIRECTIONS FOR USING THE PORTABLE CUP AND DIAL ANEMOMETER.

THE instrument is to be fixed, with the axis in a vertical position, in as exposed a situation, and as high above the ground, as may be consistent with convenience in reading. The readings are taken in the same way as those of a gas-meter, commencing with the dial to the *left*, or farthest from the endless screw on the axis.

There are five dials. The figures on the first dial (to the left) indicate so many hundreds of thousands of revolutions; those on the second dial so many tens of thousands; those on the third, thousands; those on the fourth, hundreds; and those on the fifth (or right-hand dial), so many tens.

The instrument should be read every morning at 9 o'clock; and, usually, it will only be necessary to read the first three dials. The figures can be entered as they are read off. Should the index point *between* two figures, the less of the two is to be taken.

For example, if the first dial points to 7, or between 7 and 8; while the second dial indicates 4; and the third, 5; the entry to be made is 745 (indicative of 745 *thousand* revolutions).

Every time the index of the first dial is found to have passed zero (0), a cross or star is to be prefixed to the next (a lower) reading.

To ascertain how many *thousands* of revolutions have been made during the month, it will simply be necessary to subtract the first reading from the last, and prefix to the three figures thus obtained a figure corresponding to the number of stars in the column. For every *thousand* revolutions there are two miles of wind: we have therefore only to multiply by 2 to find how many miles of wind have passed during the month.

Two entries should be made for the last day of each month (the one being written under the other), so as to bring the readings down to 9 A.M. on the 1st of the following month. The same entry which ends one month will therefore begin the next. This repetition of one entry is necessary in order to prevent losing a day's wind.

The accompanying example of the readings of an anemometer for 13 days will illustrate the method of making the entries, &c.

In this instance the first reading (687) is less than the last (793). When the first reading is greater than the last, it will be necessary to borrow 1,000 in making the subtractions, and then deduct one from the number of stars. Thus, if the first reading of the series on the margin had been 887, the result would have been 906 instead of 1,106.

687
773
822
855
900
953
990
*066
197
323
414
597
712
793

1,106 thousands of revolutions.
2
13 | 2,212 miles of wind in period.
170 miles of wind per day, on an average.

[N.B. This small but accurate instrument may be used at sea, if duly managed, and is very convenient for any place on land. It has been well proved *experimentally*.]

The foregoing directions are all which require to be regularly attended to. But it may be interesting at times to find the velocity of the wind during a period of a few minutes. This may be ascertained, by observing the difference of two readings of all the dials with an interval of some minutes between them, when a very brief calculation will suffice; but perhaps the simplest method that can be adopted is the following:—

Take two readings, with an interval of 12 minutes between them. The difference of these readings, divided by 10, is the velocity of the wind in miles per hour. Thus—if the reading of the five dials (from left to right) at noon is 15206, and at 12 minutes past 12 is 15348, the velocity of the wind is 14·2 miles per hour.

The following is the principle on which the instrument is constructed :—

It has been established, both by theory and experiment, that the centre of any one of the cups moves with a third of the wind's velocity. The dimensions of these instruments are such that the circle described by the centre of any cup is $\frac{1}{1500}$ of a mile. The amount of wind required to produce one of these revolutions is three times as much, or $\frac{1}{500}$ of a mile. Hence 500 revolutions of the cups are produced by a mile of wind, or 1,000 revolutions by two miles of wind.

In round numbers, the action of the wind on one concave surface is *four* times that on its opposite convex: the antagonistic forces being the action of wind on three convex surfaces of the four hemispheres, and a very slight amount of friction.*

Velocity and Pressure of the Wind.

The pressure varies as the square of the velocity, or $P \sim v^2$. The square of the velocity in miles per hour multiplied by ·005 gives the pressure in lbs. per square foot, or $v^2 \times \cdot 005 = P$. The square root of 200 times the pressure equals the velocity, or $\sqrt{200 \times P} = v$, and from this formula the *second* table is calculated. The *first* is obtained directly from it, conversely, and both ought to accompany every cup anemometer.

* See Robinson and Lloyd in Tr. R. I. Academy, vol. xxii. With due allowance for length of arm (or radius) which may be greater or less than that here mentioned, this applies to the large, and self-registering, as well as to the small portable Cup Anemometer, and likewise to the miniature instruments used (on similar principles of construction) for measuring draughts of air in buildings.

VELOCITY AND PRESSURE TABLE

Conversion of Hourly Horizontal Motion into Pressure per square foot

Miles	lbs.	Miles	lbs.	Miles	lbs.	Miles	lbs.
1	·005	26	3·4	51	13·0	76	28·9
2	·020	27	3·6	52	13·5	77	29·6
3	·045	28	3·9	53	14·0	78	30·4
4	·1	29	4·2	54	14·6	79	31·2
5	·1	30	4·5	55	15·1	80	32·0
6	·2	31	4·8	56	15·7	81	32·8
7	·2	32	5·1	57	16·2	82	33·6
8	·3	33	5·4	58	16·8	83	34·4
9	·4	34	5·8	59	17·4	84	35·3
10	·5	35	6·1	60	18·0	85	36·1
11	·6	36	6·5	61	18·6	86	37·0
12	·7	37	6·8	62	19·2	87	37·8
13	·8	38	7·2	63	19·8	88	38·7
14	1·0	39	7·6	64	20·5	89	39·6
15	1·1	40	8·0	65	21·1	90	40·5
16	1·3	41	8·4	66	21·8	91	41·4
17	1·4	42	8·8	67	22·4	92	42·3
18	1·6	43	9·2	68	23·1	93	43·2
19	1·8	44	9·7	69	23·8	94	44·2
20	2·0	45	10·1	70	24·5	95	45·1
21	2·2	46	10·6	71	25·2	96	46·1
22	2·4	47	11·0	72	25·9	97	47·0
23	2·6	48	11·5	73	26·6	98	48·0
24	2·9	49	12·0	74	27·4	99	49·0
25	3·1	50	12·5	75	28·1	100	50·0

PRESSURE AND VELOCITY TABLE

Pressure in lbs. per Square Foot	Velocity in Miles per Hour	Pressure in lbs. per Square Foot	Velocity in Miles per Hour	Pressure in lbs. per Square Foot	Velocity in Miles per Hour	Pressure in lbs. per Square Foot	Velocity in Miles per Hour
oz.		oz.		lbs.		lbs.	
0·08	1·000	10·00	11·180	2·25	21·213	5·50	33·166
0·25	1·767	11·00	11·726	2·50	22·360	5·75	33·911
0·50	2·500	12·00	12·247	2·75	23·452	6·00	34·641
0·75	3·061	13·00	12·747	3·00	24·494	6·25	35·355
1·00	3·535	14·00	13·228	3·25	25·495	6·50	36·055
2·00	5·000	15·00	13·693	3·50	26·457	6·75	36·742
3·00	6·123			3·75	27·386	7·00	37·416
4·00	7·071	lbs.		4·00	28·284	7·25	38·078
5·00	7·905	1·00	14·142	4·25	29·154	7·50	38·729
6·00	8·660	1·25	15·811	4·50	30·000	7·75	39·370
7·00	9·354	1·50	17·320	4·75	30·822	8·00	40·000
8·00	10·000	1·75	18·708	5·00	31·622	8·25	40·620
9·00	10·606	2·00	20·000	5·25	32·403	8·50	41·231

PRESSURE AND VELOCITY TABLE—*continued*

Pressure in lbs. per Square Foot	Velocity in Miles per Hour	Pressure in lbs. per Square Foot	Velocity in Miles per Hour	Pressure in lbs. per Square Foot	Velocity in Miles per Hour	Pressure in lbs. per Square Foot	Velocity in Miles per Hour
lbs.		lbs.		lbs.		lbs.	
8·75	41·833	19·25	62·048	29·75	77·136	40·25	89·721
9·00	42·426	19·50	62·449	30·00	77·459	40·50	90·000
9·25	43·011	19·75	62·849	30·25	77·781	40·75	90·277
9·50	43·588	20·00	63·245	30·50	78·102	41·00	90·553
9·75	44·158	20·25	63·639	30·75	78·421	41·25	90·829
10·00	44·721	20·50	64·031	31·00	78·740	41·50	91·104
10·25	45·276	20·75	64·420	31·25	79·056	41·75	91·378
10·50	45·825	21·00	64·807	31·50	79·372	42·00	91·651
10·75	46·368	21·25	65·192	31·75	79·686	42·25	91·923
11·00	46·904	21·50	65·574	32·00	80·000	42·50	92·195
11·25	47·434	21·75	65·954	32·25	80·311	42·75	92·466
11·50	47·958	22·00	66·332	32·50	80·622	43·00	92·736
11·75	48·476	22·25	66·708	32·75	80·932	43·25	93·005
12·00	48·989	22·50	67·082	33·00	81·240	43·50	93·273
12·25	49·497	22·75	67·453	33·25	81·547	43·75	93·541
12·50	50·000	23·00	67·823	33·50	81·853	44·00	93·808
12·75	50·497	23·25	68·190	33·75	82·158	44·25	94·074
13·00	50·990	23·50	68·556	34·00	82·462	44·50	94·339
13·25	51·478	23·75	68·920	34·25	82·764	44·75	94·604
13·50	51·961	24·00	69·282	34·50	83·066	45·00	94·868
13·75	52·440	24·25	69·641	34·75	83·366	45·25	95·131
14·00	52·915	24·50	70·000	35·00	83·666	45·50	95·393
14·25	53·385	24·75	70·356	35·25	83·964	45·75	95·655
14·50	53·851	25·00	70·710	35·50	84·261	46·00	95·916
14·75	54·313	25·25	71·063	35·75	84·567	46·25	96·176
15·00	54·772	25·50	71·414	36·00	84·852	46·50	96·436
15·25	55·226	25·75	71·763	36·25	85·146	46·75	96·695
15·50	55·677	26·00	72·111	36·50	85·440	47·00	96·953
15·75	56·124	26·25	72·456	36·75	85·732	47·25	97·211
16·00	56·568	26·50	72·801	37·00	86·023	47·50	97·467
16·25	57·008	26·75	73·143	37·25	86·313	47·75	97·724
16·50	57·445	27·00	73·484	37·50	86·602	48·00	97·979
16·75	57·879	27·25	73·824	37·75	86·890	48·25	98·234
17·00	58·309	27·50	74·161	38·00	87·177	48·50	98·488
17·25	58·736	27·75	74·498	38·25	87·464	48·75	98·742
17·50	59·160	28·00	74·833	38·50	87·749	49·00	98·994
17·75	59·581	28·25	75·166	38·75	88·034	49·25	99·247
18·00	60·000	28·50	75·498	39·00	88·317	49·50	99·498
18·25	60·415	28·75	75·828	39·25	88·600	49·75	99·749
18·50	60·827	29·00	76·157	39·50	88·881	50·00	100·000
18·75	61·237	29·25	76·485	39·75	89·162		
19·00	61·644	29·50	76·811	40·00	89·442		

H

VAPOUR IN AIR

The elastic force or 'tension' of aqueous vapour, at different temperatures, has received the attention of some of the most sagacious and distinguished experimental philosophers.— Dalton and Ure, in England; Gay Lussac, Dulong and Arago, Kaemtz, Magnus, and Regnault, on the Continent, have taken the lead.

Dalton experimented at temperatures below the boiling-point of water, and from the deduced law he inferred the law above it. Ure included high temperatures, and proved that the *inferred* law of Dalton does not hold good.

Regnault's experiments (of comparatively recent date) were conducted with great care, and improved instrumental agency.

The tables obtained by the several experimenters present discrepancies of sufficient magnitude to prove the difficulties that beset the investigation; and, as might be expected, the discrepancies are greatest at the high temperatures. The meteorologist, however, has to deal only with the range from 0° to about 120° Fahrenheit, and within this interval the approximation lies within narrow limits. It is true that, by means of the condensing hygrometer of Daniell, or the more accurate of Regnault, the temperature of saturation, commonly termed the 'dew-point,' can be reached by direct experiment, without reference to a tension table; but here we stop, for without a knowledge of the elastic force of the vapour suspended in the atmosphere, we can neither calculate its absolute quantity nor the ratio of its pressure to the total pressure of the atmosphere; and as the quantity of moisture the atmosphere can carry depends upon the temperature of the atmosphere, the quantity is a function of the hour of the day, and the humid or dry character of the ground underneath. Therefore, because the pressure indicated by the barometer is the sum of the pressures of the dry air (oxygen and nitrogen) and of the amount of vapour suspended in it, an atmospheric tide is masked by the *casual* amount of vapour. Hence, in the close investigation of atmospheric currents and disturbances, it is necessary to separate the influence of the temporarily suspended vapour.

As by experiment, the elastic force of vapour appears to be nearly the same in a vacuum and in air, the obvious method for testing the accuracy of a tension table, for meteorologic purposes, is to compare the temperature of the observed dew-point derived from the condensing hygrometer, with the dew-point deduced from theory, combined with the observed temperature of evaporation, by means of the well-known Mason hygrometer — assuming the law of latent or specific heat to be known with sufficient accuracy.

Of the several theoretic formulas that have been published, the following, by Dr. Apjohn, is perhaps the most simple, namely :—

$$f = f' - \frac{d}{88} \times \frac{h}{30}$$

where f is the elastic force of vapour at the temperature of the dew-point; f' its elastic force at the temperature of the damp-bulb; d the depression of the latter below the temperature of the air; 88 a coefficient depending upon the specific heat of air, and the caloric of elasticity of its included vapour; 30 inches being taken for the *mean* height of the barometer, and h the height at the time of experiment.

Let us suppose, for example, the following simultaneous observations :—

Dew-point, by condensing hygrometer, 53°·5, temperature of air, 61°; temperature of damp-bulb, 57°; barometer reading, 30·14 inches. Then if we adopt Regnault's tension table, ·465 inch (f') corresponds to temperature 57°, and

$$f = \cdot 465 - \frac{4\cdot}{88} \times \frac{30.14}{30}$$
$$= \cdot 465 - \cdot 046 = \cdot 419$$

Opposite to ·419, in the same table, we find temperature 54°·1, whereas the observed dew-point was 53°·5. And if the other elements were correctly assumed, and no error of observation was committed, the computed dew-point is too great by six-tenths of a degree, equivalent to ·009 inch in that part of the table. This is a solitary observation, and no opinion should be grounded upon it. Repeated experiments in the casual temperatures throughout one year, at least, are necessary, before adopting the table that may be safely used for deducing the temperature of the dew-point from the indications of the damp-bulb hygrometer. The tension table first adopted at the Royal Observatory, Greenwich, was derived from a discussion of Dalton and Ure's numbers. It may be proper, however, to keep in mind that the coefficient 88 is liable, perhaps, to a small correction.

If the difference between the observed temperature of the air, and the observed temperature of the dew-point, be divided by the difference between the observed temperature of the air and the observed temperature of the damp-bulb, the quotient obviously represents a factor which may be employed in a similar temperature for converting a dry and damp-bulb observation to a dew-point observation by inference. Thus, at Greenwich, a long series of observations of the dew-point by means of Daniell's condensing hygrometer, were compared with the simultaneous observations of the damp-bulb thermometer; the quotients for the several temperatures were arranged, and the means taken for the coincident temperatures. By this proceeding, a march is gained upon the tension tables and formulas, such as Apjohn's, for deriving the dew-point temperature from the damp-bulb temperature; since the calculation is reduced to the multiplication of two numbers, and the subtraction of the product from the temperature of the air — no tension table being needed, nor any necessity for considering the laws of specific heat.

A table of the factors derived from the Greenwich experiments is given in the second edition of Glaisher's valuable hygrometric tables, from which we extract the factor for 61°, in order to exemplify the simplicity of the calculation by means of such factors, taking the temperature of the damp-bulb thermometer, as in the preceding example, thus: — Let the —

Temperature of the air be	=	61°, Greenwich factor, 1·87
Temperature of the damp-bulb,		57
Difference	=	4

4° × 1·87 = 7°·48, which, subtracted from 61°, leaves 53°·52 for the temperature of the dew-point.

The range of temperature at any station being limited by its geographic position, elevation above the sea, and local circumstances, does not afford a sufficient number of observations near the limits of temperature, to obtain a mean at these points, comparable with the means for points about the centre of the range: for example, the groups of partial observations at Greenwich crowd about a much lower point on the thermometer scale than elsewhere in a warmer climate; therefore, in order to obtain a complete table of dew-point arbitrary factors, it is necessary to experiment in both warm and cold climates. The laws of latent or specific heat, and of elastic force, are universal; hence, there is no reason why the factors should not be universal in their application also. If a factor, derived from a large number of trustworthy observations made at one station, is employed for calculating the dew-point at another station, and the result is not in close accordance with the dew-point derived from a formula at the other, the cause should be sought for in the numerical elements of the formula, the qualities of the thermometers, their position with respect to reflected heat, or heat from the person of the observers when reading their indications, or ordinary radiation from any substance near.

By whatever step the temperature of the dew-point be obtained, whether by direct experiment by means of a condensing hygrometer, or from the temperature of a damp-bulb—by a table of factors, or from the same by the calculation of a formula—a tension table is needed for computing the *quantity* of vapour existing in the atmosphere at the time of observation, and its ratio (per cent.) to the *maximum* quantity the air could carry at that moment. This ratio is termed the *humidity* of the air—an arbitrary expression, adopted for convenience, which is intimately connected with *weather predictions*.

If the maximum quantity of vapour the air can carry at a given temperature be expressed by 100, the elastic force at the dew-point temperature divided by the elastic force at the temperature of the air, multiplied by 100, gives the humidity, namely:

$$\frac{\text{Dew-point elastic force,}}{\text{Dry-bulb elastic force,}} \times \text{by } 100 = \text{the humidity.}$$

All thermometers should, when practicable, be compared with a well-known standard throughout each five or ten degrees of their *whole* scale. The celebrity of the Maker is not always a sufficient guarantee for the zero points, nor for the calibration: especially of Boiling point thermometers.

The celebrated meteorologist and philosopher, Mons. V. Regnault, published in the 'Annales de Chemie et de Physique' for July, 1844, an admirably-conducted series of experiments on the elastic forces of aqueous vapour and cubical expansion of air, executed by himself, from the former of which he derived a table which is, probably, the most correct that has hitherto appeared. His Paper has been translated into English, and published in the fourth volume of the 'Scientific Memoirs.' The temperatures are given in terms of the centigrade thermometer, and the corresponding forces in millimetres; but Mr. Glaisher has adapted the table to Fahrenheit's scale and English inches, published in the second edition of his valuable hygrometric tables.

The expansion of dry air, which had generally been considered $\frac{1}{480}$ for an increase of one degree of temperature, appeared, by Regnault's experiments, to be $\frac{1}{491 \cdot 13}$

On comparing his table of elastic force with that of Kupffer, and two others, the differences are considerable for temperatures above 55°. At the freezing point, Regnault and Kupffer are identical; at 40° Regnault exceeds Kupffer by ·002 inch; at 50°, by ·006 inch; at 60°, by ·010 inch; at 70°, by ·022 inch; at 80°, by ·037 inch, &c. The effect of these differences in calculating the absolute amount of vapour is obvious; in calculating the 'humidity,' it is small for ordinary ranges: for example, the 'humidity' from Kupffer's tables throughout the observations of four weeks, taken five times daily, exceeds the 'humidity' calculated by Regnault's table by only one hundredth on each observation.

The following are tables usually employed in the several

reductions: — For reducing barometric readings to the temperature 32°, the barometer frame being of brass — Table II., given in page 82 of the Report of the Committee of Physics and Meteorology of the Royal Society of London, in 1840.

For calculating the dew-point — the Greenwich factors.

And for calculating the 'humidity'— Regnault's tables of elastic force of aqueous vapour, to which, if ·01 be added, the numbers will be expressed in terms of Kupffer's tables.

Regnault's elastic force tables are useful for obtaining the barometric pressure of the air freed from moisture.

[N.B. The principal part of this paper is a transcript of one drawn up by Sir Thomas Maclear, for use at the Cape of Good Hope Observatory, and by him kindly sent to the present writer, in 1861. A few minor, and chiefly verbal alterations have been made, in order to render it of more *general* utility.]

I

SCIENTIFIC FORECASTING.

NATURALLY a truly scientific man inclines to doubt the character of any treatment of an abstruse and rather complicated subject which is not defined by number, weight, and measure. Opinions, speculations, and discussions are unsatisfactory when not based on facts of which others can be judges rather than a theorist himself, who may be misled exceedingly.

Hence it is, undoubtedly, that some of the first mathematicians have undervalued the science of Meteorology, esteeming it almost empirical to foretell atmospheric change, and unwise to attempt more than the observation of facts, with their registration. Without affecting to argue against such legitimate opinions — even with electricity and magnetism advancing so rapidly, by irregular flashes and darts, instead of formal and proved steps — the writer will now attempt to approximate toward a method of reducing fluctuating atmospheric elements to manageable quantities, such as may enable even ordinary mathematicians to calculate their relative values in a determinate manner.

What are the *qualities* and *values* of meteorologic elements, essential to the scientific forecasting of weather (as described in in this book) which should be measured by weight, tension, number, heat, extent, and dynamic force, or ('potential')?

They are pressure (or tension) of air — its area, depth, and cubical content — temperature, dryness (or moisture) of air, and its electricity (or electrical condition).

Direction of wind: and its force and *degree* of purity, or of combination.

These are the *statical* elements partly *measurable* now at any place — partly approachable only by tolerably near estimations.

Having these amounts at *various* places, more or less correlated in climate, important dynamic considerations appear before us, such as *relative* tensions and consequent horizontal pressures: differences of temperature: differences of humidity: and differences of electricity. Directions of wind currents, also their forces, the amounts of interference on the surface, and *above*, with their respective *electricity*.

For *each* of these fluctuating, flowing, or dynamic effects, a '*potential*' may be obtained, depending on their quantities, weights, measures, qualities, and velocities.

Due combination of such potentials, in equations and formulas, should be so arranged as to enable tables and brief rules to be established, from which any moderately educated person might draw results (as the junior officers of ships are in the practice of doing, in navigation at sea), even before having accurate knowledge of the theory, or basis, of the rules and tables used by them habitually.

The limits assigned to a very brief paper exclude further examination of this interesting question now. Indeed it would be more appropriate to the pages of a mathematical essay, than to those of a popular exposition.

Some idea, however, may be given, *briefly*, of the *notation, units* of scales, and expressions, at present thought to be appropriate by the votary of this unfolding subject. He would propose that P should represent the polar air-current, and that its unit of scale should be one mile (geographic). P would stand for a true N. wind, P_2 for NNE., P_4 for NE., and P_8 for E.

Similarly, if p_2= NNW., p_7 would be WbN. Also, if T be taken for tropical or true S., T_1 to T_8 may be SbW to W., and t_2 to t_7 SbE to EbS.

The unit of atmospheric pressure or tension may conveniently be C (compression), and equal one-hundredth of an inch.

Heat (H) may be indicated by the degree, as a unit (tenths not being yet necessary).

Dryness or dampness (D) may be shown similarly, and Electricity (E) may be represented, for the *present*, by an arbitrary scale of 1 to 9, 5 being considered par, or *equilibrium*, numbers *below* it indicating what is usually termed negative, or *minus* electricity, and those above, namely 6 to 9, showing degrees of positive, vitreous, or *plus* electricity.

F may stand for force of wind, the unit being one—of the Beaufort scale (1 to 12).

Disturbance of equilibrium in any or each of these forces being followed, or attended by motion of atmosphere to restore it, the direction, amount, and duration of such motion must depend on the *resulting* effect of all *potentials*; and as each is more or less nearly calculable, *now*,—the dynamic *consequences* of a material change of weather appear likely to become within the grasp of a mathematician.

By *potential* (a new word to some persons) is here meant the momentum (occasionally but erroneously called *inertia*), or the moments of flowing (moving) energy,—measured in ponderable inelastic matter by weight multiplied into velocity, but in air *differently*, and in electro-magnetism by a totally dissimilar treatment.

Of course the greater the *differences* of equilibrium, in tension, temperature, and electricity, and the *larger* the area affected, the more extensive will be the resulting movement, but the longer will be the *previous* interval of *time*. Small areas, however much affected, are sooner moved, and again regain their equilibrated condition proportionally sooner.

Beyond this point the writer is not now prepared to go in the present paper; but he trusts that advances will be made, by *others* (so much more competent) toward accurately scientific investigation of this practically useful subject.

K

EARTHQUAKE ALARUM — LIGHTNING AVERTER.

THE Alarum used in Japan to give warning of earthquake, consists of a large magnet fixed horizontally across a support which rests on the earth. Attached, by attraction only, to the magnet, is an iron half hook, or claw, whence a silk cord depends that is wound on a revolving wheel of which the axle works, or rests, in the upright stand (or support of the magnet). To and round the axle there is another cord, holding up a circular (bell-metal) clapper, below which is a gong.

The rationale of this arrangement, as explained to Lieut. R. O'B. FitzRoy by the Japanese Ambassadors (through their interpreter, on board H.M.S. Odin, when *quite at leisure* during their voyage), was this:—'Before an earthquake, the ground being full of electricity, the attraction of the (bowl-shaped) gong becomes greater than that of the magnet, the claw falls off, and the clapper strikes the gong with a loud reverberating sound, audible at a considerable distance, and warning all to fly into open places.'

Now, without attaching undue weight to this very curious, rare, and ancient Japanese invention—said to be many, many centuries old—used only by the most scientifically learned men, and not even known to exist by the great majority of their countrymen, let us examine the Japanese explanation, before offering another.

Direct reference to *electricity*—not to magnetic action (about which those very well-informed, able, and penetrating gentlemen of Japan were *closely* questioned)—and *their* references to lightning, with its action on magnetised iron, in compasses, showed an intelligence of the subject worthy of those with whom (it has been said) the steering compass originated (taking them and the Chinese as one people — in *ancient knowledge*).

The correlation of magnetic action and electric may admit of either *term* being used in explanation; but *is there* any change in electro-magnetism at or before an earthquake? The writer believes there is; because he has witnessed, and collected descriptions of, extraordinary effects on animals and birds *just before* an earthquake—giving the *first* premonitions to human inhabitants *accustomed* to such visitations. Such effects can only be attributed to electrical agency; as atmospheric tension, temperature, dryness, and motion, have been repeatedly recorded as *unchanged* during even some of the severest earthquakes—such as that of Chile, in 1835; although, at times, *coincidences* (however *casual*) may have been noticed, and, naturally enough, connected with earthquakes.

There is something more in the subject, possibly. In earthquakes a most curious circular, or twisting, motion occurs occasionally. At Concepcion, in Chile, some of the great pyramidal stones (surmounting the angles of those very massive walls, four or five feet thick, of the most solid brickwork, which, in the Spanish *cathedral*, were thought to be proof against any such convulsion) were *twisted round* on their bases without being thrown down; while *from* the walls, on which they remained, huge buttresses had been severed and *partly* demolished — great masses of the walls themselves having been torn out, dashed to the ground, and scattered into fragments.

Mr. Mallet, in his seismologic investigations, has made some exceedingly interesting observations about twisting, or circular actions, in connection with *earth-currents of electricity*. And they, again, appear to be so intimately allied to the *atmospheric currents*, that it would ill become the writer of these notes to do more at present than advert to a field so widely extensive.

In contradistinction to the Japanese view, it has been urged, by high authority, that trembling, or vibration, of the ground, may shake off the claw before it is sensible to inmates of a house, and that a simply mechanical effect may be thus produced, entirely independent of electricity or magnetism. But to those who have been accustomed to earthquakes by long residence in the countries afflicted by them, this suggested explanation appears insufficient. So delicately sensitive does the human nervous system become, after *experiencing* earthquake convulsions, that the very faintest tremor, insufficient to ring a bell, or ruffle liquid in an open vessel, is felt by human organisation.

Were these alarums used only at night, during hours of sleep, such an explanation might have more weight; but, since it was first kindly offered, further enquiries have been made, from which it appears that the instrument is as useful by day as by night, and that *ordinary* vibration or tremor of the ground, such as carts or horses, or other passing weights cause, does *not* affect it in the least.

Directly connected with electricity—as considered in Japan, China, Cochin China, Siam, Burmah, Ceylon, and other eastern countries—we may advert here, in passing, to the system that has prevailed there, from time immemorial, of placing lumps of glass, either shapely, or irregularly massive, on the pinnacles, or other highest points of buildings, to *avert* lightning.*

About the beginning of this century, the Japanese added tc some of their *Averters* European conductors, and now have buildings supposed to be thus *doubly protected.*

One word about the *origin* of steering compasses.

Some still ascribe their invention to Chinese, and think Marco Polo brought the discovery to Europe, because the first used were shortly after his return, or about that period.†

But the Italian compass had the North end of the needle marked, and the card was *attached* to it.

The Chinese compass has an *independent* needle, marked at the *south* end, and not carrying a card.

One refers to the pole, the other to a *meridian* sun.

In Russian Tartary, at the very earliest date known to men learned in the history of Scythic migrations, a magnetised bar of

* Some of the British lighthouses had similar *averters*, even in this century—doubtless suggested originally by captains of East Indiamen.

† In about 1260.

iron was used to direct the course across *steppes* offering no distant object but a boundless horizon,—like the Pampas,—or the Prairies. This bar was *suspended.* (General Sabine would doubtless admit it to have been the original *Unifilar.*)

Considering the constant intercourse of Europe with those countries adjacent to the north-eastward, and that the first keenly felt want of such a guide as the magnet was occasioned by immediate predecessors of the great Columbus, whose voyages extended much farther out of sight of land than any since those of Carthaginian or Phœnician adventurers, it does seem natural to suppose that ingenious artists of Italy (birthplace of inventive and imaginative mind) should have adapted the *land* directing bar to the *sea compass.* Long after, when its *variation* was detected by Columbus, Italians *first* made a due *average* allowance for it, in the Mediterranean, by so fixing the needle to the card, as to show *true* bearings, variation being allowed for, by placing the needle at a certain angle on one side of the north point.

But this method, being only applicable to the Mediterranean, was not adopted elsewhere. Within that limited extent such compasses are still used, and not many years ago a Trieste vessel got into difficulty near England, in consequence of her captain using a Mediterranean compass so constructed, being himself unacquainted with its peculiarity.

A sea-compass is *said* to have been known to the Chinese more than a thousand years before the Christian era. Gioja, of Naples, certainly *improved* a mariner's compass in 1302. The Swedes used a needle laid on *floating wood* in 1250. Although neither Homer nor Herodotus, nor other early writers, even of the Scriptures, say anything on the subject, it is not impossible that Phœnician navigators may have had some such indicator.

L

CAMPHOR GLASS.

HAVING often noticed *peculiar* effects on certain instruments, used as weather-glasses, that did not seem to be caused by pressure, or *solely* by temperature, by dryness, or by moisture—having found that these alterations happened with electric changes in the atmosphere that were not always preceded or accompanied by movement of mercury in a barometer, and that, among other peculiarities, increase or diminution of winds, *in the very 'heart' of the trades*, caused effects on them, while the mercurial column remained unaltered, or showed only the slight inter-tropical diurnal change (as regular there as a clock*), we have long felt sure that *another* agent might be traced.

Considerably more than a century ago what were called 'storm glasses' were made in this country. Who was the inventor, is now very uncertain; but they were sold *on old London Bridge*, at the sign of the 'Goat and Compasses.'

Since 1825 we have generally had some of these glasses, as curiosities rather than otherwise, for nothing certain could be made of their variations until lately, when it was fairly demonstrated that if fixed, undisturbed, in free air, not exposed to radiation, fire, or sun, but in the ordinary light of a well-ventilated room, or, *preferably*, in the outer air, the chemical mixture in a so-called storm glass varies in character with the *direction* of the wind — not its force, *specially* (though it *may* so vary in *appearance* only) from *another* cause, *electrical tension.*

* See Humboldt's 'Personal Narrative.'

As the atmospheric current veers toward, comes from, or is only *approaching* from the polar direction, this chemical mixture—if closely, even microscopically watched,—is found to grow like *fir*, *yew*, fern leaves, or hoar frost — or like crystallisations.

As the wind, or great body of air, tends more from the *opposite* quarter, the lines or spikes — all regular, hard, or crisp features, gradually diminish till they vanish.

Before and in a continued southerly wind the mixture sinks slowly downward in the vial, till it becomes shapeless, like melting white sugar.

Before or during the continuance of a northerly wind (polar current), the crystallisations are beautiful (if the mixture is correct, the glass a *fixture*, and duly *placed*); but the least motion of the liquid disturbs them.

When the main currents meet, and turn *toward the west*, making *easterly* winds, stars are more or less numerous, and the liquid dull, or less clear. When, and while they *combine by the west*, making westerly wind, the liquid is clear, and the crystallisation well defined, without loose stars.

While *any hard* or *crisp* features are visible below, above, or at the top of the liquid (where they form for polar wind) there is *plus* electricity in the air; a *mixture* of polar current coexisting *in that locality* with the opposite, or southerly.

When nothing but soft, melting, sugary substance is seen, the atmospheric current (feeble or strong as it may be) is southerly with *minus* electricity, unmixed with and *uninfluenced* by the contrary wind.

Repeated trials with a delicate galvanometer, applied to measure electric tension in the air, have proved these facts, which are now found useful for aiding, with the barometer and thermometers, in forecasting weather.

Temperature affects the mixture much, but not solely; as many comparisons of winter with summer changes of temperature have fully demonstrated.

A confused appearance of the mixture, with flaky spots, or stars, in motion, and less clearness of the liquid, indicates south-easterly wind, probably strong — to a gale.

Clearness of the liquid, with more or less perfect crystallisations, accompanies a combination, or a contest, of the main currents, by the *west*, and very remarkable these differences are — the results of these air currents acting on each other *from* eastward, or entirely from an opposite direction, the *west*.

The glass should be wiped clean, now and then, — and once or twice in a year the mixture should be disturbed, by inverting and gently shaking the glass vial.

The composition is camphor — nitrate of potassium and sal-ammoniac — partly dissolved by alcohol, with water, and some air, in a *hermetically* sealed glass vial.

There are many imitations, more or less incorrectly made.

M

As the very recent storm of October 19, 1862, has been much noticed, and its effects in some few places (*comparatively*) have been calamitous, tabular records of weather statistics for the 19th, 20th, and 21st, of that tempestuous time, are annexed — *following this page*. It was stated, in the 'Times,' that 40,000*l*. loss, to underwriters, was caused by the wreck and damage of vessels — out of the Tyne alone — in the gale of the 19th, and that a great many (*uninsurable*) lives were lost.

WEATHER REPORT, 1862.

October 19. 8 A.M. Sunday.	B	E	D	W	F	X	C	I	H	R	S
Nairn	29·21	40	2	SSW.	6	8	2	b	—	—	3
Aberdeen . . .	29·16	41	3	SW.	7	5	7	c	—	—	4
Leith	29·32	47	3	SW.	7	6	3	c	—	—	5
Berwick . . .	29·33	48	4	WSW.	4	3	5	c	—	—	1
Ardrossan . . .	29·13	49	3	SW.	7	7	8	r	—	—	5
Portrush . . .	—	—	—	—	—	—	—	—	—	—	—
Galway . . .	29·01	50	1	S.	8	4	8	r	13	0·70	6
Valentia . . .	28·84	52	2	NW.	10	7	9	r	—	—	8
Queenstown . . .	29·24	52	0	W.	9	4	8	r	5	0·47	6
Holyhead . . .	—	—	—	—	—	—	—	—	—	—	—
Liverpool . . .	29·58	47	2	SSE.	2	4	9	o	1	0·05	3
Pembroke . . .	29·45	51	1	W.	5	4	7	o	—	—	2
Penzance . . .	—	—	—	—	—	—	—	—	—	—	—
Plymouth . . .	29·53	52	1	SW.	9	6	9	r	—	—	6
Jersey	29·90	53	3	SW.	9	6	9	o	—	—	7
Weymouth . . .	29·75	52	3	WSW.	5	5	9	r	—	—	4
Portsmouth . . .	29·76	49	2	SW.	6	6	7	r	—	—	5
Dover	—	—	—	—	—	—	—	—	—	—	—
London . . .	29·76	46	1	S.	4	8	4	m	7	0·71	—
Yarmouth . . .	29·72	43	2	SW.	3	3	7	o	—	—	2
Scarborough . . .	29·52	45	2	WSW.	4	3	7	o	—	—	4
Shields . . .	29·36	44	3	SW.	4	2	2	c	—	—	4
Heligoland . . .	—	—	—	—	—	—	—	—	—	—	—

PROBABLE.

From Weather Report of the previous day (Saturday).

Sunday.		*Monday.*
	SCOTLAND.	
SW. to NW. and NE., a gale. Rainy.		W. to N. and E., strong. Snow or rain.
	IRELAND.	
SSW. to NNW. and NE., strong. Squally.		W. to N. and NE., strong. Squally.
	WEST CENTRAL.	
WSW. to NNW. and NE., a gale. Rainy.		W. to N. and NE., strong. Showers.
	SW. ENGLAND.	
SW. to NW. and NE., strong. With squalls.		W. to N. and NE., strong. Squally.
	SE. ENGLAND.	
SSE. to ESE., a gale. Rainy.		SE. to NE., strong—to fresh.
	EAST COAST.	
NW. to NE. and SE., strong—to a gale. Rainy.		NNW. to ENE., strong—to fresh. Snow or rain.

Explanation.

B.—Barometer corrected and reduced to 32° at mean sea level; each ten feet, of vertical rise, causing about one hundredth of an inch *diminution*; and each ten degrees, above 32°, causing nearly three hundredths *increase*. E.—Exposed thermometer in shade. D.—Difference of moistened bulb (for evaporation and dew-point). W.—Wind Direction (true — two points *left* of magnetic). F.—Force (1 to 12 — estimated). X.—Extreme Force since last report. C.—Cloud (1 to 9). I.—Initials: b.—blue sky; c.—clouds (detached); f.—fog; h.—hail; l.—lightning; m.—misty (hazy); o.—overcast (dull); r.—rain; s.—snow; t.—thunder. H.—Hours of R. = Rainfall, or snow or hail (melted), since last report. S.—Sea-disturbance (1 to 9). Z.—Calm.

N.B.—Warning Signals shown last Sunday, Monday, *Friday, and this day*, round the coasts.

WEATHER REPORT, 1862.

October 20. 8 A.M. Monday.	B	E	D	W	F	X	C	I	H	R	S
Nairn	28·61	39	3	SW.	8	4	1	b	6	0·50	3
Aberdeen	28·59	40	5	W.	8	9	4	c	9	0·76	5
Leith	28·78	42	3	W.	7	9	9	o	—	—	6
Berwick	28·78	45	4	WSW.	3	6	6	c	6	—	1
Ardrossan	28·80	45	4	NW.	9	9	8	r	18	1·08	6
Portrush	29·39	46	2	W.	8	9	2	b	—	—	9
Galway	29·27	43	3	WNW.	6	8	5	c	18	1·13	5
Valentia	29·39	47	4	NW.	10	9	9	h	10	1·40	9
Queenstown	29·30	42	1	W.	3	8	4	c	3	0·31	3
Holyhead	29·10	47	4	WSW.	7	10	7	c	7	0·30	4
Liverpool	29·08	47	5	WSW.	6	10	6	c	4	0·17	4
Pembroke	29·38	49	1	WNW.	8	9	3	b	19	0·92	2
Penzance	29·45	48	2	NW.	7	9	4	c	15	2·08	5
Plymouth	29·40	47	2	NW.	9	8	9	r	27	1·81	6
Jersey	29·47	61	2	WSW.	7	9	8	o	23	1·40	7
Weymouth	29·37	52	5	WNW.	7	9	6	c	18	1·02	5
Portsmouth	29·31	48	2	W.	6	10	3	c	24	1·82	5
Dover	29·27	49	4	WNW.	5	8	5	c	35	1·90	8
London	29·25	45	3	W.	5	11	6	c	16	1·72	—
Yarmouth	29·17	46	4	W.	8	9	1	b	10	0·70	4
Scarborough	28·91	45	4	W.	4	7	1	b	—	—	4
Shields	28·87	41	3	NW.	4	7	1	b	—	—	2
Heligoland	28·92	51	0	SW.	11	9	7	r	10	0·48	8

PROBABLE.

Tuesday.		*Wednesday.*
	SCOTLAND.	
W. to N. and E., a gale. Rain or snow.		NW. to NE., strong. Snow or rain.
	IRELAND.	
WNW. to NNE., gale. Rain.		WNW. to NNE., strong. Squally.
	WEST CENTRAL.	
W. to N. and NE., strong. Squalls.		NW. to NE. strong — to fresh.
	SW. ENGLAND.	
As next above.		As next above.
	SE. ENGLAND.	
NW. to NE., strong.		NNW. to ENE., strong — to fresh.
	EAST COAST.	
NNW. to ENE., gale. Squalls.		As next above. Some snow.

Explanation.

B.—Barometer corrected and reduced to 32° at mean sea level; each ten feet, of vertical rise, causing about one hundredth of an inch *diminution*; and each ten degrees, above 32°, causing nearly three hundredths *increase*. E.—Exposed thermometer in shade. D.—Difference of moistened bulb (for evaporation and dew-point). W.—Wind Direction (true — two points *left* of magnetic). F.—Force (1 to 12 — estimated). X.—Extreme Force since last report. C.—Cloud (1 to 9). I.—Initials: b.—blue sky; c.—clouds (detached); f. fog; h.—hail; l.—lightning; m.—misty (hazy); o.—overcast (dull); r.—rain; s.—snow; t.—thunder. H.—Hours of R. = Rainfall, or snow or hail (melted), since last report. S.—Sea-disturbance (1 to 9). Z.—Calm.

WEATHER REPORT, 1862.

October 21. 8 A.M. Tuesday.	B	E	D	W	F	X	C	I	H	R	S
Nairn	29·27	41	1	W.	5	7	6	c	4	0·20	3
Aberdeen	29·20	43	3	W.	8	7	1	b	—	—	5
Leith	29·39	44	4	W.	5	9	2	b	—	—	6
Berwick	29·36	44	3	W.	2	4	4	b	—	—	1
Ardrossan	29·47	47	4	E.	6	8	4	r	7	0·44	4
Portrush	29·31	45	2	W.	11	11	2	b	—	—	9
Galway	29·80	49	2	WNW.	2	6	6	o	3	0·25	7
Valentia	29·98	52	1	NNW.	5	10	9	r	3	0·26	8
Queenstown	29·94	54	3	W.	5	6	6	o	—	—	3
Holyhead	29·66	54	3	WNW.	8	9	6	c	—	—	4
Liverpool	29·57	50	3	W.	6	10	9	o	4	0·20	4
Pembroke	29·80	53	3	WNW.	9	9	6	o	—	—	4
Penzance	29·99	53	1	WNW.	8	9	9	o	4	0·30	6
Plymouth	29·90	51	1	WNW.	8	9	9	r	3	0·28	5
Jersey	30·00	52	2	WSW.	9	9	8	o	8	0·29	8
Weymouth	29·82	52	2	WNW.	7	8	5	m	2	0·12	5
Portsmouth	29·81	48	3	WNW.	6	8	6	o	2	0·13	5
Dover	29·79	46	3	NW.	4	5	9	o	—	—	6
London	29·74	46	4	W.	3	7	8	o	—	—	—
Yarmouth	29·62	44	2	WNW.	8	9	6	o	—	—	3
Scarborough	29·45	44	3	WNW.	4	6	8	r	—	—	4
Shields	29·41	44	4	NW.	5	9	5	o	—	—	4
Heligoland	29·37	50	5	WNW.	9	9	7	o	10	0·53	8

PROBABLE.

Wednesday.		*Thursday.*
	SCOTLAND.	
NW. to NE., strong. Rainy or snow.		NE. to NW., fresh. Some snow.
	IRELAND.	
WNW. to NNE., strong. Squally.		NNE. to WNW., strong to fresh.
	WEST CENTRAL.	
WNW. to NNE., strong. Squalls.		NE. to NW., strong to moderate.
	SW. ENGLAND.	
NW. to NE., strong—to fresh.		ENE. to NNW., fresh—to moderate.
	SE. ENGLAND.	
As next above.		NNE. to WNW., fresh—to moderate.
	EAST COAST.	
NNW. to ENE., strong. Squally.		NE. to NW., strong—to fresh.

Explanation.

B.—Barometer corrected and reduced to 32° at mean sea level; each ten feet, of vertical rise, causing about one hundredth of an inch *diminution*; and each ten degrees, above 32°, causing nearly three hundredths *increase*. E.—Exposed thermometer in shade. D.—Difference of moistened bulb (for evaporation and dew point). W.—Wind direction (true — two points *left* of magnetic). F.—Force (1 to 12—estimated). X.—Extreme force since last report. C.—Cloud (1 to 9). I.—Initials: b.—blue sky; c.—clouds (detached); f.—fog; h.—hail; l.—lightning; m.—misty (hazy); o.—overcast (dull); r.—rain; s.—snow; t.—thunder. H.—Hours of R. = Rainfall, or snow or hail (melted), since last report. S.—Sea-disturbance (1 to 9). Z.—Calm.

N

EXPLANATION OF DIAGRAMS.

THE Diagrams from I. to V., inclusive, show the actual oscillations of a Milne self-registering barometer, a barograph, during twelve consecutive months, from January to December 1861.

As the instrument was then newly invented, and not quite accurate, the points are only *near approximations*.

On the scales—showing days, *horizontally*, and inches, *vertically*—extremes of wind forces (maxima and minima) are given, for each day, at the top. *Directions* of wind (as *general* about London) are at the bottom of each scale; and *mean* temperature, during each day, is shown by a broken line.

Diagrams VI. and VII. illustrate the meetings of polar and tropical currents—one or the other, or a combination of both, being supposed to cover the *whole space* (outlined *beneath* them) between Ireland and Western Continental Europe.

A *few* arrows show average directions of the two currents—those for polar having full barbs and feathers—the tropical ones only half of each.

The features are taken chiefly from actual statical facts, as recorded. The second (VII.) may be compared with XIII., the Royal Charter storm—as illustrative.

VIII.—Is intended to show how cyclonic eddies, or curling *sweeps* of atmosphere, affect each other at times;—and how winds veer to the right, or *back* to the left, in *ordinary* conditions of weather.

IX. and X. illustrate Howard's nomenclature of clouds, with twelve additional varieties.

XI. relates to tides. (It *might* precede IX.)

XII. and XIII. are taken from Mr. Babington's Atlas of the Royal Charter storm, published by the Board of Trade in 1860.

XIV. and XV. were drawn, in 1857, to illustrate the apparent advance of (barometric curves, like) waves, and their approximation to synchronism — from Scotland to the British Channel (inclusively). Spaces or intervals horizontally, represent days,—and divisions of the vertical scale show inches and fractions—vertically. The *length* of a *day* space is insufficient to show *much hourly* variation of barometer; therefore the *apparent* progress eastward of the maxima and minima seems more nearly synchronous, on *paper*, than it was in reality. The so-called *waves* actually advanced from the *south* of west.

They are placed in this volume *now*, to show a few of the periods, or periodic times, about equal in *duration*, on an *average*, to those of the moon's phases.

For similar periodicity, reference may be made to our year's series, for 1861,—to Webster's work on Recurring Periods, and to Espy's *Fourth* Report.

XVI.—As a *form* for registering observations of weather is often required—by persons who may not have been accustomed to tabulate their records systematically — in as short and explicit a manner as may be desirable for really *practical* use—perhaps these Diagrams may be appropriately closed by such a *frame* as is used at the Meteorologic Office of the Board of Trade

O

NOTE TO PAGES 223 AND 224.

Extract from Mr. Glaisher's *Letter respecting his Balloon Ascent of Sept. 5*, 1862.

Blackheath: Nov. 22, 1862.

Our elevation on September 5 was, at least, 36,000 feet, and very probably exceeded 7 miles.

The lowest temperature of the air I noticed was, at 29,000 feet, minus 5°. The lowest registered by a thermometer was −12.

The temperature of the dew-point must have been—50.

You will be pleased to learn that most important results will spring out of those experiments. For instance — the theory of decline of temperature of 1° in every 300 feet of elevation must be abandoned.

In a clear sky I found 1° in the first 80 feet; becoming less and less to about 0°·3 in 100 feet at 5,000 feet.

In a cloudy sky there was about 4°·5 in first 1,000 feet, 4°·3 in next, and reducing slowly to no more than 3° between 4,000 and 5,000 feet.

In a partial *clear* there was between 7° and 8° decline in the first 1,000 feet, 5°·3 in second, 4°·6 in third 1,000, 3°·4 in next, then 2°·8; 2°·7 slowly decreasing to 0°·8 in 1,000 feet, at 30,000 feet high.

We had in the first 1,000 feet a decline of 1° in 137 feet, and of 1° in 1,250 feet at 6 miles.

This result is most important: as it affects Refraction, Wollaston's boiling-point theory, thermo-electricity, &c.

I.

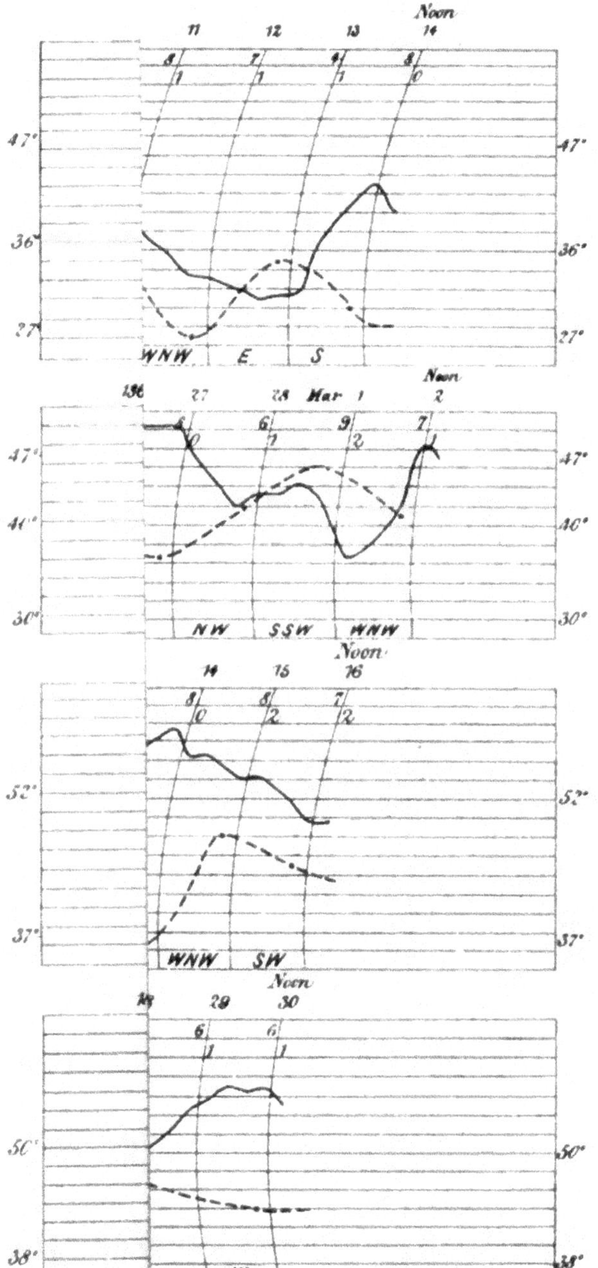

Martin & Hood, Lith. 3, Gt Newport St London, W.C.

INDEX

CPSIA information can be obtained
at www.ICGtesting.com
Printed in the USA
LVHW111947130522
718423LV00014B/175

9 783375 004422